Malama Katulwende

Bitterness

Bitterness

A Novel by

Malama Katulwende

MONDIAL

Malama Katulwende: Bitterness
© Malama Katulwende – All rights reserved.

First edition

This paperback edition of "Bitterness"
© Mondial. New York, 2005

www.mondialbooks.com

Library of Congress Control Number: 2005929567

ISBN:
978-1-59569-031-9
1-59569-031-X

For Nona

Chapter 1

Concerns the curse

Now I know, my son, that you have betrayed this land, this Ng'umbo[1] country, for which I am cursing you, you traitor of my own blood.

If I'd done some wrongs in my life, wrongs that darken and pain my heart, the worst was fathering you. I wish you hadn't been born; then you wouldn't have known the odour of this life. Yet by fate you came into this world, and brought with you a pit of a mouth that has consumed my energies and times to waste. When you knew you had learning enough, you became deaf to our wants. We turned into a son, and you into a father, a bad father untroubled by the nakedness of his house. What use is there, then, in having children that cannot even see your works? Didn't our fathers teach that old monkeys are fed by their young?

Earth has ended and light and virtues have fled her lands; chaos and darkness have come in their stead. Yet no matter how many seasons are to pass, the clouds of strife that shall bring pains and tears will certainly have hung in the sky long enough for you to see and to bear. These would have been my fears for you. You have shattered the calabash of our laughs and joys. May misfortune now possess your feet.

O Spirits of my Fathers, you who have since departed, take him away with you. I believe he will go; courageously will he meet his dreadful end. Take him, my Fathers, you who long ago went. Do not spare him. And since he did not know that I held the winds of life in him and sent witches to sleep when they longed to lick his blood during the night, let him know as I stand before his very eyes, that I was his father, his own father. I enabled him to see the sun, and I now put an end to his earthly days.

Chapter 2

Concerns the meditations of Musunga Fyonse,
priest of the ancestral shrine,
about certain things which threaten his peace,
or the oneness of the land

In a mango shade where Musunga had been resting for the latter part of the afternoon, a strong breeze rustling over the land awoke him from a forest of thoughts in which he lost himself. Until then he had wandered in those solitary shades like a hermit in search of the self, reliving the past in an attempt to see for an explanation of the rages his body alone found too hard to contain, and of the confusion cast over his mind like a spell. He was sure he no longer owned himself. The forces wrestling within had already found a home, and now he just had to endure the torture they bred.

Turning in a chair to make himself comfortable, the old man watched the world of objects that had been difficult to assimilate, wondering whether there might be found some certainty and meaning in the flurry of these things and events. Trees and houses were standing tall and erect; dust was rising and leaves were flapping in the breeze; specks of clouds hung in the sky amid the spectacle of twilight...whereas men, bent under years of dreams and labours, dreamt and laboured for the future without cease.

Musunga abandoned his perch and went into his house, troubled and lonely at heart. A fire glowing happily on the family hearth cast knotted shadows on the walls, dark varied patterns that were intricate and confused. He spread a mat not very far from the fire and thought of nothing in particular. Then he pushed dry wood into the heart of the flames and watched them leap into the air. The flames were always changing shape, colour, and length, and he wondered how very useful fire was, or how darkness and light inspired the creation of the arts. The more the fire intrigued him the more it became a source of veneration and wonder. Suddenly, however, the man ceased to think about the fire as such. Instead, the smoke gave his thought patterns a different direction.

The room was diffused with a thin cloud of smoke. Looking up at a triangular shaped window, chest-high, Musunga noticed that the air from the outside was blowing in and twisting the smoke like an invisible spear. The smoke spiralled around the spear, though some of it only curled very slowly. The old man questioned himself:

'Is what I have just seen not pregnant with some significance, however faint, or a revelation of myself and what is around me?'

To him it was, for he was a man whose soul found peace in the things and the ways of the past. His whole being was there at the shrine, miserable and crying out to *them*, pleading with *them* that the past would be now. His heart was with his fathers, begging them to see (as though they did not!), the smell of poverty that was already more than enough to fill the air and everything with the poison of death – while a few, those who had gathered about themselves things that enabled them to refuse to go beyond the lips of misery, boasted of the goodness and the passage of the time. This unearthed a voice. It had rung somewhere from his memory in sharp and clear torrents of vibrations, calling for the oneness of people in everything. The voice sung, pleadingly and passionately, about the magical works that would take place if people returned to the past and embraced it as their present, for the life to come would shelter *all*. The voice mourned as it sung, and poured out its dream for all to hear. It sung on and on, and on still, and he flew to it so that the voice would be a part of him. Yet without warning the voice stopped its beautiful singing and calling. He felt terribly distressed and began to look for it in the present days, but the voice was not there. It was one in the past, and that past was enshrined in his soul. Could then those who had killed the voice in surrounding things go unpunished? He did not think so, for they were the ones drunk with the obsession of each soul for a pursuit, the fruits of which only fed that mouth. This was not the way of life of his people. They were many and yet they were one.

Peering down into his inner self again, Musunga observed that each time his feet carried him to the shrine, his beliefs glowed more firmly in his heart into a fire of exalted conviction that nothing would dare put out, for its physical presence was perched within, burning and razing to the ground everything that anchored the present order of things. Thinking over this again, had he not witnessed how – across the plain of his mind – the Spirits and the ancestors battle it out with the evil fathers who wanted to put into permanence *this* rotten life he still saw, get crushed! by his forefathers, by the mighty hand of the past? How could it not be said that there were seasons in this life, and also that past days were not coming again?

Thus it was so at the shrine. His ancestors were always triumphant, and Musunga went back to the village bathed in this courage of working for the fulfilment of a better time shortly to come. He looked radiant and was ready within. The Spirits both lived in the past and in the present, and he had lived and was living with them. The invisible owners and guardians of the land and people would see to it that things had to change. He was ready.

As he stayed his prolonged days, however, he began to see that the world outside the shrine would only greet him, as though in mockery, with the usual happenings and other things his eyes found too ugly to look at, and his heart too heavy to hold. The readiness he thought was there within him in each falling day sundered mercilessly, and whatever he stood for all his life disgraced and belittled. It was as if he was living merely to witness his own life and the power of the Spirits defeated. With them gone, his dream would also fall apart, the bitter fear, which took him to the shrine again and again, to ease the flaring helplessness inside, this agony of having to face two things.

Presently a voice removed him from his thoughts:

'Musunga, Musunga,' cried mother of Besa. She was shaking him by the left shoulder. 'Musunga-'

'Hmm?'

'Are you well?'

He blinked a few times. He saw, when self-awareness returned, the fright and concern on the face of his wife.

'Musunga, you were like one dead all this time I was watching you. Are you certain you are well?'

He nodded in irritation.

'What is it that is in your heart, causing you to stay alone for long times?'

He said nothing to her, to her who did not understand some things that it was not given her to understand.

'Father of Besa,' she besought him again, 'as your wife I have to know. I have to know what is troubling my husband's heart. Perhaps it is I who has done you wrong. Musunga, what is it that you cannot say?'

No word fell from his mouth. She had been watching him like a child, and he hated her for it. He stood up silently and went to bed. As his eyelids felt heavy with sleep, Musunga decided that he would go to the shrine some time this week.

Chapter 3

Concerns the journey to the shrine

The sky was clear of clouds, and a few persistent stars he saw were barely gleaming shyly across the hollow space above. Here below it was unbearably quiet. The whole village was not yet on its feet.

Musunga threw a sack of cassava over his shoulder and set out for the Boma[2]. He went past a few houses, their backyards a garden of bananas, and looked out for a shorter path that would take him to the bakery shop where loaves of bread and buns were sold. From there, he would be able to see the snaky corner of the main road winding its way through forest and bush up to Katanshya.

There was a path to his right, and Musunga bent as he walked under a mango tree so dense that its thick, dark leaves and branches darkened the underneath even more. He came out and found his way shortly, and treaded the path while he pushed the sack over to the left shoulder as the right was starting to hurt.

An early morning wind had started to blow. In the distance he heard the hooting sound of *fwifwi*[3], the bird of misfortune, and repeatedly spat on his chest to fend off potential evil. Musunga approached the shop. Glancing at the building for some time, he recalled that Leleke Bakeries had stayed in business for many years now, whereas other bakeries and retail businesses in Mwense village had collapsed after some time. He neared the bakery and saw its large window now open, a hole through the wall before which people queued up each time when there was a dearth of bread and buns. Musunga stared intently at the window and beheld the owner – chest upward – stretch his fat arms and yawn. The man turned his back to Musunga and started counting loaves of bread and buns.

Trivial though this incident might have seemed, it nonetheless induced some remembrances of a painful past. Images of clashes with the colonial police flashed before his eyes. He remembered Mpanga, Kaminda, Teula and others who had died for the Blackman's freedom and government during the *Cha Cha Cha Campaign*[4]. Once this freedom was won from the Whiteman, however, his own people began to recreate exactly those institutions and things that had inspired the struggle for freedom. Who could comprehend why Leleke Bakeries would still sell their goods through a burglar barred window? Was it not common knowledge that the government had now reintroduced the colonial law that prohibited the freedom of assembly and discussion of matters of common interest?[5] The blood of our fighters had never been given proper rest and respect, save for a few mouthful of short, hurried mutterings thrown about by those who were eating well in the land, and these were said in mocking praise of the warriors that were dead.

Musunga listened to the burst of wind whipping everything in its path. As grasses and leaves of trees waved merrily about him, he had a sudden burst of thought. It seemed as if in a certain respect, these vibrant notes of sound were akin to a metaphor of a people crying against a stream of oppression plunging them headlong into a canyon. No matter how loud they wailed the gods and those with ears stayed aloof and unmoved. These were moments when he doubted the existence of *Lesa Mukulu*[6], for how could *He* be silent about matters as heavy as this?

Musunga walked along the left side of the road heading for Samfya Boma. He passed some crumbled buildings and stopped at the summit of a hill to regain his breath. A swampy space started out towards the forest in the distance beyond, and he made out some huts and plots of rice at the fringes of the marsh. He turned where he had come from. Mwense, his own village, was lying silent and asleep. It would soon come to life when the children resumed the playing, the women their daily chores, and the men their beer drinking or their work. And there would be other noises of speeding vehicles, too, and all activities would melt into one solid noise that would resist all effort to be put down, even when others cried over their dead.

He felt restful within. He bent down, gripped the sack by the mouth, lifted it over his head and was on his way again.

Musunga heard the deafening sound of an approaching truck at his back. He stopped to glance behind him and saw an old lorry also lumbering uphill, running out of breath so that he was afraid it would stop and crush into the marsh to the left of the road. The truck's movement was uncertain, and there were times the driver brought his head out of the window to stare at the back. Just when Musunga thought the vehicle would stop, something cluttered underneath it, shaking the lorry several times in its motion. It went on shaking but luckily found its steady sound again. Behind the lorry swirled a very thick cloud of black smoke. The truck's arrival stirred *ba igoigo*[7] to excitement. They whistled and screamed after the truck:

'Imilima! Imilima![8]'

'Imilima are your mothers!' shouted back two men who sat atop an anthill of bundles of fish the lorry carried. 'Imilima are your parents! Sleep with your mothers!'

'Banana eaters!'
'Are your parents!'
'Imilimaaaaaaaaaa!'
'Are your parents! Sleep with your mothers!'
'You have finished our fish, you gluttons!'
'You'll die an *igoigo*!'
'You have a head like an Ifa truck!'
'Go and sleep with your sisters, you sufferers!'

Musunga saw the back of the lorry but could no longer hear the retorts of the men. The truck had, without doubt, left some stimulation at the bus station since *ba igoigo* and *bana maliketi*[9] were all laughing and chatting merrily.

Turning off to the left of the road, the old man walked between houses in the Suburbs Compound, remembering his life in Kankoyo Street where he worked as a houseboy in the Copperbelt. Police beatings, passes, slave work and workers' strikes were some common events that everyone witnessed every day. But those days were now gone. Others like ghosts had come and would come. And yet again, the days that had seemingly gone were not really gone. They shared a likeness with these present days.

'Odini kuno,' Musunga called as he approached a house, the handiwork of terrible people. Colonialists had built *it* like all other houses in the Suburbs Compound. They were reminders of past pains. 'Odini bane,' he called again and lowered his load on the ground.

A fat woman who had been singing softly as she cleaned the veranda vigorously jerked her head to see who was calling and then exclaimed:

'Iyee! Is it you, father of Besa? You are like rain – you come and go!'

'We are all the same. We come and go.'

'We may be like that but it is worse with you. You are like a sweet potato buried into the ground. No one will see it till harvest time.'

'Some potatoes are always on the surface for the blind ones to see them – like me!'

'You have started,' she laughed. She stood up and walked down the steps to greet him. A wide smile was spread over the rest of her face.

'Mother of Mweni,' Musunga said, pointing at the sack on the ground, 'your cassava has hurt my back. If I die you should remember to come for my burial.'

'I refuse to listen to you today. Don't I know how strong the back of my young man is? I cannot be cheated.'

'He is ageing fast, though.'

'*That* is also not true. He sloughs off his older skin like a python.'

The two cousins laughed and shook hands like great friends who had come into each other after many moons of absence. She was eyeing him very closely now, as if to be sure he was very well.

'My great friend, my husband,' she said. 'How are you?'

'I am well. The Spirits are keeping me.'

'And the children at home?'

'They are all well except Besa. He has a cough.'

'Iyee, your Mweni is also suffering from a cough! Two whole weeks have passed and the cough doesn't seem to heal.'

'This is bad,' he lamented in a lowered voice. 'What could be the cause of these coughs? Is it the dust?'

'It could be the dust. That is what everyone is saying. Coughing is now everywhere.'

'What you're saying is true,' he nodded in gloomy agreement. 'At this time of the year when the air is dusty, most people suffer from coughs. Things will change very soon after the start of rains.'

'You have spoken well. During the season of rain there are fewer coughs. But there are also other diseases such as diarrhoea! Do you know how many people died of diarrhoea alone last year?'

Musunga expressed ignorance.

'Many! It is just that you cannot raise a finger to count the dead.'

'Indeed many of our people have died. The only reason why we haven't finished is because our spirits always watch over us.'

Mother of Mweni hurried back into the house and said, 'I am ashamed, what daughter of a father am I, making you stand there like a tree!' over her shoulder. Musunga awaited her outside. After a little while the woman emerged out of the two bed-roomed shelter with two wooden stools she clamped by their legs. Her husband came out also, but stood in the doorway and was smiling very broadly. He said:

'I heard the voice of the witch outside, and I knew instinctively that things were not well.'

'Then you are also a witch. Only a witch can see another,' retorted Musunga with a smile. 'I am told that the witch finder divined that your fellow witches had to fry you many times before you were hardened. You people who get charms from Congo are very treacherous.'

The other laughed. 'It must have been somebody else, not me. I am a child who was only born yesterday, and I don't know about things as deep as these. Witches are old people who have travelled far.'

'Listen to the liar,' Musunga said to mother of Mweni who was handing him a stool to sit on. She placed the other next to him for her husband. 'Father of Mweni is saying he is a child, but what child can smell a witch unless he too is so? Let me alert you that since the witch finder is coming next moon, you should leave this compound or else you will drink *kalola*.[10]'

The three laughed heartily, and there were tears in the woman's eyes. She told Musunga, 'You will kill me with laughter if you continue with your jokes.'

'Yes,' Musunga added quickly. 'He ought to be told the truth. *To teach a child is to be honest with them.* We do not want among us people that send thunder and lightening across great distances and fly at night. Father of Mweni, do you still use your owl? At least say the truth this time!'

They were laughing again.

Father of Mweni climbed down the steps and went where the other man was seated. Soon they were shaking hands and asking about each other's health.

'Son of a chief,' said Musunga, 'you look thinner than you were a few moons ago. What is happening?'

The other man clapped his hands to express dismay and said nothing.

Musunga cast an accusing glance at the woman seated beside her husband on the ground. She was breaking small lumps of sand with her fingers, her head bent down.

'Perhaps it is my cousin starving you?' he said uncertainly. 'Sometimes women neglect the stomach of their husbands by forgetting that *that* is where all marriages are strengthened.'

'No,' said the other man. 'Mother of Mweni keeps me well. It was just a strange illness that came upon me.' Then the wife took over from him and explained the nature of the illness. 'He was vomiting every time and his body was always hot.'

In this reflective moment, Musunga had visions of pains and miseries that sickness always left behind, including other misfortunes that could have taken place had death struck. Seeing before his very eyes the man's wife who might have been a widow, Musunga felt a gratitude to Lesa Mukulu, The Great One, for preserving the life and happiness of his beloved friends.

'The illness lasted three weeks,' said mother of Mweni. 'During that time I was afraid that things would never be the same again. Fortunately, however, Mulungu helped us. Father of Mweni survived!'

'May the Spirits of our fathers be praised.'

'May they all be praised.' Husband and wife answered in unison.

'I heard,' father of Mweni began to say in a cheerful voice, 'that Besa has been called to study at the place of higher learning.'

'*I* told you so,' the wife corrected. 'It was I who heard – not you.'

'Father of Besa,' the husband appealed, 'did I say I heard the news from the air?'

'A quarrel tastes sweeter indoors. Mother of Mweni, how often do you beat this sick husband of yours?'

They laughed again but were soon quiet.

'Both of you are right in your hearing,' Musunga consented. 'What you heard is true. Besa received a letter from the University of Zambia requesting him to go and begin his studies there. He will go in three months.'

'This is very good news,' they said, clapping their hands. 'This is a blessing from Lesa Mukulu. A great favour has been done us.'

Father of Mweni lapsed into a short, deep thinking that ended with a slow nodding of his head. 'I knew he would go to university. Besa was always studying and asking questions. I am not surprised. Something like this had to happen.'

'I too knew it,' the woman also confided. 'As father of Mweni said, Besa was always reading things. There was a time I came to your house and found him and his mother arguing about his study habits. His mother explained to me that she was very worried about him. Besa forgot to eat every time he was studying. He slept little and refused to play with his friends. She also told me that Besa had given a friend two pairs of trousers in exchange for a book. His mother said to him: "Besa, it cannot be many moons ago when your father and I were very angry with you for giving away a good pair of shoes in exchange for a torn book you have been reading without showing any signs of tiring. See what you have done again. You have given away your cloths! Very soon you will walk about naked. Are you not envious of some of your friends who dress well and look like government officials?" And Besa replied, "I don't really need cloths and shoes but I need these books to pass my examinations." His mother shook her head and said: "All my children have hearts that I don't understand. I am not fortunate in my child-bearing.""

As she narrated this story, mother of Mweni gesticulated and shook her head in a show of incomprehension. 'Besa is very strange and difficult to understand. However, whatever he did could not have come to waste. Something like this had to happen.'

'You have spoken well, mother of my children,' said her husband. He shifted about the stool and addressed her: 'We should slaughter two chickens for him and make him a feast to show that we are very happy for him.'

'O yes we should,' she answered most readily. 'Anyone who works as well as this ought to be rewarded. This is how fortunes begin.'

Satisfied, the man turned his countenance towards Musunga. 'When did you say Besa was leaving for the university?'

Musunga hesitated and decided to count his fingers instead. 'This is June...In the moon of August!'

'His going is very near, then. Preparations must start right away!'

'That is right. This is why I want to buy some fish and sell it so that Besa will have enough money when he goes.'

'You shall do well,' the woman said. 'He mustn't be made to regret going to the university because of a lack of money. He should have everything he will need.' She paused and asked Musunga: 'Father of Besa, does our child know anybody at the place of higher learning that might be a companion?'

'Eee,' Musunga consented. 'There's Washaama. Besa and he are childhood friends.'

'Washaama. That name sounds familiar.'

'He is a son of Sokoshi, the hunter. The one who was nearly beaten by a cobra a few moons ago.'

'Can Sokoshi have a son at university?' asked father of Mweni. 'I am quite surprised.'

'You too did not know, mother of Mweni?'

'No I didn't.'

'Well, now you know. Sokoshi has a son at university. This year will be his second.'

'His *second*?' asked the woman in amazement.

'Yes, this year will be his second, though I hear from Besa that Washaama still has three more years before he completes his studies.'

'Iyee!' the woman was again astounded. 'Couldn't someone grow very old in school - having spent seven years in primary, five years in secondary, and another *five* years at University? What is it that takes so many years to learn?'

'This is why,' her husband quickly took up from her, 'those who go to university and finish their learning are made as great as any chief.' Now he paused to let his words be understood and continued:

'You know, students from university are truly educated. Their English is not like that which is spoken by the Standard Three and Six each time they are boasting about Roy Welensky[11] and colonial education in beer parties. *Their* English is heavy, full of well-chosen words and wisdom. It is as though you were speaking with a white man. When you hear them talk of what they have learned, your heart trembles in fear and astonishment for you have met people who have what the white man praises – knowledge. Do you remember Mumbwe Chibale who worked for the Council?'

They all remembered.

'Well, Mumbwe had a son who used to talk about his life as a student at the University of Zambia. He would say that things there are not easy because teachers make students study all the time. If you woke up after midnight, for example, you would still find students studying and discussing! Life is very difficult for both men and women.'

'If there are women at this place,' mother of Mweni said, 'they will be too old to see marriage!'

'Women are also there,' her husband continued. 'Sometimes some become mad while others behave like the things they had been reading about. It is not uncommon, therefore, to hear of students being taken to Chainama Mental Annex for treatment. But after they have completed their education which might take seven years – '

'*Seven* years?' the woman said, confounded.

'Yes, seven years. When they complete their education they are given papers that say, "This person has finished his studies at the University of Zambia, give him work. These are the people the country needs." They are offered big jobs with very good salaries akin to what any white man gets. They are also offered cars, large houses, servants, watchmen and other attractions. They are given all these things because of what is in their heads. Who can turn their knowledge to nothing, the same that the white man himself praises? I swear, father of Besa will throw away all his old cloths when Besa completes his education.'

'What you say is true,' Musunga smiled coyly. 'However, you mustn't speak as though I bore Besa alone. Don't you, father of Mweni, know that a child belongs to the tribe?'

'Yes I do.'

'A child belongs to the clan because it is the clan that bears children. If a child is like a bitter musuku tree bearing bad fruit in the forest, people will see a shadow of bitter fruit over that forest. But if a child is like a sweet musuku tree bearing sweet fruit in the forest, a sweet taste will remain on the tongues of the people each time they go into the forest. This is true of Besa. He has born a sweet fruit for his people, and therefore bears this fruit for the tribe. When we bear children we bear them for the tribe, and this is why a child will call any man, "my father," or any woman, "my mother". Others the child will call "my sister" or "my brother". And any person should be regarded as though they were the child's real mother, father, brother or sister. This is the teaching our forefathers have always taught us - or am I speaking like a child?'

'No. You are speaking for the tribe,' answered both husband and wife.

'If I am speaking for the tribe, I should therefore not behave like a dog that keeps bones for itself since *those who bear, bear for everyone.*'

The others nodded in unison.

Staring out to the bus station, Musunga beheld an old open Land Rover pull up in front of the *chitenge*[12] where bus tickets were sold, and also where passengers spent their miserable nights stretched out on the floor. Perhaps excited by the vehicle's coming, *baigoigo* started shouting, 'Mansa, Mansa, Mansa! This is Mansa!' and thus woke travellers who paid heed to their cries. In a very short time the suddenness of moving feet, shouts and laughter spat a confused noise upon there, a noise that stayed and heightened for some minutes. With heavy luggage in their hands, travellers bound to Mansa limped to the parked Rover while others who had lighter things to carry sprinted forth and tried to force their way through the slower ones who clustered around the Land Rover, struggling to jump in. The strugglers pushed, grabbed, tore and shouted at each other angrily, oblivious of the two fallen ones upon whose bodies many feet crushed. As these people fought and fell to the ground, *baigoigo, bana maliketi* and some travellers not bound for Mansa held their breaths. Then the Rover reversed and drove out of the station.

Mother of Mweni stood up. Her countenance bore fear and anger. She was also perspiring heavily.

'Father of Besa, I am going into the house. I fear to see more mis-fortune. I wouldn't want to witness another person crushed to death at the station. How could people live like this as though there was no government? It is as if whites still ruled us. Nothing has changed.'

'Mother of Mweni,' her husband stood up to calm her. 'Stop say-ing such things. We are not alone here!'

'I don't care. Let them arrest me if they want to. It pains my heart to see my own people suffer because of one man who stole public money that was meant to build a better station. What did he say when we asked him, "Where is the money?" He said nothing! But we hear that when government officials go to the land of the white man, they are treated like chiefs. They lie to the white people that they speak for us, and the whole world believes what they say to be the truth. Village people cannot be heard. But what have they done since independence? Nothing!'

No one answered her. Her husband pleaded with her: 'I don't want to go to prison, mother of Mweni. Please go inside.' The woman went into the house.

Father of Mweni explained.

'It started after they beat her.'

'After they beat who?'

'Mother of Mweni. These people from the Party flogged her and some of her friends for refusing to dance for the Party officials and our Member of Parliament at a meeting. Their stalls at the market were confiscated and they were arrested and locked up in police cells for one week. The women were charged with hating the Party and the president. They were tortured and abused and it appears some of them were even raped by the police officers. They were asked to plead guilty to the charges or spend their lives in police custody. They refused to confess and this earned them more beat-ings from the police. If you had seen her when mother of Mweni came out of the cells, you would have wept as I did. She was swol-len and very sick! When I imagine what she went through I want to take up a gun and fight. Why must women be beaten and abused for refusing to dance to what is not well? Why should anyone be forced to dance to these politicians who are corrupt and do little for their people? Don't people have a right to say no?'

Musunga said nothing.

'Ever since that time, mother of Mweni has never been the same. I don't blame her for how she feels about the Party and the Gov-ernment. How could they expect respect and support from people whose dignity and rights they tread on every day?'

Musunga shook his head as if he did not want to hear any more. He stood up and said to the other man: 'Your wife wanted cassava and we dug up some for your homestead.'

'Thank you very much.'

'It is a small thing for which I needn't be thanked. But I ought to go now. Look, the sun has risen. We shall have time to speak another time.'

'Walk well, father of Besa. Walk well.'

'You and your house, stay well.'

Then he set out again for the shrine.

Musunga felt sore inside. He was obviously disturbed. Yet he had to go on, he reminded himself, his thoughts adrift into the past, a past from which he had often wanted to flee. Transfixed by the weight of a large burden, the old man heard his father's voice for a thousandth time:

My son, I leave you this load to carry, for my time in this earth has ended. It might be today, or tomorrow, when I shall be reclaimed by the soil. Please do not cry! I want you to hear this.

You were named "Musunga", because your work shall be to hold things together in harmony. You are one who holds. Starting from the first recollections of our social memories, our fathers say that this shrine and many others have meant a lot to our people. Spread the teaching of our ancestors, or else the tribe will drown. And, my son, slave for your people as you saw me do. The survival of our people rests in the things that are ours, in the works and thoughts that are cultivated here. You should harden your strength and endurance. Walk well in all paths. The Spirits of our fathers will richly bless you. You shall fulfil your works according to the oracle of Chipepa.

Environed there and then in a gruesome world, Musunga heard a cool wind rustle through the grove in small ripples of whispers, and time seemed to be dragging away very slowly indeed.

There were some birds that had been singing and flying about in the morning when they came to the shrine, but all were now gone. The last three that had been playing and chirping in the branches had just stopped and, like the others, also flown away, perhaps unable to bear the heavy, forbidding quietness anymore.

By midday the silence in the shrine was far and wide, and the immense aura of mystery, too, was about them. His father sat at a small distance away from him: legs crossed, eyes closed and his hands clasped over his chest. Just when fatigue was imposing itself on Musunga, he heard the priest mutter:

O you Spirits of the Land and the Skies!
You, Mweela, the Serpent of the Lake!
Chundu, Musepa, Mukolo Chipande
And other shrines!
O you, Gods of the Tribe, we evoke you.
We evoke you, Spirits of our Forefathers!

Intercede for us to the Great One,
Lesa Mukulu Nsafyamanika,
So that blood, misfortunes and anything which
Brings tears and pain
Will not stain the continuity and unity of goodness.

Let the rains always fall.
Let the fishes be caught.
Let the seed always grow.
Let ill health be far away from us.
Let there be dance and song in the Land.
Beget wisdom in your people...
Spirits of our Fathers,
Our stomachs have kissed the ground – we plead:
Our stomachs are full of want – hear us:
Please hear us.

The whistling, lamenting wind through the grove, as though in answer to the priest's invocation in such lonesome cadence as this, suddenly rose and fell to a gentle steady blow. The solitude was frightening. Yet in notes of irritable defiance against the loneliness, a bird started singing very sweetly on a branch so that the wind dispersed her melody far and wide.

The priest built a fire and began to wave a short broom over it, accompanying each wave with rehearsed ancestral utterances. From time to time he would dip the broom into a black pot at his side and sprinkle shrine water into the burning fire and also about them.

Yellow fire, of you
Once I was a part,
But now I am joined to the bosom of the earth,
To feed and to resign,
I resign to the lullaby.

Chundu, Musepa and other shrines,
My priestly name write in your veins,
And duties entrusted to me by my Fathers
To Musunga now I leave:
Yellow fire to be lit by him,
And you too administered by him.
Spirits of our Fathers
Hearken and concede.

While Musunga lived and witnessed each moment of this day, there was scarcely any inkling in him of the great responsibility that was in store for him as a priest-to-be. A sacrifice was offered to the spirit world. Quite late in the night, they rejoined other elders who awaited them after all shrine rituals to the continuity of the tribe were performed. 'And tomorrow,' he thought, 'the drums will sound for everyone to know that he has been initiated into the mysteries of the shrine.'

There was a shrieking cry of agony behind. Stopping to stare at his back, Musunga saw a frail looking middle-aged woman lying in agony on a dirty wheelbarrow that had just broken down. Relatives who attended to her anxiously encircled her.

'People of my clan,' wept the sick woman. 'My head…my stomach…O mother death, take me. Why have you taken so long to meet me?'

'Mother of Chisanshi,' said a man who was bending over her. 'Mother of Chisanshi, everything will be well. The hospital is now near. You'll get well soon.'

'Nooo!' resisted the woman. 'Just take me home, my people, for I have already died. Take me home, my people.'

The man straightened up and sorrowfully looked at the others, his head moving side-ways in great despair. 'This earth is cruel. How they have done this to her, I do not know. This is the work of wicked people, for how could someone be suffering like this?'

The elders nodded their heads in agreement. Suddenly someone spoke:

'Father of Chanda,' it was a young man who had a container of water in his hands. He seemed uncertain of what to say.

'Yes, my son, what is it?' demanded the man who had spoken to the woman. 'What is it that you want to say?'

'I have water here and it would cool our mother if we splashed it on her body. I have seen others do it.'

Everyone who had heard this was shaking his or her head, wishing the young man hadn't spoken at all. Yet it was father of Chanda who answered him calmly, saying:

'My child. What you say is true, but this thing cannot be cooled down with mere water. It is of hands of men who hate us! Father of Moose, am I not saying the truth?'

'You are saying the truth. Our sons are young, and this is why they may not know things like these. But speaking as we are doing right now, we are wasting time. Our wheelbarrow has broken down, now we should just carry her on our shoulders before it is too late.'

Father of Chanda tore away from them and stood with his hands at the waist, and his face drooping to the ground. When it was raised again Musunga saw large grains of sweat breaking and rolling down the face of this man. He seemed as if he would faint any moment.

Just then, a Toyota pickup full of singing children was slowly coming along the road, and the singers would not hold their mouths even when their car neared where people gathered round the wheelbarrow on the left of the road. Father of Chanda hurried to wave the vehicle to a stop, hoping the driver would help. It came to a standstill and the man had to shout above the noise of the engine in order to be heard.

'Ba driver,' said the old man, 'we have our mother over there who is very sick. Please help us take her to the hospital. We have travelled very far, and our wheelbarrow—'

'Do you want booking? If you have money then let's go.'

'My son, we too are your people. Your mother here is just a hair length away from death. She is vomiting and has terrible stomach pains causing her fall in small deaths. We have no money, but please help us!'

'Aah, if you have no money then I won't help you,' said the driver, wearily. 'I am a busy man. Why didn't you call an ambulance?'

'That we did, my son, but you know how misfortunes come. Your brother went to the hospital to ask for an ambulance, and he was told that it was being used for bigger things. What can poor people do? So we decided to use a wheelbarrow and laid your mother upon it. And as you can see,' father of Chanda pointed in the direction of his people, 'the wheelbarrow is broken.' He waited anxiously.

'Well, this is your problem. You'll know what to do. This is a private car, so I can't help you.'

'My son, *Laugh not at my death because yours too is in a pot.* In this earth we do not live alone. A time will come when you too shall plead for the help of a stranger. Our fathers said that —'

'It's your problem,' the driver declared firmly. His car began to move off, yet father of Chanda still clung to the window, begging to be heard. The driver shouted obscene words in his face and sped off, almost felling father of Chanda.

He stood dejectedly, lost in the contemplation of the going car, unable to believe what was happening to them. Now he dragged his feet back to the others and said: 'We are unfortunate. We have to carry her to the hospital. But how could he do this to us? What is it that has hardened the hearts of people so that we are no longer what we used to be?'

The others heard him and were wagging their heads in the agony of disappointment. Yet their whole attention riveted to the woman again, and there was a moment's panic when one ear went down to hear the beating of her heart and heard nothing. Then the same ear went down again, staying there a little longer this time – and again there was nothing it heard. Another that thought it would hear better came down over her chest to listen for the remains of her heart - and heard nothing. At last, the woman had found her peace.

Musunga plodded on. He passed the council chamber, the post office, the government administration buildings, the bank, the magistrate's court and police station, respectively, situated on both sides of the road. When he reached the structures that had once belonged to the CMML Church but which the government had turned into Chibolya primary school and a clinic, Musunga stood motionless and agape. In front, a great swarm of people had gathered around a classroom on the left side of the road, brandishing stones, sticks, bottles, axes and hoes in their hands. They were obviously very agitated since it became apparent that the crowd's patience was weakening. A number of voices soared up and demanded:

'Open the dooooooor!'

'Open the doooooooooooor!'

'We want the thief to come out now!'

'If you don't open the door we shall stone the classroom down!'

'Yes, we shall stone the classroom down!'

The crowd echoed this strong, fervent demand for the thief, and when he was finally given unto them, the clamour was suddenly warped into one continuous howl that shrouded everything with violence. There were two crowds here, really. A smaller one whose soles were most active and rained on everything it possessed, especially, upon he who tried to break into a run but fell and rose and fell. The larger crowd, providing the former with sticks, stones and

other objects, closed every opening through which it was feared he
would escape, and it were they who struck up a song in encouragement of such gallantry as here was found.

> Cipaye,
> Nolamwina!
> Cipaye,
> Nolamwina!
> Cipaye,
> Nolamwina!

The song was sung over and over again, as they pelted all sorts
of objects at the thief. When they let him stagger to the Boma where
other wraths probably awaited him, this huge crowd surged with
him, singing and showering missiles at him. Behind them were dis-
ordered trails of weapons that had been picked up wherever they
had lain, and these were used to kill a single soul.

Twice he dropped on hard tarmac like a bundle, and there were
many hands to flog the thief so he could get up again. He was up
now, swollen and drenched with blood, wobbling along insensi-
bly as a flurry of blows rained upon him again. The crowd started
another song that informed the police that another thief had been
brought them.

> Sakala,
> Nalelo twaleta!
> Sakala,
> Nalelo twaleta!
> Sakala,
> Nalelo twaleta!

Chanted with a religious passion, the song was sung a number
of times. Fortunately, however, the barbaric ritual came to an abrupt
end when teargas canisters flew into the air to disperse the crowd.
Goaded by the nearness of death, Musunga also took to his heels
like a hunter after a chase, and ran and ran till he slowed down on
feeling a sharp finger of pain pricking the inside of his chest. He resumed his brisk walk through Mwamfuli village.

A small group of people had collected about Nsemukila Bar.
They were recounting what had happened.

'He was nearly dead when the police fired gas.'

'They beat him like a dog.'

'What did he steal?'

'Some people are saying he stole six cobs of maize.'

'It was a bag of mealie meal.'

'I was there when everything started. This boy did not steal any-thing. He was merely asking for some cobs of maize when a woman cried, "Thief," to scare him away. But people took it seriously and ran after him without understanding why.'

Musunga passed them, the echoes of their words closing upon his soul with such heavy insistence that he wanted to run away. He walked faster now, hoping for some distraction around him. All he saw was Mwamfuli market. As he walked by through the crowd, the old man stopped near a small group of people who were attentive to a thin woman. She was saying:

'This earth is bad. You see, the young man *you* have killed with beatings is an orphan who had no one to look after him. It is a beg-gar you have killed, not a thief. Now tell me, people. Has the earth become so selfish and cruel that a life will cost six cobs of maize?'

'He also stole a bag of mealie meal, don't forget.'

'It was a woman who spread that lie,' replied the thin woman. 'There was no truth in anything she said.'

'The young man you seem to support is a thief,' said a man, 'and the reward given thieves are beatings so that they don't steal again. What are you saying?'

'What you say may be true. But have we become so inhuman that we cannot feel pity for the most poor? Everyone who is born into this world has a right to live in it. No one has a right to kill an-other person.'

'What you are forgetting is that the people from whom he stole needed those things just as much.'

'O yes,' she retorted, 'this is what you will be saying to hide your guilt. You have also forgotten that food is never little. But even if he were a thief, he would still be human. It is foolish to pay evil for evil. He needed our help, *your* help. Instead, the whole village fell upon him like dogs just because a poor hungry man needed to eat in order to survive. No one was born a thief. It is the earth that makes people the way they are. *You* are no better than he is.'

After the thin woman had left the group, the listeners squarely looked into each other's eyes and saw some marks of remorse en-graved upon their faces. They went off saying:

'You mustn't listen to such people. She thinks Jesus Christ will save her.'

'Everyone is selfish. Why should I worry?'

'In court she and her husband the thief will lose. He stole.'
'He will be given three years in jail. We will see.'
'The new magistrate doesn't play with thieves.'
'He's dead.'
'Are you sure?'
'Yes,' said a man. 'Could anyone have survived after the way the entire village flogged him? But even if he had survived I doubt whether he could have lived much longer, anyway. *They* had slit his belly open and his intestines were falling out! He was bleeding very profusely and one of his eyes had popped out! I have never seen anything like that. How could they murder someone as if he was an animal? What the woman was saying is correct. It appears the young man was not a thief!'

Musunga walked away from them after the group had broken up, for the way was now cleared. He plodded on and looked at the sun. It was between the horizon and midday. Its rays were already quite warm, but they could not penetrate a coldness spreading all over his inside.

A feeling of being pursued by things with nameless faces came again and he started running, running past many houses and people he did not see. He stumbled over something along the way but kept up his running since he desired to stretch out his arms to the ancestors who would give his soul a greater amount of peace. So Musunga sprinted forward and felt more and more strength possess his feet, for he was leaving disorder behind him. He ran on and was soon out of the Mwamfuli village, going to the shrine where *all* things would be restored - *where* his hopes would shine again.

Chapter 4

*Concerns some possibilities of the future
and the letter from university*

Sometimes, particularly on weekends, when it felt too tiresome to
stay home, or when there was need for a long walk to ease body
stiffness, Besa Musunga came here to pass some time looking at the
water and the people crowded on a strip of beach sand. It amused
him to watch different people doing different things at once. It made
him feel happy and human, although there were times, when he
truly felt, in such easy delights and crowds, a fear he could neither
suppress nor understand. Yet what had started as an occasional visit
to Samfya Holiday Beach soon became an obsession. It was no longer the crowds who urged him to come away, nor the boredom, nor
his friends who sometimes asked him to come along, but a certain
disquietude that bade him to seek a place where he could be alone
to think about his future, his uncertain future. Although Besa did not
know what he truly wanted to be, he presumed that the footprints of
his destiny were already marked upon his forehead.

Since the beach was usually deserted in the mornings, Besa had
decided to walk over in order to think more about *this* future, despite his parents' insistence that he goes with them to weed their
cassava gardens and also inspect the traps. He had feigned sickness and fatigue; he needed a break from everything. His parents
eyed him with mistrust and surprised concern, and though they finally left him alone, Besa was admonished for laziness and the un-
healthy habit of desiring to be alone. His eyes brimming with tears,
the young man criticised his elders for berating what he did for the
family – such as chopping fire wood, mending fish nets, working
in their gardens, buying groceries from the market, cooking and
drawing water from the lake, growing vegetables, hunting, thatching and also fishing! Why couldn't they leave him alone for once?
His parents were speechless and awed by the new firmness in his
voice. They left him and went into the bush. Besa buried his head in
his palms. Alone and troubled by the sense of being a *nonentity*, he
now faced the task of defining that future by himself.

Besa Musunga was a shy, beardless nineteen-year-old youth
with suspicious eyes cast in a concentrated repose. He was very intelligent, handsome, tall and slim, and was presently walking from
one end of the deserted beach to the other. His hands were thrust

deep into his pockets; his bare feet kicking sand and enjoying the gritty feel of it. Besa was looking at the glitter of waves in the morning sun, listening to the sound of the water beating and sucking the shore of the lake, and the steady rush of wind.

He was solemn but contented, contented because his exceptional performances in the examinations were already producing results. All the six colleges where he had applied had offered him scholarships and were awaiting his confirmation, though Besa was not sure which career best suited him. Ill-advised by 'career guidance teachers,' he had written to tertiary institutions without prior, sufficient information about the colleges and the actual programs they offered. He was compelled to fill out application forms because this was what 'Ama saz'[13] said.

And so Besa had settled for Everlyn Hone College (where he hoped to read pharmacy or personnel management), Natural Resources Development College (Water engineering or Crop science), Mindolo Ecumenical Centre (Journalism or Graphic design), Northern Technical College (Automobile mechanics or Electronics), Zambia Consolidated Copper Mines College (surveying and mineral science) and finally Chainama Health Sciences College, where he would pursue studies in the sciences of health.

Reflecting on his choices (the first of his choices), Besa imagined himself a personnel manager – balancing a phone and giving orders to his secretary behind a huge desk covered with a litter of paper, dressed in a suit and looking arrogant and officious, growing fat and lazy in a spacious office, spending an entire life thinking about his company and its performance – and he would have been a *deportee*, a man exiled from himself. He shuddered at the vision of it. Nor was he comfortable with the pharmacist who spent his work life in the lab, nor the graduate from Chainama who examined patients until retirement. Besa saw himself as a crop scientist, crossbreeding different species and working with peasants to increase their production, or perhaps as a water engineer in the ministry of agriculture, and he wondered how he would endure the corruption, inefficiency and bureaucracy of the system. He then considered graphic design and thought; 'Would I be content with this?' but Besa doubted it. Journalism appealed to him, though it wasn't altogether satisfactory. Would he be a reporter, photographer, or public relations officer in a company? Would he be a staff writer, columnist or editor at a reputable paper? He doubted this, too. Then he remembered automobile mechanics and brushed it aside. The world was certainly greater than that, though he could not define what he meant by 'world'. Besa imagined himself a surveyor in helmet and mudded boots, making calculations and pondering their consequences, and he felt helpless. Perhaps he ought to apply elsewhere, he thought in desperation, like to some colleges offering aeronautical engineering, carpentry and bricklaying, architecture, forestry and other courses that paid well, or perhaps join the police force, army or air force as an officer. Yet these choices also exasperated him. What then did he want?

Besa supposed that if he looked deeply at the reasons why these careers did not excite much interest in him, perhaps he would understand what he really wanted to be. Could it be that his interest lay in the totality of all these careers and others besides? How would he be defined, then?

Walking up and down the beach, the teenager wondered what future he had to create. Of all the options open to him, however, Besa favoured journalism the most. He would take it and surrender himself to this fate, regretting nothing since he could choose but one thing. Besa stopped to stare at his fingers. They were long and thin – long, bony fingers of self doubt and coyness, certainly not those of an artist who created literary images that exuded confidence and effortless ease, images created with a sense of complete apartness, as if they were just the sort of things they were ordained to be. 'I have no career,' he asserted suddenly. 'This is a very terrible way to be.'

After carefully tying the laces of his shoes, Besa looked about him: he was no longer the only person at the beach. Besides two young women descending the steep steps of the rest house and hurrying towards him in the sand, there was a couple holding hands as they strolled leisurely along the beach, and some three men seated outside the bar and staring covetously at the girls. He wanted to avoid them. Most women he had known burdened him with their frivolous attentions and were generally boring. He had nothing in common with them, and Besa could never endure the monotony of their gossip and lack of a clear purpose in life. They were mostly interested in marriage and having relationships. Besa's life was above this.

Glancing long at the girls, he decided that they were whores who had left their rooms to come and stretch out on the sand and talk about their night – a thought which nauseated him – their night of love making. Besa did not want to be anywhere near them.

As he started off towards the road, he cast furtive glances at their approach and, after he had passed them, caught one of the girls looking at him. Briefly they held each other's gaze. She wasn't beautiful, and yet there was something about her that seemed aglow with a rare loveliness of its own, something that bewildered and attracted him. He caught his breath and quickly moved on again, surprised at the suddenness of his emotions. Again he looked over his shoulders: the girl was walking beside her companion, her feet planted in sandals, her short skirts opening at the back and revealing and concealing something of her brown thighs, and lovely were her hips and her shoulders and those shapely legs, her bare arms, her narrow waist, and the small breasts that proudly pressed against her T-shirt. Besa stood rooted to the ground, watching, and dazed by that female radiance that held him like a spell. Never in his life had he felt, in a breath of a moment, enigmatically drawn to a woman. She seemed to have reached some deep part of him that, absurd though it was, suddenly became alive. *What was happening*, he wondered silently, scratching the top of his head. He dared not speak to the girl. He went into the bar for a drink.

Besa was sharing a joke with the barman when, to his horror, the two young women entered the bar and made for the counter where he sat on a stool. He shifted uneasily, watching their reflections in the mirrors, without directly looking at the girl who had enchanted him. Why was he gripped – and suddenly! – by these emotions when he should be thinking of proper thoughts? Who was this girl to excite him?

Besa was now courageous enough to observe them. Her companion bought four Coca-Cola drinks and asked the barman how far Kasanka National Park was from Samfya. The man shook his head and turned to Besa for help.

'Slightly over a hundred kilometres,' he answered in Bemba, 'or probably less. I am not very sure.'

'It's not very far, then,' she said in Njanja, which he understood. 'Are you a resident of this area, by any chance?'

'Yes.'

'Do you know the place very well?'

'I hope so. Why do you ask?'

She hesitated for a moment. 'We're college students from Chainama on field attachment at the clinic. We came in yesterday and we hardly know anybody, but we love this town and would like someone who knows the place very well to take us around and have some fun. Someone acting as a tour-guide. We're willing to pay for the services.'

'We're interested in the local history and wildlife,' added the girl who had enchanted him. Then she looked at Besa and asked, 'Will *you* be our guide?'

'*Me?*' asked Besa, confused. 'How can I be your guide? You hardly know me!'

'We can trust you,' said the other girl. 'We also want to be friends.'

'You want to be friends with *me*?'

'Yes,' she said, thrusting out a hand for him to shake. 'I am Gertrude. This is my friend, Musonda. What shall we call you?'

'Besa,' he responded, still unsettled by their boldness and straightforwardness. They were not like the girls he had been used to in the village. These were certainly different.

'What do you say?' asked Musonda, the girl who had enchanted him. 'Don't be shy. You'll be perfectly safe with us.'

'Did you say you were students?'

'Yes,' they said.

Besa took a gulp from the bottle and set it down. He looked at them and said, 'How much will you pay me?'

'A fair amount,' said Gertrude. 'We'll cover the cost of transportation, lodging, food and entertainment and leave something extra for your pockets. Your job will be to take us out every Friday evening, Saturday and Sunday by involving us in exciting activities such as sightseeing, sports, disco and anything interesting . We want to visit some waterfalls, archaeological sights, game parks, islands and all the towns in Luapula province before we go back. These activities must be packed in thirty-six days spread over three months. You'll plan and manage everything and make sure we have a memorable experience or the deal will be cancelled.'

Besa laughed. 'Are you serious about all this?'

'Of course.' replied Gertrude. 'Do *you* accept?'

Besa considered the situation. He wasn't in the least interested in the money they were prepared to pay him. He was, instead, interested in who they were, for not only were they unique, good looking, friendly, adventurous and liberated young women, they were also college students who had something he lacked. They were more knowledgeable than he was, so he could learn from them and perhaps get to understand the heart of a woman. All his uncertainties about them vanished.

'Alright, I accept,' he said at last. 'As long as you can pay. Today's Tuesday… I'll make an activity plan with the estimated budget and then present it to you for consideration on Thursday. We could begin to put the plan into effect by Friday.'

'Great!' they said, very excited about the news.

Then the girls invited him for a drink on the beach and led the

way out of the bar. Expansive and happy with this incredible stroke
of luck, Besa nodded and accompanied them to a thatched hut.

The talk was open and very relaxed. Besa questioned them about
their college, private lives and what they hoped to achieve in life.
He was very impressed by their clear sense of purpose and direction, intelligence and extensive knowledge of tropical medicine. In
their presence he felt incomplete and insignificant. He seriously
lacked a certain necessary sort of disposition – lacked too many
things to be definable, though they appeared to be content with his
inadequacy.

Besa gave Musonda special occasional glances when he thought
she wasn't looking. Surprisingly enough, though, she seemed to
sense the adoration in his eyes and returned those glances with a
gentle look and a smile. He felt clouded in a strange sensuality, an
urge to have and love her unashamedly and completely. Who was
she to have inspired in him these warm feelings of love and content-
ment? She was speaking to him now!

'What about you? You haven't said anything about yourself!'

'There's very little about me. I live in Mwense village. I am the
fourth child in a family of five. I finished school last year and I am
about to go to college.'

'Which one?' Gertrude pursued softly.

'I don't know yet. I have a few offers but I am not sure what I
want to be.' He paused and went on, 'My father wants me to read
law but one can only read law at the University of Zambia – and I
may not be accepted there. I have to see in a few weeks.'

'Is your father a lawyer?' asked Musonda.

'No,' he laughed. 'He's not even educated – formally, that is.
He's a priest.'

'Which Church does he belong to?' Gertrude said.

'He doesn't belong to any Church. He belongs to a line of religious leaders who look after our shrines and cults of traditional religion and philosophy. He preserves the link between the people and
the spirit world.'

'Isn't that rather strange?' asked Gertrude. 'One would hope that
all people embraced modern values of public worship and accept-
able standards of beliefs. Shrines and cults are old fashioned, if you
don't mind my saying so.'

Besa took some time to respond. 'I am not a theologian, but I
don't agree with what you call "modern values of public worship."
I think you underestimate the complexity and unitary structure of
traditional African religious experience. I doubt if there is anything

"modern" about Christianity today. Take an example of Catholics. Most of their rituals are a reminiscence of some ancient Egyptian, Greek, Roman and even Hebrew mysticism and superstition. Who is a more rational person – the one who believes in rivers, hills, waterfalls, trees and other unique features of landscapes as aspects of divine reality, or is it the one who falls before a wooden cross in an act of worship, and passionately believes it to be Jesus Christ? How do you explain the placing of bones of a deceased person called a "saint" on the altar where the chalice sits during mass, and the belief that the bones will "carry" all the prayers to God?

'In my view both may be wrong. But I think we should also appreciate that possibilities in which different realities may find existence and representation are quite varied. Where does the truth lie? I would rather not condemn but remain open to the possibility that I may be wrong.'

'I think you're right,' said Musonda. 'We should be slow to condemn and be tolerant of other people's beliefs in case ours are also wrong.'

Besa decided to tell them a short story.

'I once went to see a man who carved masks. As I was busy admiring his works of art which were truly very good, he suddenly looked up from his work and said: "Do you know that *everything* is in a mask – the water, trees, people, and fire and so on?" When I said "No", he studied me with a shocked expression and said: "You must be mad." But I challenged him and said: "If everything is in a mask, how is it possible that you are *outside* the mask?" He replied: "That's because I am the *creator*. But I tell you – everything else is in a mask." His reasoning defied logic and common sense, but suppose I adapted his viewpoint? The point is – our beliefs may be in error. We have to look at life with humility.'

A few days after this sudden encounter, Besa walked back home with a vast feeling of hope and enjoyment of life. He had taken the girls around Samfya on their first outing and shared a packed lunch with them at the Harbour. They could be very witty, affectionate, considerate and understanding. Wherever they visited the girls asked the local people probing questions about their lives, though they were more interested in women and children. They often scribbled notes and took pictures of situations they considered important. Proud and very happy to be with such precious friends as these, Besa was upset when it was time to say goodbye. Fortunately, however, there were more weekends to look forward to and he vowed to enjoy every moment with them.

As he hurried along the village path, Besa saw everything about him as though he was seeing them for the first time. There were clusters of small, thatched houses with low cupping roofs belching columns of smoke skyward. Simply designed and constructed using perishable materials such as mud, grass, fibre and wooden poles, the houses reflected the settlement patterns of people whose main economic activities were fishing, farming and local exchange. He passed a group of small children playing football amid the cheers of their companions; short-tempered goats mulling grass and doing play fights; old men seated under mango trees watching the ageing world deceiving itself; young girls skipping ropes and others playing waida; four men staggering home and singing a wine song; a communal gathering with a headman speaking; chickens pecking among dry leaves and grass for food; an elderly man carving a mask as he sung imipukumo (the lovely work songs that evoked pleasure in the work and the beauty once made), some girls washing kitchen utensils at a bole hole; the rhythm of pestles as women pounded cassava or millet; a woman suckling her baby and others chasing after their children refusing baths; some men busy thatching a roof and others coming back from their gardens (tired and desirous of rest); and two men mending a fish net. They looked up from their work and greeted Besa: 'How are you, our son?'

'I am very well, my fathers.'

'Is your homestead also well?'

'It is very well, my fathers.'

'That is good. Don't forget to carry our greetings to your house. We too are well, though your mother, Mumba has a fever. Don't forget to take our greeting to your house.'

'I won't forget, my fathers.'

'Walk well, our child.'

'Stay well, my fathers.' He walked away home, always staring about him and very happy to merge into the life he knew so well.

When he finally reached home, Besa went to his room and stayed there for some moments, gazing into the thatched roof as he missed the girls in silence. Although he was attached to both of them, he was particularly attracted to Musonda in a way that still baffled him. Was she flirting with him or was this just a figment of his imagination? Yet he had seen how she stole subtle glances at him and blushed when he caught her looking. Curious and inviting, the girl's lovely eyes emanated warmth and vivaciousness that aroused him, and he secretly yearned for an opportunity to put his arms around her and kiss her on the lips. Yet he curbed such unruly impulses because it betrayed the trust the girls had in him.

Besa went into the kitchen. He found his mother and sister, Maliya busy cutting meat into little pieces they piled into a heap. He sniffed about him and said:

'What meat is this?' A sudden fear seized him. 'I hope you haven't slaughtered one of my goats again without informing me! Maliya, is it one of my goats?'

'Why are you upset?' his mother answered. 'You're not the only person who owns goats and sheep in the family. Maliya, hold the knife properly! Do you want to cut my fingers? I told you that you didn't know how to cut meat but you wouldn't listen. Besa, come and help us.'

'No, not until you've told me.' He paced the kitchen listlessly. 'Maliya,' he threatened her, 'if you don't say anything I won't talk to you again. Whose goat is it?'

'It's not your goat, it's mine. A lorry killed it today,' and the poor child burst into tears. Their mother was irritated:

'You're just foolish. You have been crying over this goat as if it was a human being that had been killed. We shall see whether you won't lick your fingers when the meat is cooked, and you know how well I cook!'

Besa stifled the urge to laugh. He felt relieved though he was very sorry for his nine-year-old sister who loved animals and never went to bed until she was sure that all the family livestock were safely back from their grazing.

'It's the brown one with white patches on the sides and stomach,' she told him. 'She was pregnant and she died with her baby.' The girl wept. 'I am unfortunate, Besa. All my goats will finish!'

Besa wanted to cry with her because he understood the pain of losing an animal that had been a part of you. He tried to soothe her, calling her by her pet name:

'Don't worry,' he said, 'you who has the grace of the katutwa[14] bird. I'll see if I could give you another beautiful brown goat you'll love more than the one you have just lost.'

Maliya sprung up and leaped into the air, in a sudden show of happiness.

'When will you give me my new goat?' she asked anxiously.

'Tomorrow, honey bird. I promise.'

'Give me the goat now!'

'No, not now. It'll soon be getting dark. I want you to see your goat in the morning and take it to feed. Let's wait until tomorrow.'

'Tomorrow is too far away.'

'I know but when I give you the goat you'll have it forever. Look, let's just be patient and wait, okay? I won't run away.'

'Are you sure you'll give me the goat?'

'Yes.'

'Swear by your navel!'

'I swear that if I don't give a beautiful goat to she who sings and trails like a honey bird, then I am a dog.'

She looked at him with affectionate, trusting eyes, and said: 'That's why I love you!'

Their mother gave out a grunt. 'If you say you love him then why do you like troubling him all the time? '

Maliya's eyes dropped to the ground.

'I know you well. After one or two weeks you'll forget and start refusing to do small things for your brother when he asks you to.'

'I won't, I swear!'

'You speak as if we don't know you. You'll soon forget.'

'Noooo!'

Their mother smiled and shook her head. 'We shall see. But if I were you I would sometimes do chores for people to show my gratitude for what they do in my life. When did you last help clean Besa's room? You often refuse to run small errands for him despite the constant kindness he bestows upon you. All you know is play!'

'I have changed, mother,' she said. 'I will never refuse to do anything for him.'

This satisfied their mother, yet Besa was uneasy. He said:

'Mother, I think you're wrong. I didn't give Maliya a goat because I expected anything from her in return. I have given her the goat because I know how she feels, how she must feel. She doesn't have to do anything for me except out of her free will. You heard it – she said she loves me, and that's enough.'

'Don't spoil her. She must learn to do things for her own good. Remember that she is a girl and she will soon be a woman. How will she wash her husband's cloths if she doesn't know how to wash her brother's cloths? How will she keep her house if she doesn't know how to clean this house?'

Besa said nothing. He squatted down to help with the meat. Afterwards they began making little heaps their family would give out to their relatives.

'This is for father of Mweni,' their mother said, 'and this will go to your uncle, Bwaale. Your grandfather Kasuba will take the head because it is what he likes.'

'What about our elder uncle, Chisala?' Maliya asked. 'Also my brothers Mwape and Chizindo.'

'And don't forget our father Chanda. We didn't give him anything last time we slaughtered my goat,' added Besa. 'Maliya, throw this bit of meat on the fire to roast. We should eat something before the meat vanishes out of our sight.'

Their mother lamentably agreed. 'It is true. We have so many people to share the meat and I fear this house will get nothing. *The divider always thins.*'

Besa shared her concern. 'Let us make the heaps smaller and tell everyone that the goat was not enough to –'he didn't finish speaking when suddenly someone crashed into the house and banged the door shut. The intruder tripped and gave a cry: 'Why do you put stools all over the place? Besa, where are you?'

'I am here,' Besa called back. It was the voice of his brother, Chizindo who worked as a forester and lived with two other brothers, Mwape and Chisala. Perspiration on his face, he ran into the kitchen and held out his hands: it was a letter.

'You have received the letter! You have received the letter!' he exclaimed in frenzied excitement. 'You have received the letter at last!'

Their mother was angry. 'Chizindo, do you have to come into this house like a thief under pursuit? Look at him now – he's dancing. I always tell you that drums don't beat to announce that you are of age. Get married instead of dancing in our eyes like a child. You found us working – but see how you have disturbed our counting!'

Yet Chizindo ignored her. He danced and circled around, which made their mother angrier:

'Chizindo, I am begging you to leave this house now before a misfortune befalls your head. You haven't read the letter yet, but you are dancing as if you already know what is inside it. And Besa, let him be. You'll read the letter another time, if it is really yours. We have work to do. Where did we end?'

'I was trying to suggest that if all our relatives should get some meat, then we have to make the heaps smaller.'

'That is true. But some will think badly of us. They will say we gave them little because the rest of the meat we hid for this house.'

'But we are only being generous,' Besa said. 'We haven't slaughtered a cow. Whatever we give them will be enough. After all, some of our relatives are selfish. They give us nothing whenever they kill their goats or catch fish and yet-'

Chizindo grabbed and lifted Besa to his feet. Besa was annoyed.

'What are you doing?'

'Read the letter now,' he said. 'You must read it.'

'Is it my letter?'

'Yes.'

'Well, if it's mine then it can wait. I'll read it some other time. Can't you see we are busy?'

'Go and wash your hands, butcher of goats,' bellowed Chizindo. 'Wash your hands before I smash your face. Do you think I ran all the way from work for nothing?'

'Leave him in peace,' said their mother. 'He has told you that he will read the letter another time, and you shouldn't force him to do what he doesn't want done. What is so important about the letter?'

Chizindo was silent. He picked up a cup and filled it with water, pouring the liquid onto his hands and wetting the floor.

This was too much for their mother. She took an axe from one corner of the kitchen and waved it at Chizindo:

'What is the meaning of this? You started by coming here like a confused wind, then you started dancing like a drunk because of a letter whose contents you don't even know, and now you have wet my floor that you don't sweep or mop! I warn you, go out of this house before I strike you with my axe.'

Chizindo broke into a deep laughter.

'Oweee, I bring everyone some good news and you begin to lift axes? What a great day this has proved to be!'

Their mother gave up. 'Besa, do as he says. Read the letter now. *To prove the impotency of a man is to spread your thighs.*[15]'

'Mother!' Maliya reproached her for obscenity. 'You shouldn't say that!'

'Yes, and *to see the ends of the plain is to walk it*[16]. Read the letter, Besa.'

Everyone now drew around him. His hands trembling, Besa seized the letter from his brother and ripped it open. It revealed a white sheet of paper with very clear prints:

Dear Mr Besa Musunga Fyonse.

The Senate of the University of Zambia wishes to inform you that your application for a place in the Bachelor of Arts degree Course has been accepted for full time study.

As everyone waited for him to speak, Besa reread the letter several times and could still not believe it. In that instant he remembered those strenuous days when he studied with fanatical zeal, when the world around him ceased to exist as he lived perilously amongst ideas and concepts that excited and bewildered him, tortured and gave him little peace. That time had now passed: another life had opened up for him!

A cry of triumphant joy and ululation sounded in their house, and all had begun to dance. In the ecstasy or confusion of the moment, their mother rushed to the hearth and, scooping some cassava meal from a nearby basket, returned (her face struck by the pride and joy of motherhood), and threw some of it about them as a sign of blessing. She smeared some cassava meal about Besa's head, and circled around him as she sung a song everyone took up:

> Today the drum has sounded
> For becoming-of-age,
> The drum has sounded, the drum has sounded!
> Today the drum has sounded
> For becoming-of age,
> The drum has sounded, the drum has sounded!

For several minutes at least, as though overcome by a relentless frenzy they could only express through the dance, the four of them clapped their hands, shuffled their feet, circled around and raised their voices to the thatched roof. Their waists vibrating rhythmically in the paths of the song, the dancers were only interrupted by some of their neighbours who flocked to the house with concern showing on their faces.

'Mother of Besa,' said grandmother of Mutale. 'What is this singing we have heard? What is happening in this house?'

'Yes, indeed, what does this all mean?' another woman also asked.

'Perhaps they are just drunk,' someone suggested. 'Mother of our children. Did you brew beer secretly and forget to invite we who live with you? Can this house be like this?' asked a man. 'If everyone begins to drink beer in secret...'

'It is not the beer, my relatives,' Besa's mother said. 'We are not drunk.'

Everyone was quiet, waiting.

Her face was animated by a smile, and she looked around her and tried to explain. 'The singing you have just heard is because of a letter. We have received an important letter.'

'A letter, mother of Besa?' echoed a woman in surprise. 'What kind of letter can have caused this dancing and singing?'

'Your son, Besa, has received a letter from the place of higher learning. They want him to go to Lusaka to learn more things.'

'Are you saying the truth, mother of our children?'

'It is the truth,' said Chizindo, pointing at a white paper in Besa's hands. In a moment everybody closed around the letter to read its contents, and all congratulated Besa on being accepted to university. They promised him gifts in the days that were to come.

'This house is greatly favoured,' observed a man seriously. 'A son who goes to the place of higher learning is someone to be venerated, for he will be a king when he finishes his studies.'

'Your words are true,' a woman said. 'This homestead will not walk naked or live hungry. It is only us who bear children who have no beads, who will suffer in old age. For what goodness is there in having children who fail in school, play about like dogs, smoke dagga and drink beer as if …as if this is the meaning of life? Of all great things a son can do, he chooses drinking beer and troubling his parents!' She gave her head a vigorous shake and continued speaking. 'If child bearing could be repeated, I would choose better children who – '

'Eei,' a man cautioned her. 'Do not curse the fruits of your womb for every child is a gift which is precious!'

'You say this because some of your children are in college. But if you were I you wouldn't say a child is precious if he insulted his parents and behaved as though he brought himself into the earth. But if a son could work as hard as this and be called to the place of higher learning, what couldn't I do for such a child?'

'True,' said another woman. 'I too would do everything for him. I would love him, give him my blessings and everything he needed for his education. But what can you do for a child who beats his parents, makes girls pregnant as if pregnancies are a proof of greatness, and brings shame and misfortune upon his homestead? What could you do for such a child, father of Chilufya?' she asked angrily.

Chapter 5

Concerns Musonda, the path of his longing,
and some attentions the letter has wrought,
one of which is to have sent to his uncle, Bwaale

That Wednesday afternoon, after the return from the hospital where he had been to see Musonda again, Besa sneaked into the house through the back door with a feeling of dismay, for she who had the colour of ebony, her life a tale of the forest (beautiful and frightful) and her eyes a glowing flame (brown and enchanting), had nonetheless rejected him, and he felt worthless and defeated...

'I like it better when you're saying something...anything,' Musonda reminded him as they left the hospital building, a relief for both of them to be out in the sun, away from the terrible stench of drugs, sickness and death. Leading the way to the kiosk for drinks, she continued, her eyes betraying anxiety, 'I am freer with you then...but not when you're brooding about something and paying me little attention. It sort of worries and makes me uneasy.'

He did not reply.

'I thought you were happy to meet again?'

'I am but...'

'But?'

'I am not just sure if I am in the mood to...to talk over much. I am sorry.'

'Well,' she sighed. 'There isn't much sense in meeting if we can't talk, is there? Not that we must talk all the time, but when you act grim and absentmindedly I feel helpless and out-of-the-way, if you see what I mean. And yet I'd like to be taken into your confidence – as a friend.' She tilted her head sideways and hesitantly asked, 'Are you perhaps upset because of what I said the other day?'

It took some time before he replied. 'Partly, yes.'

'We can still discuss – you know. If you wish.'

'I doubt if we can. Your ego and mine will always clash.'

'So you think it's hopeless?'

'I don't know. I've no idea. I've stopped thinking.'

'What do you want me to do?'

'Nothing.'

'That's not helping much. If there's anything I can do I'll do it.'

'I doubt it. You're very proud. You don't take me seriously. You think you're too good for me. Let's just forget about everything.'

The girl stiffened and stopped walking. She released his hand and said plaintively:

'Besa, I don't know why you should say such terrible things about me. If I were proud or too good for, do you suppose I would be with you now? I would be with someone else! Everyone here knows by now that you're after me but I don't mind the gossip because I like you very much and I always look forward to being alone with you. Sometimes I sacrifice a few minutes of work to talk to you each time you pass through! What more can I do that I haven't done? Doesn't this say anything to you? Look, we could still talk and come to some understanding. We could make the peace.'

Besa was still not sure. 'Have you ever heard of the story of Tantallus?' he asked her suddenly.

'Never. Can I hear it?'

'Tantallus is a name of a king in a Greek story. As a punishment for his deeds he was made to stay in the water, which, whenever he wanted to drink it, disappeared from his sight. Each time he wanted to reach for the fruit under, this too disappeared. The verb *tantalise* draws its connotation from this story. Sometimes I feel the same way.'

Musonda shook her head. She held his hands by the wrists.

'Besa, you know I like you very much and I want to stay close and see you as often as I can. I always say yes whenever you want us to meet privately. But this is all I can do at the moment, though you seem to expect more than I can give you. Sometimes I have a feeling that you want me to be suddenly in love with you but I am not there yet. No, Besa, I am not proud nor anything. It's just that I feel we have to wait to see whether we're going to be serious with each other. But if you feel anything for me, then the feeling must be strong enough to wait. I'll not rush into a relationship for our own good. Do you understand?'

He nodded. She said reassuringly:

'Be a little patient with me. It's going to be all right. We don't have to rush because we have a lot of time on our hands. Can we now go and have a drink?'

Besa nodded again.

They had their drinks in silence. For some moments his eyes settled on her white lab coat and contemplated the body that filled it. What tender yearnings, what fancies, and what hopes lighted her steps and visited her in her morning dreams? What fears clouded her life, and plucked tears from her eyes? Besa observed her curiously. He was not particularly concerned with a thousand trivial things that they had lived through but, instead, with just that palpable feeling in which his attraction for her subsisted – whether she was there or not – though he was presently confused by what seemed to be beyond him.

She chatted about her work at the hospital, a few friends she missed in Lusaka, and their next outing, which, she confessed with a mysterious smile, was often on her mind and upsetting her concentration at work. She could not wait to see what Mansa looked like.

Besa offered no comments. He was enwrapped in who this woman was – in her words, gestures, moods and special smiles which, at certain moments, set his heart aglow with a deep longing to seek in her a pure simple rest sustained in the unity of love and understanding.

An elderly man stood in the doorway and peeped into the kiosk. He lingered there for some moments but, upon recognising Musonda, decisively stepped inside and exclaimed in glee:

'Miss Musonda, long time no see! You're looking good! See what Samfya has done to you!' For a few moments he looked her up and down appreciatively, laughing and beaming at her, holding her hand with a possessiveness, which offended Besa. He resented the man immediately.

Smiling shyly Musonda shook hands with him. 'It's good to see you, Doctor Katiiwa. How are you?'

'The same.'

Musonda laughed, and Besa couldn't help smiling at the ludicrous figure of this man whom it would have been impossible to suspect as a medical doctor. He looked ordinary enough, though his character seemed accentuated by certain traits that removed him from the ordinary. He had that rare stamp of the eccentric – a quality Besa would subsequently observe in the finest lecturers at the University of Zambia.

'The hospital is shambles,' remarked Doctor Katiiwa. 'We have no more drugs, and patients have threads for their blankets! The wards are congested. Lice, bedbugs and mosquitoes are all over the place. We are managing an institution that pretends to provide health but actually does the opposite.'

Besa was speechless. Musonda was embarrassed. She said, 'Doctor Katiiwa, I want you to meet my boyfriend, Besa.'

The man withdrew his hand and offered it to Besa to shake. For a few moments they scrutinised each other curiously without saying a word. Then the man said: 'Good to meet you, my friend. I am Doctor Katiiwa.'

'Doctor Katiiwa is our District Planning Unit Co-ordinator based right here in Samfya.' She explained to Besa. 'Apart from his other normal duties, of course.'

'I am pleased to meet you, too, sir.'

'Thank you.' A silence prolonged itself. Then the man asked Besa, 'Are you working or are you still in school?'

'I am not working. I am a school leaver. I am considering what to do.'

'He will be going to university soon,' Musonda interjected. 'He's been awarded a scholarship.'

'That's very good news,' Doctor Katiiwa observed, fixing him with a look of fresh interest. 'It's always a great thing for me to meet young people trying to further their education. Nothing can be nobler than that especially in country where over sixty percent of the population is illiterate. What do you intend to read?'

'I am not very decided.'

'You should be decided by now.'

'I have a few ideas but somehow I can't choose which program would be the best for me. I have conflicting interests.'

'Have you tried counselling? It's not everything but sometimes it clears your mind.'

'I have had some discussions with my former teachers but I am still not very sure. I want to do something that will retain its essential meaning in my life no matter the changes in circumstances. I want to do something that will make me happy. Not something sought after by reason of obligation, compulsion, blind chance or the like. It has to come from myself and has to be larger than life. I don't see any point in following the beaten track when everyone has been there.'

Doctor Katiiwa fell silent. Later on he said,

'I have a feeling that you know where you stand. What you perhaps lack is the courage to stand by what you believe in. But don't worry. Sooner or later you'll encounter exactly what you must do. Follow your heart and the dictates of your reason with unshaken humility, sincerity and persistence. I wish you the best.'

'Thank you, sir.'

'I should be on my way now,' he said and shook hands with them. After the man had left Besa said to Musonda:

'He's a nice man, your Doctor. Is he always like that?'

'Like what?'

'Like someone ready to listen to people's problems?'

'That's his job, but I see what you mean. Yes, he is a good man.'

'What is he specialised in?'

'He's a surgeon.'

'Are you serious?'

'Yes. What did you take him for the moment you saw him?'

'I thought he was from the streets.'

'Most people think like that. They think he's mad.'

'If he's a surgeon he must be very learned. Why is he here at this tiny clinic?'

'He was working at the University Teaching Hospital until recently when he lost his job.'

'Why?'

'It was an order from the President,' Musonda explained patiently. 'According to the story, Doctor Katiiwa had operated on some political detainees from Kamfinsa Maximum Security Prison – those who were on death row. He wrote a paper to the authorities on the living conditions of the prisoners. When government failed to act, he passed on his work to international human rights organisations and pleaded for some form of sanctions against the Zambian government for its failure to meet the minimum conditions of human rights requirements for prisoners. Locally, however, his good work and intentions were interpreted by politicians as trying to discredit the image of the Zambian government and getting the international community to interfere in the internal affairs of a sovereign state. Because of this the authorities felt Doctor Katiiwa was a threat to the Party, so he was thrown to a remote place like Samfya where the police and special branch would always monitor him. He's very lucky to end up this way. At least he has a home, a job and he's a bit free – though they have confiscated his passport, practitioner's licence and other documents so that he doesn't leave the country.'

Besa said nothing. He thought about the doctor and others like him who desperately wanted change. Perhaps they had realised that since their happiness depended upon occasional efforts to clean up the vast, vile surroundings of dirt, then their fates were entombed in the places they sought to change, in the very things they were against. He felt for the learned doctor a terrible pity.

'I am sorry for him.'

'We could pay him a visit if you like.'

'Do you know each other very well?'

'Well enough, I believe. I have met his wife and children. They are a wonderful family.'

'We could pay him a visit.'

'When?'

'I don't know, but certainly not this week. We have the weekend for a trip to Mansa and I have to spend a day or two at a rest house to be by myself. That's Thursday and Friday.'

'Are you still decided to go to the rest house?'

'Yes, I have to. I have to think.'

'If you wanted to think home would be as good as any other place.'

'You still don't understand. All I want is the feeling to be in a different place, a feeling to help me see things from a distance.'

'You could also imagine it without having to be at a rest house.'

'I want to leave my village and home behind. I want to live in a different place for a while to see where I am.'

Musonda shook her head. She still could not understand.

'Everything changed the moment I received an acceptance letter from the university. Suddenly, everyone started giving me respect. My former classmates are uneasy in my presence, and village girls are flocking to me more than ever before. It appears as if I am elevated to a status of a god, and this frightens me. Why should people adore me as if I am special? They treat me with so much respect and I don't like it!'

'I can understand your feelings of anxiety but this is just a passing phase in your new life. I am very sure you'll come to terms with what's happened. It's not something that should worry you.'

Besa assumed a thoughtful expression.

'You still want me to come with you to this rest house?'

'Yes. We could be together and talk.'

'I am sorry I can't accept. I don't think it's right.'

'What do you suppose is right?'

'Anything other than that.'

Abruptly he announced his leave. 'Thanks for the drink. It has been a wonderful day. I have to go home now. I'll see you on Friday afternoon.'

'You're angry with me?'

Besa did not respond. All he wanted was to leave this place and the woman behind. He started towards the door but stopped. Musonda was holding on to his hand.

'O, come on. Don't make a fool of yourself. Please let go of my hand.'

'No. You must first tell me why you're angry.'

'Okay. I am angry because you doubt the sincerity of my feelings for you.'

'It isn't me you really want.'

'Fine. You're not the one I want.'

'All you wanted was sleep with me and forget.'

Besa fixed her a hard, shocked look. 'If what you say is true, it would have been easier to ask one of the village girls to sleep with me than go through all this trouble.'

'What do you want from me, then?'

'I want to be with you. I want to whisper in your ears and hold you in my arms. I want to share my feelings with someone who understands me – the way I think you do. But I also appreciate your suspicions and will respect your decision. I'll be fine by myself. Perhaps I don't really have to be with anyone at all.'

Besa pushed her slightly; she was holding back her tears. For a few moments he had an impulse to shout at her and go. Thus they stood facing each other like complete strangers, neither understanding nor knowing what was exactly happening to them. Musonda made an effort to say something but couldn't. She was bewildered and crying. The sales woman was speechless. Besa left their presence.

Back in his room, he riffled through their meeting and wagged his head. In after-thought it seemed Besa had been unfair, childish and irresponsible, whereas the girl had been calmer and wiser. She hadn't rejected him as he had imagined. All she had pleaded was patience and understanding. Nor had Musonda said (now he remembered) that he meant nothing to her. She reminded him she always said yes whenever he wanted them to meet, sincerely confessed that she needed to talk and stay close to him and, what was more, had introduced him to Doctor Katiiwa as "my boyfriend", though Besa didn't know what this term exactly signified. And why had he forgotten? Musonda sometimes permitted him to take her in his arms – but only when they were sheltered away from the eyes of everyone: He fondled her hair, slid his fingers between her cloths, and touched her breasts as she made room for him to caress her thighs and what was between them. She once said, "I enjoy being in your arms like this", yet would not allow him to go beyond caresses and kisses. That would have been a crime, and yet she surrendered herself to him as if she would have wanted to. But why had he behaved that way?

Although self-criticism wasn't easy for him, it now occurred to Besa that quite contrary to what he had believed in himself, he was immature and needed so much to learn. His early loves were sweet but trivial. They were incapable of arousing in him feelings so rich as to be immortal. When he came face to face with a girl who could decide for herself and fight him, Besa blamed her for what she was, excusing his impatience, intolerance, lack of understanding and his feelings of inadequacy. He had perhaps hoped to recreate her in the image of something he could do things with – like the girls who did exactly as he asked – forgetting she was different and had to remain so since this was her worth and the ultimate thing she had to be. Besa was alarmed by his blindness.

Leaving his room, after having finally and sincerely resolved to apologise or risk the loss of a sweet woman through impatience and ineffectual arrogance, Besa strode across to where his mother sat peeling cassava in a mango shade. The moment she saw him she pulled her face in an expression of contempt and waved a knife at him.

'You're rarely staying at home these days,' she said. 'Very soon you will bring trouble into this house. Where have you been?'

'To see friends.'

'Which friends?'

'New friends.'

Besa sat down on bare ground and leaned against the mango tree. His mother asked him to take a stool to sit on rather than lie on the ground like a duck, making his trousers dirty. He had to think of the cost of washing paste! He went into the house and returned with a stool.

'Are you unwell?' she asked. 'Long breaths like yours are a sign of ill health.'

'I am very well, mother.'

'Have you eaten your nsima?'

'No. I am not hungry.'

'What have you eaten?'

'Nothing. Why are you asking me such questions?'

She stopped peeling cassava and stared at him. 'If you don't like being asked questions, then you should at least say to us, "I am not eating anything today," so that no food is wasted. But if you say nothing then you should eat your food. Throwing away nsima is bad because there are many hungry people who need it. This you should never forget, even when your stomach is full. Just wait until you're married. Your wife will hit you with a cooking stick to teach you that refusing food is bad. It hurts those who took care to pre-pare it.'

Besa regretted what he had done and apologised to her. Afterward he asked her, 'Where is father? Is he on the lake?'

'I don't know where he is. Men have dogs' feet that carry them
very far. It is unwise to follow the path of wind. You might lose
your way.'

Besa laughed with her. He watched his mother work with that
peculiar concentration in her eyes that pushed her forward, often
against barriers and obstacles until what she had to do was realised.
He admired her forbearance, persistence and her uncompromising
nature and the faith she had in herself. In spite of what people told
him Besa tended to suspect that he inherited most qualities from his
mother. He favoured her presence and confessed everything to her.
Musunga was often aloof and preferred to be alone, though he offered him some very useful instructions on various livelihood skills
such as net making, fishing, hunting and herbal medicine.

'Are you listening?' his mother asked him presently.

'Yes.'

'I am saying that mother of Mweni came to see us this morning. What she said also agrees with other whisperings I have been
hearing lately about you. I do not know what has come upon your
head, but you have started doing things that will not take you anywhere. What if your father was to hear of this? He would blame me
for bearing bad children.'

She gazed at him with feeling. Besa was now uneasy in her presence. For a hundredth time her voice vibrated in his ears as she admonished him, repeating to him the necessity of always acting in
the way that was praise worthy and guided by the counsel of elders since *fire surrounded by elders does not burn.* Did he perhaps
want to disgrace his parents by doing outrageous things? Was it not
his wish to bring joy to their family by doing good works? Wasn't a
good child the envy of everyone?

'Perhaps you have forgotten. I am the woman who conceived
you and believed in the treasure I carried in my womb. We raised
you well, but you have now started spitting in our faces by doing
things that are not well. I have heard many things, some of which
darken my heart with sadness. For how could you fall into the paths
of fools by drinking beer at your age? Are you of age to start smoking and sleeping with women? If you feel you are now a man, why
don't you say it so that we choose a respectable woman for you?
There are many good girls in this village to choose from. Do not
bring shame upon us by walking about with these women. You
know your father, you know who he is. Do not let his anger fall like

a roof over our heads. Your father loves you and has a lot of faith in
you. Please, Besa, do not kill this or you will kill it for everyone in
this house. Do not cause us to weep.'

'I don't drink beer,' he said in self-defence. 'I don't smoke cigarettes either. What you heard is not true.'

'What about women? I hear you have befriended two women
who are working at the hospital.'

'That is true, but what's wrong with having friends?'

'They are female.'

'O come on, mother. I have always had female friends. What
about my classmates? Look, my new friends are very good people.
I learn a lot from them and I love them. What use do I have for people who are treating me as if I am a chief? I need people who can
build me up.'

'I don't want you to befriend women,' she insisted. 'Your father
would also not advise it.'

'What's wrong with having female friends?'

His mother did not reply. Besa was silent. He would not drink
beer nor touch a cigarette, of course, yet when he remembered Musonda and her life enhancing presence (and to hear her name rejected merely because only parents could rightly decide what was
good for their children) his heart tumbled in terror. It was unjust to
lose her forever and deny them something that might have been, yet
Besa would do nothing against his family. He would do nothing to
disappoint them. He would have to give his first and only love neither thought nor care... she who (dear God!) had pressed her tender lips upon his feet. With her whims she coiled her precious arms
around his neck and held him tight, whispering intimate things
though she would not let them commit the crime. She would not let
him live the beauty of her nakedness.

'There is something more,' his mother pursued in another tone.
'It's about your uncle, Bwaale. He is also worried about you. Not
just about your behaviour but also about what some people in this
village have started saying about your going to the place of higher
learning. Do you now father of Nkoma?'

'Yes. His daughter is Maliya's friend.'

'Do you also know that he's a dangerous witch?'

'I've heard him spoken of as a witch.'

'He's a witch, and it is he who has started whispering things
against you and our family. Father of Nkoma is not happy that you
are going to university. He and others like him are saying it was the
teachers and your father's powerful charms that made you pass your
examinations.'

'Is this what is worrying you?'

'It is what is worrying me every day.'

'You need not be worried by what isn't true. Whatever people are saying about me is not the truth.'

His mother shook her head. 'It doesn't matter whether what is being said about you is true or false. What matters is what people feel about your going. You see, my child, people are difficult to understand. Yet I have come to learn that they may be as treacherous as a lion. And so a child must always understand the earth in which people live. What preserves their land and peace is also what destroys it. Now since everyone's death is in the surroundings, a child's eyes must always look outside for things that can threaten or protect the peace. This is the wisdom by which people live.'

Besa was restless. Although he did not believe his going to university could upset anybody, he at least understood what his mother meant. It was stupid to suppose that charms or the help of his former teachers had made him be where he was. Parents had to urge their children to study with constancy until they had mastered concepts and their applications and, changed by what they had truly learned, the learners would be able to reorganise their experience and bring the world to their command. He doubted whether there could possibly be any lucky charms or shortcuts towards knowledge. One had just to study with ceaseless patience in order to bring oneself closer and closer to what reality was.

'So you see, you have to be protected. Your uncle has agreed.'

'What do you mean?'

'You should be protected from such people who could do you harm through their hatred. You must be protected.'

'I don't need any protection. If you and uncle Bwaale are afraid that people will bewitch me, let them. What have I done?'

'You haven't done anything, but to others you have done something they cannot bear.'

'I am not to blame for the failure of others. People are responsible for who they are. I did not prevent anybody from passing examinations. They did not just study hard enough. But if I should succeed at doing anything at all, why must I be hated when everyone had the same chances?'

He got up on his feet.

'Where are you going?'

'To my room. I can't hear more.'

'You're behaving like a child.'

'I really don't need any protection. Tell that to your brother.'

Chapter 6

Concerns the rich words
imparted for him who has done well,
and the flight in search of where he stands

Dressed in a clean, brown suit the family had bought him recently
from Mansa, Besa stepped out of the house accompanied by a cluster of women who led him into the open air amid the joyous, up-
roarious ululation. Suddenly the slow and cautious throbbing of
drums filled the air, overwhelming everything with the vibrancy
and tension of sound. Rising above the trembling beat of the drums,
a woman's voice cried out a song that everyone took up, as hand-
fuls of flowers and cassava meal were thrown about him. The celebration had now begun.

> Sekela seke ee
> Natemwa!
> Sekela seke ee
> Natemwa!
> Nganamona mankangala
> No mutima munda
> Watemwa![17]

They walked unhurriedly towards a large stool planted in the
centre in the crowd, the slowness perhaps prolonged in order to
heighten the sense of welcome and importance the occasion demanded. Besa sweated profusely. He hesitated before he finally sat
on the stool with some elders at his sides. The women were singing another song.

> Emfumu yesu
> Eyeyi
> Ngawamona imbi
> Yabene.

> Emfumu yesu
> Eyeyi
> Ngawamona imbi
> Yabene.[18]

Song followed after song, and sometimes the drums sounded fast and inharmonious. The drums were always apace with the gracious swaying of the women's waists. Then the beat softened and slowed as though in final tired descent, and was joined by the deliberate, hesitating shuffle of women's footsteps. Fainter and fainter grew the pants of the drums, till they reached their own rest and the dancers made the last sequence of footsteps. The women were given a riotous cheering.

Oozing exuberant joy, his father stood up to speak when all had quietened down.

'To my mothers, my fathers, my uncles, and indeed to you, my clan,' he said. 'As I stand before you now, my heart is filled with happiness, for there's always gladness when a child has grown and is initiated in the ways of the clan. Today we are celebrating, my clan and I, the works of this child that have shown themselves to our eyes. What he has done is not little, for if it were little who would have gathered here? Our ancestors said, *A finger points where a garden is*, and they also said, *A pestle does not stand where there is no pounding*. Therefore, it is because there is something here that we are with laughter.'

Musunga paused briefly before he resumed.

'When our warriors came back from battles, our people celebrated their victories over their enemies in songs and dances at gatherings like this. However, times have now changed, for battles are no longer fought with spears, knives and shields, but with pencils, pens and paper. It is with the power of the pen that both poverty and misery may be defeated. Those that are not learned will be slaves of their friends, and a slave is one who refuses to know what they must know, or one who doesn't know how to use the wealth of knowledge around them.'

Again he paused and, picking a small branch of a bush tree, turned to Besa and said:

'Take, take this;
It is what I have that I can give.
You are also the shade, my son,
For we, in our ancestry,
Are the blood in which people shelter.'

Like other gifts that he would be given, the branch was put on a mat before him. His uncle Bwaale had now stood up to speak.

'My relatives and my clan,' he said. 'I have very few words on my throat, for father of Besa has said all the rich words that should be said. And I need not waste your time since I can see that father of Chungu is thirsty. He looks as if he wants to start drinking *katubi*[19] now.'

He waited for laughter to die and went on.

'My nephew, Besa. See what you have done: do not destroy what you have started. In our clan you are the first child to be called to the place of higher learning. Our people have born sons and daughters but none of them, if my memory is my true witness, has reached where you are. It is also because of this that we are celebrating. Other clans have sent children to university and they laugh at us and say, "Your children are without any use. They are just good at beer drinking, witchcraft and akaleela[20]. But now that we have a son who is due to go, our other children will start looking up to him as their light, which will guide them. They will be strengthened and work hard, and those that mock us will be ashamed.'

He observed the crowd briefly and went on:

'Before I end my words, I wish to thank all our people for coming to celebrate. I am also giving words of encouragement to this child – and others like him – to struggle to learn the things of the white man, for these also are wisdom. May the Spirits of our fathers be with us always.'

His uncle was silent at this moment. Glancing at what was in his hands, the man looked up and faced Besa.

'In my hands I have a wrist watch, Omeka (Omega), given me by Bwana Olotoni (Mister Halton), who came from Safa Filika (South Africa), when we both worked in Mufulila Mine. He told me this watch would help me keep time. Besa, I am giving you this watch to help you keep time. This watch, Omeka is not like these tins I am seeing on people's wrists. This is Omeka. It has the strength like kaimbi and outlives times and changes. Take it. It will help you keep the time.'

There was applause. From now onwards, his relations would come into the circle to offer their gifts and words of advice, and Besa listened attentively.

'Have your seen these eggs on my plate?' His grandmother, Chola, said. 'My grand child, before a hen sees her chicks, she must first incubate her eggs until they have hatched. Great things carry long times to ripen. And so you too, must have the courage to wait when you begin your studies. Patience brings good things.' The eggs and plate were left on the mat.

Now his cousin, daughter of his uncle, Mwansa, said:

'Don't our elders still say, *Sleep, O my witchcraft, so that we may observe the habits of the natives?*'[21] She paused and went on. 'My brother, Besa. I have nothing to offer you but my words of humility. When you go to university, do not show off what you know until you have understood the ways of the people around you. Rashness destroys.'

'My…my…my brother, Besa,' stammered Maliya. 'I know you like reading much but you should also find time to play. Please take this pillow I made you; when you're tired and needing sleep, rest your head upon it.'

A blind man, guided into the circle by his stick, said:

'If I could see with my eyes, I would show others the way. You, who have eyes, use them well to lead others along good paths.'

A woman with a honeycomb said:

'My child, the sweetness of honey comes from dirt and other uneatable things. There would be no honey if the bees shunned these. Therefore, you too must never forget what has made you be the child that you are now.'

Now his mother danced about in the circle, singing,

'See not scales on my back,
It is I who mothered the great one.
See not scales on my back,
It is me who bore Besa.'

'My son,' she said. 'I give you this white chicken and many blessings. May you always walk where there is light.'

Then Chanda, a close cousin, said:

'Can you see this scar across my forehead? It was a girl who did this to me when I was your age. My friend, when you see that your eyes have started jumping, close them and remember my scar. Learn from the misfortunes of others. Women's breasts may be sweet to touch, but they are also fires that burn you little by little. Only those who hear live in the earth. I have nothing but these words to give you.'

And an old man said to him, waving a book:

'What is in every book can heal or make sick. When your head is full of learned things, do not forget your land, your tribe and your navel name as this would be sickness. May we always be your land and your relatives.'

Two women came into the circle and sung two songs for him.

Cibuluma pakulya
Witumona ifi fyebo
Tulibengi.

Cibuluma pakulya
Witumona ifi fyebo
Tulibengi[22].

And also:

Abakumulume nga baisa ati,
Nafwa umutwe;
Nga banoko bese ati,
Yande bamayo,
Yande batata,
Yande bayama.

Abakubakashi nga baisa ati,
Nafwa umutwe;
Nga bawiso bese ati,
Yande batata,
Yande bayama,
Yande bamayo[23].

'Besa,' said one of the women. 'When you complete your studies we expect to visit and live with you in your home. We hope
you'll not be selfish and abandon your relations.'

And then at this moment Chizindo and Mwape staggered inside
the circle, each holding a parcel. They danced ludicrously. Chizindo said:

'We love you, Besa. We will always love you!'

Two days after the ceremony (during which his relations feasted
– drunk, ate and danced contentedly), an acute sense of apartness
and loneliness oppressed him again. He was restless and fed up.
Their unceasing attentions and words of advice that narrowed experience and diminished possibilities burdened him. The way they de-
scribed him defined him. He was the end of their feast, the feast at
the end. Instead of the peace and joy that it was believed he would
feel, Besa only felt a responsibility and fear crush him. Yet an impetuous voice, heedless and fierce, impelled him to go away and find
some peace in flight. He could not see who he was in the crowd.

Besa packed a few articles in an old travelling bag and checked
in at Bangweulu Rest House. Surveying his new surroundings with

an air of disapproval, the teenager considered whether this was the right place to be or feel or reflect in, as the room was rather too small. He felt cramped or bounded by these impenetrable walls and the low ceiling. Yet he thought, 'I am not going to stay here forever. It's only two lonely nights and I will be gone,' and the feeling of being limited disappeared. He then dived on the bed on the single bed to test it. The springs compressed from his weight and something creaked underneath the mattress, but he paid no attention. He jumped up to open the windows to air the room, switched on the light, inspected the wardrobe and washbasin, and began to unpack. He put on his shorts and went into the bathroom. He lay naked in the tub, like what Archimedes must have done several times, pursuing his thoughts.

A stream of affection and gratitude inundated him when he recalled Gertrude and her confidences. The minute she had seen him she dragged him into the corridor and said, 'What the hell is going on? Musonda won't eat and she's crying most of the time. What did you say to her?'

'We had a fight.'

'I know, but you love her, don't you?'

'Yes.'

'You don't want to lose her?'

'No.'

'Listen. Musonda cares a lot about you. She's as much worried about you as you are about her. She loves you and doesn't want to lose you. She's hoping you'll want to sort things out amicably and start afresh. But she's not courageous enough to come to you, so you have to make the first move. Go to her and tell her that you love and want her in your life. Tell her what you feel exactly about her. She has realised that she needs you to be happy. But don't push her too hard, give her some space.'

'Can I leave her a message?'

'You don't want to see her right now? She should be in the ward.'

'No, we'll talk over the weekend. But I'd love to leave her a poem.'

Gertrude promised to deliver the message and Besa disappeared from her sight. 'She has a face of woman who tries to live her life immediately,' he thought presently. 'She lives, loves and toils with a will, placing no faith in tomorrow. She understands that once the clock of life is wound, it may come to a stop any time!' Yet Besa was not like that. He revelled so much in the past to enjoy the present. His thoughts returned to the present. He was in the tub, he was immersed in the water, he had left home behind him, and he now had a problem of managing the time. What was he going to do? There were many things to do, and Besa would do them all. The early morning hours would be consecrated to self-introspection when he would encounter, or be deluded by, what he really was. He would then go to the lake to exercise on the beach and have a swim. By lunchtime he would have read some pages of the prospectus from the University of Zambia in an effort to decide which courses or programme he would pursue. The afternoons would be different. He would wander aimlessly about the village like a vagabond and submit to the dictates of events. In the evening he would retire to bed and think of the day as having been well lived as no day is empty of content.

As Besa dried himself, it suddenly occurred to him that he had made no plans for Musonda, nor even considered the possibility that she might decide to be with him, assuming, of course, that the poem affected her so seriously as to risk caution and danger. At the remembrance of the girl warm feelings stirred in him. For an instant he lived a vision of the woman – enticing yet eluding, just as if her lucent loveliness to which she attached importance would never yield to the blind hurrying of time. She walked up to him with eyes uplifted, her shoulder bag dangling on her side, and Besa felt whatever beauty he perceived in her very sharply so that he closed his eyes as if he sought to contain it. They did not speak. Theirs was a world in which speech or the mere language of humans had little function. A deep thirst of her consumed him. The closeness, the intimacy with what was happily had, the reasoning obstinacy to love and protect rested on her radiant face. They did not have to speak. Gazing into her tear filled eyes he saw and understood her surrender that, like his own, was the highest joy. He gathered her to him in a long dream-of-embrace, burdened by an inexpressible ecstatic rapture she had aroused in him, the tenderness and sweetness of love.

'What if she doesn't come?' Besa suddenly realised. He shivered at the thought of it, yet had to caution himself against expecting too much for fear of disappointment. He changed his thought patterns and was resigned to what he truly had – a tiny room for two solitary nights, some books to read, and some time to spend as he liked. Outside of this there was clearly nothing.

He idled about the market place in Mwamfuli village observing people going about their businesses. He studied their faces and contemplated the consequences of their lives. Weariness, courage and a sublime calmness etched upon each of these faces reminded him that happiness did not consist in the quantity of material possessions one had. It consisted, instead, in cultivating friendship and lessening the burden of the people around you.

Besa went in the direction of the shops, following behind three male delinquents who endlessly jabbered about prostitutes, drugs, beer and money – but happily from whom he learnt about a disco at Buyantashi Bar. He decided to go and see for himself.

Inside it was sultry, very crowded and dark, and the air smelt of cigarette smoke, liquor and body odours. He threaded his way to the counter and ordered a mosi beer. Looking about him Besa was surprised to see as many women as men dancing on the floor. He felt a sense of relief and relaxation. He scrutinised the faces to see if some were familiar and there were none. He ordered another beer, and then another, and again another. Three women had already tried to entice him but he courteously declined, saying he had no money. In any case, he was waiting for his girl friend that would join him any time. The three prostitutes disappeared. The evening was going very well. He was content with the beer in his hands, the flow of sensual music, the on-and-off flickering of lights, and he enjoyed seeing people dance.

Mosi lager in his hand, Besa hurried across the bar towards the door, aware of his light feet lifting very easily – was he getting drunk? – and smiling to himself. He smiled because he was edging towards the extremity of freedom, disorder or possibility, the condition of chaos out of which thought was shaped in any form. In this state of being, life (or whatever life purported to be) lost its austere aspect and became a dear friend.

Outside the bar it was less noisy, though there were some people clamouring to get in through the door. Along the wall was a line of women and small children selling cigarettes, eggs, groundnuts and fried fish, meat and chicken. Lifting a chunk of meat with a fork and eyeing it critically or drunkenly, a man screamed a protest at an old woman who suddenly sprung to fearful attention and waited.

'Woman!' shouted the drunk, 'Isn't this killing? Why are your prices high?'

'Don't you know that prices of everything have climbed? You must be a stranger on earth. Even small children know that the price of something today will go up tomorrow. You shouldn't complain.'

'You must lower your prices or people won't buy from you. Do you know how to do business?'

'Bwana, if you don't want to buy go somewhere else where meat falls from heaven. See now. You're chasing away my customers!'

'These Zambians!' he retorted with great distaste, dropping the meat back on the tray. 'They all want to be like Ba-Kasai[24] or Indians. They want to get rich in a minute, even small people! What's wrong with this country?'

'Don't insult me,' the woman said, trying to keep her temper down. 'I don't want to pick up misfortune. What others do when they see that they have no money in their pockets –'

'You think I have no money?'

'Yes. If you really had, why haven't you bought anything? You're just walking about here, harassing people. Those who have money don't waste time. They would have bought something by now.'

'Eeee,' said the man, trying to reassert his dignity. 'You take everyone to be fools. You suppose people should spend money without thinking of the cost of things. I am not that kind of customer.' And he retreated back into the bar.

'He's stupid,' said the woman bitterly. She was very hurt. 'When it sees that its pockets are now full of holes ... Why can't it ask such foolish questions to those who rule the country? Am I the one who controls prices? Does it not know that when we fry meat or fish we use cooking oil, tomatoes and onions? Who doesn't know that the prices of everything are going up every time? Why can't it ask such foolish questions to those who rule the country? Am I responsible for the increase in prices to deserve this kind of abuse? Atase! Men are fools. Ask those questions to those who have destroyed the country. If I sell at the price it wants, how will I make a profit? Does it want me to live on faeces?'

Several people laughed.

Besa traced his way to the toilet, chuckling in the night. A strong, exuded stink of shit and urine made him stop and turn round in the doorway. He headed back to the shadowed trees and shamelessly spouted out a jet of urine. Across to the road a car came to a sudden halt. A few minutes later two people got out, repeatedly said, 'Thank you very much,' closed the doors shut, and watched the vehicle scream towards the bridge. The two dark figures were women coming to the bar, as silently as ghosts, their footsteps unhurried. Besa did the zip up and waited for them to pass. When they had passed him, the women left behind them whiffs of some strong perfume he supposed to be very expensive. He sipped the beer in the dark – four mosi and he was already feeling very drunk, though he liked the feeling of having lost all concerns.

In the night Besa asked:

Why am I here? Where am I supposed to be?
He replied:
Nowhere. I am a young man who doesn't know where he ought to be.
Again he asked:
Why don't I know where I ought to be?
He replied:
Because I find no peace anywhere I happen to be.
He thought:
So much is outside. The sky, the stars, – you name it. I am also outside, I am a public face, and yet I am the sculptor's mask: I do not make myself. But I am inside myself, I am my own content. I revolve upon myself.

Besa thought of home. Like everyone else in the village, his family was impoverished and could barely make ends meet. Though the levels of poverty were already quite high, his people had the courage and calmness to wait for the harvest of the seed that had now been sowed. *He* was that seed. They had built their dreams around the graduate whose magical powers would transform their lives once he completed his studies. Their laughter, courtesy, gifts and the ceremony all attested to it. Besa was the feast; he was the feast at the end.

Then he remembered something else, too. After his restless waiting had ended, Besa went to the grove with his uncle, Bwaale. As they left the village behind them (following a footpath into the heart of the bush), the teenager glanced at the vast stretches of tall, elephant grass and stunted savannah trees. It was hot and cloudless. Except for the sharp twittering and chirping and hooting of bush birds, there was a great veil of impenetrable silence about them. They passed many cassava gardens. Sometimes, though, his uncle startled him when he suddenly stopped to listen for sounds. Like a man who had clearly discerned danger, he would dip his right hand into the medicine bag for leaves or roots that he chewed hurriedly before spewing the spittle about them, saying, 'The winds are not well. My chest feels heavy,' though there was really no wind to speak of. All was very still.

On the way to their destination his uncle spoke to him of the depth and complexity of traditional medicine. As they approached the grove, however, the passionate voice of the herbalist faded into silence like everything else, and Besa sensed the presence of mysteries shrouded in the thick, interwoven branches of trees and long, coiling creepers. His heart pounding on his tongue, the teenager felt

as though he was about to encounter the primeval forces of nature –
the secrets and spirits that inhabited and guarded the land.

They sat down on the ground denuded of any foliage, on a layer
of moist, dry leaves in the centre of an irregular clearing bounded
by closed-up trees, creepers and wild grasses, and shaded by a
dense canopy above their heads. It was a dark world unvisited by
streams of light in their full intensity and splendour, a sombre place
reeking of an ancient mustiness of its own – a guardian of odours,
secrets, darkness, isolation and inaccessibility, a place permeated by
strange, entangled harmonies.

Besa gazed at his uncle with an expression mingled with fear,
mistrust and even hatred. He felt very weak. A dumb sense rooted
him to silence.

'Do you know why we are here?' asked the man at length, pouring the contents out of the medicine bag.

'Partly.'

The old man explained. 'Your parents told me everything. You
see, my nephew, people's hearts are not alike. There are those who
are filled with thoughts and wishes of destroying children of their
friends, and these will not rest until their evil intentions are fulfilled.
This is how things are. But for this very reason every child should
know where to tread in this earth.'

Besa was already sweating.

'It is not goodness or innocence alone that may help a person live
happily in this life. It is also what the person is, or what he promises to be, that decides who must be his friends and his foes. Every
moment of the day we are walking into things that may hurt us, and
this is why our ancestors created different medicines to shield themselves from evil of their enemies and from life itself. Are you listening to my words?'

'Yes, my uncle, I am listening.'

'Let me now tell you something about yourself. As far as I can
remember, death has always been at your feet. Of all the children in
your house you have been the sickliest, and Kalumba the great diviner had asked the same thing. "Why is this child sick almost all
the time?"

'I recall when you were born. You came into this world too early
– a little after seven moons – and we were all very surprised since
no woman in our clan had had too early a birth. But it did happen.
Our fears were that you would not live many days. This was why
your father, your grandfather, Kasuba, who recently left us, and I
busied ourselves with finding herbs. It was not easy, but we tried

our best. We were fortunate because you recovered after some time, though your health was still very delicate.

'But perhaps the saddest time of all was when a strange sickness possessed you shortly after you had started crawling. Seeing how things were going, we all had a big fear that everything was about to end, for we were putting our ears on your chest and were just waiting. The herbs we had used had refused to work, and even Milimo of the hill-clan, whose knowledge of such matters is respected and trusted everywhere, could do nothing but shake his head. Your mother thinned as a stick. Despite reproaching her that cries hastens the end, she cried every day and refused meals. Then, one day, when it was evident that one full circle of the sun would not pass, your mother strapped you on her back and started off to Lubwe hospital on foot. We were shocked by what she did. And I remember elders asking themselves, "How can a white man pass where we the elders had failed? How could he heal our child when our powerful herbs and sacrifices could not? Could the white man tread the path unpassed by the feet of the wise?" Such were our doubts. Yet it was agreed that since we had tried everything perhaps the hospital could help, though we all sincerely doubted it.

'This was how we found ourselves on the way to Lubwe. We reached the hospital in the night. We found a white doctor called Father John. When he looked at you and saw the way you were, he became furious with us as though we had done some terrible things to a child of our own. He removed the beads around your waist and called us foolish. Had it not been for the others who restrained me, I would have beaten him in the presence of everyone. For how could he insult us like that, we who had travelled far and had a death in our hands?

'We subdued our angers and waited, expectant of women's wails any moment: there were none. We became very anxious and pleaded with the nurses for the news of our child. When the white man permitted us to see you the following day, we were very shocked to see you alive! Yet we could not forget the fears we had passed.

'Soon after this worse things happened. Your mother became a Catholic. She had you baptised secretly because she believed it was the white man's god who had saved you. But we told her that if our medicines had not worked at all, you could not have lived. We further said that it was true there were some works the white man could boast of, but certainly not everything. Yet your mother started speaking badly of our ancestors and shrines. She believed in the magic of the stranger. But how could someone lose faith in all our ways? Your father said he no longer had a wife, since she stood against everything he believed in. He could not live with a woman who had trust in the white man's medicine and religion, and who insisted that our herbs and ways of life could not equal those of the stranger. How could he permit himself to eat her food?'

The man was quiet again, remembering. When he seemed to have recovered from such memories his eyes settled on Besa.

'Perhaps you may see it strange that I should be saying all these words to you. Yet I meant to show you how your parents have been concerned about you ever since you were born. Yours has been a troubled path, a passing through the night, a scream for help inside the storm, and a keeping of a fire in the rainy winds. It has not been easy, but the crops you have planted must be tended. How can your parents go to sleep when the lives of their children are in danger? No, my nephew, we cannot leave you unprotected.'

As the resonant voice lapsed into yet another silence, Besa could but feel resigned. His uncle made a fire from dry twigs and leaves. Gazing dreamily into the flames leaping into the air, the medicine man fell into a self-induced trance. His body shivered, grains of sweat appeared on his forehead, and his breathing became irregular and hurried.

The words were inaudible at first, but the man was uttering something. He recited a prayer to all the Gods of the tribe, exalting and trusting in their existence and mercies that befitted these psalms of praise. Imploring the ancestors to hear him, the man evoked their very names – that of his father, Kasuba (who revealed medicines in his dreams); Mulonda Mulonda (whose spirits originated from the Katanga); his grandfather Mulenga (the diviner who dwelt in the forest); Chipango (the teller and pronouncer of oracles); Mwila (the prophetess who remained unblemished by the desires of men); Nchike (the maker of rain, fire and sender of pestilences when provoked); Mwaba (the invisible one and watcher at the village shrines); Kolwe (who, as the name signifies, was reputed for killing monkeys with knives of lightening); Mpiwe (he who dealt with every sickness and slept under the river water); Chibale (the witch finder who often sailed on the lake on a mat); Kaoma, Yaluma, Kabende and other healers and seers of the lands whose names and wonders were worthy of praise and emulation, calling upon them all to safeguard the life of the child.

After the recitation of the prayer, Besa was requested to undress and lie down on the ground. Using the magic stick the man marked an eccentric circle around him, and almost simultaneously dropped thumb-full of impande[25] along the drawn line to repel evil spirits that might render everything ineffective. This was very important. He then clasped a whisk and chanted, like a canticle, other ritual words, dancing and gesturing with his arms, uttering shrill cries to invisible forces the way a witch finder went about his work. He entered the circled area. Crouching down beside his nephew the herbalist, with a razor blade in his hand, cut some tattoos on his forehead, below the breasts and navel, on both kneels and feet, and some on his back as well, ignoring Besa's stifled cries of pain. He rubbed into the bleeding cuts a powder concocted from different things such as barks, herbs, roots, a cobra's head, and the excreta of a dog. Besa was given a witchcraft antidote to swallow – the taste of which made him queasy.

'One important thing,' said the herbalist. 'There are some prohibitions that must be followed every day of your life. You shall not sleep with another man's wife or a pregnant woman unless she is your wife, or eat any food prepared by a woman who has seen her menstrual blood. Never fill your stomach with food from a neighbour's pot or fire, or eat your food cold. Refrain from eating meat, chicken, bubble fish, okra and sweet potato leaves. You shall not touch a dead body or sleep in a funeral house, unless the deceased is your relative. You shall not drink katubi. Whenever you cut your nails or shave hair from any part of your body, be sure these are burnt by you. And finally, if you break any of these prohibitions something terrible will happen to you. You shall always be pursued by misfortunes. Have you understood?'

Besa was listening.

Hardly a moment passed when he started shaking, sweating and panting. A deep drowsiness seized every part of him in an instant. Before his eyes objects seemed blurred, distant and distorted, often shifting positions. His tongue dried up; he gulped for air; a wave of panic filled him; he tried to scream, to open his lips to protest or rebel against this man and his family, but he could not. All the strength had deserted him. He lay there abandoned, his consciousness retaining the last awareness that he was dying, plunging easily into a deep abyss that obliterated all memory.

Besa presently lifted a fist into the night and said:
So much is outside. My life is there, too, suffering the sculptor's knife. I am the same as clay. Mould me now, you who are outside, that I may find in this moment some hope to be.
He lurched forward and said:
What am I doing here at this bar?

Early this morning, a feeling of unsurpassable sweetness such as he had never experienced before seized him by storm. Leaving the room to savour it in solitude, Besa, calmed and awed by this state of inner repose, wandered down to the boats anchored at the dock and for a while perched on a rock halfway immersed in the water, his eyes scanning the stretch of the rippled lake apparently touching the horizon, and waited for the sun to appear. In that moment, the rare moment when he encountered the ecstasy of thought merged with more stable emotions, Besa reached a certainty that time had now come for him to go, and so he would go. He would leave behind him a closed life the beauty of which had been the simple remembered pleasures of childhood and innocence (a life plagued by sickness, poverty and unrest, a haunted life permeated by doubts and the ravings of his uncritical sense), and would, in surrender and closeness to every essential circumstance to be disclosed, create a critical life standing apart from itself, a life aware of itself a truly living.

Unable to bear such feelings any more, Besa rose from the rock and strolled up and down the Small Beach, reaching as far as the reeds sometimes, envisioning university life beckoning to him to come away and shelter in the light of thought and contemplation. He fell on his kneels, overcome by an inexpressible joy, and murmured to himself, 'I am an initiate,' an initiate whose soul was athirst for the eternal and abiding. He would be heedless of intellect, satiating curiosity by frequenting the library, the treasure of books, whiling away long hours of his life browsing through works by authors with whom he would become acquainted. He would read their works piously, for such works could not be uttered by commonplace minds, yet by the race of men and women who had tasted or alluded to the higher realities and forms of thought that neither time nor place could diminish or obliterate…the chanting fruit, the chanted harvest and feast and radiance of lofty intelligence. Besa gave out a cry, a psalm for those gallants in all centuries who, despite the constant siege of ever day distractions, had nevertheless fashioned with their hands works of such stature as to defy temporality, the abundant souls who had dared throw their lives into the burdensome expansion of their consciousness.

His cheeks wetted by tears of mystic rapture, Besa stared over the lake and entreated the sun (now rising over the horizon), or the idea of it as a causation or effect, that some of its power be apportioned to him. He said:

O glorious light, primal source of what was, what is, and what is to be. I as an existent worthy of nothing prostrate myself before

*you, you who are the way and the ultimate. In the blindness of our
youth we have stumbled along our ways, surrounded as we are by
the veil of darkness. We know not where we come from, where we
are nor where we should go, for uncertainty and the forest of night
have enveloped us. No one will heed our cries, and yet we cannot
wait to find our way. If we should wait, our life will fall from us. If
we should take our steps, our lives might plunge into the unknown.
We therefore stand as a challenge in a world we scarcely know, yet
in a world in which we must act. May we learn to love the best in us
– the imperishable – or live by that which consciously and really is
so that, would our world collapse in our sight, we would stand unshaken and never perish with our bodies. O wondrous light, hear
the pleas of your child.*

Besa woke up with a frightful start, after what seemed to have
been a very long time, and only to find – what a miraculous day! –
Musonda giving his shoulders a vigorous push.

'Wake up, wake up,' she urged, squatting beside him.

Besa blinked and rubbed his eyes with the back of his hand. He
was momentarily disoriented; he didn't know where he was.

'Are you all right?'

He raised himself on his elbows. His gaze fell on her arms and
shoulders, her puzzled expression, and then on her chest. He imagined her breasts veiled behind her garment, and a rush of memories
made him quaver with desire.

The girl must have felt the same sensation, too (in a moment
vibrant with doubt, momentary unease, bewilderment and finally
happy relief, a moment made wholly new by this unsuspected encounter), for she flushed and moved even closer to him so that
their bodies touched. As if in a trance, in a voice strangled by emotion, she echoed his name, 'Besa' at least twice, then in an impul-
sive movement reached out her arms and took his head between her
palms (and kissed him, deeply on the lips), before they slumped on
the sand in a wild embrace. She was shaking against him. She was
sobbing quietly now.

'I missed you very much,' she murmured softly when they sat
up. 'I didn't know what to do. I felt lost without you.'

Besa smoothed sand from her hair and face and pressed her to
him. It was sudden, how they had met again, yet he was very glad to
have her back in his arms. She was warm and nice. Her arms were
wrapped around him like creepers of the grove, and he thirsted for
the glamour of this woman with whom he would share, now and
forever, the storms of life in their fullness and diversity. It was in her

that his feelings would grow, deepen and extend. She was his end, she was his commitment.

'I missed you, too,' he confessed, remembering their recent past. 'I am very sorry for what happened. It was all my fault. I am usually arrogant but it didn't take long to see how foolish I had been and what I had lost. Please forgive me. Let me be your best friend to stand by you forever.'

'It wasn't entirely your fault. I am also to blame. I was nervous and mixed up. I hid the truth from you and me until you left. Then I realised how much you meant to me and that nothing would be the same again without you. Please forgive me. Let me be your friend to be by your side till the end of time.'

Her words wrung tears from his eyes. She wiped them with her hand and thanked him for the poem. 'I really love it. I didn't know you could write poetry.'

Besa sighed. It had been almost fictitious, and yet the girl was there all right. He cuddled her in his arms and said he loved her.

She kissed him. 'I believe you. I love you too.'

Besa stood up and held out a hand. Musonda got up too. She clung to him but he had to disengage them as some people were watching.

'They have been watching us all the time,' she protested. 'Another kiss won't make any difference.' She searched his lips and kissed them again, lightly.

He clasped her hand and pulled her to his room.

'How did you find me?' he asked her.

'The people at the reception told me your room number. When I got there the door was locked. The watchman said you might be at the rocks or small beach, so I decided to try the small beach first and found you snoring.'

'I had drunk some alcohol last night and was feeling rather sleepy all morning. I spent some time at a disco.'

'Was it good?'

'Somehow. It wasn't too bad.'

The girl nodded enthusiastically. 'What about finding where you stand? Has it helped to be here by yourself just as you thought?'

'I think so. I hope so. I feel great to be by myself.'

Musonda threw him a smile and squeezed his hand. They collected the key at the reception and headed to the room. She watched him unlock the door and told him about the change in her schedule.

'I have a day off today, thanks to my sickness.'

'Are you ill?'

'No,' she laughed. 'I am okay. I only got a sick note just to be with you.'

The door unlocked. Besa said, 'Well, this is it. This is my place. What do you make of the room?'

Chapter 7

Concerns the meditations at the shrine

If the place of sanctuary consists in what we are and not what others persuade us to be, then it is not so with me. Entering this earth in nakedness soon after the Spirits of my Fathers bade me farewell, I began to live my destiny in the land and ways of life that have now almost fallen apart, though my soul still extols and exults in the humanity and generosity of a life more preferable than this – our cultured spirituality, our abundance of love and gentleness, our reverence for what man is – while I yet suffer pangs I cannot here tell. My memory is my grave. In these unrelenting returns to the days behind me, and many struggles to see in these days things of worth and finding none, I am led towards nothing but confusion, and sometimes this confusion weighs over my heart like a huge burden, yet I cannot speak of it, only how it sets me apart from everyone, I who feels like a stranger in my own land.

That I, and perhaps others like me, should feel strangers in our own land is perhaps proof that not everything is well. We are outcasts. Denied the chance to speak and be heard, we live outside of everyone – our thoughts too heavy to carry – and yet would be happy if, one fortunate day, our own people took pains to be where we are, since we ask nothing but their ears, that they listen to us and see for themselves the wealth entombed in what they hold to be true – there is nothing, their feet have condemned them.

In this aloneness of being, removed from the whirlwind of the village-life, I find some peace here at our dear shrine. Behind me, however, people are living their usual lives. They shall accept new tongues of speech and new ways of doing things, and will be glad in such things unheard of. Like slaves shadowed in the darkness, they, believing to be free, will bow in obedience to what they hardly know, and they together with their leaders will walk towards a pit. Who can warn them? What can I tell them? What is the shrine to them? What is the past to they whose eyes are cast in an opposite direction where the only things that are *white* are the only things to store? What use is there in evoking a memory that has no place here? What are ancient words but untrue gossip drivelling out of blind old people with nothing to do? Am I of any use to anyone?

I am nothing here. My body is my tomb. With most of its dreams unrealised, my life has almost neared where it should now cease.

I am nothing in the eyes of everyone – including my wife, mother of my children. O Spirits of the land, a man is unfortunate if he should live his life with a woman who cares nothing for what he is, for this would only bring into their lives tears and differences.

'I was asked today,' my wife started, a long time ago, 'that I should speak to you about the Church and Yesu Klistu.[26] Yesu is a Son of God who died for us. He died for you and me in order that we receive salvation. His blood was shed for sinners. Yet if they rejected him they would burn up in a lake of fire at the end of time. There shall be no mercy for the Children of Lucifer, for those who disbelieve in Him. And you, my husband, are such a child. But there's still a small time for you to repent of your sins. Do you desire to burn in this lake of suffering and pain?'

I cleared my voice to speak.

'Why are you telling me all this? For how long will you preach to me what I cannot understand and accept? Can't you leave me in peace?'

'Musunga, Yesu Klistu is calling out to you to be saved. Stop worshipping your shrines and your relics and return to Yesu. In Him alone will you find peace. You're a troubled man. Give yourself up to Him and all your troubles will leave!'

'I don't want your salvation. I can't abandon myself to Him. There is no meaning in your words.'

'You perceive no meaning because you always harden your heart. Would I ask you to do something if I knew it would not be good for you?'

'What if you asked me in ignorance?'

'I am not ignorant. Everything I say is written in the Bible.'

'What is the Bible?'

'It is a book in which the Word of God has been revealed. How He created the world in seven days, how He made man and woman, how our first parents sinned and, because of it, how He became angry and punished them and their descendants forever...up to the present day! All this is written in the Bible.'

'Did you say God punished them and their descendants forever?'

'Yes.'

I could not believe what I heard.

'Your God must have a very cruel heart,' I said. 'How can He punish the innocent? Am I to believe that it is just to punish a man's children and grandchildren, for crimes they did not commit? Is this what you are taught?'

'It is what we are taught.'

'And for sins that the descendants did not commit, He sent his Son Yesu to die on the cross?'

'Yes, that was what happened.'

'What is the meaning of sin?'

'It is doing what God does not like.'

'And *what* does your God like?'

'He likes honesty, loving one another, caring for the sick and doing many other good things.'

'*That* is not new to us. We have always lived that way even without your Bible or God's assistance. We don't need Him to learn those virtues.'

'Our ways are not enough. You must also accept Yesu as your personal saviour. You must let Him lead your life.'

'Why should someone lead my life as if it is not mine?'

'It is not your life!'

'It is my life! I care for it, I suffer for it, and I do what I choose with it. I concern myself with it – because it is mine.'

'You are proud.'

'No I am not! I have just failed to see why it is important to believe in Yesu Klistu. What can He do for me that I cannot do by myself? Does He know me?'

She would not answer.

'What if I refused to accept Him? What would He do to me, and why?'

'He would punish your disobedience.'

'Have you ever seen or heard of anyone punished because they refused to accept your God? I would like your God to speak to me face to face.'

She would not answer again, so I went on:

'Mother of my children. You speak to me of strange things like fire (which you haven't seen), and of the Bible (which you can't even read, or if you can, cannot question.) You speak to me of Heaven (where you haven't been) and of Yesu Klistu (the man who is neither from our tribe nor lineage) and then desire that I feel guilty for sins I did not commit. You say He came to save me though I cannot see what He has saved us from, or what changes He has brought in this world.'

'He has brought us light. His death and teaching are what have saved us. You should just believe.'

'He did not die for me, or for you!'

'He died for us!'

'He did not die for us. *We* are not the reason why they killed Him. Why should we bear upon our shoulders the blame and guilt of His own people? He did not come for us. He came for Himself, and died because of what He was. It is not because of us!'

'You have a devil in you. A devil that does not want you to obey God.'

'You are wrong, for I have no devil in me. Whatever I have said it was I who said it – and not your devil. Or do you want me to believe everything without thinking? Why should your God punish me for my desire to understand what He wants us to believe?'

We looked at each in hatred. I said:

'This man you're bringing into this house will cause ruin upon our hands. He is not one of us. He cannot be our eyes with which to see our way. We have to look to our ancestors and ourselves for guidance.'

'Our ancestors are dead. They cannot lead us. We need something stronger than ourselves to show us the way. We need God and Yesu Klistu. We need a rock of all ages.'

'If we ceased looking to ourselves for what we have to be and entrusted our paths to someone else, how could we be sure that He would lead us where we wanted? We might be too weak or frail to rely on ourselves, yet there's nothing else to rely on beside ourselves. We are the steps to what we want.'

'Your speech is the speech of arrogance. You know it inside yourself – everyone needs God to be happy. Without Him the earth becomes dark and frightening!'

'Your God cannot lead us. He can only divide us. We have our own gods and mediums to venerate. We need nothing else.'

'Worshipping skulls of your ancestors will lead us nowhere!'

'You cannot understand. My words are greater than you are.'

'You worship rivers, lakes and relics and other dead things.'

'You don't know the meaning of death. If the lake and rivers and the grasses were not there, where would you be? Must I curse my land and praise a God to receive food from your heaven? Must I scorn the presence of what is, and abandon my life to what is not there? Must I lose this life in the hope of another that may not be there?

'Mother of my children, it is not Klistu or your new God who made you. This land and what it is, is what made you. Are you not ashamed of walking to Church? Do not forget that even the white man is laughing at you because he knows what you have lost. The shrine and your tribe are closer and more meaningful to you than what you now believe – as if you were the creators of his religion!

Our true life does not consist in becoming what other people tell us to be. Our life is the root of where we are, since what surrounds us is what creates us. A person without a navel name is lost, just like someone who despises his or her roots is dead. Finding security in other people's works and forgetting to create your own is foolishness. Our ancestors were not wrong to teach that *akacila kasengula apo kekeele.* Therefore, you may only trust those things that are truly yours. You cannot trust the words of a foreigner.'

'Our priests are children of God who only speak the truth, and white people are better than we are. They have brought us the light. We should be thankful.'

Her words filled my heart with anger. I stayed for some time without speaking, not knowing what to say to help her understand. Nonetheless I pleaded for her to see the meaning of my words.

'Mother of my children, is it very difficult for you to understand? Do not curse the memory of our Forefathers, saying it was darkness. Do not belittle your land!'

She shook her head at my speech, as if I had been uttering words that befitted the countenance of fools. In this silence, I clearly understood that our lives would never be the same again, a realisation, which filled me with terror, for, I loved her as much as myself.

'You speak like a mad man,' she said suddenly, unafraid to berate me with words such as these. 'Other people have now believed in the new God. Churches are being built, people are learning how to read and write while you seek the past. You're not even afraid of the wrath to come. What is it that hardens your heart?'

'It is the truth that dwells in me. A truth that says, I can choose between things.'

'What truths have you been speaking here?' she asked. 'I heard nothing except the utterances of your falsehoods.'

I wanted to argue that our past as a people could not have originated from the Bible or the speech of the white man. I also wanted to show her that the stranger, whom we had received in our midst like our relative, could not completely be trusted as he had deceived our chiefs and stolen our wealth. He had also taken our people into slavery across the seas. What was there that he couldn't do to us if he had done terrible things with the blessings of his God? Why then should I be asked to kneel before his God, if such a God had looked at our plight in silence? Was this not enough proof that He cared nothing about us?

I looked at her open-mouthed. She could not understand, and a deep sorrow engulfed me. I knew it would be useless to speak. How could someone like her ever understand? My eyes tear-filled, I went outside into the night because I needed to be away from her. This was the only thing to do.

These were moments when, alone and wondering what misfortune had fallen over my house, I whispered to myself, 'I have to divorce her. I cannot bear to live with someone who is a traitor of my own land,' yet such feelings brought other fears as well, such as those of my children. I went over to see if they were well. I patted the shoulders of my first born child, Chizindo (who was eight and already running errands for elders), and asked about school. I looked at Mwape: he was six, mischievous and difficult to appease, and asked him if he had caught any grasshoppers this morning. Chisala moved closer, his face bearing an eager smile. He informed me that Besa, the youngest, had wet his shorts. I stared at the boy: he was a pitiable sight, he liked to play alone, and he resented others. I called his name but, surprisingly, the boy started crying. 'Stop crying, for my father's namesake,' I said, and picked him up from the floor. I gathered the children around me and told them humorous stories. They listened. They seemed to understand.

Now I said to myself, 'What would be the lesser evil: to divorce so that I might have some peace but at the same time throw the children into the grave of suffering? Or should I let myself suffer while I stayed in a loveless marriage, so that the children might grow well, even when they would be affected by their parents who lived many distances apart?' Such were my troubles. Yet I had to decide. I decided not to separate from her for their sakes, on the faith that the little ones would grow to be greater than I am, and that perhaps my wife would change.

I waited for her and saw no change, while she fervently prayed to her God for my lost soul to see the light and follow in her footsteps.

Watching this earth changing always in my eyes, I have wept over what had once been ours has now been swept away. Money has become a God to be respected while humanity is no longer the centre of our lives. I am living in a world I can hardly understand.

Old men are sleeping with their daughters without shame; mothers with their sons, sisters with their brothers, uncles with their nieces, while marriages break like glass. Babies are drinking beer, smoking dagga, playing at night like ghosts, assaulting their parents – spitting in their faces and saying, 'You did not bear us!' Women are sleeping with strangers in the length of a single sigh, abandoning their babies, and walking naked and smiling at confused children, bleaching their skins to remove the 'curse' of being born black. Deceit is honesty and honesty is abhorrent. Funerals are laughed at. Thieves are praised and the victims are despised. Poverty is everywhere. Leaders are stealing from their people when the people are singing or asleep. The law is an axe against the weak and the poor. Crime is a common sight. Police officers and judges protect criminals. New roads and thoughts are created but lead nowhere. And as people queue for mealie meal or protest against prices, politicians are chanting, 'This is development.' Men are drunk in the morning when they are supposed to be working. Beer drinking has become our culture. Children are scolded for speaking their language but praised and rewarded for speaking the language of white people. Beggars are everywhere. Disease is our companion. Police officers walk about with guns to impose terror in the people they are supposed to protect. The Party has become very powerful: the cadres will not tolerate opposing views. Chiefs have lost their worth. Fish in the lake has almost finished. Our Gods are dead... And schools, where children learn what alienates them from their people and surroundings, are collapsing. The armpit is now higher than the shoulders, the tongue may touch the forehead, the eyes have surrendered their sight, and the voice has rebelled against the mouth, as the law of confusion besieges the earth of the wise!

Yet as I watch things come to be and then pass away, I am consoled that it is in their coming that the same things will pass away, and I throw my eyes to the eventuality of this, though with a small fear that in our cherished wisdom or self-righteousness, others will see nothing but our foolishness. And where we thought we were right they would show us how wrong we had always been – and we will be defended by nothing.

O Spirits of my land, my eyes thrust into the gloom of the falling day, or the coming dusk. At these searches of inward and outward realities, I see my confusion deepen, yet no fears are born, no losses are felt, except perhaps a lament in my time, that silent are the ancestors' bleak confinements, and dumb and quiet are their stirrings. We partook of the wrong, and yet today we are right.

Chapter 8

Concerns a sudden visit, memories and images,
And Besa meets Shantiee again

The idea to work for a newsletter hadn't come by storm. It had been – at least for him – a slow process of understanding during which Besa Musunga realised the ineluctable need to express the creative urge in him, the essayist in him. Thus shadowed by the suspicion that he could write, the second-year history major submitted essays to the Vanguard – the most controversial student publication to date – as yet another way of exercising his intellect on diverse issues through critical discussion. Little by little he mastered the art of criticism – and words, mere words that were once vaguely and carelessly used now seemed imbued with conscious meaning, intention and rigour. The most important thing for him, however, was not the social praise or censure which resulted from his works: rather, it was the value contained in the act of realising the labours of his mind, the value had in that which was self-sufficient and required no justification.

But though essays generally gave him satisfaction or the experiences of joy in the contemplation of aesthetic beauty, the task was not only demanding but risky as well. The PIG – or the Party and Its Government – had made it clear to silence, expel, or in some cases imprison, any student writer found guilty of 'offences against public order', even when such 'offences' were genuine criticism of government policy. Such students, therefore, were often warned against 'interference in politics' and sometimes 'tried' at Special Branch cells for their 'irresponsible' actions that tended to cause the public to view the government with ridicule, hatred or disfavour. On the other hand, as one student rightly reminded a visiting government official who had come to warn 'trouble makers', the statement, 'Don't interfere in politics,' was, to many such, clearly irrational, since that by which 'politics' was defined could not possibly exclude students from its ontological implication. Moreover, as every citizen had the natural right to participate in the affairs of the country, it was absurd and discriminatory, therefore, to cause some to lose this right merely because they were students. At the same time, it was equally contradictory to ask students to rally behind the Party for 'peace and development', as this was an acknowledgement of that right to participate in the affairs of the country.

What, then, it was often asked, was the position of the student with respect to what existentially concerned them?

Such were the uncertainties that Besa, this Saturday afternoon, laboured on the last draft of an essay on the economics, politics and ethics of education from the point of view of historical mutation. Sensing for 'offences against public order', he was disconcerted as much that had been written was sceptical of recent government educational reforms. Cautiously the young author examined the work from the context of content but found nothing inconsistent again. Like a valid syllogism, facts naturally led to their logical conclusions by which Besa bared the inadequacies, contradictions and lack of vision of the present education system. Yet the artist's consciousness of the State made him determine the legality of the essay. Hence he pored over law books, emitting occasional grunts whenever he came across clauses or legal instruments that, in all sincerity, were repressive and did not permit the writer to write what he liked. The historian asked: 'If the structure of the Law is designed to protect and sustain the interests of the ruling class, why should I be obliged to obey the law? As the case is, my right to express myself on matters of importance is almost non-existent.' Besa frowned at the pages: 'The Law cannot explain nor defend itself. It cannot account for itself, and yet it sanctions statutory obligations upon everyone.'

Afraid he might tear the script, the historian took a break from his work to put his thoughts back in order as panic, or the fear of the State, had gripped him now. He mounted the stairs and stayed awhile at the rooftop, watching students march to makumbi dining hall for supper. They filed past the School of Mines like ants carrying responsibilities of existence upon their shoulders. They did not see him, of course, they were too intent on themselves to feel noticed. They were a strange lot, and their collective lives were justified by a multitude of heads bending over pages of books – reading, calculating, memorising, or impertinently enacting the monotony of the academic ritual. To what end? – Possibly knowledge in some sense, or the prospects of a job after graduation. Besa focussed his mind on it – on precisely what end education purported to achieve if should retain relevance and meaning, and thereby broached the teleological dimensions of his essay again. Inspired by fresh ideas, he descended the stairs and shut himself in the room to finish the work.

He was hunched over the table, refreshed and ready to start. Besa wrote sentences. Time had stood still; time flowed without his knowing of it. As he riffled through note cards and piles of paper, a knock (like an echo far away), sounded in the room. Besa ignored it: the sound must have come from somewhere else, he didn't expect anyone. Yet there were several other taps on the door – on his door, for sure – this time louder and more desperate, so that he answered irritably, 'Come in!', and waited in annoyance.

It turned out that the caller was a woman. She was coloured: a self-confident girl between eighteen and twenty with strands of brown hair reaching her shoulders. She had barely stepped in. She forced an apologetic smile, revealing a row of white teeth. Where had she come from? He would have liked to give the stranger no serious attention but... the suddenness of her visit and, he dared not admit this to himself, the fact that Besa was physically attracted to her in an instant, perhaps kindled his curiosity in her: a slender, well formed body, a very beautiful face, and a nature that was very new to him.

He gazed at her curiously, lured away from his work, a cluster of questions stuck on his throat. Was she lost or looking for a boy friend who had gone out? He strained hard yet could not remember ever seeing someone like her in this block. Or had he not just seen her? If she had a boy friend in this block, their relationship was most likely just beginning, otherwise he might have seen her at least once. He knew most of the girls who frequented the block. Or could it be that he hadn't seen her though she had been coming here regularly? The historian doubted this too. She was probably just a girl from off campus or a new student looking up a friend for the first time. He explored these possibilities in detail but none fully satisfied. Abruptly, however, the image of the Nigerian student to whom girls flocked like flies flashed in his mind. Besa resisted it – and yet – more and more insistently, the image asserted itself. Was she one of them? Like a fall of rain, a lamentation of Shakespeare rung in his ears: 'O thou weed, who art so lovely fair that the sense aches at thee, was this most goodly book made to write "whore" upon? Heaven stops the nose at it...' He flushed and corrected his feelings: 'I mustn't look at women in a sexually oriented way. It doesn't matter what life they choose to live. I am not called upon to judge them.' Deeply ashamed, Besa was cold and indifferent: his feelings for her vanished.

He caught her admiring species of tiny crystals mounted on a large, thick cardboard paper hanging by the thread against the wall. He was fond of this treasure. It had taken him one and half years to collect. Some were imitations while others were semiprecious stones anyone could buy on the streets. He loved to see them there.

He appreciated their symmetries and the stones interested him in the mathematics of patterns and space.

When their eyes met at last there was, in the ensuing moments, suspense and anticipation. Besa judged the moment well; he was resolved to be rid of her and go back to the essay.

'Can I help you?'

'Yes, please,' she replied, taking another step into the room. 'I am trying to locate someone. This is Soweto 2 room 22, isn't it?'

Besa said it was.

'Do you live here in this room?'

'Yes. I share it with someone else, though. A fourth year vet.'

'O, so you must be the person I am looking for!'

'Me?'

'Yes!' Her eyes gleamed in triumph. 'Aren't you Besa Musunga?'

The historian hesitated: he eyed the girl mistrustfully, and for reasons that were obscure at the moment denied his own identity.

'I am afraid you've come to the wrong place. I am not the person you're looking for. Try other hostels.'

'But I thought…' she stammered in astonishment, glancing back at a piece of paper wedged between her fingers. 'I thought this was the correct address?'

'Well, I don't know about that but the fact is I am not the person you want. There's certainly a mistake. Or do you want me to accept that I am Besa when I am not?' He fidgeted with a pencil and went on relentlessly: 'If there's nothing else I can do for you then you'll have to excuse me. I've work to do.'

A few minutes later Nchike – a friend and third year economics major who also contributed work to the Vanguard – found Besa sullen and disgruntled by the absurdity of what he had done, though the friend paid no notice of it at first.

Nchike said:

'Are you coming to the meeting, Ferio?'

'Which one?'

'The Vanguard meeting, of course. We're to review our next publication tonight. Had you perhaps forgotten?'

Besa had forgotten all about it.

'Are you coming, then?'

'I hope so.'

'Fine! Now I must run along to have others confirm their attendance. The venue is the same but the time is different. Be there by twenty thirty. I'll see you later. Goodbye.'

'Nchike...'

'Yes?'

'Don't go away yet. I have something to tell you.'

'You're not about to start another lengthy discussion, I believe!'

'No. It's something different. Did you meet anybody on your way up?'

'I did. I met a girl at the ground floor landing. She's coloured. She was asking for directions.'

'Where?'

'I wouldn't know. She was talking to a guy and I was in a hurry.'

'Do you know the guy?'

'I don't know him, man. Why are you asking?'

'Be patient. I shall soon explain...Had you seen this girl before or was this the first time you had seen her?'

'I had seen her a good number of times before, usually in the company of her friends. She's a first year. Why are you interested in women all of a sudden?'

'You'll probably laugh at me if I tell you.'

'Perhaps you proposed to her and were rebuffed?'

'No.'

'Well?'

'She was here to see me and I more or less dismissed her. I thought she had come from the Special Branch.'

For some minutes Besa narrated all that had happened without seeking to excuse himself. When he had finished, Nchike threw him a look of disapproval.

'The first thing you should have done was ask who she was or where she had come from. You should have queried her if you were suspicious. Why didn't you?'

'I only wanted her to leave.'

'Ok, but why, Ferio? Why?'

'I don't know why. I acted on impulse.'

'Your reaction, assuming this incident really took place, was based on an assumption, however false or farfetched. Didn't you see about her something that made you suppose she was from the Special Branch? Her appearance or the way she behaved, for instance?'

'No. As a matter of fact we hardly spoke for more than two minutes and I never paid her particular attention.'

'How would you justify your behaviour in that case?'

'I don't know. I just reacted, that's all.'

Nchike lit a cigarette and watched rings of smoke twirl and disperse. He rose to pace the room, the expression on his face alert and critical as he considered the situation.

'There are two possibles. Either she's from the Special Branch or she's not, and I am ready to admit both as real possibilities. Yet for some reasons I am more inclined to the second than the first. The girl just came to see you, and that is that.'

'What makes you say so?'

'It's clear, isn't it? She knew where you stayed; she came to the right person. She had reasons.'

Besa regarded the argument too weak to justify belief, yet did not interrupt.

'Perhaps she had heard of you and wanted to ask a few questions. Perhaps she needed help from you.'

'She had never heard of me and didn't need any help.'

'She had read your essays and had been inspired by them. She asked around and found you. She wanted to meet the mysterious man who writes under the pseudonym "Ferio". Or perhaps she had been sent to you by someone – some of your class, for instance!'

'Perhaps you are right.'

'I am damn right. As far as I am concerned there is no real basis to suppose that the girl is an agent. The problem is you. *You* are fucked up and need your head examined.'

Besa smiled in spite of himself.

'You're irrational. You took for an agent someone you never sufficiently observed. You acted on impulse – on no grounds at all. And what's worse – you weren't even curious about someone as beautiful as she whereas any normal young man would have been interested in her and only been too glad to help.'

'Perhaps...but I was busy and she happened to come at a time I was reflecting the legal implications of my essay. I must have been thinking of freedom of conscience as well. You know as much. Student authors are watched by the security system, and we can't create without wondering how the Party will react. We write in fear. We're not really free. We're afraid of criticising the State...When she came I naturally assumed she was from the Special Branch, given this psychological background. It's perhaps outrageous, but that's how it happened. I've no other explanation.'

'You have no other explanation, you say,' Nchike argued, 'but you should also admit that you're paranoid.'

'Paranoia,' Besa countered, 'is a mental disorder characteristic of people with intense delusions or types of imagined fears having no basis in fact. But this case is radically different because persecutions of students by the State are a physical fact in our present political system, a thing no one would dare deny. And let me tell you something. Why are some students beaten on suspicion of spying for the Office of the President? Why do we flog and treat them like traitors? Is it because we are paranoid?'

'To some extent – yes, since you cannot just pick on anyone and assume they are agents and start beating them up. It is illegal, barbaric, and dangerous.'

'So you still insist that I am -?'

'No no no no. Don't get me wrong. I appreciate your points, really, all of them; though I also feel you should at least have waited before kicking her out. She could have been an agent or couldn't, that's clear, but to act on one assumption rather than another without sufficient evidence is not very wise, just as it isn't wise to overlook instances that can be credible. Between two or more conflicting hypotheses under consideration, there is a conscious process of elimination by way of *testing* each one of them. The one that looks more probable than the rest becomes the basis of further researches. In other words, my friend, one must be cautious before acting in order not to make too many mistakes. The consequences may be very great.'

'What do you advise me to do?'

'I suggest that you search after her and see what happens. If she was looking for you it can only be that she has a message, but what that message is I leave it for you to discover...'

* * * * *

A long time ago, Besa led his beloved to a room at the rest house. She inspected it like a government official, her gaze probing everywhere before settling down on a single bed with blue rumpled sheets. When the woman faced him again, she seemed to have lost her vibrancy and natural ease, Besa decided sadly. He went over and rested both arms on her shoulders, glad to have recovered her to him.

'Well,' murmured he, turning his head slightly round. 'What do you make of the room?'

'It's small but nice. I suppose I like it. How much did it cost you?'

'Almost nothing.'

'How much is "almost nothing"?'

'Does it matter how much I paid for the room?'

'To me, yes.'

He withdrew his arms and moved away from her. Leaning his back against the wall, Besa studied the girl in amusement. Of course Musonda had the right to know yet the least thing he wanted discussed was money. He knew how she would react: she would think he was crazy.

'Well?' she pursued hopefully. 'Won't you tell me?'

'It's not important.'

'How can you say that?'

'Alright. The bill is over there…next to the books on the table. You may look at it if you like.' He slumped on a chair, swung both legs over the edge of the bed and closed his eyes. Abruptly he was tired. He didn't feel like arguing.

Musonda whistled in amazement.

'Just like I thought. It's quite expensive.'

'Think of the nice things we could do together before saying anything more. It's not a question of expense – it's a question of having fun for a few days.'

He heard her giggle: he opened his eyes. She had assumed a serious expression again.

'Your mother,' she said softly. 'What did you say to her was the reason you would be out?'

'I told her a few lies. I said I needed to see a certain teacher about university.'

'Did she believe you?'

'I am sure she did. She had no choice.'

'What about your father, did you lie to him too?'

'My mother explained for me.'

The girl was quiet. She came and perched on his lap and kissed his forehead. Then, in a voice full of apprehension, she said:

'About the money you spend as like, Besa. Where did you get it?'

'Are you suspicious?'

'I am afraid so. Because you don't work.'

He indicated the savings book with a finger:

'Perhaps it'll answer your questions… Muzo, I am not a delinquent. I do things with a purpose, and it's very well for me to be here. I know it's important.'

She was warm and strong: loyal, loving, perhaps needing someone to trust.

'I love you very much,' Besa declared suddenly. 'So much that I wish you could stay with me.'

'It's not possible.'

'Why, I thought you said you'd come to stay?'

Musonda would not speak.

'Why won't you stay with me?'

The girl was still silent.

Besa was mystified. He wanted her very much. In that instant he was so wronged that he only longed to shed tears of relief. He excused himself and made towards the door, very worn and angry. At the same time he was tempted to say, 'You're going nowhere', yet remained passive and silent. Let her be. She had the right to her life. What would be the use of forcing her against her will? Besides, Besa had no desire to persuade her: she could decide the best for herself. It wasn't fair, though. He had almost excluded her from his life when she discovered him on the beach. She had come freely with open eyes, knowing what to expect, and had made her confessions there. And now – she wasn't even sure about anything.

A suppressed sob startled him: the woman was crying!

'Why are you crying?' Besa demanded in alarm.

Musonda did not reply. How tiresome everything was! Truly this was too much. She had looked formidable the first time they met – now she was weeping like a child, a little child (miserable and defenceless), for no apparent reason. Out of politeness he retraced his steps to comfort her, though he felt quite ridiculous. He wasn't used to fussing over a grown woman. Besa assured himself: 'She's nonetheless a nice girl. She'll soon be composed, she left her patients for my sake – now see what has happened. I don't understand it at all, yet I am bound to accept the situation. I am responsible for it. I hope things will be all right.'

Perhaps because of caresses or soothing words of assurances, the girl responded by way of flinging her arms round his neck. They rolled onto the carpet, humility and longing visible in her eyes. He slid his hand behind the blouse and found her breasts. As he squeezed or stroked them, she dug fingernails into his flesh and made purring noises like a cat. She shut her eyes. She clutched at his clothes, wound her legs around him – and Besa, inundated by her eager responses and breath-taking kisses, bent as if to an impetuous wind.

He rose to the call of her body needing to be filled, like a plant thirsting for sunlight, sighs of pleasure gurgling from his throat. For in tender moments such as these, lamentably rare and fleetingly long, the girl had – so to speak – offered him the best gift of herself by teaching him to recognise what he lacked in himself. He was eternally grateful. He racked his mind for a present to give to Musonda. He settled for a necklace and, taking pencil and paper by the bedside, scrabbled at words in order to leave some likeness to this moment behind. Yet he couldn't. No single line issued from his hands in a flow of poetic verse. Besa whispered a short prayer to the Heavens:

I thank you, God,
For having brought into my life such a good friend.
Help me learn to love always
    Thy precious gift;
And to cherish her life and mine.
I ask this through Christ, our Lord. Amen.

Naked they lay together, touching and speaking in undertones. She rolled over him and laid her hand upon his chest. The girl was newly pleased.

'What could be the time?' she said.

'Probably after twelve.'

'That explains why I am famished.'

'We can order our lunch or go out to eat. Whichever you please.'

'Let's go out and stretch our legs a bit. I would like some fresh air, too.'

They got up on their feet, looked deeply in each other's eyes, embraced in silence. Tears had now trickled down her cheeks. She tightened her hold on him and kissed his lips again. She was in earnest.

'Besa,' she said with a new gentleness in her voice. 'I'll stay if you still want me to. I've changed my mind.'

Some few weeks before Besa was to leave for Lusaka, it became routine for him to find the girl patiently waiting for him at the hospital, ready to be taken 'home'. Once they were in her tiny room in the Beach rest house, she would lock the door and ask to be undressed. She would kneel to unlace his shoes (muttering in frustration whenever she failed to undo a knot), remove the socks torn in some places, unbuckle the waist belt, pull his trousers down, unbutton his shirt…and show him to their bed. There she would smile in his face and wrestle with him – and would, in moments so joyously ardent as to be sublime, sacrifice for love the best moments of herself. Besa was content. She had helped him understand or taste

– what could it be? – the experiences of love in their eternity and wonder.

They sometimes took walks into the village and sampled fruits at the market. As they made their rounds, the girl impressed him with her new boldness in public since, at times, she often tugged at his elbow or got him to share a banana she had peeled for them. Her attention was fixed on him: she was affectionate, protective, responsible and generous. The girl matured in his eyes. She sensed his moods, appreciated his strengths and weaknesses and, perhaps more importantly, grew to love him every coming day. On the other hand Besa liked to let her do things the way she wanted them done. He took joy in her interests and learnt to see life from her point of view. He realised later on that the meaning and value she attached to different things were not quite the same as his. Thus he became cautious, tolerant and perhaps a little human.

As days drew closer for him to go to university, Musonda became unusually quiet, remote and petulant. Of late she had been talking about her childhood and how much she missed her family in Kasama. She hadn't paid them a visit for a long time, and this saddened her.

'I come from a family of four girls. I am the first-born child. My sisters wrote me – two of them, asking why I no longer visit during vacations. I never wrote back.'

'Tell me why?'

'I forgot to until recently when I seriously started thinking about the way you talk about your family. You're so close together, whereas I am very far away from mime. Perhaps being away makes me feel dissociated from them. Perhaps I've lost touch. But I've had strange dreams lately. Did I tell you?'

'No.'

'I keep dreaming about my mother and I am worried about her. Do you suppose she might be sick?'

'It's difficult to say.' He cupped her head in his palms: 'Muzo, perhaps the best thing to do is going home and staying with your family for some time. They miss you, too.'

'Yes, especially my sisters.'

'When did you last go home?'

'Almost a year and half now.'

'You see? You've been away too long, and this may explain your dreams. You are home sick and need to go back to your roots. It's not enough to have a sense of where our home is. We sometimes need to be physically there... otherwise we'd always be rootless.'

'Yes,' she sighed. 'You're right. I've been away too long. This is why I am so ashamed.' She lowered her eyes and propped her head against his shoulder and promised to go home.

'When?' Besa demanded.

'There will be two months between when I complete my field experience and my first appointment. I'll go home then.'

'How long will you be here before you finish your programme?'

'About one and half months.'

He sharply looked at her: the full implication of their future hit him with such force that his body quavered in fear. The thought of being separated from her for months was intolerable.

'Do you know what this means?' said Besa. 'It means that by the time you've started work I'll have been into the second term – so we shan't be able to see each other for at least six months!'

The girl did not look perturbed. 'We'll bear it,' she relied confidently. 'Six months isn't much so long as we keep in touch and care for each other.'

Besa was silent. Things were easier said than done. Life was complicated yet he could do nothing but hope for the best.

'What's the matter? You're so quiet!'

'I've just realised how little time is left to be together. One would wish we had done more with it. You know when I am leaving, of course?'

'Yes – you told me. This Sunday, isn't it?'

Besa nodded. 'Five away before we part!'

'We'll see each other again after my field experience because I shall have to go back to college to report and collect all my things. After that it shall be as we plan. But my home will always be open to you any time you feel like coming to see me. I would love to look forward to this.'

'Where will you be posted?'

'I don't know yet. But I might work anywhere in the Copperbelt. I'll let you know once I know for sure. Are you worried about us?'

'Yes.'

'Why?'

'Because I love you. Because I'll now have to live away from you.'

'Be positive. We shall be meeting from time to time. Just let us keep in touch.'

'I'll certainly keep in touch.'

'Write to me as soon as you arrive.'

'I hate letter writing. I'd rather we just phoned because it's easier and faster.'

'Phones here aren't very reliable.'

'And letters take too long to arrive!'

'How shall we communicate then?' she asked in horror. 'I'll need to know how you are or else be anxious!'

'Ok. I'll write and see about the phones.'

'Do you know the hospital address?'

'I'll look it up in the directory.'

'No. Much better if I give it to you when you go back – with the phone numbers, of course. They keep changing numbers all the time.'

A gentle smile brightened his face. He was lucky to have someone like her at his side.

'What are you smiling at?'

'At you – or at nothing in particular. Are you suspicious?'

'Sort of.'

'No need to be. I just had a pleasant thought...It's nice to be with someone who's positive and forward looking.'

'I only needed to be sure we'll stay in touch.' She trustfully looked at him: 'You wouldn't like to break the ties between us, would you?'

His head shook. 'I'd never do that.'

'Nor I.'

A hand fell on his thigh – a feminine hand groping everywhere: subtle in touch, gentle but persistent, a hand that aroused him to heights he had never known. Mind and heart reposed in a unitary feeling of oneness with her, in an affinity to love and trust her always...even where he wasn't always and completely loved and trusted in return!

Besa stood up and yawned, viewing the scene once again. They were at the Small Beach, a short strip of sand studded with sparse grasses, reeds and bushes. A stream flowed on nearby. In the far distance to the right, following the shore line of the lake, he made out the pier, the boats, the radio transmitter towering over iron-roofed structures close by, and some grass thatched houses partially shaded by bananas and mango trees. It was a charming sight. Yet as the gaze shifted over the lake – presently calm and deceptively infinite in extent – there was to be experienced again (in this liquid sunset), a sensation of finality without an end, for an ominous gloom and shadows had descended upon the very roots of things.

One Friday evening, the historian was seen in the Zambezi Common Room waiting for his turn to try a call to Samfya. Immedi-

ately the girl replaced the receiver back on the hook, he stepped
into the booth with a decided air about him, dialled the number, inserted three tokens into the slot, and listened for the dialling tone. It
hummed for some seconds: then a male voice boomed into the ear-
piece:
'Samfya Holiday Beach. Good evening.'
'Good evening, sir. May I talk to Miss Musonda Matipa? She's a
student clinical officer from Chainama doing fieldwork there... Yes,
she's booked in room six... Besa Musunga. I am calling from Lu-
saka, University of Zambia...Thank you!'
He gripped the receiver more tightly than before and waited. Af-
ter about a minute, her familiar voice – although distorted slightly
– came on the line:
'Hello?'
'Hello, Muzo...Guess who's calling?'
'Is that you, darling?'
'Yep!'
Sounds of excitement, hysterical laughter.
'You bastard, why didn't you call sooner? You had me wor-
ried!'
'I thought you despised phones so I –'
'Idiot!'
Besa laughed in delight.
'Sorry, sweetheart. I couldn't contact you earlier because I was
running up and down. I needed to settle down first.'
Silence.
'Are you there or do you want me to hang up?'
'I am still here. Don't hang up or I'll kill you. Tell me every-
thing.'
'During the past week there have been a lot of activities for the
first years. We had to apply for bursary schemes and this took days.
We also had to attend an orientation programme and workshop on
how to use the Library and take lecture notes. We then had a tour of
Lusaka for students who'd never been to the city so they wouldn't
get lost if they decided to come into town on their own. We also had
a buffet and speeches from distinguished members of the University, and much more!'
A moment of silence slipped in.
'I am almost settled now after days of bewilderment. Lectures
start next week, Monday, and I am nervous!'
'Have you been accommodated?'
'O yes, I am in the New Residence. Can I give my address?'

'One moment, mister. Let me collect a pen and paper. I'll be right back!'

She returned:

'Your address again, please?'

He repeated it slowly until she had written it down. There was another voice in the background. He asked who it was.

'It's Gertrude,' she answered excitedly. 'She wishes to say hi to you.'

'Alright, but not for long.'

Two seconds passed, and then he said:

'Hello, Gertrude?'

'Hello, Besa. How are you?'

'I am fine, thank you. How are you?'

'Great.'

'How's Samfya?'

'Samfya is okay except for a recent outbreak of dysentery around Mwamfuli and Chipepa areas.'

'That is news to me. Is the situation serious?'

'Not really. The spread is contained at the moment and we are doing all we can to educate the people on sanitation. So we are mostly travelling around. It's quite interesting, clinically speaking.'

Besa laughed.

'What's funny?'

'Nothing. It's good to hear your voice again.'

'Did Muzo tell you I have a boy friend now?'

'No she didn't. Who's the lucky fellow?'

'His name is Peter. He's an accountant working in Mansa. We met at the Post Office and that started it. He's a nice guy. He's already met Muzo and she likes him. I hope you'll also like him!'

'I am sure I will. I am happy for you. I wish you the best with Peter.'

'Thanks a lot. I also wish you a good time at university and love and happiness with Muzo. She's here now – very anxious to speak to you. Goodbye from me and thanks for talking!'

'Goodbye.'

Musonda said:

'Well? Here I am for whoever wants to talk to me.'

'Are you alright?'

'Aha.'

She explained briefly what she had been doing the past one and half weeks.

'I am usually working in the children's ward. O, I almost forgot!
I saved some good news for you!'

'What is it?'

'Some UNICEF people are here and there's a possibility I may
be sponsored to study in England for two years. Doctor Katiiwa has
recommended me for a UN programme aimed at training potential
students in various fields such as cell biology, nutrition, and tropical medicine and so on. I have been asked to submit results tran-
scripts to the Director in Lusaka for consideration as soon as possible. I haven't done so yet.'

'Why?'

'I needed to talk to you about it before making a decision.'

Besa was quiet. He thought: 'She doesn't need me to make decisions about her life – it's her life.'

'Are you around?'

'Of course, I am listening.'

'So...what do you think. Should I go ahead?'

'Yes, go ahead. I've no objections. I'll give you all my support.'

'Please be honest. Tell me anything...anything!'

'I am being very honest. Make the submissions today and let's
hope for the best.'

'I thought you'd be upset if I left. I thought you wouldn't like
me to.'

'Ever heard of St. Augustine, Muzo?' he asked after a short pause.

'No. Who is he?'

'He was a theologian and author of the *Confessions*. He was can-
onised by the Church as a saint. He said, *"Love means, I want you
to be."* If I understand him correctly, he meant that we have to allow
and help those that we love and respect to be the people they must
be, as this would coincide with their happiness and essence. How
else would I show how much I loved you? I only wish you the best
because this is what you need!'

Silence.

'Have you written to your parents yet?'

'No, not yet.'

'Not yet, Muzo, why? What have you been waiting for?'

'I've been busy. I'll write them anyway. I promise.'

'This will be the second time you've promised me.'

'Yes, I know.'

'It's not that I am criticising. I just feel your parents deserve to
know what's happening in your life. In my case I've had to send let-

ters and pictures to my family so that they are aware of where I am and what I am doing with myself.'

'What about me, did you also write me?'

'Yes. Expect your mail any time soon.'

'Thanks a lot.'

'You're most welcome, Muzo.'

'You're very kind and considerate to me.'

'You're flattering me.'

'I am serious.'

'What makes you think so?'

'You've written me a letter as promised, you've taken the trouble to phone as promised, and you've insistently been asking me to contact my parents. And what's more – you'd like me to go abroad for further studies.'

'Does this surprise you?'

'It does – in a way, if I recall the person you used to be just after we met. You weren't as responsible about other people's feelings as you are now. You were mostly cynical, indifferent, headstrong, and often immature. Just someone who pestered me about being his girl friend without giving me a break, so that I sometimes wondered if I was making a mistake. I had doubts about you.'

'Do you still have some of those doubts?'

'Maybe one or two.'

'Do you regret us?'

'No! I don't regret anything between us. I am happy with the way things are at the moment. I love you!'

'I am glad to hear that.'

'What are your plans for the evening?'

'I am not very sure. I might either read in my room or perhaps go to a disco at the Student's Centre. It seems everyone is flocking there for a good time. What about you?'

'I'll sit on the veranda to watch the lake in the moonlight and think about my life and you.'

'In that case I'll walk around in the moonlight and dream about my love for you!'

'That's poetically said. Do you miss me?'

'I do. I look forward to the time we'll see each other again.'

'It's only a month and a week away.'

'I'd be very happy to take you around and introduce you to all my friends.'

'That'd be very nice. As soon as I finish work I'll jump on the first bus and come over. I'd love to meet your friends and see where you live.'

'You've been here before?'

'Only once. We didn't stay longer than we would have liked, though. Do you like the place?'

'I think so. I have an opportunity to lead a more varied life and I am freer in my mind than I ever was. I also like the fact that there's the Library with good books that I can use.'

'Speaking of books, Besa. Doctor Katiiwa has a collection from undergraduate days that are no longer very useful to him. He said to ask if you might like to have them. Should I say yes?'

'If the books are not about surgical techniques or neurology, say yes and tell him I was happy for the gift. I'll write or send him a card. How's he?'

'He's okay.'

'I am surprised at his gift. Had you perhaps talked him into the idea of sending me books?'

'No,' she replied. 'As a matter of fact Doctor Katiiwa is very fond of you – judging from the way he likes any opportunity of discussing you. When I told him that I was sure you would accept the gift from him he looked relieved and said, "There's something special about that boy. I can only hope the books will help him." He is a very nice person.'

'Does he know about us –that we are lovers?'

'Yes, he does. I told him everything. I hope you don't mind?'

'No,' Besa said, glancing at some two students waiting for their chance to take a call. 'I don't mind…Only – there are some two fellows here desirous to phone. They are gesturing to me to hurry up. Can I call you again tomorrow at about the same time?'

'I'd rather I called you instead so you wouldn't have to pay always. What's your number?'

Besa gave her the number. 'It's a pay phone located in the Common Room. There are few pay phones here so the booths are usually crowded. But let's try it, all the same. I'll wait for your call between nine and nine-fifteen. If you fail to come through I'll then try to reach you. Okay?'

'Okay.'

'Another thing. I am not sure I'll spend my first vacation in Samfya but I'd like to see those books. Ask Doctor Katiiwa whether it may be possible to load them on one of the hospital vans that come here once in a while. Give him my address also.'

'I'll do as you wish though it'd also be possible for me to deliver the books to you next month. It would also give me a perfect excuse to see you!'

'You're sure you can manage with an extra load of books?'
'I can manage all right. But I'll still talk to Doctor Katiiwa and see what he says. If he can't send them then I'll take them with me on the bus. Is that okay?'
'Yes, Muzo. That'd be all right. Thank you.'
'Is there anything else I can do for you?'
'Nothing.'
'Nothing at all?'
'Nothing at the moment.'
'Are we about to hang up?'
'Yes,' he said. 'I am sorry.'
'Expect my call tomorrow at the same time and be there for it!'
'Yes, yes. I will be there for it.'
'I love you, sweetheart.'
'I love you, too, with all my heart. Take care!'
'Take care! Goodbye!'
'Bye!'
And the line was cut.

Besides communicating by phone once in a while, Besa received a letter from her after this. It read:

'I was shocked to learn that my first letter hasn't reached you yet. I wonder what happened to it. Please don't be angry with me because I did write and I was the one who physically posted your letter! I used the same address you read out to me on the phone.

Sorry for not being there to talk to. As I write I am at Chilubi Island with five colleagues of mine from Samfya Health Centre. We're here to conduct a series of workshops on the importance of breast feeding, under-five clinics and family planning. Although everyone may attend such meetings we are for the most part interested in women because they play a leading role in child parenting and health care. Since our arrival three days ago, we've made some good progress even though we've also met with some discouragement. The most serious problem has been how to persuade women to speak their minds on intimate issues relating to their reproductive lives. Either they're too shy to share their views or simply terrified of their husbands. What complicates matters is their lack of a basic education and proper cultural attitude to life. Can you imagine a situation where women are generally agreed that having ten or more children is okay? If they were asked, "How will your families survive?" they would say, "God will care for us." But how does God care for them if they are so poor?

According to our schedule we should be back in Samfya af-

ter two and half weeks. We must visit all the islands and parts of Chinsanka and Katanshya. As you can imagine it's a laborious work. The worst I don't like about it is having to move just when you were getting to know a place a little – and having meals at improper times. But this is another chance for me to visit and be of some help to our people who need us most. There's is so much to do and so little time!

I was very happy to receive the beautiful necklace as a present from you. Thank you very much! I have other ornaments, too, but yours is different. It has a unique design that I like and the gift is precious because it came from you. On the other hand a cheaper necklace would have done! I honestly appreciate the gift but feel you needn't have bought an expensive item for me. You are a student and you need every coin you can get.

How are your studies? Hopefully you would have settled down into the academic life by now. I wish you the best, and do hope that the courses in which you are registered are those that really interest you. This is important, but equally important is for you to realise that your family and friends expect a lot from you. I believe in you and expect you to do your best. I look forward to the time I shall give you roses on your graduation day.

Darling, I am about to end this letter. Someone crossing over to Samfya will post it for me. Despite the distance, I am just as close to you as I have always been. You are with me every time, and you are the reason I want to live a successful life. I can face anything with you by my side. And if this is of some comfort to you, I want you to know that if ever there was someone I truly loved and cared for, that someone is you. If ever there had been days in my life when I was loved and happy – when my heart overflowed with gratitude for what life was giving me – it was when I listened to your voice and obeyed. I thank God for granting me the chance to love and be of some good to my best friend. I thank Him for letting me share my life with someone who is truly great. You make me have the courage to see that our love will never die.

This was all I had for you. I will never stop loving you.'

She had signed her name in capital letters.
He slept with this letter under the pillow.

Besa was seated at the centre table in the Mingling Bar, enjoying a morning cup of tea. He retrieved a packet of cigarettes from the right breast pocket and lighted one. He drummed a finger absently on the table, observing other students laughing, shouting or arguing unrestrainedly as if from force of habit. They looked a little tired, eccentric and somewhat suspicious. They made him want to laugh.

A ludicrous figure of a man cut across his view just then. It was Washaama, an old friend and second year student of civil engineering. He was undoubtedly agitated. Besa whistled to draw his attention and beckoned to him.

He said:

'Looks like you're moving against the current, my friend. What happened?'

'I am going to quit,' Washaama declared bitterly. 'I am just wasting my time at this fuckin' place!'

Besa laughed hard.

'I am not kidding.'

'I know. If you should quit nobody will prevent you. You're perfectly free. But please do sit down.'

'Do you have a cigarette?'

'Sure,' he answered, handing him a packet and a box of matches. 'There. Help yourself.'

The young engineer puffed at his cigarette as though he were famished. He surveyed the Bar with shifty, uneasy eyes, and sighed in astonishment.

'What happened, Washaama?'

'Two of my lecturers have resigned from my department for good! This makes ten the number of teachers who have left to join other universities since I came. Should this continue at this rate I doubt whether educational standards in the faculty will be what you'd expect of a university. We're in a lot of shit.'

'Don't despair. Perhaps the university will recruit other lecturers.'

'Undoubtedly. But the reputation of the institution will still be at stake. And we mustn't forget: Given the present rift between lecturers and their employer over conditions of service, coupled with student dissatisfaction with allowances and government interference in the Student's Union, the chances that we might witness another riot are almost certain.'

'Can there be another riot?'

'I don't know. One only senses certain things. One only tries to interpret events.'

'Surely there can be better ways of resolving conflict than stoning buildings or setting everything on fire. Personally I'd hate to see my studies interrupted. What would I say to my family and my girl friend? They'd be very upset.'

'Naturally,' agreed Washaama, trying to appear calm. 'Whenever there's a riot everything is disturbed and everyone is a loser. On the contrary such disturbances often force government to listen to students' grievances. Perhaps we need another riot to change things!'

'What things do you wish to change?'

'Anything which stands in the way of good education and students' welfare. Just the whole system.'

'But, Washaama, although riots may be means to force government to listen, I don't think they are the best way to resolve conflicts. I am sure you will agree with me.'

'I wasn't referring to means but to ends, and as far as most students are concerned the ends are more important than the means. You should also understand that dialogue with government might not always achieve desired results. There are times when violent protests may be considered necessary and perfectly legitimate. Students decide things and bear the consequences.'

'What about the courts? Are you not afraid of the rule of law?'

'I may be afraid but what does it matter? More than anything else we are concerned about creating better conditions for the University. And don't be blinded by "the rule of law". Some rule of law is unjust and its legitimacy should be called into question. It has little to do with right.'

'So you wouldn't be sorry if students rioted, is that correct?'

'I wouldn't if circumstances permitted it, if government continued to ignore students' demands.'

'I don't understand you. At first you spoke as if you were only disappointed as an individual but you're now attributing your feelings to everyone else and talking about students' demands. What demands? Are you not just mistaken?'

'I see. So you haven't read the notices!'

Washaama smiled. He searched among the papers in his file and held out a notice:

'This lists all our demands,' he continued. 'The most urgent one is to persuade government to revoke Statutory Instrument 100 that forbids students to choose their representation. In other words, we want them to lift a ban on Unzasu[27] without any conditions attached, and we also want government to recognise the Union as the only student representative body at this University.'

Besa absorbed the so-called 'demands', returned the notice and looked regretful:

'I am barely a month old and already there's talk about riots or violent protests. I couldn't have believed it.'

'What did you expect?'

'I expected to live in a place where I could study and use my mind in peace.'

'You could still do so.'

'I could – of course, but surely not when there is trouble or fear of it. Now I am beginning to have doubts about the future. I may not even graduate.'

'That's a possibility,' Washaama replied with a nod. 'But look at it this way. No one is really interested in making trouble or closing university for good. On the other hand when trouble starts you'll be a part of it. There are no outsiders. Everyone is in it.'

'I may not be in it if I decided against.'

'In that case you would be fighting students' interests and would be torn apart. When students agree on a certain course of action everyone is expected to be in support and whoever is opposed is considered a sell-out. Students might even kill that person.'

'I don't think in groups. I think alone – and nobody will change that.'

'Students can. Remember the gestalt: the whole is greater than the sum of its parts. I respect individual freedom but when the general consensus says –'

Besa got up abruptly. 'I must be off to a lecture. I'll see you in the evening!'

Perturbed by what Washaama had confided he scarcely listened to the lecturer's exposition. The historian reflected: 'Washaama isn't exactly the person I used to know. He is radical in his views and rather impatient. He has certainly changed. He even disregards the law and its consequences. What could have happened to him? Why do students seem radical and uncompromising?'

A female secretary advanced towards Professor Watson, whispered into his ear, thrust a note in his hand and slipped out of the lecture theatre. The lecturer was briefly puzzled: then he recovered his composure and said:

'The gentleman by the name of Besa Musunga, please follow the secretary upstairs to receive some urgent telephone call from Samfya...' After a short pause he went on with the lecture.

Besa proceeded to her office in a dreamlike way, confused and fearful of the worst. When the lady pointed a helpful finger towards the telephone handset and took her place by the typewriter, the young man hesitated and mutely looked at her. Then he reluctantly reached for the phone with trembling hands.

'Hello,' he said in a strange voice nobody could have recognised as his own. 'Hello!'

'Besa?' answered a female voice. 'Is that you, Besa?'

'Yes, please. Who's calling?'

'Gertrude!'

'Gertrude?' Then he gave out an exclamation of surprise and relief. 'Gertrude, what the hell. You nearly terrified me!'

'Besa,' she mourned on the line. 'Muzo is dead...she's dead... They are looking for her everywhere. They've discovered her things but her body is still missing...People are asking me questions as if *I* killed her. They keep saying I should have prevented her from going to the islands... I can't take it anymore. They make me feel guilty and I am so afraid...'

He would not speak. He was too benumbed by the news.

'Are you still around, Besa?'

'Yes. When did this happen?'

'Today, morning...She died together with five clinical officers when their motorboat capsized on the lake as they came back from the islands. Two bodies have been recovered but hers and three others haven't yet. Fishermen are searching everywhere and the whole of Samfya is at the Beach. I can't believe this has happened. I can't believe Muzo is dead...The night before she left we discussed our boy friends and plans for the future – and you were at the centre of her life! She had great hopes...To hear that she's dead? ...What shall we do now? I can't live without her! I am seeing her everywhere! I am going to hang myself!'

Large drops of tears rolled down his cheeks. He appeared stunned and bereft of something immeasurably rich as inexplicable pain and sorrow shrouded him completely.

'Are you coming?'

'Yes,' he said. 'I am starting off right away.'

He replaced the receiver back on its cradle and turned to the secretary.

'You know already, don't you?'

'Yes. Your friend told me. I am very sorry.'

'I've got to go home – to see my girl friend.'

She nodded understandingly and rose to her feet.

'First you'll have to obtain leave of absence from the Dean to avoid problems when you report back. Come. I'll personally take you to his office and help you process your leave.'

It took them half an hour to do so. He would be in Samfya for two weeks.

Besa went back to his place, tears still running down his cheeks. He stood before the portrait and examined it at length: her outlines were duly proportioned and beautiful to the sense, and he recalled her life and what it might have been. Then he looked for the knapsack and began to pack, his conscience revolting against the mortality and futility of existence. As he was about to leave for home, Besa took another glance at the picture and shuddered from head to foot. If Muzo had waited for him ... if only she had – since he neither saw anything to long nor hope for save the hurt and loneliness. Huddled in a corner of the room – engulfed in an extreme sense of unreality and wretchedness – he fell to dreaming of the girl who had inspired the happiest moments of his life. Yet he could not (as happened when they were estranged or circumstances prevented them from seeing each other for days prolonged) find the means to reach and put his arms around her. Nor would she now (because they had lived far too long apart) seek repose in their embrace and request them never to be separated from one another again.

'Poor Muzo,' he cried a thousandth time, wishing for her return. 'I have no one to tell my thoughts to. You're the only friend I have, the only one I love...'

* * * * *

'Where can she have gone?' Besa thought in perplexity. He had looked in almost all the male hostels but to no avail. It now seemed probable that the stranger had disappeared without a trace. 'This is impossible,' he affirmed quietly, stopping before the entrance into Soweto 4. 'Everyone stands out. You can't evaporate without leaving your prints behind – however vague.' Three girls descending a flight of stairs stood aside at the third floor landing to make way for him. They fell silent at once, perhaps sensing the severity of his nature, the fixed inward gaze in his eyes, the stamp of torment and fatigue marked upon his face. Besa passed them – heard their footsteps and lively chatter recede, and paused at a door marked 22 in black prints. A coloured poster reading

> *Umkhonto we sizwe*
> *Long live the struggle*
> *Long live Azania!*

and another ad with the words

Moma na Monko Investments Plc

On offer:
Sausages, sliced bread, eggs, buns, groceries
And much more!

Working Hours: 17.00 to 23.00 Every Day

Other outlets:
New Residence: Kafue 3 -6, October 2-19, Zambezi 1-4,
*   Kalingalinga 2- 7,*
The Ruins: International 2-6, Kwacha 6-4, Africa 2-3

Beat inflation with our prices!
Buy the best and shun the rest!

Moma na Monko Investments Plc
at your doorstep!

glared back at him. He smiled at the ad and knocked. The door swung open. Besa was admitted inside.

The historian found himself in a room that had undergone a radical transformation. Gone were the beds, wardrobes, study desks or anything typical of a student's room. Instead there were shelves along walls stuffed with foods and groceries, and there were two deep freezers, a fan, a chair, and a wooden counter running across. The walls were adorned with wrapping paper on which were pasted written notices, quoted texts or annotations, cartoons, news paper fillers, colour pictures, portraits and other visual images collected from the outside.

These filled his vision. However, although pictures of nude women torn from pornographic magazines attracted him, Besa belittled such pathetic arts as intellectually and morally degrading in their effects. He studied the women in their various postures – some lying on their backs displaying their genitalia, others showing off their breasts or their behind – and wondered what was the matter with their minds. He fixed his eyes on abstruse questions – namely, on mathematical symbols scrawled on the notice board and recognised sigma, lambda, delta, pi, kappa, epsilon, mu, gamma and many more from the Greek. He marvelled at their use in conveying simple ideas, which, as premise piled upon premise, culminated in the most complex mathematical arguments. Following a series of

deductive steps intended to introduce the idea of gradient, Besa remembered having read Kant's transcendental aesthetics or the great
man's attempt to establish the possibility of mathematics, but nothing came of it. Then his eyes moved off to another picture that disconcerted him with its captured, horrific illumination.

Here was contained the experience of a single moment. For in
a shroud of swirling dust, Black people regardless of age and sex
were scampering away from a terror behind them – the arm of apart-
heid in pursuit. The stutter of gunfire, hissing bullets tearing human
flesh, the crackle of riot batons, sjamboks and tears gas! Fallen bodies were run over, lying prostrate in puddles of blood. A child bending over corpses seemed to be stammering protestations against de-
cades of oppression. The wounded either crawled or limped away
in fright – but where would they go? – While a woman caught in a
kneeling position with a lifeless body of a child in her arms continually wailed amid the shouts and stampede. Below this was the foot-
note: 'Behold, the people that shed rivers of blood shall be free.'

There was yet another image – a small map of Africa without political boundaries encircled by crude portraits of Kwame
Nkhrumah, Julius Nyerere, Jomo Kenyatta, Nelson Mandela, Haile
Selassie, Kenneth Kaunda, and some quotations from such notable
figures as W.E.B Dubois, Edward Blyden, L.S Senghor, Cheik Anta
Diop, Mahatma Ghandi and Steve Biko. The map was fitted with
thin, cardboard legs starting out below the Cape, and short arms
protruding from the west and east coasts clasping begging bowls in
emaciated hands. Underneath the abstract were the words: 'Poverty
and Darkness, Africa's finest dreams.'

Besa grinned at a newspaper photograph of Beyani (President
of the country), taken at a recent political rally when his rhetoric
had given way to suspicions and threats: 'Comrades,' he seemed to
be saying to his followers, 'the Party and Its Government has im-
plemented economic policies that are intended to promote development and prosperity, but there are subversive elements in league
with some countries in the West that are trying to undermine our efforts and the fruits of the revolution. But thanks to our vigilance and
nationalism, the enemies of our country have now been identified.
We shall flash them out, for we believe it fitting to protect, defend
and uphold the liberty and interests of this nation here and abroad,'
and there was thunderous applause as the blind citizens chanted slogans against imperialism. 'Long live the Party! Long live Beyani!'
they cried frenziedly, waving placards. At the foot of this historical
picture was a list of twenty titles conferred upon Beyani – and the

words, 'Be a success, be a profound man without a face. Be everything and be a success!' crowned the potentate.

Briefly passing over other images crowded over the wall in silence, sometimes amused by their comic effect or benumbed by
their allusions, Besa read the cartoons or such snap sayings as:
'University education has gone to dogs,' 'Release funds! We're
barely surviving. We need all the basic essentials!' 'God looked
at the plight of Zambians and – how touching! – the poor fellow
started crying,' 'Castrate politicians,' 'No student allowances, no
lectures,' 'Stupid are you who hunger, for the kingdom of hell is
your creation,' 'Tighten your belts: inflation might pull your trousers to your ankles,' and so on, and reflected that the images – in a
stammering fashion – were nonetheless commenting on the realities
of life... depicting its varied moods and content.

He turned to the student-grocer and said:

'Sorry for breaking in like this, my friend.'

'We're not yet open,' replied the student. 'The exact time is indicated on the door and it's now sixteen thirty. Come after thirty minutes.'

'Actually I am not here to buy anything. I've a question to
ask. Did anybody come to this place asking for a mister Besa Musunga?'

'No. Nobody came.'

'Are you sure?'

'I am sure. I cannot lie to you.'

'You've been in doors for the past hour?'

'Yes.'

'Thank you very much.'

Besa closed the door behind him. He leaned against the wall and
felt rather foolish: he had overreacted and driven the girl out of his
room for reasons he himself did not fully understand, though he
supposed the trouble to have resulted from the confusion between
living and writing. How many times had Besa caught himself trying
to live what he had written or written what he had lived? In a single burst of creativity that sometimes percolated the physical, the
creator mistook work for living and deluded himself! 'Oh well,' he
sighed in terror, and then suddenly laughed. 'I am a besotted sort of
fellow, I cannot even understand myself.'

But whether by sheer luck or at destiny's behest – for it was impossible to tell – they met again in the Library's Short-Loan Collection two days after that unhappy event, when every hope of ever

seeing the girl had waned. Besa spotted her first, watched in tense silence the bearings of that female form seated a couple of tables away from him (taking in the strands of hair touching her slim shoulders and back in soft falls, the adorable face presently grave but naturally harmonious in repose, the smooth, yellow skin without a blemish and seemingly elastic and transparent in the pool of light), and for some moments sat rigid in his chair, entranced, beguiled by the features of one so incredibly attractive that to think otherwise would have been preposterous. He stood up, repressing a stirring of emotions somewhat resembling a mild seizure, and walked the length of the passage towards a table at the far end of the crowded, study area, callous to the furtive, inquisitive glances from other students. When he pulled an empty seat and sat on her left side, the girl looked up at once, gave her head a quick sideways tilt and stared him in the face. Besa was uneasy. For what seemed a very long time his mind reeled in the abysses of space, yet while he gathered his wits or grappled with the fragility of the moment, the young woman's look hovered upon him, steadied its focus, found the eyes of a man who had refused to see her but whom she would choose to love, and recognised him instantly. After another pause Besa, stiffly seated in a chair, with what little courage he could master, cleared his voice and said, in a whisper:

'Excuse me. Are you the girl who came to my place looking for Besa Musunga?'

'Yes. What is it?' she replied with some fear in her voice.

'Don't be alarmed. I have come to apologise for what happened that day. I think I lied to you. I was the person you were looking for.'

'I know that. Someone told me afterwards. But...but I don't want to talk about it if that's the reason you are here. I'd rather we forgot about everything.'

'Are you still angry with me?'

'No. Why should I?'

'You're not in the least interested in knowing why I behaved that way?'

'Maybe I am but what difference would it make if I did?'

'Shss,' he said, trying to quiet her down. 'Don't raise your voice or we'll disturb the others.'

'It's your fault. I really wanted to see you but you lied to me and sent me to other hostels where you knew you couldn't possibly be. I wished to speak to you then – now I don't, and this isn't the right place to chat.'

Besa tried to explain in a reconciliatory voice:

'I am sorry for what happened but there were some reasons which led to it. This is why I am here, and this is why I have had to look everywhere for you. I feel I have to explain so you wouldn't think I am a jackass or someone who was unkind to you. Please let me talk to you – here or anywhere else.'

'I am sorry I can't,' she answered coldly. 'Just leave me alone. I want to study and you are disturbing me.'

'Very well,' Besa sighed and stood up. 'You're obstinate and won't speak to me, and I mustn't ever know why you came. Goodbye and thanks for your hospitality, Miss first year!'

Thus hurt and puzzled by the girl's reaction, the historian returned to his table and was set to work but couldn't. Images from the text fell apart and left no impression on his mind, except, of course, the woman's form, the beauty of which was certain and conspicuously expressed, the essence of which he was unwilling to forget. He closed his eyes: the girl was everywhere, flaunting her looks which appealed but never actually invited, a fixed expression of reproach and resentment etched upon the otherwise, cheerful and sensuous face, and her unreasoned arrogance which pained and frightened him. He tried to concentrate, stole glances at students bent over books like scholars enwrapped in the interiority of thought, and became restless. Besa got up and left the library.

He emerged into the light of the setting sun feeling cold and solitary. He peered into the sky: it would soon be dark, strings of stars would stand out, humanity would fall asleep, – and the world, racing through space and solitude, would shoulder existence alone as there was no choice. Besa lit a cigarette. A group of friends perched on concrete slabs invited him to a debate on the role of concepts in the acquisition of knowledge but the historian politely declined, not being in the mood for discussions. Holding onto the railings, he descended a series of steps that led up to the front of the library, made a turn to the left, and moved in the direction of the university main entrance.

Released from unrest since he was no longer with the girl, Besa Musunga cheered up as soon as he had put some distance behind him. The pleasures of perspective and relaxed movements of arms and limbs created sweet sensations mingled with literary thought. A flux of words – would he write tonight? – enshrouded in being and becoming intelligible hastened his steps, so that with the eyes of his mind he beheld clearly the ideal form the next essay would take. With proud affection he remembered the pseudonym, 'Ferio',

a nonsensical-word Besa had borrowed from one type of argument
in the first-figure of Aristotelian logic (in which the major is a universal negative while the minor and conclusion remain particular
and indefinite), even as he shuddered at the difficulties writing entailed: a sedentary lonely life, a cold encounter with words and their
ontological meaning, a passionate thirst for truth made explicit in
the light of reason.

By now he had turned right. The Students Office towered over
by trees stood on his left. A chilly wind had started to blow. Street-
lights had now lit up. Pervaded by night, the lustre of the sunset
against land and sky was about gone. Further up the road, a horde of
student-Christians filing out of the Ecumenical centre soon filled the
way. And then, as if by mutual assent, their voices billowed out as
they broke into a hymnal, which seemed both pathetic and futile.

> *Ukwisa kwakwe eko ine*
> *Ndolela,*
> *Ukwa Mulubushi wandi, Yesu Kristu.*
> *Mu caalo ca 'mfwa na masambi*
> *Nshifyaya kwikala,*
> *Mu ng'anda ya Mfumu mwaliba*
> *Imiputule 'yingi.*

> *Shi isa we Mfumu yandi,*
> *Shi isa, we Mfumu Yesu Kristu:*
> *Ukwisa kobe 'ko ine ndolela*

His coming is what I
Await,
Of my Saviour, Jesus Christ.
In the world of death and sin
I desire not to live,
In the Lord's house there are
Many mansions.

Please come my Lord,
Please come, my Lord Jesus Christ:
Your coming is all I await.

Besa stopped awhile to watch them pass. They paraded along like
an experienced choir, going the way he had come, singing beautifully in the virgin night, their minds upturned to the vaults of heaven
for divine intervention in human affairs. Recalling Deucalion and

Pyrrha in the *Metamorphosis*, however – 'If the Gods may be touched and softened by the prayers of the righteous, if divine anger may be thus turned aside, tell us, O Themis, how we may repair the destruction that has overtaken our race. Most gentle goddess, assist us in our distress…' – he questioned the origin, nature and utility of the religious sentiment in understanding the world of fact and, finding this deficient and illusory, shrugged his shoulders and resumed the leisure walk back to his room in the New Residence.

The student soon disappeared into the hostel, a flight of stairs he climbed in an absent-minded way. Propped against the wall, a woman waiting by the door of his room stood to attention the moment she heard footsteps in the corridor. Startled, Besa stopped instinctively, unable to believe his eyes. Although light was scant *she* was visibly recognisable – all too familiar, in fact, that he hardly knew what to think! What did she want if she had declined to see him? Why had she refused to talk if she now wished to see him? He made straight for the door, plunged the key into the lock, and asked idly:

'Are you looking for someone?'

'Yes,' she replied, seeming remorseful. 'I was waiting for *you*. I came to apologise for what I said in the Library. I felt bad after I'd seen how you left and knowing that I was the one who had started everything. I thought I wasn't being just to you.' She eyed him with feeling: 'I bet you are still furious with me?'

'I was, actually,' he smiled at the girl. 'But not so anymore. Not after what you've just told me.'

'Thanks a lot,' she said. 'I was worried. I had to come.'

'Have you been here long?'

'Maybe five minutes, or probably less.'

Besa opened the door, switched on the light and invited her in. That she had decided to see him again was almost incredible. Her candour and concern impressed him. Things were now beginning to fall into their proper place. 'The order that we create in our mind,' he thought quietly, 'must necessarily accord with the facts, or else we risk displeasure and disillusionment.'

'I also wanted to show you these,' she held out papers to him. 'It was the reason I sought to speak to you in the first place. A friend of mine told me you're the Vanguard's publishing secretary and would be interested in seeing my work. I have two essays that I would like to see in print.'

'Please do sit down,' he said, accepting the scripts. He skimmed through the works, noted the author's name and place of residence, and met her eyes. Besa adopted a serious tone.

'Your work looks good. I shall pass it on to my friends and report back to you. We would certainly like themes on the environment.'

'How long will it take to contact me again?'

'About a week at the most. If your material is accepted we will probably ask you to check one or two things out before a firm offer of publication is made. This is normally the case, though acceptance may not actually mean seeing your work in print. We have a backlog of scripts and we're limited by space on the newsletter.'

'What d'you look for in the material submitted to you?'

'We generally accept anything that directly or indirectly focuses on student life even though there are exceptions to this rule. We like scripts to be good and well informed, and we normally consider submissions mainly on the basis of their application rather than theoretical value. We want to encourage students to extend their theoretical knowledge to practical demonstrations. Topics may be diverse – politics, economics, education, ethics, medicine and so on. The most important rule is that the author should be able to interest us in his or her work.'

She smiled at him for the first time, a slow gentle smile that charmed his heart. Besa added hastily: 'As regards what you get after we've used your work – in case you didn't know – I am obliged to tell you that we don't pay royalties to our authors because our newsletter does not run at a profit. We welcome contributions from our readers, of course, but make it known to them that they may not expect to make money on their submissions. But we do give, as a token of appreciation, free copies of the Vanguard for each accepted, published submissions, and we sometimes offer a small award to the best essayist. In general, therefore, we give nothing back in return. The only reward for our writers is the satisfaction had in expressing themselves and tasting print. Their work is not copy righted, either – it belongs to the public domain – and the readership is extremely small. But our authors continue to write and provide a small voice that is very important to our country and history, even though outsiders give them derogative names!'

'I wasn't actually thinking of royalties or anything of that kind,' was her rejoinder. 'What I have in view is the passion to share certain of my impressions with students. I am honestly not out for money, if this is what you think.'

'Please don't be upset. I didn't mean it that way,' exclaimed Besa, seeing how she now looked. 'I was merely explaining our situation so that everyone is aware. You see, in the past we've had experiences when some students demanded payment for the use of their work and caused us much trouble when we refused to pay. In short we make our stand very clear right at the beginning to avoid problems later on…And everyone has to sign this.' He rose from his seat and recovered a file from the bookshelf. Then he handed her two author-publisher agreement forms. 'Fill out where appropriate and return them to me. We'll give you a copy for your file.'

'When would you like the forms back?'

'As soon as possible.'

'I'll read through tonight and bring them over tomorrow about this time.'

'That would be very fine.'

The girl stood up also. She brought out her hand for him to shake: 'It's been a pleasure talking to you. In a way it's quite a relief because I didn't expect to be spoken to again after the way I reacted in the Library.'

'It has been nice speaking to you. You're most welcome to submit *any* of your writings to the Vanguard.'

'Thank you very much.'

She moved towards the door but turned round to face him again.

'You have a beautiful name. I like it.'

'Yours is also nice.'

'Thank you. I'll see you again tomorrow. Goodbye.'

'Goodbye.'

He closed the door. He went over to gaze at those exquisite crystals – and was there for some minutes noticing, as always, their flatness and regularities imposed upon them by the unbreakable properties of the three-dimensional space. When he had tired of the stones Besa picked up the essays and began to read them in his leisure, often showing amazement at the subtle perceptions and powers of expression in so young a girl – or, for that matter, in a first year!

This was how he met Shantiee Perroni, the second and last love of his life.

Chapter 9

Concerns the tutorial
during which that which history seeks to illuminate
is approached ...
then another argument erupts in the Mingling Bar

On the second floor of the New Education Building (in a room marked 2A), a group of students had convened a tutorial as was usually the case every Friday afternoon. Checking his watch, their tutor, Professor Owen, ordered all to silence, spoke briefly about yet another assignment to write before the end of the month (copies of which were available in the Head of Department's Office upon request), and finally asked Besa Musunga to begin the presentation. The student shuffled some papers and rose to the presenter's place at the lecturer's table. The tutorial was now in progress.

'Good afternoon ladies and gentlemen,' he greeted.

'Good afternoon, sir,' they said, hiding their grins.

'Before I begin today's presentation, allow me to inform the house that my co-presenter, Miss Miya Muchimba, is taken ill and admitted in our clinic. She has malaria but her condition is improving. I was informed by the Sister-in-Charge that Miya would soon be discharged as soon as she completed her medication. We can only wish her a fast recovery so that she joins us in our studies. As everyone knows, Miya's contributions have proved very intelligent, interesting and fruitful, and I dare say that I shall miss her this afternoon. But I'll try to do my best to discuss our assignment. I only hope that Professor Owen and discussants will accept this apology as genuine and excusable.' To which everyone consented.

'Today's discussion, ladies and gentlemen, is about capitalism. I shall first trace the origin and development of this important phenomenon. Then I shall discuss some basic features of capitalism such as private ownership, markets, labour, international capital, banking, tariffs, the State, and so on, to help us understand capital polarisation or the global economy – the Poor and the Rich, if you wish. My focus of attention is England, though I shall also feel at liberty to cite a few experiences elsewhere, particularly in Russia and Germany. Finally I shall demonstrate how western capitalism under-develops the world. I shall use India and Africa as examples.

'From my discussion it will become apparent that I have relied on Karl Marx, Walter Rodney, Rosa Luxemburg, E J Hobsbawn, Joseph Stranger, Cole and Clough, Maurice Dobb, R Coulburn, Sweezy and Wallace K Ferguson. I have also used some journals and world financial reports and some lesser texts.'

Then he caught the attention of the audience by his persuasiveness and show of inter-relatedness of ideas and significant facts for almost three quarters an hour. When he finished speaking, there was a spell of silence save the sound of pens scratching paper as other students jotted down relevant points. Besa waited for the worst part – answering questions from his interlocutors. A hand was up already.

'You have a question or a comment?'

'I have a question,' said Muchacha. 'I need a clarification on some of your sources. I notice that you have also included two books by Russian writers whom I believe are very great. Yet I wonder whether the authority of your references is not undermined by the use of fiction in a serious academic work like this. Do you think such an inclusion is scholarly legitimate?'

'Well ...I suppose so. One author I just referred to lived at the time feudalism was still existent in Russia. To the extent that the work in question was, at least in part, influenced by feudal conditions ... yes, the inclusion is legitimate. Moreover, Leo Tolstoy was not only a writer but a landlord and reformer. The book cited is on land reform in Russia.'

'What about the other book – the novel? It is a fictitious book.'

'Undoubtedly, Mister Muchacha,' replied Besa. 'I quoted Dostoyevsky's novel, *The Brothers Karamazov*, to shed light on the social context in which serfs generally lived.'

'You quoted a book of fiction that cannot be relied on as a historical document,' the same student insisted. 'The word "fiction" is derived from the Latin word, "fictio", which means an invention or something imaginary, something which is different from what reality actually is. Fiction merely distorts and falsifies reality – it cannot therefore be used. This is why Plato condemned the arts.'

Besa took some time to respond:

'In a certain sense you are right: we must be careful which written sources to use in our research. I understand this very well – the dangers that are inherent in using artistic materials. But I also think your working assumption, "Everything fictitious cannot be used as a historical source", may not apply to every case. Some seemingly fictitious books have turned out to be invaluable sources of truth. For example, Sol T Plaatje's novel, *Mhudi*, has provided us some information about Southern Africa. Other books such as Peter Abrahams'

Mine Boy, Stephen Mpanshi's *Chekesoni Aingila Ubusoja* (Chekesoni joins the Army), and Ngugi's *Weep Not Child* provide historical information in a guise of a simple narrative. In a word, therefore, while it may be admitted that some fiction can deceive, it may also be affirmed that some other may not. The reason is simple. When an artist forges in his soul a work of art, the work so produced does not evolve from nothing. It is generated from concrete conditions of existence in which he is located, and creativity is not an unconscious act. Like crystals or other objects the author is subjected to the properties of space and time – which is why novels can be differentiated or classified on this basis. Ultimately there is no fiction, and you'll perhaps recall that Freud's research method as tested on the wandering psyche rested on his belief that whatever a person says or does has meaning and relates to his total personality, personality being the function of the environment. When one takes care to scratch the surface of Hellenic myths or the African mask, for example, one discovers – if not actually the truth – at least some likeness of truth.'

Nobody dared contest him now. They were all quiet.

'As for your allusion to Plato,' Besa continued, 'the fact that he despised the arts or called them *imitations* or *shadows* of reality does not render the arts, or poetry in particular, false in every case. Art sometimes represents reality or what I may call "reality", since there seems to be a difference in what constitutes what is real. In the Platonic sense, art is condemned and banished because it concentrates on empirical being and only in exciting the senses rather than the intellect. Because of the nature of his epistemology Plato calls inferior anything which does not tend to the world of Ideas in which, according to him, reality and true knowledge subsists. But in the sense in which I am using the word "reality", art represents that reality which is particular, contingent and concrete, which is what history seeks. That which is historical can never be found in the Platonic Ideas. For if it was, it would no longer be historical. History concentrates on change without seeking laws that regulate these changes, laws that are characterised by necessity and universality, laws beyond which there is nothing. History stops at the empirical or at facts that originate, have a duration and an end, whereas the philosophical-reality that led Plato to condemn the arts transcend the historical. Therefore, in supporting Plato's theory of art and your condemnation of what is "fictitious", you are not exactly being historical. Perhaps you should redefine your terms of discourse or tell me clearly what is meant by historical truth and the means by which to reach it.'

'I raised an objection to your fictitious material because I believe it is not correct,' said Muchacha. 'We're not free to use any relics anyhow.'

'I agreed with, sir,' responded Besa, 'though only to a limited extent. But look, when I used Dostoyevsky's scene of a child torn to pieces by the general's hounds, I sought to show the relationship between serfs and their masters. I started my presentation with this prelude in order to capture your imagination of the conditions on the manor. Serfs are generally hungry, landless, and unfree and are often conscripted into wars or crusades even without their consent. Perhaps most importantly, they don't own the means of production but merely sell their labour for nothing. Like characters in George Orwell's *Animal Farm*, the oppressed are not in control of their destiny because of a conscious decision of other people. The manor as a social, cultural, military and economic unit was the starting point in tracing the preconditions for capitalism, conditions which Europe exported to the Americas and else where.

'When you said, "We're not free to use any relics anyhow," you were perhaps right. However, to write a history is to reconstruct and give meaning to important events and changes, which affected man as he was in the past under consideration. This process is an abstraction, as when you reduce a concept down to its real connotation by choosing only those attributes that are sufficient and necessary, and nothing more. It is a human abstraction – and as a result no history is ever complete. There are glaring gaps just as there are on a number line. Again, depending on the answer to the question, "Why write this history rather than another?" the historian is led to choose necessary facts available from different sources. He sees areas of agreement or disagreement and then proposes an interpretation that accounts for the facts. Where does he collect them? Well, from sources such as sculptures, paintings, architecture, oral and written literature, photographs or pictures, and so on. The history of N'gombe Ilede as commercial site in precolonial Zambia, for example, was constructed from the study of the material culture there such as pottery pieces, copper crosses, beads and human skeletons in different burial sites... This is all I know. But if you still insist, then you ought to explain your position, Mister Muchacha. Or – why does Andrew Roberts, in his study of the Bemba, use oral stories as his source?'

Another hand was up. It was Gloria Njira, widely known as The Young Lady by all her course mates.

'Yes, Gloria?'

'I have an observation to make about the role of religion in the development of capitalism,' she said. 'But before I do so I would like to agree with you on your use of some fiction in research. As Mister Muchacha will remember, research in history, as a social science, demands an inter-disciplinary approach or openness. This means there are no precise guidelines for data collection provided the material is relevant and collaborated by other sources. I think Besa has demonstrated this very well – considering the fact that his citations are quite impressive. My disagreement with him, however, is on that part of the paper which relates religion and the growth of the capitalist spirit; the part in the presentation which establishes a necessary link between the capitalist spirit and such religious movements as founded by Luther, Calvin and Zwingli...It's about this I want to speak...'

After the tutorial, Besa and two friends went to the Mingling Bar for drinks. It was quarter past sixteen and crowded in the Bar, yet they managed to find a vacant table and smoked cigarettes in silence, each engrossed in his own thoughts. Besa looked at his companions and voiced his lament:

'I forgot to add something in the tutorial. Do you remember what Aristotle said was the weakest point in his master's metaphysical system?'

'He said Plato's chief deficiency was in the relationship between Ideas and phenomena,' replied Nalumino. 'He couldn't clearly resolve the contradictions between being and becoming, a problem already paused by the pre-Socratics but which the Stagirite was to attempt to solve later.'

'Precisely. And with regard to the arts you'll recall that Aristotle commends the use of comedy as a means to represent truth. For him the arts do not wish to imitate the contingent but the universal, intelligible and rational. Art has an educative value... Perhaps I should have found some way of applying this to the argument about the use of fiction. What do you say?'

'I say, brilliant ideas always come after a fight,' Nalumino grinned. 'Anyhow, you did your best and got away with a B plus.'

'Girls normally get B pluses and better without any effort,' Sichone interjected quickly, 'while you guys sweat it out in the Lib trying to extract data.'

Everyone laughed. Nalumino then said:

'Beware of your insinuations, boy. Someone might overhear.'

'I don't give a shit. Who doesn't know that some lecturers here give good grades to girls in exchange for sex? There is a lot of fuck-

ing going on in these offices. My niece, Georgina, was telling me
the other day that one of her course mates is getting As from a lecturer she sleeps with. Now do you know what grades that lecturer
gives the monk who lends out his assignments to the same girl to
copy? He gives him C pluses and Bs – if he's lucky!'

'Never mind grades,' said Besa. 'We're concerned with Aristotle and not trivialities.'

'Oh, you and your little gods!' Sichone answered with a wave of
his hand. 'I bet you dream about him every night!'

'He's better than all of us,' Nalumino asserted proudly. 'And we
mustn't discuss him as if he were just any ordinary person.'

'He's just as human as you and me,' Sichone returned, visibly
offended. 'Just as human as anyone else. No one should be raised
on a pedestal.'

'True,' Besa added, 'but then some humans are lepers, lunatics,
imbeciles and foolish, while some others are not – so that distinctions between species in the same genus may sometimes become in-
evitable.'

'Such distinctions are superficial and accidental. You said as
much yourself when you discussed the real connotation of a term
during the tutorial.'

'I made that reference specifically to one type of definition …
definition per genus et differentiam…because it is analogous to the
writing of a history – as this requires a process of selecting just
those facts which are significant in fixing a historical situation in its
proper context. This is what I meant, nor did I deny the existence of
different histories.'

'All human beings are *human* without distinction.'

'No doubt about that,' Besa said. 'But seriously speaking no co-
ordinate species is ever alike in every respect.'

'And there are no such things as categories and universals. We
live in a world of particulars in which similarities among observable
phenomena is a fiction,' Nalumino laughed.

'Perhaps you don't realise the implications of such a grand idea,'
Sichone protested. 'Your thinking is just as destructive as that of
the British empiricist Hume who thought Blacks to be inferior to
Whites.'

'Just because we can't discover *horseness* in individual horses?'
Besa asked. He had seen David Hume's work, *Essay of national
characters*, and considered it unworthy of a man who opted to remain rational.

'What do you mean?'

'In an argument with Plato about the nature of concepts, the empiric nominalist, Antisthenes, told the former: "O Plato, I see the horse, but the *horseness* – that I do not see," and Plato replied: "You do not see the *horseness* because you have nothing but the eyes of the body.'

'Yes,' Sichone looked pleased. 'You have nothing but the eyes of the body.'

'It's difficult to infer with certainty the particular from the universal or pass from the particular to the universal. Such a passage is illegitimate, illogical and unreal. It is akin to a leap from the logical to the ontological plane. Perhaps the most we can do is propose a world of concepts to which nature approximates – just like pure mathematicians do. In Bertrand Russell's words mathematics is "the subject in which we never know what we are talking about nor whether what we are saying is true," which is exactly the point. We can never assimilate the world in its absolute uniformity, essence and entirety. Such a world is closed to us because no passage from the particular to the universal ever exists!' Nalumino explained.

'You're a bunch of nuts,' Sichone snared. 'Your theory only provides a basis for all forms of anarchy and cannot even be useful to the spirit of Negritude that every Black person should profess.'

'The spirit of Negritude you've just mentioned,' Nalumino answered again, 'is admittedly a genuine problem in African thought. But every individual is the shaper of their destiny and should therefore rise to the demands of what they choose to be provided their choice truly coincides with their individual essence. Africanness or the search for an African identity does not consist in a collective attempt to become one prescribed ideal. It consists in an attempt by individuals to live their lives as fully developed individuals who can't help becoming individuals and can't apologise to the world for what they truly are. The interiority of this essence, then, is the starting point, so that no one is allowed to look further than themselves – to Negritude or Europeanness or any other idea flavoured with a vague universality. No one should hide from themselves in preference for some recommended ideal that may not actually exist.'

'Moreover,' Besa took up the argument, 'since universality cannot be made to discover particular objects in their fullest individuality, it follows that Africanness cannot describe *me* as completely as I am. Someone is not everyone, he's *someone!*'

'You have misunderstood me,' said Sichone regretfully.

'No we haven't,' Besa claimed. 'Our position is the refusal to raise the universal to the level of primacy. The particular is the starting point, and you cannot abolish that.'

'Themes about Negritude or the Black experience as elaborated by Senghor, Nkhrumah, Kaunda, Fanon and a dozen others are not just particular themes about a *particular* sort of people. They echo real experiences of people who have been tied by a *common* doom – slavery, racism, colonialism and underdevelopment,' Sichone said. 'So when we define Africanness as a historical fact or phenomenon, we're talking about the African personality as a *collective* person pitted against his past, his present and his future. We're saying, "What are we about in relation to what we have gone through?" This is a question that exacts answers. It is a *general* question.'

'Without doubt you're right,' Besa agreed. 'Yet remember that our argument, if there is an argument at all, is not about Negritude as such but concerns particulars and universals. In your case you perceive resemblances among things that we presume to be unlike, whereas in our case we perceive differences among things that you presume to be alike, and there is a supervening suspicion that since both these cases cannot be true at once,' and Besa recalled the Stagirite's attempt to resolve the problem of being and becoming by recourse to the idea of potency and act, the metaphysical disputations of Suarez, the concept of association of David Hume, and Kant's struggles to unite rationalism and empiricism in a more advanced type of phenomenalism, 'then surely one of the cases must be true, the other false…Your position reminds me of the one posited by realists who maintained that because universals exist in individuals' things – as, for example, Africanness in individual Africans, therefore all differences between individual species are accidental as the genera is prior to the individual or the particular, and by implication individual existence is thus denied. On the other hand our position in this regard is somewhat similar to that of the nominalists in so far as we consider the universal to be something posterior to the individual. In other words nature does not in itself contain the universal, but the mind, like Russell's definition of mathematics, forms universal ideas, which try to correspond to reality or individual things. The individual is *prote ousia* or the primary substance of all modes of genera and species, as Aquinas and Aristotle also teach. The universal as an idea of a class is simply the manner in which the thinking-subject may relate individual things to itself. It is an abstraction on the basis of some characteristics in common. But the general idea or universal, taken as such without particular things, cannot be made to discover the nature of reality. It possesses the qualities of universality and necessity but cannot, according to Kant, lead to any true understanding of nature…'

'I don't quite understand you,' Sichone observed with serious air about him, 'though I admit that our present problem is such as you have stated it. But if the individual is the primary reality or *prote ousia*, as you would have it, how can the objectivity of knowledge be guaranteed? Nalumino has denied the existence of categories and universals and called them fictitious, while you, Besa, have been silent about the origin of universals in a mind, which is itself actually particular and part of nature. I appreciate your arguments but feel they are fraught with contradictions. Was it not Kant who found empiricism unsatisfactory since it lacks necessity and universality, the basic elements all true knowledge must possess? Does knowledge consist in the knowledge of the particular?'

'The question we're answering,' Nalumino answered, 'is not the one about what constitutes true knowledge and what does not, but we're questioning particulars and universals. I have personally denied the existence of universals and categories because these are not subsistent entities as such, but are concepts of particular things that are considered alike in some manner, the likeness being a pure abstraction since the mind may *choose* to adopt itself to the things differently...'

'I cannot understand you,' Sichone repeated wearily. 'I believe discussions about particulars and universals imply the types of knowledge that necessarily correspond to each?'

'Somehow, yes. But we wish to determine whether things that are radically different may be taken to be the same, or whether things that are apparently the same may be considered to be different.'

'And the answer to the former is still affirmative. All humans are the *same*.'

'Perhaps you're right. But Lenshina was a politician but she was quite *different* from other politicians. She committed crimes that none dared commit... and happily ended up in jail.'

'You're misplaced. Lenshina did not end up in because she had committed that you would properly call crimes. She was jailed because her religious fervour was seen to be a threat to the government.'

Nalumino's voice then soared: 'Are you denying this too? Are you refuting historical facts?'

'There are no historical facts as far as this is concerned. Much of what had been said about and the Lumpa Church is cheap propaganda aimed at justifying government brutal force against the sect. I am surprised that you should be a victim of rhetoric!'

Nalumino stood up trembling. The debate had now taken a more heated bent as the two students indulged their emotions and clashed like protagonists.

'I despise President Beyani and his repressive regime,' Nalumino was heard as saying, 'yet on this point I am prepared to defend the State against false allegations...Alice Lenshina was just a misguided religious who, together with her followers, committed acts that were not only illegal but morally outrageous as well. They drunk urine freely like beer and ate their own excrement, and to test their faith in God sometimes jumped from rooftops believing angels would catch them in mid-air. But this was not all. Besides portraying Jesus as a Blackman or praying naked in Church, the sect shunned singing the national anthem and belittled formal education like the Jehovah's Witnesses, and finally advocated civil disobedience for no good reason. Her teaching had neither sound doctrine nor support from the mainstream Church. It was no wonder the sect received little sympathy from the people.'

'You're totally mistaken,' Sichone contradicted. 'To say the truth Lenshina represents those unusual leaders capable of challenging existing politics even in the face of political intolerance. If her teaching had no appeal, why did the State send soldiers to slaughter many of her followers and destroy their homes? The fact is: she did have some influence and government felt threatened because she was becoming too popular. She spoke out against dictatorship and at times hinted at an alternative government representation...but for which no one in power was prepared. It was not surprising, therefore, that she should be imprisoned. And many of her followers fled to Congo and neighbouring countries for fear of the State.'

'The woman was religious: she had no reason to meddle in politics.'

'But religious experience cannot be divorced from politics. Both are social facts. But even admitting this to be false, Lenshina had the right to profess any system of beliefs that she chose and discuss affairs of the country any time she wished.'

'It was her system of beliefs which made people do outrageous acts, though.'

'Everyone is free to express their beliefs.'

'Some beliefs are dangerous and cannot lead to good ends. The constitution may guarantee certain rights to the citizens. On the other hand it is the duty of the State to uphold law and order or even withdraw those very rights from the citizens, especially if those rights are exaggerated and wrongly exercised.'

'The present regime does not represent an ideal type of democracy that upholds the liberties and freedoms of the people. It is characterised by censorship, the state of emergency, detention without trial, police roadblocks, mass fear and the use of the security forces to crush any opposition to the status quo. It is therefore morally wrong to defend such a government that does not respect the natural rights of man. The American Declaration of 1776 asserts, "...whenever any form of government becomes destructive of these ends, it is the Right of the People to alter or abolish it..." – 'The American regime is not the ideal type of democracy either,' Nalumino maintained. 'So your analogy is weak and cannot be made to appear as a standard against which lesser democracies may be measured...If that nation was truly a democracy, it would not have sustained a deliberate policy of discriminating against Blacks and other minority groups. Your Declaration only applies to Whites – or to those who should rule the country. America only succeeds in laughing at herself.'

'But in speaking of democracies or lesser democracies, you are referring to the gradation of democracy and, consequently, to the *essence* or to that which qualifies democratic nations in its extension. And when you speak of outrageous acts, you are distinguishing between various acts (some outrageous and some not) and you are again implicitly referring to a quality or qualities that make some acts outrageous and some others not. You are talking about the essence or universal.'

'I am referring to the essence only secondarily. As to the particular, it is the starting point and constitutes the fullest knowledge possible. Essences are not in themselves knowledge of anything at all, but may only be used to understand particulars. On the other hand particulars are particulars as such, that is all. Nor are particulars subordinated to the universal, as is sometimes said of the part to the whole...'

The argument raged on unabated, drawing the attention of other students in the Mingling Bar. As they flayed each other thus, Besa eyed his companions helplessly, remembering the story of two Greek thinkers who, after failing to agree on the precise nature of the ego for several days and nights, finally decided to use weapons in order to settle their dispute forever. And he thought: 'Soon there'll be a fistfight where reason has given out. But, surely, entities are alike as to their essence and unlike as to their accidents. One recalls the problem of monists like Thale and Anaximander who asserted that natural phenomena, passing from one state to another, is nonetheless governed by some fixed law by means of which pro-

cess can be derived or reduced. That is to say, they explained varia-
tions in terms of a single substance which, in Thale's case, was *water*, and in Anaximander's case the *indeterminate*...Or is not the
question somewhat similar to the search for the Socratic concept,
by virtue of which a mass of instances are united into a single definition? How problematic, profound everything really is!' For Sichone, implacable in his arguments, looked for the underlying quality in things whereas Nalumino, equally unappeasable, emphasised
the empirical or the flux of Heraclitus, though both alluded to the
quest for certainty and the absolute.

'I beg your pardon,' Besa stood up abruptly. He picked up his
books and said, 'You guys are behaving like jerks and doing your
best to attract attention. I am getting out of here.'

'Hey, wait a minute! Where do you suppose you are going?'
asked Sichone. 'The discussion isn't over yet!'

'I am taking a break and I must speak to someone. The girl that
has just passed.'

The undergraduate caught up with Shantiee, as she was about to
go into the LT1 (Lecture Theatre 1) and privately drew her aside.
Clad in a flowery dress falling in pleats midway between her knees
and ankles, the girl emanated freshness, glamour, rarity and innocence (qualities pleasing to the sense!) and listened to him with a
reserved expression in her honey-coloured eyes, her manner neither
welcoming nor forbidding.

'I saw you pass by so I ran up just to say hello. I am with friends
in the Mingling Bar. I hope you don't mind me stopping you for a
greeting?'

'Not in the least,' she replied, looking him full in the face. 'It's
good to see you again. How are you?'

'I am ok. You?'

'I am ok too. I was just about to go in a lecture. My last for today.' Shantiee glanced anxiously at a group of first years filing into
the lecture room like sheep, an eccentric figure of an old man following behind. 'That's our mathematics lecturer, Professor Powell.
I think I'd better go in now. I'll see you later.'

'Just a minute, Shantiee. Have you heard from the *Vanguard*
yet?'

'O yes. I was going to tell you but forgot. Someone wrote me
about meeting to discuss my essays ...but we haven't yet. I am still
considering.'

'Why? I thought you'd already made up your mind to publish
with us?'

'Of course, but that was before your friend contacted me.' She touched his arm, and peered nearsightedly at him. 'I am afraid to publish, Besa. I am ashamed of what I wrote.'

'Nonsense,' he exploded. 'You're not ashamed and we're going to print your material. You're very intelligent and I hope you will write vicariously, write and always write! I liked your work and I would like you to produce some more. I'll not let you give up the promise of a great talent like yours. You're just a first year and yet you seem to write with authority. You seem to know much already. No, we'll do everything to expose your work to the public. In the meantime enjoy your lecture. Goodbye!'

'Wait!' she cried, her face newly flushed and elated. She hesitated: 'I...I want to see you again soon. Privately. When can we meet?'

'Anytime you wish.'

'Can we have supper together and maybe share a drink in my place? I have a bottle of wine.'

'That sounds great, but when?'

'Today! I'll come to your place at eighteen and we'll go to makumbi.'

'That's okay with me. So we have a date!'

She smiled beautifully at him – and whispered:

'I'll see you later. Take care.' And disappeared into the LT1.

Besa returned to his friends and said, almost to himself:

'Here's a point for you to consider, my faithful friends! What the one desires, the other wishes, and both delight in the other's good and will not, as Kant advises us to do, treat the one as a means but as end in themselves. Do you suppose this is possible at campus?'

'What are you talking about?' asked Sichone.

'I am talking about Immanuel Kant and his Categorical Imperative.'

'O well,' Sichone sighed. 'Fuck Aristotle, fuck Kant, and fuck everyone...'

'Come on, let's go,' Besa said. 'You guys need some rest.'

'I suppose you're right,' said Nalumino. 'I feel awfully tired.'

Chapter 10

Concerns requited love.
And the justification of student's protests

Shantiee Perronnie, a first year student in the School of Natural Sciences, entered the lecture theatre looking happy and excited by the prospect of meeting Besa again. She sunk in the back row of benches and, for several moments at least, daydreamed or thought longingly of the time she would be with someone she really liked. Someone intelligent, handsome and understanding. Someone who believed in her, someone worth listening to. Yet Professor Powell, his emphatic voice issuing from the lecturer's podium, intruded on her pleasant thoughts, so she must now concentrate and write notes!

'You'll recall that it is possible to represent species of equations on a Cartesian plane as a series of interconnected points which produce straight lines, quadratics, cubics, quartics and fancy curves of even higher degree, such as the rose of Grandi, the limacon of Pascal and the folium of Descartes.

'Through analytical geometry, then, every equation may be geometrically converted and, conversely, some geometric shape may be converted back into their algebraic form. When we think of curves as tracings made by moving points, when we think of terms in an equation as functions between variables in a fluid situation, then it may be possible to analyse the factors at work in that particular situation and to be able to get at the law in virtue of which the situation is determined, assuming, of course, that such a law truly exists, and that we have been working from some experimental data for which no empirical law has yet been pronounced.

'The technique which permits the mathematical probing of any process of change whatever, from the behaviour of subatomic particles to the forces which bind galaxies together, is called calculus. Newton and Leibnitz first developed it, respectively, though the Greeks had earlier hinted at calculus through their idea of infinitesimals. Now before we come to that, let us first review a very important concept in mathematics, that of functions. This is the theme of today's lecture. Now for the preliminary notations…'

Immediately after this, Shantiee hurried straight to her room in October 3, meditative as she visualised various geometric forms and their algebraic equivalents. She glanced around her – and, there they were, the pleasing shapes of nature's creations inseparable from the world of objects. The marvels of art and architecture came in circles, polygons, spirals and complex structures whose aesthetic forms were symmetrical and duly proportioned. Wherever her eyes fell – whether on plants, birds and people, she beheld varied shapes of such intricacy that even Apollonius – he whose flat plane sliced a circular cone at different angles to reveal conics or curves – would have hesitated to assign each one a name. From small beginnings nature creates – step by step – the mosaic beauty and an incomparable order, which never ceases to astound, and she wondered if Besa reacted as she to abstract forms, which obeyed rigid geometric rules, such as the graceful convolutions of buds in certain plants.

She stood before the mirror: a nude, slim body refreshed by a shower. She fiddled with her stringy hair, and in a sudden rush of horror stared at an offending pimple on the right eyelash. Suppose it grew into the size of an orange and distorted her face? She explored such a disturbing thought for a while, eyed her breasts for a moment. Two rounded mounds on her chest were standing proud and erect, with two brown points on it for nipples. Shantiee cupped her breasts in both hands, decided they were growing a little fuller, and turned to lotions and deodorants. She worked quickly, leaving her body scented, softer and a satin smooth. When she had slid into her lemon underwear, however, the first year was at pains as to what to put on. She tried one outfit after another, discarding them all for some reasons, until she finally settled for a white, cotton dress she hoped he would love to see her in. It had a simple cut, yet the dress gave her just the sort of effect she wanted: a graceful, erotic appeal.

The undergraduate locked her room and walked steadily down the stairway, holding on to the railing least she should miss a step. If her roommate came she would find a note which said, 'Gone to see a friend in Soweto. I shall bring him along in the evening for a drink,' and Jane would probably think of a high school friend, Davies. She had never met Besa, of course, nor had Shantiee discussed him with her. She would introduce him and add, 'Besa will be coming to see sometimes,' just to get the facts straight from the beginning. Being a senior, her roommate might try to be in the way, yet she hoped things wouldn't go so as that, or there would be trouble. Smiling to herself, she imagined how optimistic she was, yet the memory of his last look reassured her: a slow, affectionate smile from him who had now become – and what a sequence of events! – more than just a friend in her dreams.

She remembered it so well: essays in her hand, Shantiee hurries up the stairs and reaches the third floor. She hopes to find him in, taps lightly on number 22 and faces a boy working at his desk. For a moment she regards him, 'Perhaps this is Besa,' and recalls a friend's description: 'Besa is tall, slim and dark. He's a reflective type and not much of a talker. His clothes are ill worn and not always neat. They give him a queer appearance that is not uncommon on the street, so that he might be mistaken for a delinquent. He is basically shy, reserved, absentminded and antisocial, and he has very few friends. Yet he happens to belong to one of the most radical student publications at this University, and for this reason he is highly regarded by students and lecturers alike.'

'Can I help you?' the boy startles her out of her reveries.

'Yes, please,' says she, not sure he answers the description. She looks him over for some moments: he wasn't bad looking, after all, and Shantiee rather liked those inquisitive eyes and lips curved in an arrogant out. Stepping inside the room she says:

'I am looking for someone. Do you happen to live here?'

'Yes, with a fourth year vet.'

'Oh, so you must be the person I am looking for! Aren't you Besa Musunga?'

The boy wiggles his head. 'I am afraid you've come to the wrong place. I am not the person you're looking for. Is there anything else?'

She glances at a piece of paper bearing the name and address in utter disbelief, disappointed since she had come to the wrong place. Ought she to go back and ask again, or could she perhaps try all the Soweto blocks and see what happens before abandoning the search? What a waste of time and effort, mounting the stairs!

Shantiee meets a male student on the ground floor landing and asks him:

'Excuse me. Would you know this guy?'

The student examines the name and address and returns the paper.

'Are you a first year?'

'Yes, why do you ask?'

'Everyone knows Besa. Anyway, this is the very block in which he lives. Go to the third floor.'

They make way for a student to pass, and then the guide continues:

'The guy that has just passed – that's Besa's friend. Run up and ask him.'

'Thank you very much,' her voice quavers in anger and hurt. Tears stand in her eyes as Shantiee vows never to see him again.

Who does he think he is, anyway? And yet, here she was this Friday evening, barely a week after Besa had thrown her out into the corridor, happy and without any regrets.

She descended another series of steps in a trancelike state, much too enthralled by the leanings of her lively fancy to sense anything unusual happening below. When Shantiee had come to the last flight of steps, however, she heard a raucous applause that gave her a sudden jolt, and she stopped to listen. What is going on, she muttered, and then rushed down. The roar sounded again, as of voices inured to much screaming and shouting, and was followed by a loud crush – then nothing. Her heart throbbing, she passed the deserted October common room and could scarcely believe what was witnessed at the car park.

Two male students, apparently drunk and stripped to the waist, were uttering obscenities as spectators, being male and largely female (and without seeming particularly offended by such buffoonery) merely grinned, laughed out aloud and cheered at an account of some anecdote. When the pair started dancing to a beer song, the crowd went wild with hysterical excitement.

> Tukabulamo umutima,
> Mukashala amafupa;
> Tukamona inga ifibolokoto
> Fikanwa ubwalwa.
>
> Waini yaliwamisha,
> Waini yaliwamisha.
> Waini yaliwamisha
> Iyo bakumba mu Beirut[28]

Shantiee wasn't in the least impressed. She thought ruefully: 'This is a parody of how students generally ought to behave,' and she was only too glad to leave the clamour and the clownish pair behind. She turned right, then left, and then passed some female flats in Kafue before male quarters proper sharply rose before her eyes: a cluster of one-or-four-storied buildings well apart from each other – monumental, identical and austere in their aspects. Here and there the men, usually with their girl friends, would say a courteous greeting or simply pass in silence, minding their business without subjecting a girl to harassment as was often the case in the Ruins (where boys hung about the balconies or Monk Square to gossip and make nasty comments whenever a woman happened to go by.)

Here in the New Residence, on the contrary, you felt at ease with
your surroundings. You imbibed the fresh air, enjoyed the beauty
of perspective and, whenever you were in a mini or a stunner, you
could still mix without someone having to say, 'This isn't the right
way to dress', as though they had the authority to decide a woman's
taste. Here in the New Rez, the men did not look at you with hostil-
ity, as if to say, 'Where are you going? This isn't where you belong!'
but usually with kindly eyes and a gentle smile, and you felt you really belonged. So you smiled back at strangers, swung your hips a
bit, and made a lot of friends.

Purposeful and brisk, her steps echoed away as Shantiee hastened to pick up her new friend, her special friend. For some moments she entertained a fantasy, a make-believe world in which her
unrequited wishes verged on an admission of her attraction to him,
overflowing her heart with sweet hope and satisfaction. Like an artist she enriched her images with flirtatious embraces and the taste of
their first kiss, filling the canvas of her mind with an elaborate paint-
ing of some wild romance. She flushed and furtively looked round:
there was no one in sight to witness her secret whims, her quavering lips and delighted look!

By now she had reached Soweto 2. A laborious mount to the
third floor, a knock on the door... and lo, there he was before her
very eyes: handsome, wreathed in a boyish grin, peering at her in a
way, which made her feel really good. Smiling up at him, too, she
gazed into the depth of his brown, limpid eyes and said softly,

'Here I am.'

'You're looking great... and very beautiful too!'

'Thank you,' her voice was almost a whisper. 'Are you ready?'

'Of course, Shantiee,' was the reply. He locked the door and
added with a smile: 'I am very glad you came. I couldn't help wondering whether you were going to make it or not. I was very anxious, so to speak.'

'So was I. I didn't exactly think I would find you.'

'I don't break promises.'

'Neither do I,' and they smiled at each other and laughed.

She chose a table at far end of makumbi dining hall. Besides her
favourite soup and salads, her menu comprised rice and sausages.
Besa preferred nsima, fried chicken and over-boiled vegetables that
he ate hungrily with his left hand. Her appetite was generally good,
but Shantiee relished this meal more than any she had had in a long
time. She was perfectly relaxed and happy with him. In her enthusi-

asm, she forgot that they had just met recently and confided things she would never have said to anyone she was dating for the first time. She could be witty, intimate and open minded about her feelings, and in afterthought it was as if those imperishable fears, aspirations and secrets safely locked away in her heart could now be shared with a man she could trust, someone with whom she had a community of taste. On the other hand, Besa was just as fascinated with her as she was with him. She amused him or, what amounted to the same thing, really made him laugh.

Their supper now over, the two young people started off to her room in the virgin night – along a route she had suggested. The School of Mines on the right would drop behind them. They would follow a road meeting another at right angles and take a turn to the left, go past the Christian Centre and the Dean of Student Office building on the right, make yet another turn to the left, pass the Old Bridge Building, and finally reach her little place in October 3.

'We could also stop for some minutes at the Goma Lakes to see the ponds in the moonlight. I haven't been there for days and I'd love to see them with you. What d'you say?'

'Sounds fine.'

He pointed at the sky sprayed with innumerable stars in flight, and exclaimed in a voice touched with emotion:

'Look at the stars, Shantiee. Their light and presence bespeak great wonder and mystery, yet it is the awesome number of stars that is most astonishing. Besides our tiny galaxy with billions of stars in it, there are yet other gigantic galaxies in their spiral arms with billions and billions of stars in flight! Can you imagine the extent of the universe?'

'It's impossible to imagine,' she replied sadly.

'I like watching the sky in the evening but feel depressed afterwards. I get this feeling of infinite loneliness and dread when I consider our place in the universe and the way this bears on the meaning of our life. D'you sometimes feel this way?'

'Yes – at times, though I feel we are not alone in the universe. I think there is something out there watching us.'

'You mean God?'

'Something like that, but not only that. I feel there is greater meaning to our life than we sometimes care to admit. Our life is not in vain. There's reason to it.'

He sneered in distaste and shook his head. 'You sound like my mother who thinks that humanity holds a privileged place in the universe.'

'And she's right, isn't she?'

'She's just God-complex. Frankly, though, there's nothing very privileged about human life. Humanity has no better fate than a beast.'

'You're disheartening,' Shantiee replied in vague reproach, then started laughing. She recovered her serious gravity and eyed him intently: he was a sceptic, he was with her now, and he was enveloped in queer reflections about the human predicament, though Besa was right in thinking that the human dilemma was just as terrible as anything could possibly be. On the other hand, this sentiment of despair resolved nothing. One way or the other people had to get on in this world, and there was no escaping this fact!

'Anyhow,' she shrugged her shoulders, 'whether life has meaning or not, just now I wish to learn a bit about you. Where do you come from?'

'Samfya.'

'Samfya...I think I know where that is, I've been there twice. Once when my dad took my family for a day to see the lake and again when I was on a wildlife study tour from Lechwe with classmates. I still have some pictures from the trip. I'll let you see them if you want.'

'What about you,' Besa asked, nodding. 'Where do you come from?'

'I am from Mufulira. Do you know the place?'

'No. I have never been to the Copperbelt.'

'Well it's a small but beautiful mining town. This is where I was born.'

'Are you parents both alive?'

'Yes. My dad is a businessman – he's Italian. Mom is a banker and she's Zambian. She comes from Mporokoso. We're three in my family – all girls, and I am the first born child.'

'So you come from a well-to-do family?'

'You could say so. We're not poor.'

'You're very lucky.'

'It's possible to say that but we do have problems like every family does.'

'Well, in my case I come from a poor family. There are five of us – four boys and one girl, and I am the fourth born child. My parents are both alive. They earn their living by fishing and subsistence farming. They are simple people living their lives in a village.'

'Are they happy, nonetheless?'

'I suppose they are happy. Their needs are very basic but sometimes we go to bed without any food.'

'You sometimes go to bed without a meal?' she echoed incredulously. 'I hope it's not true!'

'I am afraid it's true,' he smiled and explained. 'You see, we rely heavily on farming, fishing and doing odd jobs for people. Our lives are at the mercy of the weather patterns and the availability of fish stocks. To supplement, my brothers and I have to work for money, but lately there have been fewer and fewer jobs. I remember it took me five months to raise money to buy a pair of shoes. That was when I was doing my last class in high school. Because of the difficulties we faced financially, my mother always made sure that I took off my shoes after school and walked bare foot. She said I couldn't risk wearing them all the time for fear they might tear too soon. They were the only pair I had. Some of my classmates – especially those from Lusaka – laughed at me for wearing torn shoes or a tattered uniform.'

'O no, Besa,' said Shantiee, and burst out laughing. 'I don't believe any of this. I know you are just joking!'

Besa was taken aback. He thrust her a puzzled, angry glance that silenced her in an instant, and Shantiee had to apologise.

'I am so sorry. It's just that I found all this somewhat funny and unbelievable. Please forgive me!'

'Never mind,' he replied with a wave of his hand. 'But it's true. I only had two pairs of shoes.'

Shantiee clutched at his arm – pitying him, remembering her home in Mufulira, a twelve bed roomed mansion with five servants to manage it. Her family also owned two fuel stations, three large farms, two hotels, a fleet of buses and trucks, and a company that supplied mining equipment and accessories. They also had shares in some businesses locally and outside the country.

She squeezed his palm in sympathy and said:

'What's important in life is having a positive attitude about your self, fixing your eyes on your goal. Anyone can change his or her circumstances forever.'

'Yes, that's what my mother also says. She says, "It is not a sharpened axe that fells trees for a cassava garden, but the heart." Determination is everything.'

'Speaking of your parents, Besa. I suppose you are proud of them – despite the conditions?'

'I am very proud of my parents. They have tried within their means to make me the person I am. I owe my life to them. I shall always remain thankful for what they have done for me. Poor as they are, they are my models of what I must be in this life.'

'You know what: I think you are very different from some people I have met. Most students here would never have said what you've just told me if they happened to be poor. They would rather say they are from rich families with powerful connections or that they are middle-class. For the most part they want to look rich and sophisticated, and they despise everything African as backward and primitive. They are elitist minded. Can I tell you something more personal?'

'If you please.'

'Right. You know, ever since I came to this place I've had at least ten propositions from guys who claim to love me, and none of them has been to rural areas!'

'Perhaps they were all telling the truth.'

'Perhaps they all were. But why would someone, for example, go so far as to preach about it or seem to want everyone to know that they're rich? Why would they say it so insistently?'

'You tell me.'

'Ok, I'll tell you why. I think they only want to make an impression as a way of getting some attention. They imagine that if they weren't as rich, urban or sophisticated, they would be nothing and wouldn't even show their face.'

'That's a possibility.'

'It's not just a possibility, it's the whole truth.' She gave him a side-ways glance and went on: 'Come to think of it, one of them even boasted about driving and night clubs, but what's so special about driving your *dad's* car or frequenting night clubs? That doesn't impress me.' Shantiee wanted to add, 'I have my own car and there's enough money in my account so I don't need a man for material things,' but she refrained.

'Poor guys. I hope you'll accept one of them, nonetheless.'

'No I won't, and I can't. I told each one of them politely that they had come to me late – I had someone I loved and there was nothing anybody could do about it.'

'Who's your boy friend?'

'I've none. I simply said it so they could leave me alone like you sometimes see girls wearing engagement rings just to have the men think they are married so nobody would bother them. What about you? Is there a girl in your life?'

'At the moment, no. But there *was* some time back.'

'What happened to her? Did you break the relationship?'

'No. She died.'

'She died? How did it happen?'

'It's a sad story; you wouldn't like to hear it.'

'Oh but I would. I am very interested. Please tell me everything.'

A brief hush fell upon them. They turned left at the corner, tread-
ing the empty road in the warm, beautiful night, their thoughts centred on the story of a love in wretchedness. A Toyota pick-up passed
that way, and then there was silence again. Shantiee looked dubi-
ously at him: 'It's Ok if he doesn't feel like sharing whatever he
went through. He's not obliged in any way,' yet she did not voice
these sentiments to him. She waited for Besa to break the silence.

He freed his hand from her grip and said:

'My girl friend drowned at Lunkunka on Lake Bangweulu as
they came back from the islands where she and some of her colleagues had been organising health care workshops. She was a
health science student from Chainama.'

'When did this happen?'

'Last year. Three or four weeks into the first term.'

'What about the others?'

'They also died. There were no survivors.'

'O my God, it must have been very dreadful for you!'

'It was – actually,' he said, 'and I'll never forget how very miserable I was. I couldn't eat well, sleep or concentrate on my studies. For months I felt totally lost, anguished and painfully empty,
and the bereavement cast a pall on me. In my dreams I would see
the swollen body of my girl friend at the Beach with a swarm of
flies hovering over her. I would see her grotesque body with horrifying eyes almost bulging out, and I would wake up and weep for
hours together. I loved her very much and I was going to take her
to my parents. When I saw her body I could not forgive her for dying and leaving me alone. I didn't see any reason to live on. It was
as though I was Dante's character in the *Inferno* where death ceases
to frighten and, instead, becomes a dear friend.'

'You should have withdrawn from your studies and gone home.
Why didn't you?'

'Do you know Sartre?' Besa fixed her a steadfast look.

'No.'

'He was a French writer and thinker. In one of his books he says,
"A man's self accompanies him everywhere." So wherever I might
have gone my problems would have stayed with me. A change of
environment does not always answer – but an attitude of mind.
Anyway, I decided not to lose time on my studies and stayed on.
It wasn't easy, though, because I always felt empty. But somehow

I managed to get into second year and in the chaos of this terrible time discovered what I love best.'

'What is that?'

'You're so curious! Anyhow, I discovered that if I sat at a table and endured the literary strain for hours, I could write essays, which people appreciated. This was how I started submitting articles to students' publications and finally found myself on the editorial team of the Vanguard.'

'Are you still writing? If you are, could I see some of your stuff?'

'It's possible to see my work but you wouldn't recognise me as the author. I write under a pseudonym.'

'Which one?'

'I can't tell you.'

'But why not?' she cried. 'You're my friend!'

'Ok. Only on one condition. You don't reveal my identity to anyone.'

'Ok. I promise not to.'

'I am the author of everything which appears under the *Ferio Pages*.'

She stopped abruptly. For an instant she gaped at him in astonishment, unable to believe her ears. Could he be the one who had written an essay on education reforms that she had read in the Vanguard? He'd better tell her at once!

'Besa, please tell me the truth. Are you the author of *A Crisis in the Zambian Education System* that appeared in the Vanguard?'

Besa said he was.

She was so delighted, so full of admiration and respect for him that Shantiee almost hugged him. At the same time she felt elevated to be with someone with a reputation for shrewd criticism and a flair for words.

'I think you are a genius,' she declared without hesitation. 'You are a real genius!'

'O come now. Don't make so much of this. I just write, that's all.'

'O yes you are. No one could have written anything like that unless they were knowledgeable and very intelligent. Indeed I think you are!'

Besa gave his shoulders a nonchalant shrug and resumed walking. Shantiee caught up with him. Her mind was working fast, conjuring up bits of information she had heard about him: a friend's insistence that she saw Besa about her writings, some references that he was a journalist, and several remarks by students about the Ferio Pages. On the other hand, how could she have guessed that this unpretentious, unsophisticated, poor boy from a remote village in Samfya was indeed that critic whose works had won the hearts of students and lecturers alike? Her curiosity thus aroused, Shantiee put another question to him:

'I wonder why you chose Ferio to write under. Why didn't you just stick to your real name the way most authors do?'

'I hate to be famous,' Besa answered after a while. 'Unfortunately, though, most students have found out who Ferio is so it's useless to hide from them. Another reason was my personal security as an author in a political environment where anything critical of the State may actually provoke government reprisals or sanctions.'

'You're right. When I read some of the material in your publication I asked myself, aren't these people risking arrest? In Mufulira, the police rounded up some teenagers whose paintings depicted the poor and the rich in a satirical fashion. A government official said such works could be used to make everyone class conscious and rise against the well to do. So the boys were flogged and their paintings were burned!'

'So you understand?'

'I understand you very well. Our government can be very ruthless against its enemies. I have seen this a number of times in the Copperbelt. There was a musician who recorded a single in which he protested against the rising prices of basic goods in Zambia. The Party decided to ban the song on both radio and television and the man was deported to his native village. His instruments were confiscated and he was warned not to sing again.'

'As a matter of fact, Shantiee, this was the reason why I was afraid to see you the first time we met. I was very suspicious when you said you had come to see me. We had never seen each other before – but there you were, at exactly the time I was writing the final draft of a sensitive essay. I was so distracted that I asked you to leave, thinking you were a Party cadre or someone from the *Office of the President* or the *Special Branch.*' He was quiet again. Besa averted his eyes as pain, and shame and remorse had discomfited him now.

Yet Shantiee understood. It didn't matter what he had done to her, for she had forgiven him a long time ago. What mattered was the fact that they had discovered each other – that was all.

'Don't let this upset you,' she told him reassuringly. They had come under a streetlight and Shantiee had noticed how distressed he looked. 'Whatever happened is behind us. It's gone – and you never meant to hurt me. If I'd not been able to forget I wouldn't have wanted us to meet – I'd have been elsewhere by now.' She stopped him and said: 'But I *choose* to be with you tonight because I like you. I hope we shall be great friends. Will this do for the moment?'

'Yes. Thanks a lot. I was so ashamed!'

'You don't have to feel so anymore. We have gone through this together and we have survived. We're now on our way to my place for a glass of wine. Are you coming with me? Please say yes!'

He looked long at her and laughed.

Walking by his side, she was more than contented. Her features softened: her eyes were tender, and her voice was gentler as her heart rejoiced and submitted to an influence so sweet. But her feelings, vigorous and sincere though they might have been, were still not fully drawn to dwelling upon one radiant spot. Shantiee liked him all right, yet she hadn't come to love him as yet.

They reclined on a public seat overlooking the fishponds. She drew up her legs, coiled her arms round them, perched her chin on the kneecaps and peered into the distance. Dark silhouettes of trees cast on the ground shifted in a slight breeze. The moon was full and very bright. The ponds were silvery white and furrowed with ripples, reflecting light beams. Water trickled and rushed over rocks towards the reeds. Traffic hummed along Great East Road like bees in a hive… And then, quite suddenly, her attention riveted to him. Besa was beside her – hands thrust deep in his pockets, legs slightly drawn apart, and as silent as a rock. She touched him with her elbow and whispered:

'You seem preoccupied. Are you getting bored?'

'Not really. I was just thinking of the essay I am currently working on.'

'What is it about?'

'It's about students' politics and activism. I am writing the last draft.'

'When do you plan to finish?'

'I don't know. I find it very difficult to write. For the purposes of *this* work I have to write in a scholarly fashion with historical evidence provided. I want to write about students' politics in a global context though my earlier plan was to write a purely philosophical piece based on simple axioms. The problem with the last approach was that it would have been too theoretical. So I opted to write something grounded in facts that no one will dispute. But I always find writing to be very difficult.'

She listened to him speak about the nature of his work – the objectives, the form that it should take, and the problems which confronted the artist as he tried to conform to the creative demands and every day existence. In these very moments, Shantiee understood that her life would never be complete without the boy who exerted upon her such overpowering unrest as to wish to be with him always, to lavish on him the passion of her heart and mind. And yet – she mustn't display this view. She mustn't touch with her lips that coveted sight!

'Bye the way,' his voice sounded as though far away, 'The University of Zambia has been asked to send twelve students to a three day Youth Forum Workshop to be organised by the British Council and the Commonwealth Development Corporation. Each School has chosen two – and mine has picked me with some fourth year guy reading geography. There will be other participants from colleges, secondary schools and other institutions. The main objective of this workshop is to get the youth share what they think are the most pressing developmental issues facing the world today. I will discuss the role of multinational corporations and international capital in Africa. The event will be held at Mulungushi International Conference Centre in three weeks. About forty participants are expected to attend. There will be spectators, too, and I would like to invite you to the Forum. There will be good food and plenty of nice people to meet. The University will provide a bus for any students interested in attending. Would you want to come?'

'Are you inviting me?'

'Yes. I'd like you to be there with me. I am sure you would enjoy yourself.'

She thought it over and said, 'I'd love to. I will come.'

'Are you sure?'

'It'd be a privilege for me to see you speak to a big audience.'

'It'll be tough. I have never presented at a big gathering. I keep imagining how things will be like and I get these sweats.'

She laughed. 'That sort of anxiety is normal. Just make sure you are well prepared. You could also practice in your room with a small audience of two or three people. I could provide your audience if you wanted.'

'You could?'

'Yes. I have some ideas about public speaking. I did a lot of that at Luchwe as a member of the debate club. Maybe I could be of some help to you.'

'*I* could certainly do with your help! Large audiences frighten me! Thanks a lot!'

'You're welcome. *Any* time.'

Shantiee felt ecstatic and on a threshold of a new life. She felt very content to be with him. She vowed to make him proud of her.

'Can we go now?' Besa had stood up already.

'Can't we stay on for a bit? Maybe ten minutes?'

'You really like the place?'

'Yes – very much. It's quiet and relaxing. It's also nice to be alone with you. I am enjoying myself. Don't you like it here?'

'I do. There's good company and the scenery is beautiful in the moonlight.'

'We could be coming here to be together and have fun. I find you quite interesting.'

'I hope you're not flattering me?'

'No, why would I do that? I am quite serious!'

'But a girl like you ought to associate with the sort of guys you spoke to me about, the sort that are rich and sophisticated. You shouldn't waste your time consorting with someone like me.'

'What's this supposed to mean?'

'I have had a different life. Perhaps you would be more comfortable with people who share your background than you'd ever be with me. We're very different, so to speak. We may be friends but we'll continue friends apart!'

'So you don't want to be seen around with me, is that it?'

'I didn't mean that.'

'That's what you meant,' she said plaintively and stood too. 'You should have told me this before. I can't associate with you – that's fine!' She was on the verge of tears. He had denied her and she mustn't be with him now. Shantiee started moving away from the spot.

'Wait up, Shantiee,' Besa called after her, and she listened. She looked at the dark outline of his face and felt unmoved by it, but not so much as to dislike him. Suddenly she was lonely and abject.

'You're angry with me?' he said.

'Certainly not. I just want to go home. I can't be where you don't want me.'

'That wasn't what I meant. I merely wanted you to understand that there are guys that – '

'Besa, I wish you would stop referring to them and let me choose the kind of friends I can easily relate to. All I ask is to be your friend, your very good friend – and friends can be together whenever they feel like it. Is this too much to ask? Don't I mean anything to you? What do you find wrong with me?' And she started to sob.

He drew her in his arms and held her pressed against him. She was no longer conscious of her body but of him whispering things she couldn't hear. When she gazed up at him, Shantiee saw him bend as if to kiss her on the lips. She rose on her toes, hungry and dying, athirst for that which she lacked or else in this impulse be united with him. Yet Besa would not kiss her. He was merely saying, 'Let's go now,' and she had misunderstood his intention. Confused and embarrassed, she was angry with herself for giving in too easily to her emotions. She must not let him see that in the depth of her heart, she was hurting and disheartened. She would have loved the taste of his mouth and the feel of his body – the ripples and pathos of his life. Why was he afraid to kiss her?

In her room Shantiee went to work. The small table was set aright. The glasses were rinsed, and the bottle of wine was produced. Besa opened it. He filled the glasses to the brim and, twiddling with his own, said appreciatively:

'Autumn Harvest. Looks like a nice drink. Did you buy it yourself?'

'It was present on my last birthday when I turned eighteen, but I had forgotten about the wine until this afternoon when I really felt like celebrating. You said some good things and I knew instinctively that you could understand me.'

She sighed in satisfaction, took her place on the bed, looked at him with curious attention and pointed a finger at a chair: 'Please sit down and feel at home. You're welcome to my humble abode.'

'Thank you.' He reached for the other glass and handed it to her. 'I'd like to drink to our new friendship. May we live for a thousand years.'

'May we live for a thousand years,' she answered, laughing. She took a gulp of the wine, laid the glass on the table and asked whether he liked her room.

'I think it's nice, orderly and clean. You have a wonderful collection of books, too. Are they all yours?'

'Yes.'

'Can I look at them for a minute?'

'Go ahead, though I am afraid you won't find anything of much interest. Have a look all the same.'

She knew her small library by heart. Apart from textbooks in hard cover there were – mostly paperbacks – volumes of Shakespeare, Dickens, Conrad, Joyce, T.S Eliot, Solzhenitsyn, Umberto Eco and some translations of German and Greek classics. Among Africans she remembered Ngugi, Wilber Smith, Soyinka, Christo-

pher Akigbo, Achebe, Albert Camus, Alechi Amadi, Mpashi, Mu-
laisho, Alan Paton, Armah and a few others of less repute.

'I have a lot more books that have been lent out to friends,' she
informed him apologetically. 'And some that I left at home but will
collect this vacation.'

'All the same, what you have here is quite impressive.'

'You love to read fiction?'

'Yes I do. I used to read a lot after completing my secondary education but not as much nowadays due to pressure from assignments
and lectures. There's very little time.' He pulled out a volume from
the shelf and flipped the pages, mumbling words she couldn't catch.

'What are you saying?'

'I am reciting a poem from the anthology *Oral Poetry from Africa* compiled by Jack Mapanje and Landeg White. Just listen to
this from the Sudan. The poem is called *The Jilted Man.*'

Besa read out aloud:

> O Ajok!
> Ajok whom I chose when she was carried in a sling,
> Ajok whom I chose before she could dance,
> Ajok whom I chose when she was not yet a clan beauty,
> When she grew up, another took her away from me.
> What misery! What a way to treat a man!
> God has speared me and Marang has speared me.
> For the daughter of Kat Atem I have felt misery.
> I weep and weep for the sake of Ajok the brow.

'Poor man,' Shantiee remarked sympathetically. 'He mustn't
weep too much for Ajok, though. He must rise above this pain and
find someone else.'

'I hope in time he will. Yet at this moment the poet is more concerned with making a statement about his present circumstances
than anything else. After nourishing his mind by the promises of
love and happiness, he soon realises, and probably watches, that the
girl on whom he had waited for many years has eloped with another
man. This is the cause of his grief.'

'I feel sorry for him.'

'The poet is silent about facts that led to this situation. Yet perhaps the girl was right to leave him, who knows?'

'Yes, indeed, who knows? Perhaps the poet was a nut.'

'Perhaps he really was. Perhaps he wasn't. We simply won't
know the truth!'

'Too bad for that,' was her comment. 'Anyway, whatever reasons led to the poet's plight there's nothing as heart breaking as unrequited love. You feel rejected, disillusioned and you can't see the future without the love that has been lost. You plunge into the poet's pit.'

'Have you lost someone lately?' Besa asked urgently. 'You seem to speak from deep down in your heart!'

Shantiee remained silent for some moments. She appeared to hesitate, thus keeping him in suspense. She shuddered in distress and decided to tell him everything.

'Yes,' she confessed. 'I lost someone once... We first met at a takeaway restaurant in town where he got me talking about who I was and where I lived. I asked who he was and that kind of thing, and he said Paul. He's coloured. He works for an insurance company in Mufulira but lives in Kitwe in Riverside. That day Paul left me his number and I gave him mine, promising to be in touch.

'After this he would phone me twice a week and we'd talk for about half an hour or so, though in the beginning I wasn't so keen. Yet the more frequent the calls the more I developed a sense of him, so I'd day dream about him and feel anxious whenever there was a long silence before I heard from him again.

'The first time Paul took me out was a disaster, yet the second wasn't. I was more confident, involved and better prepared to make up for what I'd done badly the last time. We drove to Baruba motel and watched a live band play music as we enjoyed our drinks. I was on softies but Paul was taking mosi or something like that. It was a wonderful time. On our way back to Mufulira – quite late in the afternoon – he repeated what he had told me earlier. That he had just completed business studies at the Copperbelt University and would like to settle down. He needed a steady girl friend whom he might marry some day, and he asked me to think this over because he felt I could be good for him.

'That night I didn't sleep. I was doing my A levels at Lechwe and was preparing to enter university. I was seventeen then, and we had been seeing each other for three weeks. I never quite seriously thought about marriage yet fancied how good it would be to have a boy friend who really loved me. You see, all my peers had someone they loved or someone they were about to love. It was an on-and-off thing for them and I was fed up of being pressured and mocked at because I was "single". So I said to myself, "Let me have a boy friend just for once. It won't hurt to try it."

'I phoned Paul this time, and I told him I'd accepted and suggested to pay him a visit over the weekend. We fixed a Saturday and I boarded a bus very early in the morning. I was there by seven.

'His house wasn't difficult to find. As I approached it my mind was in deep reverie, and my heart was overflowed with endearing words I had saved for my first love. At the same time, though, I was assailed by the fear – "What if I should him gone?" – and I oscillated between promise and disappointment. So you can imagine how happy I was to see him face to face. I flew into his arms and kissed him hungrily.'

Tears started, streaming down her cheeks as she recounted the rest of the story.

'We went inside arm in arm, and where I had recoiled from close embraces and probing hands, here I permitted them, encouraged them and indulged in my whimsies as one would a frenzied passion too long denied and unexpressed. One after the other fell my clothes off my body. It was a foolish thing to do, but there I was before him: naked. I stretched out on the bed, waiting to receive him. He would always love me, he said, and I would belong to him for as long as I chose. We made love and fell asleep.

'I must have slept deeply – very comfortable with my first love in bed – because Paul had been shaking me vigorously and ordering me to dress up quickly and hide somewhere. He looked terribly shaken, frightened, and every delay drove him further into a fury. I was so dismayed, so confounded that I could hardly think! When I protested, Paul slapped me and said, "Dress up quickly. My wife and kid have come! They are waiting outside!"

'I hastily put on my clothes, forgetting my shoes and tote-bag. Paul opened the window and helped me out, and I crushed on the ground with a thud, almost dislocating my wrists and ankles. I got up on my feet, looked about me in fright, but couldn't decide where to go. Then I heard someone scream, "A prostitute", and I started running.'

Shantiee was weeping freely now, her face buried in her palms. She mourned and tore at her hair in self-revulsion and grief, yet Besa implored her to quiet down. She put his handkerchief to her eyes to soothe them and dry her tears, and then miserably stared at him: 'I still feel dirty, cheapened, misused, deceived and humiliated. I shall never be able to forget. I did nothing wrong in trusting someone but they ran after me and called me "Prostitute". If it hadn't been for the police officer who happened to pass by just then, the crowd would have killed me.'

'It's all right now, Shantiee. Please stop crying.'

'It wasn't all my fault.'

'I know but such things do happen. Please don't cry. Look at you now. Your eyes are swollen and red!'

'I made a stupid mistake, Besa. I shouldn't have slept with him. I should have been more careful with my life. I thought he would marry me, but I lost my virginity.'

'Ssshhh,' Besa said, offering her his handkerchief. She dubbed the piece of cloth around her eyes and set her loosened hair back in place. Clasping his hands in her palms, Shantiee dismally looked at him:

'Now you know how filthy I am. You have reason to despise and walk away from me.'

'I'd never do that despite what you went through. As a matter of fact I feel I've to have a friend like you in my life. I am very happy with who you are. I can't change one bit about you.'

'How would this work after what I have told you?'

'Don't be silly. Are you suggesting that I leave you now because you are dirty?'

She did not answer immediately. To her consternation and terror Besa stood up to leave, and she eyed him distractedly, much too surprised to speak! 'O, what was ailing her tonight?' she considered in desperation. The chair would be vacant, the glasses of wine would remain full, the room would be deserted and dreary – while she, lonely, hurting and reeling, would soon collapse on the bed in floods of tears should Besa leave her now. And she didn't want that!

She sprung to her feet and rushed to the door. She leaned her back against it and cast her eyes sheepishly down. Besa stepped forward to reprove her odd behaviour.

'Honestly, Shantiee,' he started in a disappointed tone, 'is this the kind of come-together you asked me to? '

She averted her eyes and said nothing, suddenly guilty and isolated, hating herself for spoiling their evening with her outbursts. What could she do to make amends?

'Listen, I understand how you feel about your recent past, but everyone has a share of misfortune regardless of who they are. On the other hand, life is always a possibility of being willing to start something new, a willingness to take up our shattered selves and move on. If our life is already past, we can neither alter nor erase it, nor can we possibly influence it. At every instant of our existence the great comedy of our life is slowly coming to a close, and we cannot arrest events. The only way, then, is to contend with all the forces that control our destiny by taking courage in our hands and daring to plunge into the unknown future.

'This also means that we must be prepared to let go of some things engraved upon our minds if we should be free to recreate our experiences and enjoy life. Sometimes we lose some, sometimes we gain, but even if we lost some we would still have gained the knowledge that we had lost in order not to lose again, for our morality would then have been guided by our past experiences.

'Now you and I have lost some – and so be it – yet we must look to the future with openness and trust. We cannot afford to wreck our lives with vain regrets and self-recriminations since living consists in growth, in our readiness to risk ourselves in the quest to realise all our dreams. As the Indian poet, Kalidasa, said in his salutation to the dawn – that we must live well *today* because all the verities of our existence lie in its brief course – so we must make the best of today and, like Horace, be capable of saying, "Tomorrow, do your worst, for I have lived today!" Therefore, Shantiee, let's seize today and live as though the past and the future were of no consequence. Why should we mar the splendour of the moment by a thousand regrets when the past can never be changed? What do we gain by reliving our pains and clouding the moment with gloom and uncertainties? If I had kept on crying over the death of my girlfriend, I would have been a lunatic a long time ago. Time has come for you to dry your tears and put a smile on that beautiful face. Time has come to move on. Let us move on, for Christ's sake!'

Thus she listened to him – unburdened, dispelled of self-loathing and pain, her attachment to him created in these very moments. Shantiee made a bold step forward and wrapped her arms round his neck, her every thought tinged with a pious adoration of him. Taking a solemn vow and declaration, "From this moment on I will always love you, most coveted friend," she realised how lucky and favoured she truly was that the vicissitudes of life – at the moment she needed a true friend – should grant her the very wish she had often whispered into her pillows every night. Soft eyed and goaded by a feeling so true and right, she fastened her rosy lips on his mouth, drawing his tongue and inhaling his wine, scented fragrance. Then she kissed his nose, forehead, and laid her head on his chest. Her life had altered forever... because of him!

'I am crazy about you, Besa,' she confessed presently. 'You make me want to love you and I cannot restrain myself. What will I do?'

'Wait a moment, young lady,' he said. He held her head in his palms and flushed her an intense, passionate stare: 'You're sure it's not the wine, Shantiee?'

'I am sure it isn't.'

He subsided at once, his expression sceptical and yet critical. He shook his head in doubt. 'Everything is so sudden, and I shouldn't like us to start something we might sooner or later abandon. It's very easy to make mistakes on the spur of the moment.'

'But you do like me a little, don't you?'

'Yes. I like you very much.'

'Say it better than that! Don't you want me too?'

'I find you very attractive, and I think you're a very wonderful young woman. Yes, I suppose I want you, too. I feel the same things. Deeply.'

She looked open-mouthed at him, her eyes bursting with tears of hope and the faith she had in him. What prompting of shared feelings and sense were urging them on? What calls to destiny were luring their hearts? Shantiee hardly knew him, of course, and yet she felt he was perfect for her.

'Besa,' she said softly, 'you're the one I feel strongly drawn to, and I am willing to do anything to make our friendship work. But you mustn't think I am promiscuous or anything like that. I am just a woman who feels she must be with the man of her choice, the man of her dreams.'

'Suppose you're mistaken? Suppose you find out that I am the opposite of what you thought?'

'I know what I feel in my gut,' she answered. 'I know I have finally found the right man for me. I am very certain of it. It's not a passing fling or any of those feelings that come and go. It's a commitment and willingness to open my life to you, to live my life for you. This was how I felt the moment I first saw you.'

He was totally overcome, and there was a perplexed tenderness rising in his beautiful eyes. He bent to kiss her on the lips and admired her enchanted face. 'You are so gentle and yet so determined and brave,' he said affectionately.

'Am I forcing myself on you?'

'I wouldn't put it that way. I would say you have helped me see a side of you that I like. Your readiness to love unreservedly, and the eagerness with which you trust your instincts and give your heart away to the winds.'

'You make me do what I have done. You make me want to do anything for you.'

Besa reached for a glass of wine and got her to sit beside him on the bed. She clasped his free hand and waited in great anticipation.

'Life may start or end almost anywhere,' he told her sagely. 'There are no guides, no signposts, no authorities and no references other than our dreams and us. I just hope this moment will always be cherished and remembered by us for the rest of our lives. Shall we drink to us?'

As they sipped from the same glass, Shantiee fondled his hands, stared at the pools that were his eyes, and kissed the parted lips and sensitive mouth…wholly lost in the admiration of the features which were sweet and very dear to her now. A deep longing for him shook her in every part, yet she was content and happy to be with the one she would always call "mine". How often today had she secretly wished to make flattering overtures to him, dreamed to be touched and embraced by him? How very strange, indeed (and yet also very gratifying!) that what she had sought with ardour should now be within her grasp! She would keep the faith, of course, and love him truly and well!

'I feel very much like a bride,' she whispered to him, sliding her palm over the length of his arm. 'I also feel like being with you in a beautiful place with lots of people and lights and music to dance to.'

'You mean a night club?'

'Yes. Some place like that. I want to dance with you!'

'There is a good spot in town where we could share a drink and finish off the evening pleasantly. It's called Venus; it's very popular with students.'

'The name sounds weird. But is it a nice place?'

'It is, actually, and it is also safe. I am sure you would love it.'

'Only with you,' she corrected him proudly. Shantiee then stood up to her feet. Opening the door of the steel wardrobe, she retrieved a briefcase and asked Besa to open it. 'The number is 3469211905.'

Besa opened the case and whistled in surprise: 'Jesus Christ, is this *all* yours?'

Shantiee laughed with pleasure. 'You are so innocent. You ask childlike questions like my little sister, Karen. I like it.'

'Well, how much do we need?'

'You are the man. *You* are taking me out. That's all I care about.'

Besa took a ward of notes and locked the briefcase. In a few minutes they were set to go.

Shantiee threw her arms about him and kissed him again and again, smiling at him with a luscious tenderness. She was disarmed, satiated and, more importantly perhaps, very much in love with the boy whose twin eyes twinkled like jewels in the sky. She pressed her body against him, offering her heart in just the same way as she had done in her whims. Yielding her body and mind, she closed her eyes and welcomed the warm pressure on her mouth. So deliciously soft were his lips – so electric and sweet! – that she wavered and very nearly failed to arrest the effects of her strong impulses for him! And yet, recalling the lines, "The strongest oaths are straw to the fire in the blood..." by Shakespeare, she dared not desecrate their love into blind lust... at least not yet!

'Let's go out now, darling,' her voice pleaded in a sleepy murmur, 'or else I'll do something silly.'

She disentangled them, then, and ventured to raise her eyes to his enchanted face. 'Please do help me to do things right. I don't want to spoil anything between us. I want our relationship to last. Do you see what I mean?'

'Yes, Shantiee.'

'I will stand by you always. I promise.'

'What do you make of it?' Shantiee asked her roommate.

'I think it's a good thing to have a boy friend so long as he really loves you.' Jane leaned forward over the table and said: 'Did you sleep with him?'

'No, it's too early for that. We both want to wait until we're very serious about each other. Besides, I can't repeat the same mistake I made in my first relationship. I want this to be different. I want to be responsible and careful for our feelings. You see, Besa is understanding and patient and this makes him very important to me. I don't want to disappoint him.'

'Suppose he suggests to, what will you do?'

'Well in that case I'll tell him what I feel may be the best for us. I'll try to reason with him.'

'And if he still insists?'

'I don't suppose he will.'

'He just might, you know. Boys are always demanding sex. Not that your boy friend will, for sure, but you never know with men. Anything can happen.'

'In my case the situation is slightly different. I am the one who's initiating things – touching, kissing and holding hands. Besa is shy and kind of reserved in his feelings. I am the exact opposite. I assert myself and tell him what I want. But I will still try to be careful and hope for the best.'

'I wish you the best in your new love. And of course you're free to have him here any time you please. I won't mind in the least.'

'Thanks Jane. We'll try not to disturb you much. I promise you.'

Naked, alone and unobserved, Shantiee would pause for some minutes watching fixedly her own reflection in the mirror, finding much attraction in the planes or contours of the image the way Narcissus had found in the *Metamorphoses* of Ovid, though her case wasn't in the least excessive. She wasn't, to be sure, simultaneously the object of her own love, nor was she distraught with the impossibility of the perverse malady in which lover and beloved were merged into a single substantial form, yet sundered and never to reach the other even once. On the contrary, hers was a mere admiration of the transparent beauty of her body for which she was loved (though not only for this), suggested in the relations of her straight limbs, her waist, her stomach, her chest, her shoulders, her arms, her neck and (adorned by streams of hair kissing her shoulder blades) her head...all harmoniously united into what Shantiee undoubtedly was – a young, beautiful woman.

She lay nude on the bed encased in reverie... indulging in sweet remembrances of the evening she shared with him at the Venus, repeating with ardour the words she had said to him: 'We may not find the time to be together always because of our different schedules, but we should nonetheless see each other often enough or else I'll strangle you,' wondering why Besa hadn't showed up this Saturday morning as promised. Shantiee closed her eyes. They were at the night club drinking wine from the same glass, gazing into each other's eyes, drawing indescribable joy from a simple fact that they had found each other, and much comfort because they saw in every word and gesture a declaration of their love and trust.

The day progressed and there was still no sign of him, yet she was patient and hopeful. She pored over the dynamics of a particle (working through the principles of Newtonian mechanics), whiling away time in a concentrated effort to glimpse the solution to a problem their physics lecturer had paused concerning variable forces, and retired at suppertime. If he suddenly turned she would fly into his arms like an arrow once released from its sling and taunt him with, 'I warned you not to keep us so long away from each other, didn't I? Now you must pay the price!' and daub lipstick on his face with her craving mouth, her hungry kisses. She smiled at the threat and nodded to herself, 'That's what I'll do if you make a mistake of coming within my reach. I can promise you this, my boy.'

The following day was, however, unnaturally longer and more difficult to endure. Shantiee would attempt at concentration only to see her efforts in mathematics or physics shrink to nothing. 'How shall I apply the Simpson's rule to finding an approximation to this integral?' she murmured wearily, her mind beginning to boggle. She tried some more and the facts spoke a plain statement: 'You're stuck,' and Shantiee fought panic and the fear of failing examinations. She shut her eyes, remembering the words of Jean Baptiste D'Alembert who, a long time ago, had advised the dispirited Lagrange to keep trying. 'Keep going forward and faith will come to you,' yet nothing much came out of it since her problem wasn't that of concepts but the reorganisation of her mind. She had feigned indifference, erected fact out of possibility by hiding behind some fiction, and here was the result: Besa hadn't showed up as yet. Shantiee could no longer pretend: a deepening tension had descended upon her life, and fears had taken over. 'Perhaps he's found someone else and he's lost interest in me. Whatever we did the other night isn't as important to him, after all. I was just a diversion, an insignificant part of his life.' And she elaborated on this, adducing fantastic reasons, worsening her emotional turmoil. She was unfocused, fickle, tormented, moody and irritable. When she went to bed in the latter part of the night, she took to tears and bemoaned the absence of her love:

'Darling,' she whispered in her tear-drenched pillows, 'what have I done wrong? It's now two days since we last met and I miss you so. I'd be bereft of all reason if you decided to leave me now. I ate poorly today, I can't even study, nor shall I be able to find my way back to sleep. Please come to me at once! I want to hold you close and lovingly in my arms, for you're my man.'

Monday promised no better prospects, either. She attended lectures in maths, physics, biology and an afternoon lab in chemistry, but without her usual ebullience and earnestness. Her world had collapsed, the ground had gaped under her feet, the sun had lost its light, and Shantiee straggled in a darkness that would never let up. How was she to survive chaos hovering upon her soul?

'If he has ditched me,' she told her roommate in the evening, 'I shouldn't like to live anymore. I'll just have to kill myself.' She broke into quiet sobs and feared the worst. 'I went through the same thing once…It hurts, Jane, it hurts very much. I can't have it all over again. I couldn't survive another disappointment this time.'

'All you are good at is fretting and weeping and waiting for him to show up,' the friend replied reprovingly. 'Why won't you go to him and find out for yourself? You should be able to, if you really love him. Go to him this minute instead of brooding and getting nothing done.'

'I am afraid I might find a girl in his room. He might also tell me something unpleasant.'

Jane touched her on the shoulder and smiled:

'Look at me, Shantiee. Forget your fears; forget everything except the one you love. Think of him kindly and live your love if you must. If the worst happened, you would have to put up with it somehow. Calamities don't last forever: there are limits. The very worst thing is to think exclusively of the negative side of situations. Put your head up and go to see your boy friend, for God's sake!'

Drooping with fright in familiar surroundings, Shantiee stood facing the door, hesitant to knock least she witnessed what she dreaded most. She debated for some moments: 'Must I back out now after what Jane had said?' Then she ventured to tap on the door: a stranger opened it and fixed her an unwelcome look.

'Hi,' said she, trying to be gay. 'I am Shantiee. I presume you must be Besa's roommate?'

'Yes.'

'Good. Is he around by any chance?'

'Yes but I think he needs some rest. He won't see any more visitors. The anti-malarial drug he is taking can only work best if Besa had enough rest and quiet. Come tomorrow. I am sorry.'

She was totally bemused. 'You said "anti-malarial drug": is Besa ill?'

'Yes.'

'Since when?'

'Since Saturday morning. He just collapsed and we rushed him to the clinic. He was diagnosed with severe malaria. He was admitted in the clinic for two days. They released him today.'

'O my God,' she bit her lips to repress her tears. Eyeing this man, Shantiee said assertively: 'I will defy your order not to see him. Besa is my boy friend. I have to be with him. He didn't send for me!'

She walked into the room and saw him, wreathed in a blanket and sheets up to the shoulders, lying on his back and already fast asleep. A profusion of sweat over his beardless face gleamed in the light, and he was ghastly pale. His cheeks were hollowed, rendering the cheekbones more emphatically pronounced while his mouth, held in a fixed pout or careless abandon, lent his features a pained deathly appearance. Now he stirred a little, formless words passing between the dry, cracked lips, involuntary shivers running through him in short intervals. He squirmed in his sleep, flung his hands out: indistinct groans issuing from his mouth pierced her heart with grief. Why did he not send for her? She would have come to him at once!

She approached the bed, an expression of mingled sadness, sensuality and love for him filling her eyes. She sat on the edge of the bed, unmindful of the roommate observing her curiously from the threshold of the door. She looked at Besa as anger, directed at her, presently flared up with suffocating intensity. She had doubted, lowered and desecrated their love, and all her troubles had been ineffectual. What a fool she had been, wallowing in self-pity and blame while he suffered alone, perhaps even without friends to nurse and wait on him with devotion and constancy! On the other hand what irony, what unspeakable regret, what undeserved punishment, treating with doubts the faithful and true! O my dearest one, I shall kneel in abasement at your feet. I shall atone!

There was a towel on a chair, so she picked it up to dry his drawn, sleeping face, taking care not to wake him up. Yet the patient, perhaps sensing the disturbance, started in his drugged sleep, turning on his side so that his back was now against her, and began to snore. Shantiee's mouth tightened. She sighed heavily and rose to her feet. She paced the room listlessly for some moments, a towel in her hand, throwing her beloved occasional glances as she considered the next thing to do. She turned to the roommate and asked some questions.

'Has he completed the medication?'

'Yes.'

'Is the condition improving?'

'I think so, otherwise the clinic wouldn't have discharged him.'

'What about meals? Does he have a good appetite for food?'

'A bit.'

'Is he able to talk and walk?'

'Yes.'

'Good,' she said and sat on the edge of the bed again. She pushed him lightly and called out his name. Besa finally woke up.

'It's me, sweetheart. I didn't know you were ill or I would have come sooner. How do you feel now?'

' Shantiee... I...I am glad you're here. I am sick!'

'I know. But how are you now? Are you feeling any better?'

'Yes... – though I also feel very dizzy and nauseous. I am quite weak, too. It's the drug I've been taking. I always overreact with Chloroquine. It makes me feel awful. I also have terrible dreams...'

'You'll soon be fine, darling. I'll take care of you.' She kissed him on the lips and said he looked hungry. 'You need something to eat. What would you like?'

'He spilled his supper,' confided the roommate. 'I tried to encourage him to eat but to no avail.'

'Sweetie, would you like chicken with rice, or would you prefer it with potatoes?' she asked the patient, dextrously coaxing him till Besa gave in to her wishes. Satisfied, she stood up and told him: 'I'll be coming back shortly. Let me go into town and do some shopping. I won't be long.'

After about an hour later – around twenty-thirty in the evening – Shantiee returned with some pizza, fruit drinks, oranges, carrots, apples, honey, milk, mineral water and some cookies for her boy friend. She had brought her roommate, Jane, and two other female friends along to see the patient. She had also brought her camp mattress and sleeping bag so she could keep 'vigil' at Besa's place. She felt she had to be with him. Although the boyfriend had protested, her insistence prevailed in the end. Besa's roommate was sent in 'exile'.

As Besa slept quietly on the bed, Shantiee was fully awake, busy skimming through *A Student's Manual* in preparation for tomorrow's lab in Biology. She hated the demands the course placed on her ability to remember hundreds of specimen sketches in elaborate detail – not to speak of mastering Latin names! To qualify for a major in Biochemistry, however, she had to love the course and work hard to earn the minimum required points. She boiled some water and made a cup of coffee. She switched to another subject – Chemistry, and wrestled with problems associated with the mole concept, chemical reactions and gases for the next two hours. When it was 01.00 am, she felt quite exhausted. She pushed the chair and stood up. She now had to catch some sleep to keep alert for the day.

Shantiee packed her books and glanced at Besa's study desk with fresh interest. Why hadn't she noticed this before, she mumbled to herself, picking up some papers titled *The Ferio Pages*. Sitting down again, she turned over the pages in haste: they were a draft copy of the essay Besa had talked about at the Goma Lakes, written in pencil on A4 paper and crowded with arrows, erasures, insertions and references of books almost appearing everywhere. Given this amount of correction, therefore, it was obvious that her boy friend was a perfectionist. The work passed through several drafts before he was content with his labours. She went back to the first page and started reading through the work.

THE FERIO PAGES

'Viva Ba-monko:'[29] *Performance and the Politics of*
Student Revolts at the University of Zambia

Youths as forces of change have generated considerable attention among scholars. Some of the most pertinent questions about the subject are the following: What is the nature and significance of youth/student resistance to authority? Is it possible to formulate a model that explains youth activism in all its various manifestations? Are these theoretical constructs universally applicable?

In response to these important questions, the paper briefly surveys youth activism in the global context, with particular emphasis on Zambia. A summary of some theories that explain the basis and nature of youth resistance to authority are presented. The paper then relates some of these concepts to the Zambian youth at the University of Zambia.

Student rebellion against established authority is a global phenomenon. In Tsarist Russia, Germany and Bosnia, for example, youth based revolts may be traced to the 1800s and were associated with acts of terrorism, suicide and extreme forms of idealism, as in Hingley, *Nihilists: Russian Radicals and revolutionaries in the Reign of Alexander II (1885 – 81)* (1967) and Feuer, *The Conflict of Generations: The Character and Significance of Student Movements* (1969), respectively. In Latin America (in particular Argentina, Chile, Peru and Nicaragua), student radicals rose against the authorities and sometimes engaged them in guerrilla warfare especially after the 1930s. Youth opposition in Franco's Spain, the Berkeley uprising in America, and other youth-oriented resistance in nationalist and anti-colonial movements in Turkey, China, Egypt, Indonesia, South Africa, Algeria and Ghana, demonstrate the fact that student rebels (when armed with a higher ethic which was at odds with existing social systems), helped transform their respective societies by challenging the institutionalised beliefs of the status quo. This phenomenon of rebellion has not spared the University of Zambia.

Student activism and radicalism in Zambia did not start with the creation of the first university in the country [See Burawoy, *The Role of the University Student in the Zambian Social Structure*, 1972]. The youths were already involved in the struggle against White colonial rule in the 1960s. Upon enrolment of the first stu-

dents at the institution in 1966 and the enlargement of their numbers
in subsequent years, the youths slowly became an important pressure group that questioned the authorities on social, political and
economic issues.

In one of the student publications, UZ, published on 1st October
1969, Gatian Lungu (one of the most consistent writers) criticised
the extravagance of the political leadership in an article 'Luxury:
Zambia's persistent crisis.' He correctly observed that unless the executive itself reduced its unnecessary spending on luxuries it would
be a thorn in the Zambian flesh. He argued that 'an under-developed
economy like [Zambia] cannot afford the luxuries of affluent societies of the West without causing financial problems.'

In the same publication, UZ, 26th October 1970, a student writer
in an article 'One Party?' debated the disadvantages of introducing
a one-party-state system and called for the preservation of a mul-
tiparty democracy. In another article, 'What next, mother Zambia,'
Vasso, 19th November 1981, another student writer, reflecting on the
nation-wide strikes, attributed the economic collapse of the country
to the failure by the leadership to manage the economy. It should be
recalled that as early as 1971 (UZ, 29th November), students at the
University of Zambia were convinced that the nationalist leaders
had failed Zambians. They demanded political change.

Apart from the literature of protest, the youth at the University
of Zambia clashed with the police and State on a number of occasions. One instance happened when students demonstrated outside
the French Embassy on July 7th 1971, against the decision by the
French government to allow the manufacture of mirage jet fighters
on South African soil. This protest turned violent and the police and
youth fought running battles in town: 'Battle of Lusaka: Students
Storm Embassy', Times of Zambia, 8th July 1971.

The drama did not end there. In a Press Release on 12th July
1971, the President asked students to leave 'everything' to him.
Students did not like this, however. The executive of the Students
Union, UNZASU, drafted a letter titled, 'Where are we going?' in
which they questioned the President's authority to shoulder *all* the
responsibility of making decisions by himself. They argued that
since he was *not omnipotent*, there was need for wider consultation over such sensitive issues as foreign policy (Burawoy). However, the letter was considered insulting by the Government, Party
and the press. When Party cadres vowed to march on campus and
fight students there, the youths (with some 200 reinforcements from
Everlyn Hone College) manufactured petrol bombs in laboratories

and collected piles of stones in residences and on rooftops, and barricaded entry points into the university. Then they waited for the showdown. The cadres backed off. On the 15th of July 1971 police in full riot kit went into university. One of the most respected students, Mundia Sikatana read out a Government press statement which had been handed over by the police: the institution was to be closed indefinitely.

Meanwhile, the press (*The Times of Zambia* and *The Mail*) called students 'gutless', 'demagogues', 'ungrateful', 'arrogant and immature' and so on, as demonstrations against the youth raged on everywhere in the country.

However, the Vice Chancellor of the University of Zambia, Professor Goma, in his address titled *The Pressures on a Developing University in Contemporary Africa* on the occasion of the Third Graduation Ceremony 5th June, 1971, had raised the following concerns:

'Does society want to encourage conformity, regimentation and passivity? Are students to be encouraged to model themselves on their present leaders, some of whom have failed miserably to solve the problems of their country, or are they to be given opportunities to grow and mature, to decide for themselves what beliefs they will hold, what traditions they will respect and what they will discard?'

Yet the State machinery was becoming more and more intolerant to dissimilar beliefs. Rather than encourage students to expose themselves to academic debates and theoretical premises by means of which they could generate their own ideas and alternative methods of critical assessment, the authorities were moving in an opposite direction. With great subtlety, the Government employed instruments of oppression such as the *Public Order Act*, police and the One-Party-State System to check the free development of ideas. The context of dispute between the youth and the Government was now set.

Between 1966 and the present, therefore, there have been at least five closures at the University of Zambia. The first (as we have seen) took place in 1971 and was preceded by six demonstrations. As the numbers of students rose from 312 to 2576 by 1974, increasing the value of the critical mass necessary to radicalise students (Miles, *The Radical Probe: The Logic of Student rebellion*, 1971), the points of confrontation and divergence with the Party and Its Government (PIG) exponentially increased. The goals of the youth have never been static. They battled the authorities over issues of ideology (*Humanism* – which they rejected as self-contradictory) and policy, both domestic and foreign. Later on, however, as the economy declined in GDP and government funding of higher education reduced, the subject of allowances after the 1980s assumed greater importance than ever before. The February 1984 closure of the university was in part influenced by meals.

Why, we may now ask, do youths rebel at all? What is the logic of student rebellion at the University of Zambia and elsewhere?

In his work, *Essays on the Sociology of Knowledge* (1928), Mannheim posits a theory of 'social generation' which argues that when particular members exist in the same time and space, they develop a common awareness of their place in the scheme of things. They experience the same existential problems and eventually feel possessed by the same destiny: they become a *different* class.

This theory has been demonstrated by Feuer in *The Conflict of Generations*, and by Abrams in *Historical Sociology* (1982), respectively. The argument runs like this: youths have evolved a *different* set of ideals and values which are contrary to those of the elders; they must therefore impose their values on society and take over the running of things.

Moller – 'Youth as a force in the Modern World' in *Comparative Studies in History and Society*, 10(1967-8) – approaches the problem differently. He says that the bases of youth politics are to be found in population growth and patterns of age distribution. As the ratio of youth to total population increases in the context of economic and social disruption, the chances of student revolts also increase.

Hobsbawn, 'Intellectuals and the Class Struggle' in *Revolutionaries* (1973) argues in economic terms: the crisis in capitalism in the 1960s and 1970s over-produced discontented intellectuals who were alienated and facing an uncertain future. According to Bundy, 'Street Sociology and Pavement Politics: Aspects of Youth and Student Resistance in Cape Town' in *Journal of Southern African Studies 13*, 3(1987), this theory best explains youth resistance in South Africa.

In his studies of youth disturbances on American campuses, Lipset, *Rebellion in the University: A History of Student Activism in America* (1972) observes that the roots of student activism are to be located in the social, political and economic crisis *outside* university walls. Examples were the civil rights movement and the wars in Vietnam and Indo-China. The other problem is the university itself. Then there are ideological differences between the status quo and student radicals who want changes, and the idealism of youth (social generation). But Lipset is quick to point out that the sources of student unrest ought to be distinguished among different types of societies – underdeveloped, authoritarian, developed, and so on. This is because historical conditions are always peculiar to each society. There are no generalisations.

Lastly, Bonilla and Glazer, *Student Politics in Chile* (1970) identified three factors that influenced the dynamics of student organisation and structure in Chile. These were the economy, political climate, and ideological currents such as those of Che Guevara and Fidel Castro. As the economy in general collapsed after the 1930s, mass poverty, unemployment and social inequalities became everyday realities. The State failed to provide solutions and instead became even more repressive. It sought to sustain the status quo at all costs. Yet the problems of the country served as a continuous focus of concern and inspiration to action by the students. Like their comrades in Argentina, the youth resisted dictators and became victims of State persecutions.

The concepts and perspectives that have been discussed above will now take us back to the Zambian context. How do we explain student activism at the University of Zambia? Can studies of student radicalism elsewhere provide answers into violence and demonstrations which take place at the institution almost every time?

The theories above (collectively, that is) offer insights into this phenomenon, though none exhaustively explains the whole situation. The reason is simple. Like any other place, Zambia has peculiar historical circumstances that distinguish her from every other. Local conditions must therefore be taken into account.

A model to explain the dynamics of the Zambian student experience may be constructed on the basis of five determinants. These are not absolute categories that mutually exclude one another. The determinants interact and influence each other spontaneously.

– *Economy:* The worsening, acute economic crisis has had a profound effect on higher education. Reduced funding in the face of increased student enrolment and cost of living especially for Government sponsored students has become political. Most students feel they are now suffering because of the corruption and mismanagement in the country. They blame the leaders.

– *Competing ideologies:* Students were strongly influenced by the teachings of Che Guevara, Fidel Castro, Mao Tse Dong, Lenin, Marx and Engels. Through Dialectical Materialism, for example, the youths judged the political economy of their country and the world at large. On the other hand the Party espoused humanism as an official ideology. However, students rejected it as inconsistent. A student writer observed the intellectual contradictions faced by students (UZ, 27th September 1971), that: 'The university exists to teach and pursue truth. It faces all around it and within it untruths. The student is told that he must search for truth and finds around him the denial of truth of life and liberty of masses of people in his country. He imbibes doctrines of equality and human rights and sees around him incessant violations of human rights. He is told that the basis of scholarship is objectivity and finds that his life and that of his parents and society [are] based on personal pursuits and impersonal egoism [and] not sound...philosophies. He is exhorted to use his imagination as an instrument of progress and sees its methodical abuse in the...transformation of sense into nonsense and nonsense into sense.'

– *The University itself*: Problems within the organisational structure of the university have sometimes impacted on students. Lecturers' strikes, deportation of lecturers, or failure by the administration to address specific grievances of the youth have resulted in tension or violence. For example, in 1986 students protested against the lack of concern over their welfare by the Administration, which failed to buy them an ambulance and a vehicle for the Dean of Students Office. They demanded the removal of the Vice Chancellor, Professor Mwauluka, who was accused of neglecting them. In May there was a riot after the Police arrested UNZASU President, Ben Chilufya. A system that formally represents students within the university's decision-making structure is also lacking. Because of this non-representation, students do not feel prepared to ascribe legitimacy to the university authority (see Crouch, *The Student Revolt*, 1970) .

– *Generation conflict:* The experiences of the youth made them feel more qualified than the nationalists (elders) to run affairs of the nation. As the new intellectuals students identified their cause with the poor and denounced their leaders as mediocre (*Sophia*, March 1990). In the 'Balance Sheet,' (UZ, 29th November 1971), they called for far sweeping changes in leadership positions. They advocated for educated and dedicated persons to fill government posts. Leaders were seen as selfish and only interested in amassing wealth at the expense of the development of the nation (UZ, 26th April 1971).

– *External events:* The first six demonstrations were inspired by outside events such as the UDI (Unilateral Declaration of Independence by Southern Rhodesia) and Western support of the racist

South Africa. The liberation struggles in Angola, Namibia, Mozambique and Palestine also took centre stage in student politics. The massacre of students at the University of Lubumbashi in May 1990 by Mabutu convinced students of the evils of a One-Party-System of government. With the removal of subsidies on mealie meal students mobilised the masses in Kalingalinga, Mtendere and other townships in Lusaka to protest over the increased prices of mealie meal. Students therefore advocated for radical changes to transform society and the status quo (Social generation theory).

This discussion has brought out the following points: Youth activism at the University of Zambia is an aspect of the global phenomenon. Taken individually, western theories such as the 'social generation,' 'population explosion,' and so on, do explain some aspects of youth behaviour but do not exhaustively analyse the case of the Zambian youth. The permanent economic woes that brought about poverty and insecurity fixed the setting in which students tested their alternative ideologies, concepts and practical responses. External pressure and the failure by the university administration to respond adequately to students needs also contributed to youth activism. The idealism of youth – that desire for adventure that recognises no risks and defines the youth culture – has been, and will be, at the centre of student action. Students will still shout: 'Viva Bamonko, viva Moma-power,' as an expression of disillusionment with and rejection of perceived ills in society. Because of their exposure to a wide range of ideas and information, they shall continue to be a factor relevant to historical change. Their ideas shall aim to transform the status quo.

Shantiee put down the essay and bent over her beloved. Kissing him lightly on the cheek, she whispered, 'I love you, Ferio. I love you with all my heart,' and spread the mattress on the floor. She set the alarm at six and soon fell asleep.

Chapter 11

Concerns entries in the Journal,
that is all

February 24
Feeling much better after a week of illness, thanks to Shantiee
and my roommate, Muma, both of whom have been taking care of
me. They swear, however, that I am a difficult patient – often argumentative or simply 'impossible'. He reveals that whenever his patience gave out my girlfriend would take over and eventually have
her way with me through gradual approaches and firmness. 'For all
her efforts to have you take a bath, medication or food, you repaid
her with indifference, resentment, insolence and sometimes even
aggressive behaviour, resisting her all the way. I told her that the
moment you felt well again she deserved a present of some kind
from you.'

February 26
Lunched with Shantiee at her favourite restaurant in town. She's
a remarkable woman. I slipped into a Jewelry shop and bought her
a beautiful engagement ring I presented in the evening at her place,
and fled from her room: didn't want to witness her reaction the minute she unwrapped her parcel.

'Where are you off to, my dear sir?' her voice called at my back,
a glint of mockery in her eyes. She glanced at the ring already glis-
tening on her second finger and smiled. 'You'll have to excuse me
just this once, mister Ferio. Please cancel all your appointments for
this evening because you and I will have a little chat. I want to know
what this is all about.'

In her room we embraced for a long time, and I didn't have to
explain much because we understood that we would always live for
each other…even as man and wife.

March 4
There are basically two sorts of students. Those who are sylla-
bus or examination oriented (or those who will do anything to earn
good grades) and those for whom assignments, tests and exams are
not as important as the acquisition of knowledge for its own sake.
The former are merely concerned with passing and consequently restrict their studies to what they suppose may appear in the examina-

tions. The latter, on the contrary, being more adventurous and curious, desire to explore the landscapes of knowledge. They are exemplars of Goethe's verse: 'I declare myself to be of those, who from the darkness to the light aspire.'

March 5

This contrast in intellectual attitude as to the ends of formal education defines us forever (and reminds one of the reasons for existence in general), since it leads to the types of lives people choose. On the other hand, does it really matter whether someone embraced opinion and conjecture (or lived like prisoners in Plato's *Allegory of the Cave*?) or chose to live a life in which the contemplation of metaphysical realities of existence (like every philosopher does) becomes the reason for living? Does it matter (ultimately, that is), whether one lived this life or the other?

March 6

I think it does. I agree with Aristotle in *Virtue and Rationality*, though the principle of the golden mean is contentious.

March 9

After learning that I come from Luapula and therefore qualify to be labelled 'Bemba', a lecturer in African History – a Lozi by tribe – asked me privately what I thought of the Barotse Question. Do I oppose the idea that the Lozi people in Zambia have a right to self-determination?

'No, sir,' replied I. 'Everyone has a right to determine his or her own destiny. If all the Lozi people wish to separate from the rest of the country in order to create an independent state, that's their business. Personally I wouldn't mind.'

This unsettled him somewhat. A Bemba who oppresses the Lozi must feel hostile, as is commonly believed. We control everything and we have economically undermined them. We are a thorn in their flesh.

I checked some facts about the Lozi in the Special Collections of the Library. I consulted Gerald L. Caplan, L.H Gann, Richard Hall, A.D Jalla, Mutumba Mainga, David C Mulford, *The Bledisloe Report of 1939, Barotseland Agreement 1964,* and *The Constitution of Zambia.*

Theories of Lozi origin

a) Formerly known as Luyi, another Bantu people who migrated from the Congo Basin or the Luba-Lunda of Mwata Yamvo. They moved south down the Kabombo River in the 18th Century, and found other Bantu such as the Sotho, Shona and Nguni *already* living there. The new inhabitants conquered them. The Twa or Kwengo were driven south. By the 1800 AD the migrants had founded the Barotse nation. Their greatest chief was Mulambwa, who ruled from 1812–1830. The early Bantu had settled in the Zambezi by 1300AD, and these existing inhabitants called the Lozi, *Luyana or Luyi* – which means, *foreigners*. Barotseland was formerly known as *Ngulu*.

(b) Mythology. The Great God, Nyambe, founded the kingdom. Therefore all members of the royal family have divine ancestry which cannot be challenged.

Background to the Barotse Question

Secessionists claim that the Lewanika Treaty of 1900 AD with the British South Africa Chartered Company grants the Lozi a more privileged position than any other tribe in Zambia. It puts them in direct relationship with the British Crown from whom the Paramount Chief, Lewanika, had been seeking protection. Thus begun a policy of deference. The boundaries of Barotseland were equated to territories extending as far as the Pedicle in Congo and down the Lwangwa River, which included the entire Copperbelt mining area. The 1936 Barotse Native Authority Ordinance and Barotse Native Courts Ordinance and the Barotse Native Government, for the first time received official recognition and legal status under the Northern Rhodesia Law. *The Bledisloe Report of 1939* and the Federal Constitution in 1953 recognised the terms of the 1900 Treaty. Between 1945–1950 the British Government had reiterated that 'no constitutional changes affecting Barotseland would be made without full consultation with, and the prior consent of, the Paramount Chief.' Her Majesty's Government would continue to honour and safeguard all obligations to the Barotse nation.

Demands for secession were repeated several times between 1960 and 1964, and yet the colonial government always waved such demands aside. A year before the independence of Zambia in 1964, the Barotse 'government' presented a memorandum which proposed a new question of reinstatement other than secession from Northern Rhodesia, and this meant recognition of boundaries and other rights of the Barotseland, or an opposition to the transfer of British rights and obligation in Barotseland to Northern Rhodesia. In April 1964 an agreement was reached and ratified in London (*The Barotseland Agreement 1964*). Under this Agreement all responsibilities, obligations, between the British government and Barotseland were terminated. The new government of Zambia promised to treat Barotseland in the same way as other parts of the Republic.

Arguments advocating secession

The Barotseland Agreement of 18th May, 1964 was reached on the understanding that the Government of Northern Rhodesia (later Zambia) and the Paramount Chief, Lewanika of the Lozi people desired that Northern Rhodesia should proceed to independence as one nation. Although *The Agreement* was not included in the new Republican Constitution, some provisions of the Republican Constitution were included in *The Barotseland Agreement 1964*. These related to the protection of human rights and fundamental freedoms of the individual, the judiciary and the public service. On the other hand the Litunga was authorised and empowered to make laws for Barotseland in relation to the following:

- Barotse Native Government;
- Barotse Native Authorities;
- Barotse Native Courts;
- The status of members of the Litunga's Council;
- Matters relating to local government;
- Land, forests, traditional and customary matters, fishing, control of hunting, game preservation, control of bush fires, supply of beer, local taxation, reservation of trees for canoes, Barotse Native Treasury and festivals.

The Lozi Royal Establishment has since 1964 made calls for the reinstatement of *The Barotseland Agreement 1964* which has been 'breached' or abrogated by the Government of the Republic of Zambia. The calls are for 'a state within a state.' The following factors have undermined *The Agreement*:

The Local Government Act of 1965

This instrument empowered the Central Government to create local government administration structures; Part XI of the Act made special provision with respect to Bulozi. The Local Authorities created were directly under the control of Central Government, through the Ministry of Local Government. District Councils in Bulozi such as Mongu, Senanga, Kalabo, Sesheke, and so on, were set up. Funds held in the Barotseland Native Treasury were transferred to the Barotse Local Government Fund. On November 1, 1965 the new Government abolished the Barotse Native Council, which had resisted new changes. The impact was the reduction in the powers of the Litunga and his administrative structures; the Barotse Native Courts, for example, was incorporated into the Central government's Ministry of Justice, making Lozi personnel answerable to the Minister and not the Litunga. In the same year the Government announced that capital projects in Bulozi would be done through its offices and not Barotse Native Government. With regard to the Civil Service and Public sector, respectively, the Central Government also held the responsibility to appoint and control civil servants and public officers who worked freely in Bulozi on conditions similar to what obtained elsewhere in the country.

The Chiefs Act, October 1965

This instrument empowered the Republican President to recognise or withdraw recognition from *any* chief in Zambia in the interest of peace, order and good governance. The Litunga was explicitly mentioned. The Government would determine the subsidies to be paid to any chief and family and household. This made all chiefs in the country dependent on the government.

The Matero Economic Reforms of 11th August 1969

The President announced that mining companies operating in Zambia were to offer the State the right to buy 51% of their shares, while all rights of ownership or partial ownership of minerals in Zambia reverted to the State. All mining concessions obtained through traditional chiefs and other institutions before independence were cancelled. By implication, therefore, *the Litunga lost all the rights to determine the conditions for prospecting licences, mining and also the right to claim royalties on minerals.* It was determined that the rights that applied to the Litunga should not be different from any that obtained anywhere in the Republic.

Recall that in 1964 the Northern Rhodesian nationalist government successfully challenged the British South Africa Company's claims to mineral royalties in Northern Rhodesia. The Government demonstrated that Lewanika's territory in 1890 and after did not include the Copperbelt area, and therefore the Company could not lay claims to mineral royalties in that area on the basis of the Lochner Concession of 1890 and later agreements with the Lozi Paramount Chief, Lewanika, who had lost sovereignty as King to the Queen and Her Majesty's Government, by virtue of the 1899 Order in Council. The boundaries of the Barotse kingdom as, for example, reported in François Coillard's work, *The Frontiers of the Barotse Kingdom,* 'On the south, the Zambezi and the Chobe Rivers, on the west the 20th degree longitude east, on the north, the watershed of the Congo and the Zambezi rivers, on the east the Kafue river' including, later on, claims to areas as far as Lake Nyasa and the Tanganyika plateau, were criticised for their distortion and exaggeration of the extent and influence of the Lozi kingdom. Some of the tribes listed as subjects of the Litunga such as the Lunda and Luvale respectively disputed such claims.

The Constitutional Amendment Act of October 1969 terminated *The Barotseland Agreement 1964.*

In general, therefore, the 'Lozi' feel that as compared to other parts of the country, Barotseland has gained little in terms of economic development. They feel that their people have been excluded from the running of the government. Since Barotseland existed as a 'nation' even before independence, she reserves the right to secede as the present Constitution does not bind the Lozi people in their desire to be free.

Arguments against secession

- The breakaway may lead to the disintegration of Zambia and possibly a civil war as other chiefs would also want to secede. The impact may spread to other countries such as Angola and Namibia, respectively, whose small, minority populations may perhaps want to annex their traditional territories to Barotseland. Ultimately, this would lead to the redefinition of boundaries.
- Granting Barotseland complete autonomy has enormous economic consequences for Zambia, as territorial claims by the Paramount Chief, Lewanika can cause conflict. The claims extend as far as the Lamba country or the

Copperbelt and parts of North-western Provinces, respectively, which have large deposits of mineral resources. However, as far as 1904 such territorial claims were surrounded in controversy. For example, the Administrator of North-Eastern Rhodesia, Cadrington, seems to agree in an answer to Wilson Fox, Secretary of the British South Africa Chartered Company in March 1904, that such a claim was ridiculous. Note that the concessions signed in the name of Her Majesty the Queen and Her Government with African Chiefs were often deceptive and later repudiated. Lobengula says of the Rudd Concession that '[it] contained neither my words nor the words of those who got it.' And the missionary, Coillard writes of the Ratifying Treaty with Lewanika in 1900 that, 'the poor natives [Lozi] do not understand the situation...It makes me tremble...' An address to the Northern Rhodesian Parliament by Roy Welensky of March 22, 1948, echoes the same sentiments. The authenticity and authority of treaties between African chiefs and mineral hunters and companies are vulnerable to doubt.

- Demands for secession are not supported by the majority of ordinary Lozi but by the Royal Establishment of the Litunga and some power hungry politicians who have failed to influence events at the national level. Like their ancestors who were used by the Lozi royal family to provide labour for an extensive agricultural system and other public works, the descendants or ordinary people have little to gain from the reinstatement of *The Agreement*. They have a lot to fear from the absolute powers of the Chief.
- Seceding from Zambia is treasonable.

March 11

Concession treaties and the 'Queen's protection' were some of the tactics used in obtaining access to the natural resources of Africans including commercial and industrial rights to the continent. The phenomenon of deceit and plunder, which has been imposed on our people since time immemorial, is every African's problem. It should be challenged and stopped forever.

March 12

Apparently, this phenomenon which denies Africans the right to development has reached alarming proportions. Globalisation ravages peoples and their environment everywhere; it calls for the oppressed peoples of the world to assert their right to exist through the abolition of institutions such as the World Bank, World Trade Organisation, International Monetary Fund and other such transnational firms reputed for their economic policies which destroy indigenous economies and reduce billions of people to pauperism. The poor must stand up or, in John Chilembwe's words, 'fight a blow and die.'

March 14
The Lozi lecturer (what does he want from me?) spoke of the 'persecution' of his people as though the country has committed genocide against an entire tribe. This was shocking to me. I have read the *Amnesty International Reports* on Zambia for the last four years but found nothing to suggest that there's a deliberate Government policy aimed at persecuting Lozis *because* they are Lozi. I was very disappointed in him, and I said so to Shantiee.

'This doesn't surprise me in the least,' she told me. 'I know some Lozis who are exactly like that. They've got this negative attitude towards other tribes and they generally feel everyone is out to undermine them, particularly the Bemba.'

'Why the Bemba?'

'I don't know, but they think Bembas stand in the way of everything. Bembas are involved everywhere and they feel squeezed out.'

'I am sorry about that,' I said. 'But who's to blame? From the little I know of Zambian history, the influence that people from Luapula and Northern Provinces have exerted on the country should be understood in the context of the development of the Copperbelt mines from the late 1920s to the present. Studies in colonial wage-labour in the Copperbelt mines by Ohadike, Henderson, Deane, Perrings, Berger, Parpart and others, suggest that as far as the indigenous sources of labour were concerned, people from Luapula and Northern provinces provided a higher overall average contribution of all local labour supply to the copper mines. The people of Barotseland or Western province provided the least figures – followed by Southern province. The Lozi went to Southern Rhodesia and South Africa, respectively, and were hardly represented in the Copperbelt. But we must not underestimate the significance of wage employment. Apart from providing new skills and a living for the workers, it has also been a very powerful force in the evolution of trade unions and shaping a new African consciousness and an identity that transcended the tribe, thus shaping the course of Zambian politics. As a people who were probably most detribalised, the "Bembas" became, perhaps, more aggressive in addressing issues of wages, political rights and freedoms.

'Because of the social welfare programmes of most mining companies for the benefit of their workers, the largest benefits went to those who were most represented in the Copperbelt mines. These are the Bemba. They have gained from sports, clubs, schools, hospitals and other social amenities. As a result, iciBemba is the most widely spoken language in Zambia today. But things are changing, and I hope for a time when *all* Zambian shall feel equal before the law.'

We then discussed ethnicity as a handicap towards African integration, and decided that the future of the continent lay in broader perceptions that took essentials into account: economic development and the promotion of African values and way of life based on equality, mutual respect and freedom.

'If such is the case,' Shantiee remarked, 'then Zambia should resolve the Barotse problem permanently or let go of the Lozi people.'

I remained quiet for some time, and then pointed out a few obstacles to the independence of Barotseland as indicated above (March 9).

'Another difficulty, perhaps, may be the question of the constitutional status of Barotseland. How far in history must you go to fix your claims? The Lozi suppose Barotseland to be theirs by right but too quickly forget that what they call 'ours' has not always been theirs historically, nor can they justify the rational basis of this claim to the territorial ownership of Barotseland on agreements with the British South Africa Company, or the British Government. My question is, if the Lozi were called *foreigners*, why should they claim that land? On the other hand, assuming that ownership through the use of force legitimises Lozi claims, then why shouldn't the Republic of Zambia use force or whatever means to legitimise its claim over Western province? What should be the standard criteria of land ownership and why?'

Shantiee shook her head. 'It's difficult.'

'Exactly. And this leaves the Lozi people on the same level as everyone else. We are foreigners to this country and we cannot establish ownership of land on any rational foundation except on tribal wars and conquests. The best we can do is accepting the existing political structure and seek development within it; otherwise the whole thing becomes a murky business.'

Shantiee then wondered whether my overall opinion of the Barotseland Question was in agreement with positions sustained in my essay on student politics and rights, and I replied that Government had a responsibility of providing economic, social and cultural development to all. Without this the institution of governance becomes irrelevant to the expectations and aspirations of the people.

March 15

I presented my paper at The Youth Forum Workshop. Afterwards, one of my lecturers said, 'While we may blame the World Bank, International Monetary Fund and other donors for our misery, we should also question ourselves as to what extent we are responsible for our situation. I don't think African leaders are serious with development. It's time we stopped presenting history as the history of Westerners that shape African history. We should centre Africans at the core of historical change and make them responsible for everything that happens to them. If Africans are underdeveloped, it is because they allowed it. It is not circumstances that determined life: it is the *attitude* people have of circumstances that determine their life. This is what K. P. Vickery is saying in *Black and White in Southern Zambia: The Tonga Plateau 1884–1924*. Despite a number of measures passed by the British South Africa Company to protect White farmers and undermine Tonga peasant farmers, the latter managed to overcome external problems and increase their production. In his work, *The Rise and Fall of the South African Peasantry*, Collin Bundy demonstrates the impact of land legislation on the African social economic systems. Apart from several Anti-Squatting Acts or legislations passed between 1876 and 1900 to uproot Africans from their lands and turn them into a cheap pool of labour for white farmers and mines, there were the Glen Grey Act of 1894, the Native Land Act of 1913 and the Native Land and Trust Act of 1936. Although whites finally destroyed much of the African production and self-reliance, Africans nonetheless put up some resistance and were not always passive victims of western capital.'

In the evening Shantiee congratulated me by putting her arms around me. 'I am very proud of you, Mr Ferio,' she said. 'May I be allowed to kiss you on the lips?'

'No, not here.'

'Any place is good enough to kiss my man.' And she planted her lips on mine, unembarrassed by onlookers.

March 18

Perhaps it has something to do with being a woman: supervising the boy friend's life, pointing to a missing button, a torn shirt, a dirty collar, and suggesting changes to be made to his dwelling place. I welcome these new developments in my life but sometimes feel as if my identity was threatened. I enjoy living in an environment in which things are not placed in fixed positions: some experience of disorder is necessary in order to be creative. I also enjoy being alone and doing things at my own pace, and despise constant attention, association with parties, crowds or being regular in one's habits. I hate just what most women love: being an object of public interest. I prefer a quiet, simple life. Being a non-entity, sinking into the remote centres of nebula, forgotten, non-existent, like two parallel lines shrinking into nothing from the point of view of an observer, or like a stone fading away as it moves at the speed of light.

March 19

'I know what we'll do,' Shantiee observed this morning as she gave my room another check. 'We'll buy you some paintings at an art shop in town. I know a good one.'

I didn't see the point. My room was okay as it was. Why bother?

'This place really ought to look beautiful. Don't you admire rooms with art works hanging on the walls?'

'No.'

'You're crazy. Everyone wants their rooms to look nice, why don't you?'

'*Everyone?* Did you carry out a census?' I asked. 'Anyway, my reasons for my actions do not depend on the opinion of the majority. I think things out by myself.'

'I am sure you do. I wasn't disputing your having to use your mind. I just wanted your room to look nice. It's terrible the way it is, can't you see?'

'Depending on your understanding of *beauty*. Look, I appreciate your suggestions but would rather my room remain the way it is. Shall we leave it at that?'

She started to sob. I lost my cool and called her childish, and we ended up quarrelling. She accused me of being deaf to her feelings, and I attacked her disregard for my preferences.

'I don't know how to please you but I try so hard. Please do help me a little. I don't want to mess up our relationship. You are the most important person in my life. I don't want to be with anyone else.'

At such an exquisite declaration of love, my heart was overcome. I went over to her and wrapped my arms around her. 'You're right, Shantiee, you try so hard to please me, and I will help you in our life together. But you should also learn to give me some space to be by myself and enjoy arranging my life the way I want to. Individual freedom is very important and mustn't be sacrificed for the relationship. At the same time, though, I want you to know that no matter how unkind I might be to you, you are all I have. I trust you and I will always love you.'

March 20
S is undoubtedly an intellectual. Apart from her maths, chemistry, physics and biology, she also reads research methodologies of great scientists. Just yesterday I found her reading a pamphlet on John Dalton, Gregor Mendel, Johannes Kepler, John Sturt Mill and the existentialist, Biswanger. Asked why she had interest in the scientific method and research design, she said, 'I pick up anything as long as the material can provide data on how people organise their thoughts.'

'Why do you want to know?'

'Need you ask me that?' she eyed me quizzically. 'Anyway my answer is, an unexamined life is not worth living.'

That was the Socratic answer. I was quite impressed, for a nineteen-year-old girl who reads through Plato's *Phaedo, Euthyphro and The Republic* with some ease, or one who sincerely wishes to understand why Rutherfold, Einstein or Max Planck thought the way they did is quite something. She is a rare flower.

March 23
We were officially engaged at a small ceremony held at my lecturer's home. Shantiee's parents were there: they specifically wanted to see me face to face. It was very nice. Some people who were present included Washaama's uncle, Mr Bwalya, who represented my family. Mr Bwalya works for Zesco as an engineer. Others who attended the function were Muma, Jane, Washaama, Sichone, Nalumino, Miya, The Young Lady, Professor Feldmann (Shantiee's lecturer in physics), her friends and three of my lecturers, Dr Krishna, Dr Chabatama and Dr Kalusa. We also invited our special and very wonderful friend, Sarah Sinkaala, who was Shantiee's former classmate at Lechwe.

In the evening Shantiee, her parents, and I dined at Holiday Inn. Mr Perronni asked me a number of questions and seemed satisfied about me. Then he drew me aside and said: 'If you engage my daughter, you be a man and take care of her. No fighting, no beating. You understand?'

'Yes, sir.'

'Good. When you have your holiday I want you to come and live with us in Mufulira. I'll give you a job to do to keep busy.'

We had a number of presents from friends, lecturers and Shantiee's family. The best present I had was the mountain bike from Mr Perronni. I asked Shantiee how her father knew I liked cycling and she said:

'I told him, though he wanted to get you something bigger – like a car. But I advised against because I thought you wouldn't accept it.'

'He was going to buy me a *car*?' I asked in horror.

'Yes, why not?' she laughed. 'He likes you and believes you are a good young man. He's happy there are now two men in the family – *you* and him.'

'He asked me to spend the next vacation with your family.'

'*You*'ll love it. I know you will.'

March 27

Shantiee feels that it won't do any good sulking over the banning of our newsletter, the Vanguard, by Government authorities. She is also worried about me being actively involved in plans to demonstrate against yesterday's issuance of a *Statutory Instrument* that classifies the newsletter and Unza Bulletin as 'prohibited publications and offences against public order.' The situation is becoming dangerous, she contends, so it was about time I withdrew from publishing any of my writing and quit student politics. What did I have against this suggestion?

'Nothing,' said I, 'except that it's too late to back out. Everything is about ready and the guys are prepared to fight. We can't let the situation be the way it is at the moment. We've got to do something.'

She's been distant, reflective and pensive since morning, and her criticism has ended in tears and pessimism. 'I have a premonition something terrible will happen.'

'What will?'

'I don't know exactly but I have this nagging feeling that something will. I believe in what you do, Ferio, and I shall always stand by you, but I am also scared for you. I love you so much that I couldn't bear to see anything happen to you. It could be the end for both of us, and we've just got engaged. Please don't get involved in this demonstration.'

I nodded understandingly. I stroked her shoulders and remembered Jose Ortega's doctrine of perspectivism, Leibnitz's concept of the monad, and the venerable Socrates who preferred death to living uncritically, and related this to my situation.

'You're not them,' Shantiee objected. 'You're different.'

'Yes I am different; but in accepting the Statutory Instrument and doing nothing to change it, I would have forsaken the most elemental principles of my life: opposing evil wherever it manifests itself. Like Ortega I believe that every person has a mission of truth; like Leibnitz I hold that each individual must express their own content through self reflection from where they are, and like Socrates I refuse to choose silence.'

'What about me? What am I supposed to feel while you're demonstrating and risking your life for the truth?'

'Sweetheart, Zambia is our own country. Therefore, we must be prepared to die for her.'

'Don't you love me? Don't you care about me?'

'I do but our newsletter comes first...I am sorry.'

March 28

My self-centredness or egoistic nature (as she calls my recent behaviour) is still a subject of our private debate. As we argue or stand our grounds a new reality dawns on us, that in spite of our declaration of love and friendship we are (so to speak) paradoxically different from each other. The estimates we have for the value of things and the way we conceive the basic meaning of existence has bared who we really are, and it seems as if the glamour of our romance has shrivelled forever.

April 3

'Darling,' Shantiee writes me after I'd told her again that I would not change my mind about the impending demonstration, 'I am very sorry to bring you some disturbing news about our relationship, but I really have no choice. I think that at the moment we need time away from each other to see where we stand. We keep arguing all the time and I can't see why the newsletter is more important than our relationship. I am engaged to you and I should mean more than your friends. Suppose you were imprisoned how would that make me feel? How would I live? Sometimes I feel that maybe our priorities are different, but I will not accept to let my man do things

that will hurt him. You mean everything to me but maybe we need
to be apart for some time.'

April 4
Met her at the Mingling Bar. There I fumbled an apology, an
inane thing to do considering the circumstances. She claimed to be
too busy to discuss anything: what she had communicated to me
had to be accepted. Didn't want to be pushed. She wanted to be free
from me for some time. The relationship was confusing her.

I watched my girl (or someone who had been my girl) retreating
from my sight without saying goodbye. Like Akigbo's[30] watermaid
she was – 'sinking ungathered'.

April 7
I tried to speak to her again but she wouldn't let me. 'Besides, if
you really loved me you wouldn't be doing this to me.'

'I love you, Shantiee,' said I, 'let's discuss this and see what
could be done about it.'

'What is there to discuss when you are not prepared to change
your mind? Right now I just want to be left alone. And I don't want
you to bother me or come to my room.'

She slipped off the ring and said: 'Perhaps someone will have
more luck wearing this. Mine has run out.'

'Do what you want with it. I don't want it back.'

'Why?'

'It's yours forever. I bought the ring for you. I still love you.'

'I don't believe you do.'

'Don't you love me any more?'

'I don't know. I don't wanna think about it.'

I thanked her for everything she has been to me before leaving
her room, disquieted and perplexed as sorrow and grief very nearly
turned my thoughts to suicide.

April 10
Soren Kierkegaard, despairing and anguished by the dialectical
moments of living, raises his soul in faith and abandons himself to
the grace of God – but, according to Karl Barth, such an attempt is
bound to fail. Therefore, to whom shall we turn for help? To whom
shall we cry?
Evening
After discovering the *other* (writes Van der Kerken in *Love and
Loneliness*), true love is born when 'love really believes in the ab-

solute value of the beloved, who in love is always held to be greater and incomparably more valuable than the loving subject, because real love of its essence aims at the absolute...They see only the absolute value of the person they love, who is for both their all in all at which their love is aimed...'

Question:

Have I wholly lived for her whom I claim to love, or have I loved her less because she's unworthy of my love?

Answer:

My love, or that which in my eyes has passed for love, has failed to transcend the self so that my beloved might become for me the concrete reality around which whatever I call 'I' could revolve. The self is the limitation, a self-event in which my body, bounded and the same as itself, is nurtured by itself through self-exclusion and self-existence, for I am for myself and not always extended. Love is merely a possibility by means of which I may strive to be for others what I am always for myself. In every act of love, then, I imply myself, but I exist sorely for myself. I cannot desert my self.

April 11

A kind of 'solipsism' denying real contact between self and what lies around? Should explore above thought further. I am much confused.

April 12

As I sense in myself an extended, unspeakable pain, it seems as if I should be detached from the moments I loved and I was loved. And then I must, as Ovid writes, yield to the fate by virtue of which material reality is conditioned: 'Every shape that is born bears in its womb the seeds of change,' while I am yet shackled, or in thrall of she whom my heart naturally seeks.

April 13

At a meeting held today in respect of the banning of the Vanguard and Unza Bulletin by the Government of the Republic of Zambia, editorial members of the said student publications:

1. ARE AGREED that *The Statutory Order* which deems the aforementioned publications subversive, seditious, and prohibited, IS A VIOLATION OF OUR CONSTITUTIONAL RIGHTS. Under the present *ACT* [31] and the context hereto referred (Articles 13, 21, 22 and 23, respectively) the Law

provides for the enjoyment, exercise and preservation of fundamental human rights and freedoms, freedom of conscience, freedom of expression, and freedom of assembly and association. Under the present *Code* [32] and the context hereto referred (Section 60), the Law deems that a publication IS NOT seditious if such a publication is an intention:

   (i) to show that the Government have been misled or mistaken in any of their measure; or

  (ii) to point out errors or defects in the Government or Constitution as by law established or in legislation or in the administration of justice, with a view to the reformation of such errors or defects; or

 (iii) to persuade the people of Zambia to attempt to procure by lawful means the alteration of any matter in Zambia as by law established...

2. ARE AGREED that our publications and contents of such publications are not generally seditious and subversive, nor are they calculated to effect any of the matter which defines 'seditious intention' in Section 60 of the Code...Instead, our publications merely discuss various themes affecting millions of people in Zambia, in furtherance of their freedoms, social justice and development. WE ARE SHOCKED to learn that fair discussions of such matters are viewed by the State to be contrary to public interest...

3. ARE RESOLVED TO TAKE LEGAL PROCEEDINGS AGAINST THE State in order to repeal the aforesaid Statutory Order or, failing this, procure other necessary, lawful means to repeal the said Order. WE BELIEVE that we have a constitutional right and responsibility to defend and sustain our freedoms and interests, and to hold or express opinions about our country, or to extend such opinions to others as we wish.

4. ARE RESOLVED to seek legal council, protection, or whatever kind of help – if necessary – from organisations or individuals anywhere, in our pursuance of our right to self-expression. We believe that academic freedom (which includes the freedom of assembly, freedom of association, freedom of research, freedom to publish, travel and to have international contacts, freedom of thought and freedom of

opinion) may not be subject to arbitrary restriction by the State. Academic freedom is closely connected with the right to education since effective learning can only take place in an atmosphere of academic freedom. Articles 9, 10, 12, 17 and 20 of the African Charter guarantee the rights and freedoms of individuals and groups in the University to generate, receive and express information and opinions within the law (or in the context of international human rights standards!). Bared of academic freedom education becomes useless. The French Constitutional Court (1984) said this about academic freedom and the academics: 'Pursuant to their very nature, education and research not only allow but also require, in the interest of the service, the freedom of expression and the independence of their staff be guaranteed through provisions which are applicable to them.' We are therefore shocked that the Zambian Government has violated internationally accepted standards of behaviour for academicians and students .

April 16
I attended a talk in NELT on the following subjects;
✓ Constitutional review: a focus on developments in the political repression in Zambia;
✓ Functions and status of the university in a dictatorship;
✓ Evaluation of current student representation and Student Union;
✓ What is a Student? An analysis of public opinion;
✓ Student Discontent: its roots and solutions;
✓ The student: past, present and future.

The talk was organised by the Crisis Committee, the Vanguard, Unza Bulletin, Unza Watch and the Dean of Students Office. Speakers and facilitators included senior students, Professor Gehlen (Senior Lecturer in Law) and Doctor Harlan, S.J (Lecturer in Philosophy and Political Science). The presentation of themes was lively and informative, and the general attendance was very encouraging.

April 18
Prof. Gehlen and Dr Harlan have been detained, and the University Administration is panicky over the safety of other teachers and students (including myself!) who have not yet been arrested

but have received Police-call outs. Under the dreaded *Preservation of Public Security Regulations*[33], the President may authorise detention without trial of real or suspected 'opponents' of the Government outside the jurisdiction of the courts. We are all very worried, indeed!

April 19

Feeling very scared. Don't know what will happen to the sixteen of us... May face expulsion, detention, deportation, and torture or just about anything. Hopefully our lawyers Unzasu has contracted will do the best for us! Should inform Shantiee about this, just in case.

April 19, evening: TV Items

A Government Spokesperson has made a statement over the 'timely arrest of two foreign spies who worked under cover of lecturers' at the University of Zambia. The named persons had been working in collaboration with other foreign agents to destabilise the university and the nation as a whole, and would therefore be deported. He urged all Zambians (students in particular), not to fall prey to 'imperialist elements who are bent on destroying the fruits of [the] revolution.' He requested students to co-operate in helping police ferret out other foreign nationals engaged in this terrible crime. 'The evidence we have clearly shows that there are yet others who are lurking out there...so we must be vigilant!' concluded the spokesperson.

Commenting on the same, the minister of Local Affairs has claimed that students at the University of Zambia could not possibly 'start anything by themselves...some lecturers and foreign informers responsible for instigating unruly behaviour at [this] institution. How can one explain the disturbances that rock the university every day? We have information that some irresponsible lecturers use the university to propagate their political opinions. The recent seminar organised by two foreign lectures illustrates how innocent students can be used. Fortunately, however, the bad eggs have been arrested, and a possible unrest has been averted. I hope and pray that students will assist the police in further investigations... We don't want trouble, we want peace and prosperity.'

The President has denied foreign media reports that there was a wide spread dissatisfaction with the Government in Zambia, and that the Party was using the recent arrest of two harmless lecturers at the University to shift blame and international attention onto the 'imperialist elements'. 'The people of this country fully support the Party and its Government. Students are also in support of our policies. The problem we have is with the false reporting of events by some foreign media. The only thing they report about Africa is something negative. We pray to God that they will see the truth.'

Bedtime Note:

Hitler and Mussolini used the media to manipulate public opinion. What is most painful in our circumstances, however, is not the level of indoctrination but the level to which public institutions such as *Television Zambia, Zambia Radio Services, Times of Zambia* and *Daily Mail,* respectively, are used to oppress the very people who pay tax! Zambians must be some of the most docile people in the world. It is stupidity to let a Party and one man ruin an entire nation. Sometimes individuals ought to want to take up a gun and fight! Sometimes it is necessary to go to war and die for what you think is right! But Zambians desire 'peace, tranquillity and prosperity', and support Government without thinking. But how can there be peace and tranquillity when the majority of people are facing abject poverty? How can there be peace when *The Public Order Act* is used against the very people from whom a government draws its powers? Yet Zambians will allow a dog to oppress them and pretend that all is well in their country. They drink beer to forget. Like Germans who allowed the Nazi to annihilate Jews and led the country into a catastrophic war, Zambians have permitted a mad man to rule them. By the time they wake up because they prefer to be herded like sheep, this nation would have been destroyed! Foolishly some believe that God will come from heaven and help the country. Fat chance! God does not intervene in human events unless *some* people are prepared to shed their blood for their country. This is the law that governs *every* resistance and revolution.

April 21

Lecturers are demanding the immediate release of all the detained. If Government does not act, they will all resign!

April 22

It is evening. I am anxious and cannot sleep. I keep asking myself, 'What if I don't come back?' I think of my parents and their reaction, especially that of my mother. She would be devastated if someone told her: 'Your son is in prison. He's a troublemaker.' She would roll on the ground in deep mourning, she would refuse to be consoled, but father would be all right. What about the rest of the family? Maliya, Mwape, Chizindo...and my relatives. Would they ever be able to understand?

April 23, 8.00 hrs
This might be my last entry in this Journal. I'll leave it in my bag for anyone to read in case I don't return. I have no time, I have to go to the Central Police Station with fifteen other students. I love you, mother, and father. I love you, too, Shantiee: I love you very much! Please forgive me for the trouble I might cause you, but I choose to live a life that I must, and I am leaving with a quiet mind.

Chapter 12

Concerns love and freedom
both of which are in sight

News of the detention reached her in the afternoon, two days after Besa and other students had been remanded in custody. Friends flocked to her room in numbers, asking questions to which she provided partial answers. 'Yes,' she would say, 'my fiancé has been detained, but I know nothing of the circumstances of the arrest.' And yet Shantiee remembered everything. She recalled her fears for him, their arguments that resulted in accusations and shouts: 'I know you don't care much about me,' she would persist. 'All you care about are your essays and your friends. You don't love me really.' 'I love you, Shantiee. I honestly do. It's just that certain things have to be done and one feels responsible. Just bear with me for a little while. I promise you that everything will be okay. Please, sweetheart –' and she fell in his arms, craving every part of him. It did not matter what disagreement they might have had: for the moment she was there in his arms, feeling warm and safe – and that was what counted the most.

Shantiee wept like a widowed woman. 'What could the police do to him?' There had been cases of Government brutality against students. Those who survived the Red bricked Building[34] returned with nothing in their heads: they had become vegetables and were altered beyond recognition. Could the same thing happen to him? The thought was horrifying. 'O God,' she bit into her pillows. 'Please look into the bottom of my grief. Let nothing happen to him. I love no one but him. Please bring him back to me.'

She had implored her father to dispatch their best lawyers to Lusaka to study the situation and help all detained students. 'Daddy,' she had wept, 'they're going to kill him if we do nothing. You've got to do something. If Besa dies I will kill myself! I love him and I will not live without him.' – 'Calm down,' her father had said. 'I am sending some people over there and your mom's coming. Don't worry – Besa will be fine.'

In the evening she went up to his room, for this was where Shantiee belonged. She looked around her: there was the bed he slept in, there were the clothes that he wore, and there were the books he loved to read. She thought angrily: 'What has he done to deserve detention? What is the matter with African governments? A student writes essays to voice his opinions about affairs of his country, and he scoops fire on his feet.' She remembered something else too. Besa had returned from the Dean of Students when Shantiee happened to be there, embittered and shaking with rage. She had never seen him quite like this before.

'What's the matter, honey?' she had asked him then, unable to bear the silence any longer.

'It's that funckin' bastard called the Dean of Students. Nchike and I went to see him about the ban, and all he says is *forget!*'

'Forget what?'

'Forget everything – the newsletter and all. When I asked him, "What does truth mean to you?" he said: "It's not about saying the truth. It's about what Government says we should do." Now I understand why some lecturers of great promise abandon their studies and research and go to polish Beyani's shoes. Having lost sight of their noble aims by which they might have made landmarks in knowledge and helped mankind, the fools wallow in petty, temporary government posts and forget their ultimate obligations. What a life!'

She stood helplessly by, fearing, not knowing what to do. Besa crumpled some papers on the table and searched for a box of matches. 'All those hours of work must come to nothing. Perhaps this is what life is all about,' he said bitterly and walked out. Shantiee followed him into the corridor.

'Wait a moment, Besa. Where are you going?'

'I have to burn some useless papers. I am tired, Shantiee, I want everything to end. I want to be free. Perhaps I'll have more time for you. It's useless to fight.'

Shantiee was just as upset. She imagined flames engulfing sheets of paper, slowly turning them into moulds of ash. Hours of labour would be irredeemably lost; words that might have stirred students to the consciousness of their justice and rights. And she thought: 'Government does not understand us. Theories or concepts we learn are meant to advance our knowledge and understanding of the real world – but we are not permitted to discuss issues freely, and the little we know is rendered useless. Why shouldn't they just close University for good if we cannot be allowed to apply our minds? We shall pack our bags and go back to our parents...' She did not blame him since – 'No one has the use for silence. People must express themselves. On the other hand, people who will do anything to maintain their status quo confront us. They are opposed to criticism but decide policies that affect everyone without distinction.

They expect everyone to obey, yet obedience does not require intelligence.'

Her eyes were focussed on him. She felt sorry for Ferio or for all those whose lives were rooted in the quest for the truth. Presently Shantiee said:

'You can't destroy your work just like that. The situation may change for the better and you might use it.' What if nothing improves?'

'If nothing does then you could still submit your work to other markets elsewhere. Let us not restrict ourselves to the Vanguard. There are other opportunities for promising writers like you. Can I see the work now?'

'I have decided to burn the stuff and –'

'Please, Besa, let me read some. You can't deny *me* the chance.'

He agreed but reluctantly, and they returned to his room.

She drew a chair and flipped through three essays. The title of one caught her attention and she decided to read it first.

'What does *Idols of the Cave* mean?' she asked him casually.

Besa did not respond. He lay on the bed and nursed his wounds.

'You know something? There are moments you act like a kid.'

He ignored her again and said nothing. Her eyes fell on the text.

THE FERIO PAGES
Idols of the Cave[35]

...Let us again begin to examine, said **Manu** to his friend, the very premises (if at all there are any), on which our friends' convictions seem to rest. Should we find such irrefutable and certain, we shall feel obliged to renounce our beliefs and embrace public opinion. Yet should we prove otherwise and be led to think that their convictions are precarious and uncertain, then we shall sustain our beliefs and take care not to be corrupted by their vices, for we cannot entrust our life to that which prompts doubt, vulgarity and false notions. I believe this is what we will do, my precious friend?

Mwange: I should think so, too. We have no better choice than to reason through things and see if they accord with the facts. This was what I sought to remind those barbarians of, as a matter of fact.

But for this very reason, they laughed at me and treated me like a commoner, and in the end made me feel as though I was nothing. And there were spectators, too, and all of them were watching and were evidently amused by the fray.

Manu: I can understand how humiliating this must have been. However, let us not give in to despair and stray into what may not be very consequential. Instead, let us take courage in our hands and establish whether you who were laughed at were right or – if not right, wrong. I presume this to be a very serious matter indeed.

Mwange: Let us do as you wish. Let us examine everything.

Manu: Very well, then. To begin with, I desire to know why, in the opinion of your mockers, you were an object of derision. Why were you laughed at, Mwange?

Mwange: They laughed at me because I criticised some youths that love to act like African Americans. They are a disgusting lot. They hang out with their peers at street corners and play the characters of rappers and their betters. They dress like ruffians and idolise rap musicians whom they take to be authorities or their gods. And whoever tries to correct them or advise against, these unfortunate youths scold, harass or even beat them up, the way they nearly did in my case. It was only fortunate that somehow I managed to escape their notice or they might have killed me.

Manu: These youths are all Zambians, as you said?

Mwange: Of course.

Manu: Yet unlike Zambians or what Zambians generally ought to be like, they imitate foreigners whom they suppose to be models?

Mwange: Yes. They wear funny haircuts and earrings, and words such as 'fuck you', 'mother fucker', and 'asshole' leave their lips. They have such an indecent language that you would think they were insane.

Manu: Whether insane or not, let us not be too hasty in condemning our friends. Admittedly, though, they possess a different view of life from us, yet we might prove them right and discover that it were our rashness and subjectivity, and not their beliefs, which were responsible for the negative attitude we harbour against them. And so, my friend, let us guard against this and proceed cautiously. Who knows? Perhaps their gangster life has some rational foundation.

Mwange: Let us proceed cautiously as you wish, yet we shall soon discover that with regard to their beliefs and way of life, these people are absolutely mistaken.

Manu: They are mistaken, you say, but how can you be so sure? Is it not natural to make statements about the world?

Mwange: It is.

Manu: And by 'statements' we mean logical propositions that affirm or deny that a predicate belongs to a subject?

Mwange: That is right.

Manu: Then we admit that people form beliefs and opinions about the world, and that such beliefs and opinions influence their view of what their life ought to be like?

Mwange: That is correct. Their conduct and ethical valuation is as a result of the opinions they hold. In the case of our youths, their ethics is based on what their idols in Hollywood will say and do.

Manu: We shall come to that a little later. But I want us to agree on what we are saying right now. Do you suppose that in *all* cases, being in possession of *any* beliefs whatever is a bad thing, or are there *some* beliefs that ought not to be possessed for one reason or another?

Mwange: There is nothing wrong with forming beliefs and being in possession of them. What disconcerts me, though, is that some views of life are founded on a system of beliefs that are clearly false. It is vain to uphold a false belief but noble and rewarding to be guided by a belief that is true as far as material reality is concerned. In other words, my argument does not purport to deny that holding beliefs as such is a good thing to do. I only question some beliefs that are not founded on material facts.

Let me cite some examples. In Matanda village, our people believe that an earthquake – or *makumba* – is a god. Whenever there is a tremor, therefore, they all rush out to the shrine and prostrate themselves in an act of veneration as *makumba* passes. But this is not all. There is also *mweela*, the serpent and god of Lake Bangweulu, who is reputed to bring fish to his devotees. Fishermen worship at his shrine, too. Yet in both cases, the phenomena of a quake and the quantity of fish stocks do not arise from any connection with a god or a large snake. The two events have different causes. Worshipping the two divinities, therefore, is a falsification of reality and a waste of time.

Manu: In short, dear friend, you are proposing that beliefs in general should be founded on the facts of experience which are consistent with material truth?

Mwange: That is right. But those poor youths ground their beliefs on images from music movies and posters. Therefore, their convictions have no basis in fact. The things that we may trust and claim to know best are those things that we perceive immediately. We have a more stable intimacy and contact with the immediate objects of our senses. I am referring to our primary sensations.

Manu: I admire your exposition. And it now appears more likely that our friends who model their lives after musicians by imitating their manner of speech, dress, living and so on, without due consideration as to whether the imitated view of life is compatible with their circumstances, may actually be missing a mark.

Mwange: That is right. It is as though by choosing to live *other* lives, they were deserting themselves. By acting out characters from movies and posters, they are actually refusing to face the demands of their individuality – them and their immediate circumstances. Their lives are therefore ineffectual.

Manu: How can that be demonstrated?

Mwange: It can be demonstrated by employing a phenomenological analysis. Let this mysterious subject who imitates be *I*. Let us, therefore, begin by looking at parts of my body: I have fingers, I have eyes, I have two hands, I have two legs, I have a face, and I have my thoughts which, together with the parts of my body, we may call quasi-objects. But I become aware of other things, too. There are trees, people, buildings, vehicles and the like, and I stumble upon a suspicion – no, I am made to believe sincerely – that I am, after all, not quite these things. I am someone distinct from them. Then I close my eyes to aid my concentration, and I uncover treasures in my mind in the form of clusters of images. I am excited and I ask: 'Where did these images come from?' I inquire further into their origin, and I am persuaded to believe that these images have not always been with me. They are copies of my experiences in the world of fact, and each one of them has an ontological meaning. Sometimes, though, as Descartes rightly observed in the *Meditations*, such mental images do not necessarily correspond to reality, as when I think of myself as very rich, whereas in actual fact I am very poor. Or when I believe myself to be Michael Jackson, whom I take to be myself. On the other hand, such objects of my thoughts as may be encountered in my mind are ultimately rooted in my circumstances, and my world is open for me to understand or misunderstand.

Manu: Speaking of mental images, Freud's theory of dreams proposed that the psychical contents of our dreams have a meaning which always points to the existence of a real world. Mental phenomena, therefore, are not distinct from concrete events in which an agent is submerged. In the same way, Husserl's principle of intentionality says the same thing. But there is still a problem here. How do you justify the suggestion that a youth that behaves after an idol has deluded himself? What arguments can you adduce?

Mwange: The starting point is *myself*. I reach myself from the consideration of things that are concrete and outside of me. I am not such things, to be sure, I am simply *myself*: distinct, spatially defined and the same as myself. I see me standing apart from other things that surround me, and I develop awareness that I am *detached* from them. And in so far as I can realise that I am different and cannot be substituted and mistaken for anything else, then I am, for being me consists in the true understanding of the basis of *my individuality*: my apartness, my essence as I. I am because I am different: I celebrate my life because I am different. There is nothing in the world that is exactly like me. I am a unique individual that must stand out.

Again, as I consider this critical attitude to my existence – from which result art, philosophy, politics, and so on – I conceive that as far as I am concerned my life is primarily a task between my situations and I. I cannot, therefore, risk misunderstanding or falsifying myself, nor can I afford to mistake efficient and material causes for formal and final causes, as this would be fatal. In all my undertakings, then, I have the responsibility to interact with my world of fact, to discover the realms of phenomena that are relative to me. Who will offer to explain the meaning of existence from my standpoint? No one will, no one cares. And does it matter who I am? It does matter a great deal; it makes all the difference. But then, self-disclosure is something only I can do: help will not come from heaven or anywhere, nor will it help to start placing my confidence in other people to confirm my existence. And I can't desert the responsibilities of my life as an individual. I cannot hide behind excuses in order to avoid the encounter with myself. If I did, my life would have been useless, sterile or nothing. A person ought to reflect his or her being from where they stand. But if we *are* because of our individual identity, then we cease to exist when we try to be other people.

Manu: God forbid that we should attempt to be other than what we must be.

Mwange: We may also consider another aspect of imitation from a different perspective – the relationship between a cause and an effect that are concomitant.

Firstly, the cause as an event is independent of the effect, but not vice versa. Secondly, since this relation is concomitant, a variation in the cause produces a variation in the effect, and not vice versa. Thirdly, where causes and effects are arranged in a linear sequence, it is in the nature of causes to be superior to their effects. In other words, that which is imitated and that which imitates are two distinct realities analogous to the example just given. The imitated (or cause) is creative, itself, unaffected, superior and stands always indifferent and identical with itself. However, that which imitates (or effect) is uncritical, inferior and poor in relation to that which is perceived as an Ideal or object of imitation. Thus the imitator assimilates the Ideal without examination and tries to be it, and therefore remains poor, false, wretched, uncreative, inferior and susceptible to manipulation. The imitator is like someone confusing images in a pool for actual objects.

Manu: This reminds me of some African leaders who try so hard to model their countries on the lines established by Europeans.

Mwange: That is right. But we ought to reflect from where we stand. Our perspective as a people is unique and needs to be unveiled. We need to stand out as who we are. On the other hand, anyone who clouds his or her mind with such influences as foreign movies, literature and a neo-colonial education without subjecting them to criticism only succeeds in overwhelming their mind with errors and prejudices which distort objective judgement. Existential truth is always *particular* and nothing more.

Manu: Suppose these youths happened to imitate something that was intrinsically good and worthy of imitation, even if they did not have any knowledge about their object of imitation, would you still take such an act to be contemptible?

Mwange: I am sure I would. For an action to possess moral worth the agent must act autonomously with *prior* knowledge of the object and the vision of the Good always held in view. We do not applaud someone for imitating another person. Instead we praise someone and speak highly of them for *originating* an action in the face of different (and sometimes conflicting) alternatives.

Shantiee looked up from his work. She regarded him briefly; put the precious essay back on a pile of papers destined for the flames, and then stood up and knelt down by his bedside. She grasped his hand in earnest and said:

'Listen, Besa. I understand how very strongly you feel about your newsletter, but you can't let it frustrate your efforts to write. If Government or the Dean of Students Office decides that you shouldn't write any more – let them. I have read some biographies of authors who created their works under more difficult conditions than these. They were able to hold out for years and keep their literary dreams alive. But they *first* accepted silence, banishment, exile and solitude and neither cared for neither success nor failure. The most important thing for them was to realise the goals they had set themselves by making sure that no one cancelled half a line of whatever they had written. This is what I want you to do.

'Sometimes, darling, the beauty of a flower invites a careless passer by to pluck it and crush the petals in their hand, because it is by the same means that the beautiful is both created and destroyed. As a writer, I know you will make it good some day, but I am also afraid of this Government. This is why I want you to work in silence until you are sure that time is right to expose your writing. Do you see what I mean? I don't want to lose you. You are very important to me.'

Tears trickled down her cheeks as they were trickling down now. She remembered everything: they had a life that promised them love and happiness. She would have made him a good friend, let alone a good wife should they have decided to get married, but the force of events had come about them in a flash, and there was nothing left save the pain and memories. 'What could they do to him?' she asked distractedly. 'If they kill my fiancé I'll throw myself down from the rooftop. My parents will be shocked, of course, but I will have made a choice. My death will stand as a protest against the system.'

She closed her eyes. Somewhere in a cell, alone and miserable, her love was facing criminal charges in the *Penal Code*. What were these offences? They were essays on the shortages of essential goods, the misuse of public funds by Government officials, the illusions of the present education system, the lack of coherence in the President's political thought, the demand for the right to protest, the illegality of the State of Emergency, and other subjects that concerned Zambians. And there would be no judges in the real sense, except inquisitors to wring confessions from students under torture. The public must not think: they have to be protected from knowing the truth about their circumstances. They should imbibe the doctrine of the Party and repeat slogans ad infinitum.

She woke to the shrill sound of the alarm with a slight start, glanced about her room with a sort of benumbed indifference, and rose out of bed to press the stop-button. The clock stopped ringing and, though Shantiee wasn't very sure, she nonetheless thought there was some other disturbance outside, so she walked up to the window to peer down from the third floor. She was dreadfully tired too, having found little relaxation in sleep. Yet she gasped in excitement at what she beheld below!

A group of students were out at October Airport[36] this morning, singing and waving fists in the air.

> You may have plenty of guns,
> But we are not afraid.
> You may kill all of us,
> But our fight will go on.
> Beyani, watch out!
> We are coming to State House today.
> Beyani watch out!
> You will not eat your food in peace.

They were mostly 'monks' from the Ruins, stamping their feet on the ground, urging everyone to wake up and assemble at the Revolutionary Square[37]. Some of their placards read:

> RELEASE ALL STUDENTS IN DETENTION
> GOVERNMENT PERSECUTION OF STUDENTS IS
>   ILLEGAL
> DOWN WITH THE PIG
> STOP ALL POLICE BRUTALITY

They marched past the car park in the direction of the Vet, shouting as they went:

> TODAY NO LECTURES!
> TODAY NO LECTURES!

Shantiee ran to the roommate and tried to wake her up. She was very excited.

'Jane, Jane! Wake up!'

'What is it? I want to sleep!'

'No you don't! You've got to wake up!'

Her friend blinked several times, gazed uncomprehendingly at Shantiee, and ran her fingers through her tangled hair. She heaved out of bed and muttered reprovingly: 'This is quarter past six. I wake up at seven!'

'I know Jane. But students are going round saying, "No lectures today." There's to be a protest of some kind and I am going to join up!'

'Are you sure?'

'Yes,' her eyes gleamed in triumph. 'This is my only chance to help free everyone in detention, and I miss Besa terribly. I want him back, Jane. I want him back in one piece!'

'In that case, I'll join too. That sort of thing can happen to anyone. Let's spread the word around in case some girls are not aware.'

At eight hours in the morning, Shantiee joined an assembly of more than six thousand agitated protestors at the Revolutionary Square. They wore all kinds of things – from the miner's outfit to rags. An effigy of President Beyani was passed around for all to pinch, kick and spit at, before finally setting it alight. The air was imbrued with palpable rage and tension.

Gelo wandi taalipo:	My girl friend is not here:
Bonse aba ni bangwele.	All these are cowards.

Gelo wandi taalipo:	My girl friend is not here:
Bonse aba ni ba ngwele.	All these are cowards.

Lelo muledabwaa,	You'll be confounded today,
Nalamizandamuna.	I'll provoke you.

Lelo muledabwa,	You'll be confounded today,
Nalamizandamuna	I'll provoke you.

A student climbed on the dais and faced the crowd. Making a 'revolutionary sign' of a clenched fist most revered by monks from the Ruins, the student cried:

'Viva Unzasu,'

'Viva!'

'Viva student solidarity,'

'Viva!'

'Abash stooges of imperialism!'

'Abash!'

'Abash fat necks and their bellies,'

'Abash!'

'Abash colonialism, exploitation and the mechanics of robbery,'

'Abash!'

'Abash Beyanism and its cheap analysis,'

'Abash!'

'Abash the Party and Its Government,'
'Abash!'
'Abash the army, the police, the Special Branch and other instruments of mass fear and dictatorship,'
'Abash!'
And there were whistles, screams and cheers ringing in the air. But another student-leader had taken up his place to address the crowd:

'Comrades in the revolution: we have reached the highest state of political consciousness, a critical stage in our history when students' patience with the PIG[38] has run out...We have tried to understand, we have tried to obey, but time has now come to take the law in our hands...Time has come for students to say NO to threats, expulsions, detentions and persecutions...Time has come for us to oppose the instruments of oppression ...

'Comrades, even as we speak sixteen resident students at this university are now victims of the *Preservation of Public Security Regulations*. They are supposed to be with us now, but the System has locked them up in Kabwata Prison...We do not know their fate.

'Again as we speak, this university has no student union. Unzasu was banned two years ago under *Statutory Instrument 100* ... We have since opposed a Government proposed student representative body but to no avail. The PIG has been stubborn, merciless, and those of us who belong to our underground *Crisis Committee* have known no peace from the arms of the Law – the Police and Special Branch.

'As we speak, comrades, our Five-Point-Demand has been rejected many times by the Government. Our leaders who went to represent students' grievances at State House have all been suspended. But what is wrong with expressing students' opinions? Well, your Five-Point-Demand contained the following:

- ✓ Government must recognise Unzasu as the only legitimate student representation, in the terms understood by all students at the University of Zambia;
- ✓ Government must recognise the University of Zambia as a separate entity within the country; she must not interfere in the running of the institution, including the running of students' welfare. Government must recognise the Senate and the university federal system as independent and autonomous bodies, and cease forcing students and lecturers alike to buy Party cards;

✓ Government must improve students' allowances in line with inflation;

✓ Government must reinstate as lecturers at the University of Zambia, all our teachers whose contracts were terminated during the lecturers' 'equal work equal pay strike'.

'These were your demands, comrades! And even as we speak, two of our newsletters have been outlawed through the Dean of Students Office. Thus the PIG has once again demonstrated its desire to suppress students' right to self-expression and the exercise of their academic freedom. And lastly, comrades, three of our lecturers have recently been deported and called criminals of the State...Must we sit and watch these detentions, deportations, persecutions and harassment in silence?'

The orator paused and continued:

'The duty of the *Crisis Committee*, of which I am a member, is to protect students' rights in the face of Government repression...For two years our leaders have sought dialogue with the PIG over our affairs, and what has been the result? Intimidation, expulsions, detention and a negative projection of the student-image in the Government-owned media...We're childish, irresponsible and deserve lashes from the paramilitary and the police. This is what the public knows and wants...

'Yes, we desire a healthy learning environment and good relationship with the Government...but our patience has given out... and so...we must take the Law in our hands.'

The speaker took another breath and read out the resolutions passed by the *Crisis Committee*:

'Comrades, after having deeply thought about the state of affairs of the university student, your *Crisis Committee* is resolved on the following:

(1) To reopen dialogue with Government over our demands;

(2) To seek the immediate release of all the students in detention.

(3) To force Government to reinstate the lecturers deported.

'In order to induce Government to react, *all* students at the University of Zambia, Great East Road Campus, shall stay away from lessons starting tomorrow. No student shall attend a lecture, lab, workshop, tutorial, conference, discussion or seminar in the University premises. Lecturers shall be duly informed in due course. We are here to learn, comrades, but so our are friends in detention.

We are here to learn so that we contribute to the development of this nation, but this cannot be realised unless we change the political system. Our responsibility right now is to secure the unconditional and safe release of our friends. If this could happen to them, it could also happen to any one of us.

'Now for a word of advice, comrades: If any lecturer or student is seen teaching or attending a lesson, or is seen moving within the Library or the vicinity of a learning place, such a person will be very sorry: we shall consider them sell-outs. The *Committee* has instructed the deployment of members of RUPO[39] at strategic places. If there are informers in our midst, we would like to ask them to rethink concerning students' welfare. If they decide against or choose to betray our cause, we shall treat them as traitors of our country. The detention without trial of our brothers and the plight of students in general, shall be upon them. The history of students' struggle will judge them as perpetuators of the system.

'It is now nine hours, comrades. We shall await the safe return of the detained at the Main Entrance by seventeen hours today. If they do come, we shall be very happy indeed. If they don't return, however, we shall march to Central Police Station and ask these dictators to detain all of us. More than five thousand students will fill their cells tonight. The PIG will face the forces of liberty, freedom and justice. The PIG will face the ranks of young people who are determined to fight . Lastly, comrades: those students who want to express their solidarity with the cause by way of a hunger strike may see me after this assembly...I am told there are about twenty of them...In the meantime, comrades, let us all walk to the main entrance of the University...Long live Unzasu! Long live student power!'

Shantiee Perronni stood, together with almost six thousand students, by the university Main Entrance awaiting the return of the detained. The sun had beaten on them for hours, and they sweltered in the heat, watching traffic pass and the lengthening of shadows. Suspense, anticipation, dread, anger and pessimism defined these moments for nearly everyone. As the time closed on their ultimatum, there could be seen some traces of terror, doubt and grave anxiety on all the faces there. As for her part, Shantiee's emptiness, confusion, and misery intensified. She felt about to faint: but she hoped and wept for his return.

And yet she was not alone. Thousand of students glanced at their watches that said, 'Quarter past seventeen', their hearts full of despair and the firm loathing of the system, their feet ready to defy the instruments of the law, and their consciousness feeling justified to take matters in their hands. What did it matter if blood and wreckage and burning of ruin were loosed upon the street? 'Patience, comrades!' someone entreated them. 'We will wait for another ten minutes before we begin our march!'

And so they did.

They waited till someone screamed and pointed towards the bus stop. 'There they are, guys! I can see them standing in that military truck. Our comrades have returned!'

Everyone turned to look in the direction of the approaching truck, some even running along the edge of the road. There was incredulity everywhere – a great momentary unease which, if it wasn't true, would certainly break and scatter every order in this sun set. There would be terror as violent as storms! But, happily, it was true, because Shantiee saw Besa waving at them. She waved back and, standing on her toes, looked unbelievingly at the truck making its way into university. Some students were singing, dancing and waving hands wildly while others just stood like statues, unable to weep or utter any syllable. They were immobilised by a strong enigmatic emotion that was very difficult to describe – an emotion too sweet, too ethereal or too happy to last.

In the glowing candlelight in her room (far away from a thousand disturbances), Shantiee prayed that these moments should never be far too removed from her again. She sought love, understanding and companionship, and to him alone was committed her life with her hunger and all her thirst, her hopes and all her dreams.

Tears streamed freely from their eyes. There were a dozen apologies astir in their breasts, a million words to fill their night. They had suffered long and endured much, yet it was all right now. They would draw from each other or from the gourd of their love some reason to try again. The storms of life would bare the roots of their exalted love and trust – scarring them in every part, rendering them vulnerable and weak. But no matter how far apart they lived, she would always hold on and look to the skies for the signs of dawn. The way would be long and very rough, and their dreams would perhaps be scattered among millions of grains of sands, or would be dispersed by the breath of the winds. And yet she would, in loyalty and steadfastness, stoop down to find the true love of her life, never doubting the return of the signs of dawn.

'O Besa, my precious darling,' she pressed her lips to his, kissing them repeatedly. 'I was so worried about you. I was so scared something terrible would happen to you.'

'I am very sorry for all the trouble you've suffered on my account. I am sorry for everything. I will try to make it up to you.'

'It's all right now. Just let's live so we don't part again – ever!'

Her eyes were brim with tears. Although the doctor at the university clinic had said Besa's wounds were not very serious but just needed a regular check-up, she could not countenance seeing her beloved with swellings from the flogging by the security agents inflicted on his buttocks, back and legs. He seemed to have changed: his eyes seemed to envision something remote and fixed, something she could never understand.

'Am I readmitted into your life, Shantiee?'

'You've never left my heart,' she said with a grin. 'You are always adored and loved by me. You are my light from the distant stars – much travelled and unwearied by the spaces of the depths. Your lighted torches shine on me from above – and I know that your flowing streams share in the aspect of the divine. I was born to love you *alone*. I am yours for all eternity.'

'What was that?'

She laughed. 'Some lines of a poem I wrote for you. I'll show you the text.'

Shantiee flashed him a knowing smile, and then retrieved a bottle of wine from the suitcase. Besa looked for the glasses and whistled.

'How very enterprising. There's candlelight, some wine and a table laid for two. This is very romantic. I like it.'

'There's another important thing,' she informed him as she poured out the wine. 'I asked Jane to find herself somewhere else to spend the night because I figured we would need to talk through the night after your release.'

Besa was about to protest but she forestalled everything. She raised her eyes determinedly at him and said doggedly:

'Ever since we knew each other, I have always been flexible, understanding and willing to let you have your way. While you were lonely and suffering in the cell, I cried my heart out and contemplated suicide should anything happen to you. I couldn't eat well nor do anything except think about you and whether you were all right. I was so frantic, and yet so enraged with the Police that I was prepared to riot and die from bullets – because of you, my rebel and my love. I could never have imagined myself capable of doing such things. But there I was – with thousands of other students – proposing to fight the Government if our demands were not met!'

She was sobbing quietly now.

'Besa, your release means everything to me – everything! For this reason, I just want to share my bed, my time and my love with you. I feel very festive and very much in love with you tonight. I want everything – good food, some wine, some soft light and the certainty that I am with you in bed. I want to hold you in my arms the way I hold you in my dreams.'

She knelt before him and grasped his hands, and felt very strong and right.

'You will stay the night, sweetheart?'

'Yes. I will stay.'

She sighed in relief. 'Thank you,' she said. 'In a way what we've been through together is a blessing in disguise. I am closer to you than I ever was. I love you so much.'

Besa kissed her on the mouth, and she felt she was sliding and dying, dying joyously. Plunging because he loved her. She smiled and said, very softly:

'I am very happy, but just now I want us to enjoy our supper. I have something very special for you!'

'What is it?'

Shantiee giggled with pleasure and got on her feet.

'Just be patient, sweetheart, and please do sit down on the bed. You'll see your present in a moment.'

Besa sat down on her bed and waited. In another moment she had produced the parcel. When her fiancé untied the thread he discovered a small anthology of fifteen poems titled *Surrender*. Opening it at once, Besa read the dedication, 'I dedicate these poems to my love, Besa, for being a great inspiration in my life' and turned to her with a new look in his eyes: 'You never told me you wrote poetry?'

'Do you like the present?'

'Yes. It's a very special present. No one has ever given me such a gift. Thanks a lot!'

'The University Library did the typing and binding of the poems. There are just three copies in the whole world.'

Besa pulled her to him and touched her in every part, and her body submitted to him in a joyous and free expression of love. Her life was meaningless without him, for her destiny was to love him faithfully and well. In the ensuing moments she fumbled with his clothes, trying to undress him, and stared at the incredible beauty of his body. She was already wet, and she wondered whether he was perhaps not taking too long. Lying beside him in bed, Shantiee stroked him between his thighs, gently caressing and teasing him with her hands, proud of having inspired his erection. Then he was on top of her – and she parted her thighs for him, guiding him inside her. She closed her eyes and gave herself to him, urging him to reach the deepest part of her soul. Afterward she lay snuggled up to him, fulfilled and recreated into a woman who truly loved her man. She raised her head and said softy:

'Did you find me dull?'

'No. You are incredibly sweet.'

'So are you. We are perfect for each other. We are very compatible.'

Shantiee brought the food in bed and fed him chunks of it, though she didn't eat much herself. She wasn't feeling hungry yet enjoyed to see him eat. When they made love the fourth time, she was quite exhausted. Sleep touched her eyes. She coiled her arms around him and kissed him good night.

'Sleep well, sweetheart. I love you with all my heart.'

Chapter 13

Concerns various vicissitudes,
The pedagogy of the oppressed
And a suspicion that all had been mistaken

A frightened cry for succour in the night, a mortal plea of someone strangled or wounded, accompanied by a flow of screams and obscenities, robbed Besa Musunga of any possibility of a quiet sleep. He lay fully awake now, overwrought by disquieting thoughts and such feelings as to be coarse, sighing heavily in the dark and listening for sounds: sounds of terror and shouts expressing disapproval, sounds of chatter and prolonged laughter, sounds of R and B from a night club nearby, and sounds as of wind rustling leaves and sweeping over distant hills...mournfully and cadenced. He raised himself on his elbows: it was pitch dark, yet the outlines of this room stood out. It was his room. Besa was in it. Four vertical walls with a roof on top enclosed everything he possessed in this world: a wooden bed, some kitchen things carefully stuffed under it, a small table and a stool in the central area, a shelf of books positioned in the corner, and some clothes hanging on a line across this unairy room. Other than this there was nothing. Life was hinged on the barest of essentials, on the simple and elemental.

He jumped out of bed and set out on a stroll along the main road. Two dogs growled at him as he passed. Although it was night, the stranger in these parts was already familiar with the general squalor in the form of filth, squatters' homes and dilapidated roads, all of which gave his outlook a philosophical turn. 'What intelligible truths,' wondered he, 'can one draw from one's intercourse with shacks, poverty, violence, disillusionment, degradation and decay? What modes of thought can my life in Chawama inspire?'

He drew a blank and beheld only the commonplace: the empty marketplace, the corrugated iron roofed structures edging both sides of the road, and the lively people bustling about in a warm night sprinkled with million of stars. Far away in the distance stood the city of Lusaka, the metropolis of dreams and wealth, dotted with chains of light that gave one a suspicion of the intricate and profound. But Besa was *here*, he was in a ghetto, he was in a peripheral area of every kind of deprivation, and this was his starting point. 'A perspective,' he echoed in an undertone, looking far out. 'A place to stand...in the physical and psychological sense. A sure basis on which to postulate matters of fact taken to be one's percepts and mental states, for the subject must become the object of his own inquiry, the theme and plot subject to analysis.'

He stayed for some time at a roadside bar and enjoyed a cold beer quietly. The music was very good, and the people were friendly and did not look suspiciously at strangers. Besa called for another mosi and felt light hearted and merry, and was able to follow a lengthy discussion at a table nearby. There were some girls too, yet they were immodestly dressed and were percolated by everything bordering on excess and nothing that was not despicable. They flirted freely with the men, they laughed out aloud, they blew cigarette smoke in the air, and they seemed a little more reckless than their male friends, though some men were more extravagant in their spending and tended to be argumentative and somewhat disruptive.

A young woman looked and smiled in his direction then abruptly rose to her feet. She skirted around people and moved across to his table with confident, graceful steps, and took a chair opposite. She was wild enough, to be sure, judging from her reddened lips and heavily made-up face and two pencilled lines for eyebrows. And her black wig, together with the suggestive short, tight dress she was wearing, lent her an obvious whorish appearance. On the other hand there was still something gentle, friendly and human about her. In a voice edged with some mockery, the girl said:

'You're waiting for someone who won't come?'

'Not really,' he replied. 'I am quite alone.'

'Can you buy me a drink?'

'Maybe one. I was just about to finish my last beer and go home.'

'It's too early to go home yet.' She leaned forward and offered him a hand. 'My name is Aggie. What's yours?'

'Besa.'

'Besa…Somehow you remind me of someone I used to know. He had the same searching eyes and a kind of doubting face, only he was shorter and on the fat side. He used to be my boy friend.'

Besa blinked and yawned. He eyed the girl for an instant and wanted to get up. She sensed his revulsion and said:

'If you don't want me to be with you now, just tell me so and I will leave. We're not married.' She cast him a look of fear and asked: 'Can I go?'

'You may stay if you like. I don't mind.'

She relaxed and smiled at him – a female human smile in which he discerned an invitation to the delights of the flesh. He pitied her, though, and asked her questions by way of passing the time.

'You spoke of your former boy friend. Where is he now?'

'I don't know precisely. He ran off with a girl and I haven't heard from him since. It's about half a year now.' She told him confidentially.

'You sound embittered. Are you sorry?'

'I am bitter – yes. He hurt me so much. We were going to be married and he ruined all our plans.'

'That must have pained so much.'

'It did – especially in the beginning. But I am okay now and I am learning to cope. Are you married yourself?'

Besa wagged his head. 'But I am engaged.'

'You love her very much?'

'Yes.'

'Which part of town does she live?'

'She's at university. She's a biochem student.'

'I didn't catch the last words.'

'My fiancé is studying biology with a bias towards chemistry.'

'Okay,' she said uncomprehendingly, but gazed at him with some new respect. 'Your fiancé must be very intelligent and lucky. Few women reach that far. The rest drop out to get married or walk the street or simply do nothing. Women are most unfortunate.'

'What do you do for a living?'

'I am a maid. It's not a good job. But I have no choice.'

He eyed her for a moment with a concentrated look. Behind the masked face lay the horrors and persecution of all women. She bore herself erect, carrying existence with steadfastness as events moulded her furtively into the sort of person she really was. And she was, in fact, those very events. She was a sum of what she had done and what she had failed to do.

'You're so quiet. Are you missing your woman?'

'No.'

'What are you thinking about?'

'Nothing. What can you have for a drink?'

'Maybe a fanta.'

'Don't you want a beer?'

'Not now. But I could smoke a cigarette.'

He ordered her a drink, and they smoked cigarettes in silence. Besa looked round him: more people had now filled the bar, men and women of all stripes passing their evening pleasantly over drinks, sharing experiences or some anecdotes which made others laugh. Then at that very moment, three uniformed police officers carrying automatic rifles entered the bar and made straight to the counter, and there was a hushed silence as everything came to a sudden halt. The music stopped playing, and the people fled the dancing place and sat stiffly in their seats, gripped by fear.

'What do these three want?' Aggie whispered. 'I hope they haven't come to close the bar because of the curfew.'

'Is there one?'

'There's one, yes. There's always a curfew in these compounds. They are probably looking for criminals or they are just frightening everyone for money. Last night they beat up some innocent boys and their girl friends until the boys pleaded guilty of crimes no one could have possibly done.'

'Perhaps they had really committed such crimes?'

'No they hadn't. I know them all.' She was annoyed with him now. 'You seem to like the police but they'll have you locked up for nothing. Do you know how it feels to sleep in the cells? Do you know how many women the police rape?'

An image flitted into his mind in an instant. Sixteen harmless students from the University of Zambia, stripped to the waist and bare feet, sit before the Commanding Officer and some dozen armed men from the Special Branch and the Police Force, to answer charges ranging from insubordination to the State to inciting riotous behaviour and promoting unlawful conduct aimed at causing public discontent and the breach of the peace. Anxiety and tension mounts as everyone looks to the only table where the C.O has taken up his place. Two Special Branch officers exchange glances, and nod to the C.O to begin. The pot-bellied man stands up and says:

'So you are the people causing problems at the University. You are not patriotic. You despise our Government and make fun of the President, and you act contrary to what the Party wants and disturb the peace...

'I will not waste my time with trouble makers who are already damned and condemned, but I will at least ask the officer to read to you all your crimes so that you may realise the seriousness of your case, and the stupidity of your actions. After that you will all be detained indefinitely – and mind you, you are no longer students at the University of Zambia but dangerous political animals who don't deserve to live! You are a disgrace to your country and a threat to development.'

The said officer comes forward with papers in his hands. They were official documents bearing the student' names and citing the offences committed under the Penal Code, Chapter 146. He reads out as follows:

- You are charged with defamation of the President under section 69;
- You are charged with unlawful assembly under section 74;
- You are charged with inciting your fellow students to actions that are mutinous or actions likely to breach the peace, under section 48;
- You are charged with offences in respect of prohibited publications, under section 54, and of other matter proved to be seditious in intent;
- You are charged with insulting the national anthem, under section 68, and with wrongfully inducing a boycott under section 92;
- You are charged with departing from the Party Guidelines and instruments meant to promote development and peace in the country;
- And you are also charged with having participated in previous acts that were unlawful and conducted to destabilise the country, as ringleaders.

The Commanding Officer then resumes:

'You have heard for yourselves the terrible crimes you have been charged with. You are criminals, and as criminals you deserve no mercy from anyone... We have a duty to keep the rule of law that provides a stable environment in which our country must develop. However, contrary to common sense and the requirements of the Law, you act against the foundations of the State and the Office of the Presidency. Do you expect the Law to be suspended each time you are rioting or publishing defamatory matter in the name of academic freedom? Is this the meaning of being university students, or are you above the Law?

'You do not appreciate what the Party and Its Government does for you. Yet the Government pays for your upkeep and other services which you ignore to see. What do you expect us to do if you become unruly and threaten public peace? Are you asking to be set free even when *evidence* shows that you are all guilty?'

His eyes gleam with fury as he now paces the interrogation room.

'As citizens of this country you are expected to behave responsibly, but you flaunt every statutory instrument with impunity and expect the same Government you scoff at to feed and educate you. You disgrace us internationally and put the image of the President in disrepute, as though he never rules the country with love and loyalty.'

Then he calls the men with weapons with a wave of his hand, saying:

'The students you see here are arrogant, undisciplined and irresponsible. I want you to give them some good treatment until they admit their crimes and tell us who else is involved in this plot against the Government. They shall be taken separately in the cells. Please avoid excessive bleeding and needles, but you may use electricity. But before doing anything, ask each one what they know. If they tell lies do as I said: give them the treatment. I want results in two hours!'

The image disintegrated and there was nothing. Besa shrugged his shoulders as if he was scrapping off painful, shameful memories. He turned his head away from the two police officers seemingly issuing fresh instructions in rapid emphatic Nyanja, and said with a frown:

'You won't understand how the fear of bodily torture makes the most courageous of men lose their minds and hide their tails between their legs. Did you notice how those huge fellows over there had towered over everyone as if they had the world in their pockets? But look at them now: they are terrified by the policemen despite the fact that they are innocent and have done nothing wrong. That's what the system has perfected over the years – the fear to be suspected and beaten like a dog. Why can't everyone behave as before? Police officers shouldn't scare anyone.'

The girl stared at him with wondering eyes. She squeezed his hand to keep him quiet and watched the two men like every body else did. They moved in between tables and subjected everyone in the bar to a thorough scrutiny before walking back to the counter to rap out further instructions to the bartender who answered, 'Yes Bwana,' several times. There was much whistling, clapping and expression of happy relief the moment the duo had left.

Aggie looked ruefully towards the door:

'Becoming a soldier or a police officer – that's the kind of job only suitable for people without feelings for others. They victimise everyone but couldn't even fight a war. They only act tough with civilians.'

'In some countries, though, being a member of the armed forces is highly regarded because the army or the police are there to defend the country and uphold the rule of law. The situation is radically different here. Our perceptions of what these institutions should stand for are far from what actually happens on the ground. But we are used to it.'

'Not me.'

'Would you like to dance?'

'Yes,' she replied, rising to her feet with him. 'I would love to dance.'

Besa grasped her gently by the arm and led her some steps to the dancing floor. He pondered a moment and felt at fault to be where he was presently, let alone to be with a girl he hardly knew. 'I ought to be at my place or with Shantiee,' he scratched the right earlobe with some doubt. 'I miss her very much, and I am sure she misses me too.' Yet the girl had placed her arms over his shoulders and she was smiling very beautifully at him, enticing him with her eyes to seize the momentary pleasures allotted to all men. 'This is our life, this is our time,' he thought with passion, holding the girl by the waist. 'This is our life in which to meet our fate.'

'Can you tell me a little more about yourself?' Aggie said. 'For example, where do you work? You look like a worker.'

'I teach. I am a historian.'

'You like your job?'

'Sometimes. But I wish I could do something a little bit more challenging – like doing some research. I like research.' Besa wanted to elaborate but resisted the impulse. She would not understand him, and he did not want to be perceived as arrogant when he was merely stating his opinions.

'Never mind my job,' he said. 'Let's just dance and enjoy our selves. I can spare an hour and I will be gone.'

'You're leaving early because of your wife?'

'I wake up very early to go to work. So I have to have enough rest.'

She was disappointed. 'You decide to leave just when I am beginning to like you. It's not fair.'

'There are lots of men to choose from around here. You'll find someone better. I wish you luck.'

'Thank you. I hope I'll see you again.'

Besa nodded and excused himself. He walked over to the bartender and ordered the girl two more drinks. Then he returned to bid her good night. She hugged him and wished him well.

Completely engrossed in some work laid on a long bench in the Physics Laboratory, the science teacher, Mr Mweeni (alone and undisturbed for some time), stiffened for a moment and gave him a quizzical, startled glance. He straightened up briefly and drew a deep sigh, then bent over the apparatus without uttering a word. Besa had a sudden impulse to leave and come back another time, yet the elderly man stopped him with a wave of his hand and bade him close the door. Besa said nervously:

'Are you sure I am not disturbing you, sir? I could see you later.'

'I don't know. Just don't make any noise. I'll finish soon. You may hang around.'

He watched with interest. Here was a man working quietly with pendulums of various lengths and counting the number of swings with great concentration, recording their periods of the motion as the blobs approached the state of rest. What was the significance of taking pains to measure the interval of time between two observable events? Awe-struck, he gazed at other apparatus such as were designed to demonstrate the refraction and dispersion of light; the verification of the laws of motion; the determination of the load and extension...and then at such instruments as beakers, test tubes, burners, timers, holders, flasks, scales, microscopes and others of varying make and use. The equipment was for the pupils, but Besa doubted whether they could imbibe the true spirit of inquiry and discovery. Would there be a few who would truly appreciate the nature of science and the logical rules of thought upon which our civilisation was constructed? Would they not perceive some purpose to their lives as lying on the beaten truck? Recalling Cohen and Nagel on scientific method, 'It settles differences without any external force by appealing to our common rational nature...it unites men in something nobly devoid of all pettiness...' he thought: 'For every teacher there is just one pupil or there is none. The rest merely want to be adequate and care nothing about the search for the objectivity of the truth. They only want to use education for social advancement. That's just a pity.'

The science teacher asked without looking up:

'Did you see the Head teacher about your problem?'

'Yes, sir.'

'What did he say?'

'He advised me to wait until they find some money. He said there was nothing the school could do to help me. Salaries and allowances to teachers are the responsibility of the Ministry of Education.'

Mr Mweeni straightened up again and took off his gloves. He stayed for some time without replying, studying the apparatus in front of him with solemn, conscientious eyes, and then turned to look at Besa:

'What about the PTA Fund. Did he not indicate to you that it might be possible to use a bit of that money to help you settle down as quickly as possible while you wait for your name to appear on the Government payroll?'

'No sir. He never mentioned it. He simply asked me to be patient.'

'Patience is fine, but for how much longer will you wait? How are you expected to survive?'

'I don't know, sir, this was why I had to see you. As a senior teacher you could impress on the Head Teacher and members of the PTA Committee that fact that I need help urgently. I can't go on working if the school or the Ministry does not pay or advance me some money to use. How will I live without anything in my pockets? The last time I was discussing the same problem with an accountant at the mechanised salary unit, I was given assurances that it wouldn't be long before the Ministry put me on the payroll, but this is the third month and I am becoming desperate. My account is recording almost nothing now…My family needs my help, and I am anxious about my fiancé. She doesn't know where I am. I also have other problems to take care of. I need to settle my rent, buy some furniture and I have to think of the cost of food and transport!'

'Where are you staying at the moment?'

'I am renting a small room in Chawama.'

'There's a house for new teachers at school, and it's free. Perhaps you should consider moving in to keep some of your expenses down. Two of our new staff are already living there.'

'The Head Teacher informed me of that option. I turned down the offer because I needed privacy to write and I had to think of Shantiee, my fiancée. She would never be free to live in a house like that.'

'Not even when circumstances are not as good as they are now?'

'Perhaps she could bear it for some time. But even if she did I couldn't live with two teachers under the same roof. There are practical considerations to think of. Besides, the house was not designed for bachelors; it is for *one* family. If you crowd different people in a place that was created for a different specific function, then you go against the original intention of the design and you may distort the structural effects of the place and create problems. I want my own house where my family will feel free.'

'I understand,' said Mr Mweeni. 'I will speak to the Head Teacher on your behalf.'

'Thank you. I will very much appreciate it.'

'What about your lessons? How are you getting on with your pupils?'

'Generally very well, I should say, though the only problem is that I am constantly thinking of money and the future. I love teaching, sir, but if things don't improve very soon I will be forced to leave the Ministry and find work elsewhere. I have many responsibilities now and I have to look out for myself.'

'I understand your feelings. I'll try to do my best.'

'Thank you very much. Thank for you for your time.'

'Just a minute, Mr Besa. You mentioned writing. Are you writing a book?'

'Yes sir.'

'Can I see something of your work?'

Besa hesitated. 'I don't know. I would have to think. It's very private, writing, and normally I don't show my work anyhow. But I'll consider it and let you know.'

'I look forward to reading your work.'

'I'll see. Thank you very much.'

'You're most welcome.'

The Pedagogy of the oppressed

Every science [Besa writes in his notebook] starts from a humble beginning, from unsorted, unverified, empirical data. In African cultures one encounters the local world-views expressed in the form of myths intended to explain the totality of cosmic reality, the fertility of imagination similar to Homer's fables. This rich, uncritical narrative of events and divinities, coupled with other intuitive rituals invented to make sense out of chaos or disorder, is, oddly enough, the very foundation on which knowledge of the intelligible African world-view may be constructed. 'Our philosophy,' says Kwame Nkhrumah in *Consciencism*, 'must find weapons in the environment and living conditions of the African people. It is from these conditions that the intellectual content of our philosophy must be created...' What are these contents?

- The discovery of the African as a human fact in all his or her total experience – both historical and contemporary, collective and personal;

- An attitude of mind founded on philosophical statements and inviting us to act, to take the world in our hands, to discover within our paradoxical existence a living, liberating principle.

Now the discovery of the African as a human fact means taking full cognisance of the physical conditions that shape our destiny. This also means that the sources of phenomenal explanations do not lie in heaven or myths, but within phenomena themselves. 'Inquiry into final causes is sterile and, like a virgin consecrated to God, produces nothing.'[40] This also means that while being God-complex or religious is socially factual, the ultimate determinants of being are, on the contrary, the cold dialectical forces of matter, for the true understanding of being as such does not arise from an analysis of its superficial consequents but from it antecedents. The mythical sentiment that divorces the African from grasping the dialectics is like a fog that hides the real factors at work in physical experience. 'God is dead,' taught Nietzsche, so that the African ought to cease looking heavenward but to the earth or to that which immediately affects his or her existentiality.

On the other hand, while we hold the proposition that our life is a function of the dialectics[41] to be true, we also allow for the possibility of free will that contents with the forces of determinism. Our societies are evolutes of physical processes that have fixed the African in the present situation, yet historical determinism alone is not an excuse to escape from the full responsibility of self-existence and self-creation, for every individual African is engaged in a historical task of constructing a self-image and self-event. In other words we are, as Africans, authors of our own age. What does this signify?

- Given, then, whatever conditions, he or she who refuses to rise above the limitations of his or her existence does so willingly - for, as James Lane Allen writes in *As a man thinketh*, "*A man will find that as he alters his thoughts towards things and other people, things and other people will alter towards him...Let a man radically alter his thoughts, and he will be surprised at the rapid transformations it will effect in the material conditions of his life. Men do not attract that which they want, but that which they are. The divinity that shapes our ends is in ourselves. It is our very self...All that man achieves is the direct result of his thoughts...A man can only remain weak and abject and miserable by refusing to lift up his thoughts.*"

Therefore, the African should be willing to conceive that despite his or her adverse circumstances, he or she alone has the answers to unlocking the gates of the possible. Other than this the African becomes a self-made victim and not a conqueror. To them who dare entertain the thought that the possible is, all will be given. Thought conditions reality.

▪ Our historical grounding at the moment has progressed from slavery, colonialism, racialism and underdevelopment, so that we ought to take stock and ask: 'How much are we to blame for our circumstances?' The African ought to understand his or her place in the Universe. We need to understand how to create wealth and material goods for our people in a world in which everyone is against us. Western and American capitalism are only interested in the resources of Africa that they must access cheaply. Africans must devise methods of gaining a competitive advantage or else risk being wiped out as a race. They shall blame no one but themselves.

The philosophy that should guide us is that we are responsible for everything that happens to us. Our position of underdevelopment is as a result of our failure to advance ourselves. We have had opportunities, and we have so far failed to take advantage of them.

'Let me tell you what I think,' began Mr Tembo, throwing everyone in the staff room a troubled look of appeal. Everyone was now silent. They gazed fixedly back at him with eyes registering desperation, frustration and a consciousness of a shared doom. They sunk resignedly in their chair, listened without much interruption, and moved their heads up and down in agreement. When he had finished, someone reacted and said:

'I think what Mr Tembo has said is what we must do. We need to join hands together and say to our union leaders: You people have failed to negotiate for our better conditions of service, now it's our turn to react: we shall no longer go to work!'

There was a general consensus from everyone, and Besa searched their sombre faces: faces of educators, faces of destitution, and faces of bereavement.

'If we go on strike we shall place the Union in a precarious position. Negotiations over our conditions of service are still going on with the Government, and no dispute has been declared to justify a withdrawal of labour on our part. The best we can do is waiting patiently for the outcome and the white paper. After that...'

'What do we eat as we wait for them to dispute?' a teacher observed. 'You see, it's all right for the union and government leaders to spend a year or probably more talking and enjoying allowances. But as they discuss teachers are starving!'

'There's another consideration,' the previous speaker persisted. 'If we act as teachers here and in other schools want – if we go on strike, our pupils will miss lessons...but our profession demands sacrifice since without education –'

'Wait a minute, sir!' another interjected. 'The present salary scale of an average teacher in Zambia is already more than a sacrifice. To demand more from us is the same as passing a death sentence over public workers. Perhaps those who should sacrifice are managers and politicians – not us!'

'Don't you care about the children?'

'We all care, but you can't teach well if you're living in poverty. You should know this too well!'

'Also,' another added, 'we must accept that a decent and living wage is a right. Teachers can't go on being exploited. How do you survive on a salary just enough to buy a bag of mealie meal and a few basic necessities? This only means one thing: Government does not respect the dignity of its workers. On the other hand, since our work is contractual we need not feel any obligations to anyone. We must work as we earn!'

'That sort of attitude will destroy our country.'

'And being unrealistic will not help us either...We need to accept the fact that if Government is not prepared to invest in the education sector and instead misappropriates public funds on things which don't work, it is not our fault. Everyone has a duty to develop the country, but there are limits. If an employer refuses to pay well, an employee reserves the right to withdraw his or her labour and terminate the contract. Education is the key to economic development – yes, but the Government doesn't seem to understand this.'

'They have budgetary limitations.'

'What budgetary limitations?'

'Our internal revenue collection base is not sufficient to support a good budget. External sources of funds are also limited – and we mustn't forget that a large chunk of our capital resources goes to the serving of debts and the balance of payments.'

'In short you are suggesting that teachers shouldn't go on strike?'

'I want us to wait until the union tells us what to do.'

'If we do nothing Government will do everything possible to keep negotiations going on forever until nothing tangible is reached. We shouldn't also forget that the kwacha is continually being devalued against all major currencies so that, assuming an agreement was reached, we would have had no meaningful increment!'

'Apart from that,' added another teacher, 'there is a question of income tax. Take the rate of devaluation of the kwacha into the bargain and tell me what you get!'

'You get peanuts,' replied someone disgustedly. 'Everything goes into tax.'

The debate went on without the staff ever reaching a common ground. Other subjects such as work incentives, allowances, pension and Government bureaucracy crept in and, by the time the meeting was declared over, nobody could claim having full knowledge of what the teachers had generally agreed upon and what they would do next. What was obvious, however, was that everyone was frustrated with their condition of service.

Besa boarded a bus in town and lunched at a restaurant Shantiee liked. Once or twice the familiar surroundings induced a momentary vision of the girl sharing a drink with him and smiling lovingly in his face, the subtle prompting and knowledge of her every gesture so real to him now. Shutting his eyes for an instant, he saw her lying with him in her bed: she kissed with passion, drawing his tongue as she moved her soft palm over his back in small circles, groaning happily when he touched her most sensitive spots. Guiding him between her moist thighs the girl would coil her legs and arms round him and urged him on, gasping and echoing his name incoherently when he brought her to an orgasm. Thrilled by joy and contented – she would say: 'Thank you, darling,' and then fall asleep in his arms. But the vision vanished, and Besa hurt from the barrenness in his life. A lonely, miserable young man, a portrait of the poor or those with feeble prospects.

He paid the bill and found himself window shopping along Cairo Road, among an assortment of people loosed upon the streets. There were some idlers, beggars, vendors, lepers, cripples, shoppers, tourists, prostitutes, vagabonds, lunatics, delinquents and imbeciles crowded about the corridor length. At the moment he crushed into a blind man clasping a begging bowl and bore an angry retort: 'Can't you see where you are going, you dog?' roared the incensed man. He shoved Besa to one side. 'God gave you eyes to see but you don't use them!' He apologised very clumsily, yet the man dismissed him with a wave of his hand and spat on the floor with distaste. Humiliated and subdued, the young man moved off from the scene and dreaded stepping on someone's feet again. He pondered a moment: 'These people's movements are frozen like statues caught in various acts and attitudes peculiar to their circumstances, and they appear vulnerably exposed to the reach of thought. What do their faces carry?' He peered at them, and they were long columns of black ants trapped between the extremities of the light and the dark, a dispirited species crushed under by the harsh realities of a dying economy...by the final stroke of the anvil.

Besa passed some time reading the days papers in the British Council Library. He flipped through the *Times of Zambia*, the *Daily Mail* and the *National Mirror*, respectively, and as might be expected in a country where personality cults were a rule, the front pages of these publications captured 'wonders and works of the President and the Party', but confined real issues to small print between pages where such could very easily be passed over. On the other hand there was, in the *Times of Zambia*, a courageous writer who dared grumble about the 'ailing economy plunging headlong into a pit.' Citing social and economic indicators such as the rising levels of social insecurity, crime, poverty and unemployment, the author paused a simple basic question: 'Is there hope for Zambia's economic woes?' and offered suggestions no one in the Central Government would take seriously, despite the merits of the analysis. What was the relevance of numerical data to followers of Beyani (and there were many such!) who reasoned with their bellies and disputed facts with commands, threats, emotions and an appeal to religion? Besa gaped at a picture of the President flanked by Government Officials and Party cadres – and *there* was the man of the moment, quick to tears when occasion demanded him to show that he was equally affected; swift of foot when unpleasant facts required him to stamp over them and prove that some fears were unfounded, and so persuasive in the art of rhetoric that the severest of critics were left reeling and convinced.

He smiled at a letter by a pastor who defended 'the gift of speaking in tongues' in the National Mirror. 'Actually', wrote the man of God, 'the gift of speaking in tongues comes from the Holy Spirit. In 1 Corinthians Chapter 12 verse 10 we read: "To another [the Holy Spirit gives] the working of miracles; to another prophesy; to another divers kinds of tongues: to another the interpretation of tongues..." And again we read in 2 Corinthians Chapter 14 verses 2, "For he that speaketh in an unknown tongue speaketh not unto men, but unto God: for no man understandeth him; howbeit in the spirit he speaketh mysteries..." Therefore, I am not surprised that some unbelievers doubt the existence of speaking in tongues. But the Bible clearly *proves* this to be so...' And Besa asked: 'What constitutes proof?' yet allowed that for some deeply religious shadows, images, analogies and mysticism of sense passed for reason to believe, and they might be quite right.

On the international scene, humanity performed a balancing act in which racial conflicts, earthquakes, floods, wars, poverty, pollution, disease, crime, terrorism, drug trafficking and other pestilence shaped the course of human comedy. Africans called for stiffer United Nations sanctions against the White – minority rulers in South Africa; the Libyan leader Muammar Gaddaffi said, 'The United States of America is an enemy of mankind;' the Saudis were worried about the escalating tension in the Gulf; an earth quake devastated Mexico; the Chinese Government was charged with human rights violations by Amnesty International; the international community was deeply concerned about the effects on the environment of a nuclear disaster in Russia; American researchers probed deeper into the complex link between amino acids and the DNA and RNA molecules, and Europe expressed fears that a United Germany would not perhaps guarantee the future of peace on the continent. 'The horrors of the past are still alive,' argued one critic.

As for sports... – Besa suddenly looked up as someone knocked lightly on the table. Of all people he least expected to meet, Washaama towered over him with an expression of bewilderment on his face.

'I didn't think I'd see you soon,' he said and sat down. 'Where have you been?'

'I have been around,' Besa answered with a smile. 'How are you?'

'I am okay,' replied the civil engineer. He fixed Besa a look of reproach: 'You don't know how much embarrassment and worry you have caused me and Shantiee. Why haven't you cared to keep in touch or at least tell us where to find you?'

The historian refused to answer.

'I met your fiancée again the other day, and the poor girl doesn't understand what's going on.'

'Shall we go outside?' Besa suggested and stood up. 'You're getting worked up and we mustn't make any noise.'

Washaama fumbled in his pocket and produced a car-key. 'Wait for me in the yellow Toyota pick-up with a Telka Construction logo on it. The car is at the far end of the parking area. I will join you in a few minutes.'

'Where are you off to?'

'Upstairs to see my new girl friend. She works here as a programmer.'

'Is she someone I know?'

'I doubt it. By the way, it's good to see you again!' And off he went upstairs.

Besa stepped out of the Library with a clipboard held under his armpit, and for a moment looked from left to right. He spotted the Toyota pick-up without any difficulty, hurried across to the opposite side of the parking area, and waited in the driver's seat. Then as if from nowhere, a throng of youths suddenly clustered round the car with brushes, cloth and buckets of water: 'Can we wash your car, boss?' one of them asked politely. 'You can't be seen moving around with all this dirt on your Toyota. It should look clean!' They were about a dozen of them – unkempt, hungry and seeming somehow restless. 'Should we start work, boss?' they chorused hopefully.

'I am afraid – no. Maybe some other time,' he said sympathetically.

They lingered on for a while and eyed him with hatred, and then they trotted off to another prospective client.

'You've got yourself some nice place,' Besa complimented Inutu, Washaama's girl friend. They were in her beautifully, furnished two bed roomed flat in Kabulonga, talking over drinks in the late hours of the afternoon. The walls of the living room were adorned with elaborate Zambian paintings and masks fashioned out of bark and stretched over frameworks of sticks and painted with resin. Other works of art included wooden sculptures of animal and human figures in varying thematic contexts, and carved wooden stools and boxes for storing things. Their drinking "glasses" were, in fact, an exquisite creation carved in wood and featuring geometric patterns of an interwoven continuum of lines. The cups were shaped like human heads joined together and used for drinking with guests.

'This is fantastic,' he repeated, admiring a wooden sculpture of a male with a large concave oval head attached to a tiny body. The artist had made the facial features of the erect human figure more detailed and pronounced, thus rendering the fury concentrated in that face even more obvious.

'Inutu is an art fanatic,' Washaama smiled affectionately. 'She collects everything which strikes her as artistic – from children's toys to some of the most complicated forms of artefacts which would say nothing to you. You should see the damage she's done to my bathroom in Thorn Park. She's painted things on the walls that are certainly crazy, but you won't stop wondering – what is this?'

'You lie,' said the girl with a grin. She rolled her eyes and gave her boy friend by her side a special glance of adoration, then instinctively began to trace patterns over his thigh with her slender palm. A simple gesture, no doubt, but one which was fraught with meaning and conveyed to the beloved a voluntary flow of her life being lavished on him, an intimate act the essence of which was real and unconditionally given.

'You're shy, sweetheart,' said Washaama with much passion in his voice. He beamed at Besa and asked: 'What do you think of us? Don't we make a fine couple?'

'What do you expect me to answer?' he laughed.

'Really, Washaama,' put in Inutu, smiling. 'What do you expect him to say?'

He gave his shoulders a nonchalant shrug: 'Anything.'

'*Anything?*'

'Yes, why not? After all, -'

'If you don't keep quiet, Washaama, I shall go away.'

He gave a slight gasp, but remained quiet. There was a disconcerted look on his face.

Besa said cheerfully, changing the subject,

'How's life, man?'

'O, life!' Washaama exclaimed. He had already recovered his good humour. 'Life is fine. I have a good flat, I have a nice car, I am well paid, and I have a beautiful girl friend. I am not complaining. I have everything I need.'

'That's good.'

'What about you?'

A brief silence followed.

'Things are not all that good. I have a few problems.'

'For example?'

'I work as a teacher at Lusaka West Boys School – and this is my third month there – but I don't draw a salary nor receive any allowances. I work for nothing, so to speak.'

'Is that true?'

'It is – though I am not the only one. There are hundreds of new graduate teachers from University and colleges who are still not on Government payroll. We're told that it'll be some time before we begin drawing our salaries.'

'That's impossible,' cried Inutu in astonishment. 'How does one live?'

'I don't know.'

'How are *you* surviving?' wondered Washaama, staring gloomily at Besa.

'I wake up every morning and meet the day as it comes. I make small plans to be accomplished within a day and refuse to look into the future. I live a day at a time.'

'I meant, do you have money?'

'Not anymore. My account is very low and I might soon be forced to borrow.'

'Do you have a home?'

'Yes, Washaama. I do have a home. I live in Chawama.'

'Chawama?' He winced painfully. 'You can't live in a slum!'

'Why not?' he laughed. 'Lots of respectable people are living there happily and I am beginning to like the place. Look, boy, don't worry about me. I'll be fine by myself.'

'Maybe you should consider leaving your job before it is too late,' suggested Inutu. 'You can't stick to something that doesn't help you stand on your feet. You're risking your life.'

'I agree. You have to quit teaching and find a better job that pays well. I can help you look around for something. I know some guys who could push things and it wouldn't take a month.'

'I am not quitting the teaching profession. I shall hang on for a bit.'

'But surely, Besa,' Washaama protested, 'you can't hang on to a job for which you are paid *nothing*. As a teacher you'll always be poor and miserable. You've got to try something different like the banks. You have a good degree and you could start as a management trainee and climb to the top.'

'There is also another way,' offered Inutu. 'If teaching really means much to you, you could try working in South Africa, Australia, and Botswana or anywhere outside the country. Conditions there are better and Zambian teachers are in high demand in many countries. They are making money.'

'If you were in South Africa, for example,' Washaama nodded, 'not only would you earn good money but also find time to pursue your studies. You could do your master's degree and even go for a Doctor of Philosophy degree and work there as a researcher, consultant or lecturer. I can't countenance the idea of seeing you live like a pauper struggling to make ends meet. You are an intellectual, Besa, and there are very few like you. It would be very unfortunate if you were to spend your energies and mental resources on petty things like how best to save for a pair of shoes or when is the next meal coming. Your mind is above such trifles and you owe it to yourself and to the world to give your life to the most fundamental realities and not to the demands of the belly. Poverty brings no virtues!'

'I appreciate your concern, my friend,' Besa replied after some time. 'However, I have chosen the teaching profession with all its limitations because this is what I want. I certainly do not wish to live in poverty, but at the same time I believe that these are the right conditions in which to make myself useful.'

'What about Shantiee?' Washaama said. 'You are not suggesting that you'll subject her to these intolerable conditions such as face teachers and public workers?'

'I have given her much thought,' he confessed, 'and I am afraid our relationship might take a different turn. I love Shantiee very much, yet I feel she deserves a better life than the one I can offer her at the moment. She has never experienced a life of deprivation and I would like to spare her that, I don't want her to make any sacrifices for me.'

'Could this explain why you have been avoiding her lately?'

'Yes, but there's more to it than that. Do you remember our discussion at University about cargo-mentality? There were four of us: you, me, Nalumino and Sichone.'

'I don't remember.'

'We were analysing Ayi Kwei Armah's book, *Fragments*, in which an individual for whom wealth and social status mean nothing conforms to society where practical ideas for change are belittled.'

'Yes, now I remember.'

'And we discussed how, in a country which accepts corruption and inefficiency as the norm and elevates social titles and the outward shows of ornaments, he who sees beyond such exteriors and stands up for an ideal is bound to be alienated by his own people.'

'I remember that very well.'

Besa remained quiet for a moment, and said with authority:

'In the Zambian context, the cargo-mentality finds its precedents in our historical roots. At the dawn of independence there were about a hundred graduates[42], and these fortunate individuals took over senior government posts and enjoyed all the privileges which went white-collar jobs; fat salaries, allowances, loans, mansions, a fleet of cars and so on...Remember also that the larger bulk of the population were illiterates or labourers without any skills. The co-

lonial government's education policy was to offer African Natives
an inferior kind of education so that Blacks could not compete with
Whites. Education, therefore, came to be perceived as the surest
passport to social mobility, especially university education. A graduate was a chief or miracle worker in whom the cargo-mentality
was actualised. Through the power of the pen poverty and nakedness were defeated. Yet at the same time, remember that the value of
education, in the minds of our people, has never really consisted in
the advancement of knowledge and putting that knowledge to work,
but in the ability of the educated to speak good English and acquire
wealth and a social standing.'

Inutu and Washaama glanced uncomfortably at each other.

'I now wish you to contrast this with the following gloomy picture,' Besa went on resolutely. 'Excepting very rare cases, the graduate from University is no longer the disembodied spirit who com-
mutes between the land of plenty and the concrete demands of his
people. He is no longer the god who, with the mere flick of a hand
or movement of lips, summons his strength to the utmost and gives
free course to transformations of many a kind. Instead, he is a god
whose powers have shrunk considerably, a god whose feet cannot
outrun the pursuit of misfortune...as devotees, anxious concerning
their distressful state, pile prayer upon prayer and evoke frenzied
torrents of tears without cease.'

He surveyed his friends for a while, and said in a less forceful
voice:

'It is a great paradox I am in. My parents and relatives expect
me to help them now that I have completed my studies, but I cannot
fulfil all their dreams. My life yearns for the company of children
impatient to learn, but teaching offers me no prospects but fright.
My heart always longs to be with Shantiee, yet the kind of life I am
leading causes me to hesitate. I feel confused.'

'Listen, man,' said Washaama. 'Whatever situation you are in,
you've got to see Shantiee. She's dreadfully worried because you
have been out of touch for at least five months! This is an awful lot
of time, and she's very disturbed and doesn't know what to do. But
she says nothing has changed since. She loves you and will stay engaged to you unless you tell her to the contrary. You've got to see
her as soon as possible. It would be a very big mistake to lose a
woman who truly loved you. Unlike most women that contract relationships for financial gain and material support, Shantiee is neither
after your money nor any material things from you. There is *nothing* material that you can give her that she cannot buy by herself. As

a matter of fact the opposite is true: she has been giving you money ever since you met. On top of that her parents are very supportive of your relationship – particularly her father who is very fond of you. Do you want to lose all this?'

Besa guiltily looked down. 'You're right,' he said. 'I'll see her.'

'When?'

'Any time I am free.'

'Are you sure?'

'I think so. I'll see her soon. I promise.'

'Fine. I'll take your word for it. But if you don't see Shantiee soon then I'll tell her everything. It wouldn't be right to make her suffer needlessly.'

'There's another problem, though,' said Besa. 'My parents and some of my relatives – particularly my uncle and aunt – are opposed to my being engaged to Shantiee. They mistrust educated women and strongly feel Shantiee will turn my heart against them. They would rather I married from my tribe and they've already chosen someone for me.'

Washaama was indignant. 'I am learning this for the first time. Why didn't you tell me?'

'Didn't I mention it to you in Samfya?'

'Of course not,' answered Washaama. 'You said nothing despite the fact that as soon as we had written our final examinations we both decided to go home and were almost inseparable. We were there for two whole months – and all I knew was that everything was okay between you and Shantiee.'

Besa looked morosely down again – guilty and more ill at ease than ever before.

'Listen, man,' said Washaama. 'You and I come from the same village. I know your parents and relatives as well as I know mine. Your family is my family, and your relatives are my relatives. I have known you since I was very little. We had the same dreams - and your fights were my fights. You're like my own brother. Your pains are my pains.

'Now let me tell you something about Shantiee. Those girls from our village are *not* interested in you because they really love you but because of your education. They believe that with your qualifications they'll have a good life, and this is why they would not hesitate to marry you. Secondly, you have been away from the village for nearly six years. This is a long time in which to change – and you have changed. You don't know anything about this girl nor will it be possible to share your feelings about life with her. You need someone who can challenge your ideas, basic beliefs and aspirations. You need a woman who can build you up. Your wife will be your companion for life, and you owe it to yourself to choose someone who will be compatible with you spiritually, intellectually and emotionally. Shantiee is all these things: she's very beautiful, intelligent, educated, generous, patient and understanding. She understands your aspirations in life and she has supported them ever since you met. Most importantly, you've known her for all these years and she has proved beyond doubt that she can stand by you in thick and thin.'

Washaama paused and said firmly: 'You'll not ditch Shantiee for some village maiden because your parents say so. That would be foolish. Our elders say *umwela untu beema nao*[43]. You can't be very sure of strangers but of people that you have lived with.'

'I think he's right,' said Inutu. 'Choose Shantiee and weather the storm.'

Washaama stood up suddenly: 'I have a brilliant idea. Let's leave off this discussion for now and go out and see the sights. We'll hang out somewhere for dinner and come back here. Besa will spend the night at my place. I'll drive him to the school tomorrow morning.'

'Give me a minute,' said Inutu. 'I need to change into something more decent.'

'Hurry up,' said Washaama. He turned to Besa: 'Don't worry, man. You'll pull through this. Just don't make the wrong decisions about Shantiee. *Ninshi tukapusana.*'

Every day at five Besa woke to the ringing sound of the alarm. He would reflect for some moments on the demands of the day, venture outside to gaze into the sky as if to fathom a herald of hope within its depths – expectant of some small accomplishments within the few hours lying ahead – and then take a cold bath. After a dismal breakfast of scrambled eggs and four slices of white bread, he would walk three and half kilometres to school (sometimes drenched with rain), and spend the entire morning teaching. He would stand before a class with a piece of chalk in his hand, posing questions intended to pry into the thoughts and beliefs of his pupils, helping them see the paradoxes and inter-relatedness of ideas. In the afternoon Besa would offer extra lessons to some pupils at different homes and, by the time he reached Chawama by seven, he would collapse on the bed from sheer exhaustion. On Saturdays and Sundays, however, he surrendered himself to the one thing he loved best, the celebration of the word he fashioned in various forms, the fruit of thought that triumphed over poverty, affliction and weariness.

And yet Besa missed her. He might flee from the memories of their past and seek forgetfulness in a hundred distractions, but no matter how far he strayed and hid in lonely shades, she nonetheless gained on him and bound his heart with tenderness and hope, nourishing him on her feelings and love. 'O Shantiee,' Besa uttered in grief, 'I am unhappy and lonely without you! I miss our deep and lasting friendship, but love will not force me to you!'

Three weeks had passed since the meeting with Washaama and his girl friend, Inutu. Starved but resolute and purposed, Besa engrossed himself in teaching and offering extra lessons to make ends meet, holding on to his wits that were threatening to fall apart. He was heavily in debts: he had taken to drinking and frequented some of the most disreputable places in Chawama, often in an attempt to flee from the clinging shadows of his past. He had become a prisoner of the choices he had made. How was he to come to terms with the fact that the songs, dances and festivities made for the benefit of the *raised one* a long time ago were now meaningless? Would his people accept the logic that those who threw the seed into the ground did not harvest after many days? Besa wagged his head several times and thought, 'I couldn't have predicted it,' and buried himself in his work.

The young teacher returned to the staff room after his second lesson of the day had ended. It was 10.30 in the morning. He went back to his table and started going through two lesson plans and walked over to the History Department to check whether the teaching aids he had assembled yesterday were where he had left them. Mr Mwanza, one of the senior teachers in the school, pointed at a letter on the table. 'You have received a letter. It came yesterday.'

Besa recognised his father's handwriting immediately. He tore the envelope open and sat down on a chair. He started to sob after reading a few lines:

'My son,' Besa read, 'I hope that the Spirits of our fathers are keeping you well. We are glad that you have now found work. This has brought much joy in our hearts, though a misfortune has befallen our family.

Your mother is very sick. She tripped over and fell as she carried drinking water from the lake. Her spine is broken and the doctor here says your mother may not live very long. Or that if she does, she will be paralysed for the rest of her life. She will not be able to do anything that normal people do.

I have been advised by the nurses and doctors to take your mother to a better hospital but, because we have no money, there is nothing we can do. She is in much pain and she doesn't recognise anything around her. It is as though her breath has already returned to the world beyond.

We have sat as a family and decided that since you are now working, you could come home and help take your mother to a better hospital in Lusaka before it is too late. We ask you to come here immediately.

These words will be heavy for you, but I cannot make them any lighter. As a man you should be brave. For as long as your mother is still alive, there is hope! All of us here are relying on you to save her. Please do not delay. Come home as soon as you can. I am your father, Musunga.'

Besa dried his tears. He left the History Department and was admitted into the Head Teacher's office. He took a seat and said:

'Good morning, sir.'

'Good morning, mister Musunga. What can I do for you?'

'I just received some bad news. My mother is very sick.' He produced the letter and handed it to his superior to read. 'The letter arrived yesterday but it is dated eight days ago. I am scared something could have happened to her by now.'

The man put on his glasses and read the contents. His head shook in sympathy.

'I am very sorry about what has happened, sir,' he said. 'I am really sorry.'

'Can I go home?'

'Yes, you have my permission. You may leave immediately and stay for as long as it is necessary. We shall make alternative arrangements for someone to take over your classes while you are away. It is important that you should be with your family when they need you most. Your presence will bring much comfort to them.'

'Thank you. I shall hand over my schemes and records of work and everything to the Head of Department before I leave. I'll see Mister Dube at once.'

'I wish the school could help you with some money,' he said. 'It pains me to see my officers stranded like this. How do we expect you to work productively if the Government delays your salaries for months? How can education reforms work?' He removed the spectacles and stared into the ceiling without speaking. Then he asked Besa: 'Where will you find the money?'

'I have some friends who might be willing to assist me.'

'You are sure they will help?'

'Yes, sir.'

There was nothing more to say.

Besa left the office feeling a bit relieved. He spent some time with mister Dube and then boarded a bus into town. He had to see Washaama.

Grave and stately, he *imagined* his mother lying in a hospital bed, insensible and incapable of sound and movement, so that she might be taken to be dead. In another instant she *was* dead; she lay in a coffin with closed eyes. Relatives surrounded her and filled the air with their cries. 'Wake up, mother of Besa,' they entreated her. 'They are taking you to the grave!' Yet she remained indifferent and solitary, beyond the reach of love or reproach. Lifeless and transformed, her work was now complete. 'Mother of our children,' they cried, 'hurry before it is too late! You *can't* choose to live away from us. O mother, please don't be cruel. They are taking you to the grave!'

Besa got off the bus at a station in Katondo Street. Crossing the other side of the road, he threaded his way along Indian shops that were closing for lunch, unconcerned about people standing motionless admiring objects on display behind shop windows. Being a rush hour, traffic was usually dense and there were occasional accidents everywhere. With other pedestrians at the zebra crossing, Besa waited for the traffic light to change to 'CROSS NOW', and then hurried across Cairo Road as if they were pursued by danger. Another road to cross and he was finally at the Main Post Office building to make a trunk call to Samfya. He bought enough tokens and hurried out of the building to the phone booths. He remembered the Samfya Health Centre number very well. He inserted the tokens in place and dialled. After some delay the dialling tone started buzzing. There was a click and someone said:

'Samfya Rural Health Centre, good morning.'

'Good morning. May I talk to Doctor Katiiwa, please? It's urgent!'

'What's your name, sir?'

'Besa Musunga.'

'Hold the line.'

Besa held the line, clutching the handset with a trembling hand. He wiped perspiration from his face with a shirtsleeve and thought he might faint any moment. He heard the pounding of his heart in his ears and smelt blood. There was another clicking sound.

'Are you there?'

'Yes please.'

'Unfortunately Doctor Katiiwa is not in. Can you leave a message?'

'I just wanted to ask about the condition of a certain female patient who broke her spine about a week ago. Her name is Mumba Musunga. She's around forty. She lives in Mwense village.'

'Wait a moment.'

A long wait again. He inserted two more tokens and watched them roll in place. Looking about him, Besa saw traffic and people moving everywhere. He had lost the power to assimilate objects. His vision seemed blurred and vague.

'Excuse me,' the voice startled him. 'Are you related to the patient?'

'Yes. She is my mother.'

'You're calling from?'

'Lusaka.'

There was silence. Besa shouted into the mouthpiece:

'Hello! Hello there!'

'I am still on the line... I have made some inquiries about your mother...Unfortunately...she died this morning at ten-twenty. The body has been taken to Mansa for a post mortem, but I know nothing of burial arrangements.'

My mother is dead? My mother is a "body"? My mother can't die!

'Are you sure you have the facts correct?'

'Yes. For the past week we have only received *one* casualty case – a woman whose back was broken because of a fall when she was drawing water from the lake. She is a Catholic and I am told she has a son who is at the University of Zambia. She was asking about him. Are you listening?'

'Yes, yes,' he said, tears gushing down his cheeks. 'Thank you very much.'

'I shall inform Doctor Katiiwa –'

He hung up on him – he couldn't bear it anymore. His heart throbbed wildly, violently, and there was a terrible pain in his chest. Besa stared about him in shocked panic, too weak and dazed to call out for help. He crushed to the floor and fainted.

It must have been some time before he sufficiently came to. When he finally did Besa beheld unfamiliar faces anxiously looking at him. He was stretched out on the ground, in a puddle of water, and two men were shaking him rather violently. A strange, painful exhaustion had crippled his limbs. He tried to stir them to life but couldn't. He fought panic and felt those violent strokes of his heart again; a sharp pain pricking his chest made his breathing difficult. A transitory sense of being returned. He was slipping away!

A man asked him worriedly:

'Can you hear me?'

'Yes.'

'Can you stand up?'

'I feel very weak.'

'What's your name?'

'Besa Musunga. I am a teacher at Lusaka West.'

'Do you have friends nearby – here in town?'

'Yes. Inutu ...British Council. And Washaama ...Telka Construction.' Then he remembered that his mother died *today* – and his whole being protested angrily. *O for the unreality of it! There would be no life without her!*

'What's the matter?'

'It's my mother,' he said. 'She passed away this morning. Someone told me so on the phone.'

'Be brave,' they said. 'God will help you!'

Someone phoned the British Council and asked for Inutu immediately. Thirty minutes later she arrived at the scene with two men. Besa was rushed to the University Teaching Hospital.

Alone in Inutu's spare-bedroom, Besa focussed his mind on the fragility and absurdity of existence. If his mother had died, what was the point of living on? He remembered the first love, Musonda, and thought how dreadful her death had been. When he saw the mutilated body lying grotesquely on the beach sand, he could not imagine how someone he had loved could be so altered. Besa had asked God to strangle him there and then. Bewildered and hurt, he had tried to bring some meaning into his life by writing and studying but, even then, writing wasn't altogether self-sufficient and satisfactory because he lacked other things as well. On the other hand it was because of his literary activities that he had first tested the prison cell and shrieked from the flogging of policemen. He had believed teaching would satisfy him but, on the contrary, he had ended up in debts and faced a rayless future unless he changed his plans. At the same time, was it moral to accept a career as one's life-long vocation when one suffered the pangs of the belly? Teachers were right to demand better conditions of service, but Government was slow to act and you felt disheartened by waiting. Was quitting the answer? On the other hand, if everyone acted that way, how were children going to learn?

Besa considered his mother's death once again: what did it mean? She prayed every day of her life and believed that God was

on her side. Then she slipped and she was no more. Surely, therefore, God had let her down and brought suffering on her family –
there was no denying this fact. On the other hand it seemed as if
death ordered this life as everything was, without exception, imprisoned by the inescapable law of change. Saints or rogue alike suffered the same fate. Socrates, despite his inductive system, drank
the draught of poison and closed his eyes. There were other great
men such as Pythagoras, Zeno, Parmenides, Empedocles, Duns
Scotus, Copernicus, Galileo, Plotinus, Spinoza, Einstein, Newton, Brentano, Ortega, Heidegger, Gartry and many other names
who had left a spark of genius behind them and yielded their place.
Therefore, what was the point of going on if you already knew the
end? Were not plants, insects, birds, animals and other living organ-
isms also subject to the same brute force?

He thought of God and wanted to pray but couldn't. Besa was
two people: the one lying flat on *this* bed, and the other looking
down from a *distant* galaxy millions of light years away. He saw the
earth, then, a tiny negligible dot like a speck and wondered whether
anyone could possibly be concerned about its squabbles. The vast-
ness of the universe as compared to the earth was a very large ratio
so that by implication, the earth could never be more important than
the rest of the universe. In other words, the part was not greater than
the whole. Humanity was alone in the cosmos. Such a cold percep-
tion of reality, however, made him tremble as life so conceived in
mechanistic terms would be meaningless. Recalling Einstein, 'The
man who regards his life as meaningless is not merely unhappy but
hardly fit for life,' Besa closed his eyes and was suddenly trans-
ported into a dream world of sombre mists, hazy sights, changing
shapes and fantastic images, in which he bore witness to things both
ancient and modern, human and divine, and false and true.

At a graduation ceremony held at the University of Zambia,
Besa recognised the presence of distinguished faces giving a loud
applause to the dancing troupe. He nodded at Shantiee making love
to a Professor; he laughed at Musunga arranging his laboratory apparatus; he asked Sigmund Freud, whom he was seated with, to
please pay attention to the proceedings: Freud pinched him play-
fully and yawned. He saw Socrates in his robes drinking poison
with relish, and waved at the old man though it was his mother who
waved back, muttering something to Washaama in his ear. Besa
marvelled at some girls parading in the nude – among who was
the mathematician, Hypatia, whom rogues had spared in her char-
iot. His uncle ordered everyone to silence, threatening punishment

on noisy makers. Mister Bwaale stood on the dais and said: 'Comrades, we have assembled here to honour our dear graduates with certificates of excellence. As you know, the future of this country rests on the training of highly skilled young men and women who will shoulder the responsibility of propelling our nation to economic prosperity...At this juncture, allow me to introduce to you some of the invited guests from reputable universities around the world,' and he named Max Planck, Charles Darwin, Gregor Mendel, John Dalton, Gouel, Eilenburg, Szebely, Boole, Faraday, Kepler, Archimedes, Euclid, Newton, Descartes, Gauss, Mendeleev, Thomson, Heisenburg, Bohr, Moseley, Fermi, Boltzmann and not forgetting Galileo, who apologised for having forgotten to bring his telescope along. At this point, Uncle Bwaale turned to the Chancellor of the University of Zambia, President Beyani, and demanded to know why some graduates were not tattooed. 'They are all tattooed,' replied the potentate, citing Besa as an example. 'You will not blame my Government for anything. Every one of them was taken to the grove: prayers were said and sacrifices were made to our ancestors for the protection of the raised one...festivities were held in their honour, and the elders did their best. The fact that they have come this far – with the invited guests to witness this event means that all is well for our graduates.' Washaama interrupted the Chancellor and said: 'Your Excellency, Besa wishes to quit teaching despite my telling him that his work is gallant. What can we do to stop him?' And the reply: 'We don't care all that much. After all, it is cheaper to employ expatriate persons than locals. On the other hand, your friend has no reason to complain because teachers are well paid and he is a graduate. Do you suppose to tell me that this assembly, a summit of our dreams, is in vain?' At this moment Evariste Galois, the French teenager who died at twenty over a harlot but had made a reputation as a great thinker, regretted that some of the so called graduates were half baked and feeble minded, and to prove his point proposed a question: 'Can anyone of you chaps, by using Lienard's construction, obtain an approximation to the limit cycle for van der Pol's equation when $\mu = 0.1$ and $\mu = 10$?' 'Too difficult, sir' replied the graduates, and Evariste changed the question to: 'Can someone show us a method by which we can predict students' riots at the University of Zambia?' There was silence. Some of the graduating students complained of a lack of textbooks, which Descartes disputed by pointing to a copse or urging students to pose questions to nature, and someone cried out: 'Viva Unzasu! Abash capitalism and exploitation!' and the graduates sprung to their feet at once, overturning chairs, tables and benches because when reason gives out man naturally turns to violence as a remedy. Everyone fought each other as though it was a carnival, and the guests tried to scamper for their lives but couldn't. God had allowed the paramilitary police to open fire on demonstrators who tried to escape, and there was no exit! Archimedes shouted, 'Give me a place to stand and I will move the earth,' while Karl Marx and Engels laughed at the revolution of the proletariat: 'Strip them, guys!' they said, waving the *Communist manifesto*. 'Strip them and bash their heads!' Herodotus recorded everything. John von Neumann supplied the solution by the application of game theory to strategy, but Musonda, who had been quiet for a very long time and had managed to emerge from the lake without drowning, snatched the manuscript from him and shoved it in Shantiee's face. Shantiee smacked the other's right cheek and there was a fight. Besa left Freud and tried to separate them but couldn't. Tear gas canisters, stones, fire, glasses, bullets and groans flew into the air. A chopper flying overhead crushed nearby and exploded into a ball of fire. A pastor blamed the devil for everything and pleaded with God for mercy. God advised the pastor to read the papers and stop telling Him what to do. 'Humanity must fend for itself!' At this point all was helpless and confused, and the C.O ordered the Special Branch to give him twenty lashes on his buttocks. 'Because he thinks he has the right to self expression!' Besa was aghast and begged pardon but to no avail. They dragged him away, and then bound his body to a tree trunk. Shantiee laughed at his quavering limbs as he squirmed in terror from the lashes whistling through the air, while Musonda decided to fall asleep. A coffin was produced by the paramilitary and, all of a sudden, everyone chanted, 'Put him in, boys! Put him in!' Besa struggled to free himself from his captors, yet his cries were muffled and useless...They reached for his throat and tried to suffocate him and – he screamed.

'What's the matter?' said Washaama, pushing him vigorously. 'You are screaming and twisting.'

'I had such an awful dream,' answered Besa, a profusion of sweat over his body. 'They were going to kill me.'

'Who?'

'Everyone. I saw them all.' Then he asked quickly: 'What is the time?'

'It's sixteen in the afternoon,' replied his friend. 'But you must rest first. This was what the doctor advised. You're still under the shock.'

'Can you lend me some money? I've got to go home.'

'I know, man. I have worked out something already. I have some money for you and I'll drive you half way to Samfya first thing tomorrow morning. I'll get you as far as Kapiri Mposhi and then you'll board a bus from there. We'll start off around five. Is this okay for you?'

'Yes, man. Thanks.'

'There's something else, though. I think we need to inform Shantiee about what's happened. She'll never be able to forgive us if we kept this away from her. I could pick her up and bring her over her here so that you two could talk before we leave.'

'No,' he said. 'Not now. I can't face her now. She'll ask me a lot of questions. But you could inform her that I'd definitely see her when I come back. Right now I'd rather be alone.'

'Fine,' said Washaama. 'I'll explain everything to her though I am tired of the treatment you're subjecting her to. She deserves better from you.'

'I know but...just tell her we'll meet soon...Please.'

'Ok. Have some rest.'

'Thank you for everything.'

The journey to Samfya was long, wearisome and eventful, as though the gods had conspired against him. Travelling over bumpy roads for hours and almost caught in an accident involving a truck, Besa endured unnecessary delays at police posts and two breakdowns before the bus arrived home around midnight. Other passengers, loudly thankful to be well and safe, congratulated each other and could not but make exclamations of relieved happiness, whereas he did not care all that much. His thoughts were differently oriented. They centred on the pessimism felt by one whose world had crumbled under his feet, by one whose vacillating moods had overpowered his capacity to think. Who would dispel that palpable anguish evoked by the unbelievable loss of those dearly loved? Life was, indeed, a fearful dream, a series of connected events in which man were enfolded by the crashing pain beyond compare. Who would bring back his mother that she might scold and love him again? O that he might wake from this dream unscathed, and be able to feast his eyes on her presence! 'O mother,' he moaned quietly, 'you can't leave while I haven't done anything for you! How can you do this to *me*?'

The first signs of the truth dawned on him as Besa approached his father's house. He dropped the bag and stood stationary in the dark, assailed by an intolerable dread as he listened to a funeral hymn which bespoke of the human bondage and the mystery of death, while some hysterical shouts ringing in the air overflowed the village with dumb, grief and wretchedness. He picked up his small luggage and broke out into tears again, groping his way between grass thatched houses with a heart heavily weighed and broken by an incredible pain. O that these desperate groans and lamentations would be quieted at once! That his heart, crestfallen and consumed by agonies, would see some solace in speaking to her who had cared for him always, even for a single moment! Yet the sounds of mourning persisted and became clearer with each step, the words of the hymnal plunging his soul with their terrible meaning that blighted his hopes.

> Ilyo ipenga likomfwika
> Ilyakwita abomi na bafwa,
> Takwakabe ukubutuka:
> Shalenipo ine naya.

> Pamilomo ya cilindi
> Ndeshalikapo ifibusa,
> Imfwa yamfumwa pa calo:
> Shalenipo ine naya.

Besa hobbled along in the night, sobs gurgling freely from his throat. He reached his home at last. He looked confoundedly at the lighted, grim faces of mourners gathered round a fire outside the house, went in as in a trance, dazed between bewildered incredulity and frenzy. The bag slipped out of his hand.

They tried to restrain him but he managed to shake them off. Overtaken by bereavement, rage and pain, Besa made his way into the crowded, living room and knelt by the bed where his mother lay. He grasped her hand and gazed imploringly into her face – she would not look back. Her eyes remained closed, her features distant and aloof, and he was suddenly astonished that her expression should be so indifferent even to *him*! So near was he to her and yet so far away – for great spaces stretched between them! – that he felt utterly grieved: this unhoped-for tearing of sweet affection exhausted and tortured his heart, so he wept convulsively until they took him away.

From this moment on, he writhed and reeled in the regions of sorrow in which the senses refused to function. It was a gruesome

world unvisited by whisperings of hope and comfort, a solitary delusion in which only agony prevailed. O that he might free from the
hurt in his heart, that he might flee and seek flight or deliverance
upon a thousand wings! And yet he was numerically one – inseparable from the feelings he longed to wish away – rootless, exposed,
orphaned and emotionally wrecked.

He spent the night sprawled out on a mat by the funeral fire just
like other mourners had done. The sun had now risen in the east and
was slowly arching across the cloud-studded sky. More and more
people were flocking in to pay their last respect. As wails filled his
ears and some women prostrated themselves on the ground, Besa
was struck by a sudden realisation that it was all over now. Disconsolate, worn and famished, he watched in muted misery the men
taking turns to work on the coffin with a detachment that was un-
nerving. The choir sung with hoarse voices. Chizindo, Mwape,
Maliya and Chisala looked on dejectedly but were too dissipated to
weep. Musunga was stunned and speechless. His hair was dishev-
elled and his face betrayed an anxious tension…while his clothes,
bedraggled and dirty, lent him an appearance of long suffering and
difficulty. A family spokesperson stood up and silenced the women
and the choir, and then began to speak:

'Before I ask one or two close relatives of the deceased to say
something, I should like first to thank most sincerely everyone
mourning the death of our mother who has departed from our midst.
You left your homes and works so that you might be united with us
in pain and suffering, so that you might lessen the burden that death
always brings on the shoulders of those left behind. Let me also
thank the choir and the men of God for their songs and words from
the scriptures. You have calmed our hearts with promises of eternal
life and the triumph of the cross. He who assumed the aspect of man
defeated death through the resurrection, so that as believers and im-
itators of Christ we would be admitted into paradise in which we
shall meet God face to face. Even though our mother has left us, this
is not the end: we believe that we shall be with her very soon.

'For those who may not know about our mother who has died,
her maiden names are Mumba Chanda. She is from the hill clan.
She is the second child in a family of ten, and she was born forty
years ago. She married early, and is survived by four grown children – one of whom has recently graduated from the University of
Zambia – and a husband, Musunga Fyonse, who is of the drum clan.
Our mother was a catholic and she followed the sacraments with
devotion and constancy. People who knew her well will agree that

Mumba Chanda Musunga was humble, gentle, generous and help-ful. Her home was a shelter to everyone. Unfortunately, however, the good do not usually live to a ripe age, as happened on the day our mother hurt her back as she and her daughter, Maliya, returned from the lake with potsherds on their heads. She fell and was im-mediately rushed to the hospital, yet the doctors and nurses could do little to restore her back to health because her spine was severely broken. After being in the clinic for eight days, our mother left us and returned to our Lord…This is a death that is in our hands, a death that has shocked and befallen us.' He remained quiet for some moments and requested Besa's grandfather, Mpundu Chanda, to say a few words, then took his place back on a stool.

'My relatives and my friends,' began the old man, 'you who have come to mourn me. I thank you all for the tears you have shed over my daughter, Mumba, whose sudden death has been astonishing. My heart is oppressed by thoughts and sadness since mother of Besa, who was the only remaining child I had, has also been reclaimed by the soil. It would have been easier to bear had she been sick for some time, for in that case we would have anticipated her going. Yet she was well until the day she fell. Who could have believed that she could have fallen on the path she has been using for more than twenty years? But I mustn't think anything. I have lost all my chil-dren including their mother. Who am I to question the thoughts of God? It is as He wished it. We can only accept that God –'

'It is not the work of God,' retorted a relative. 'It is the wish of those who hate us.'

'What are you saying?' his grandfather asked in bewilderment.

'I am saying that this death is not natural. A magic spell was cast on our daughter and she died because of it. The day before her fall, mother of Besa recounted a dream in which she was struck by light-ening. She went into the bush to pick indale leaves and some roots as custom demands, yet it didn't help. She was constantly fearful that something terrible would happen to her – and it did.'

'Are you suggesting that our child was bewitched?'

'Yes,' replied Mpombo. 'I am also suggesting that we should not rest until we discover the truth. We cannot just sit and do nothing. We too are children of elders.'

A cold uneasiness was thrown upon the crowd, and there was a delicate tension. Another relative begged pardon and rose to his feet.

'My fathers and my mothers,' he started with humility, 'the words that are now being said openly are heavy and mustn't be uttered at all. What good can come from discussing witchcraft and revenge? Our sister has died a death that was allotted to her. She will never come back though we may decide to consult witch finders of great reputation. We should also remember that mother of Besa was a Christian whose love for God was very strong. Although she has died unexpectedly and unhappily, this was God's wish.'

'Are you telling me that the God in whom she believed is responsible for her death because He wished it?'

'No, that was not what I meant,' he answered Mpombo, unable to sense the contradiction. 'How can God permit something as terrible as this to happen?'

'Then you agree with me that it is the work of men who hate us?'

The other was now confused, since he could neither confirm nor deny. A woman came to his rescue, however, and said:

'Father of Mweela, we are all embittered by what has happened in this house, yet the bigness of death is burial. Therefore we should first rest our daughter and afterward see what to do as relatives. This is what I think.'

A murmur of agreement passed through the crowd. And then, with a Bible in his hand, a preacher stepped forward and began to administer to them, saying:

'*Let the day perish wherein I was born, and the night in which it was said, There is a man-child conceived. Let that day be darkness. Let not God regard it from above, neither let the light shine upon it. Let darkness and the shadow of death stain it. Let a cloud dwell upon it. Let the blackness of the day terrify it.* ...Words taken, my brothers and sisters, from the Book of Job. In the name of the Father, and of the Son, and of the Holy Ghost...Amen.'

'Amen!'

'Today, my brothers and sisters, something extraordinary has happened. We have witnessed a miracle of transformation in which someone whom we loved very dearly has departed from our midst. We have witnessed and felt very profoundly the anguish of Job in the eyes and hearts of all the relatives of the deceased. Overwhelmed by this terrible loss, we ask questions in order to understand what has happened. Like Job we curse this day because of the bereavement that has crushed us. However, when all is lost and pain overwhelms us, we must remember that God is on our side. Yes, God who gives also takes away, and He alone knows what is best for us! Let us now look closely at this man, Job, and see what lessons may be drawn from his life...'

Several days after his mother was put to rest, the distressful burden of unreality that had overcrowded his heart and rendered him mournful beyond solace began to ease and subside. Bent and broken-hearted still (vulnerable but not alone!), Besa thirsted for meaning in life and saw some reason to go on. He beheld the vista of his passage into the present in which everything became apparent and explicable, and remained strangely unaffected as the world around him discussed allegations of witchcraft and revenge, burial rites and widower's second marriage. Practical aspects of living were now uppermost in his mind.

His mother was dead and buried – this was the first fact. Secondly Musunga, bereaved of his wife and apparently overcome by melancholy, as well as the rest of his family, needed some financial support – was the second fact. How was he to help when the teachers, like other public workers in the country, were some of the most poorly paid people in Southern Africa? Should he embrace destitution and the deplorable conditions of all public workers in a belief that he was patriotic?

What ethical considerations would be most appropriate here?

Besa reflected that the choice he had made was the right one regardless of whether there was money in teaching or not. Opinion might shift and demean the profession a hundred times, but its intrinsic value and relevance would remain intact and unperturbed since nothing could be more superior to it. What was nobler than imparting knowledge to the youths that would take responsibilities of managing the country? On the contrary (in so far as the vocation offered little prospects in the way of social advancement), it was equally important to realise that in all sincerity sustaining one's material life was imperative and obligatory as everyone had to stand on their own feet. Given the present circumstances, however, his vocation could never guarantee this basic material existence and, by implication, actually threatened it. His colleagues at Lusaka West were now reduced to despairing beggars who extorted money and favours from pupils and ran to shylocks or 'bailiffs' for financial assistance. Not only had they lost the ethics of work but also the love for children and devotion to duty. They despised their profession, ministry, and country and did not mind missing classes. Instead – and who could blame them? – they were more concerned with managing their lives on a paltry salary whose value inflation eroded almost every day, and thus contributed to the collapse of educational standards in the country. Was quitting the answer to his problem, or was he to stay on and hope for change? How would the career and needs of his life be reconciled?

After much thought and consideration of various options available to him, Besa decided that the best course of action was to resign from the Ministry on the ground that he had never been paid since he started work. He would give the required three months notice of resignation and look for another job in a bank, insurance company, and non-governmental organisation or consultancy firm. With a better paying job Besa would be in the position to help his sister and brothers. He would help his father too, and he would ask Shantiee to marry him. They would raise a family and live in a city where it would be more convenient for both of them to pursue their lives. Besa would read a master's degree and probably work abroad for some time.

He was now contented with his new plans. He would miss his pupils and staff, of course, yet there was no better alternative. The compulsive demands of his life necessitated a radical action by which self took precedence. How was one supposed to live on less than thirty dollars a month? He had no desire to be rich, yet Besa could not fancy living an impoverished life such that all that one dreamt about was mealie meal and a few basic groceries. As a teacher, it was generally impossible to speak of buying a car, mortgaging a house, taking a life insurance policy, saving up for a holiday or planning for your children. The monthly wage was extremely limited and you were perpetually in debts. You reached a limit beyond which it was justifiably right to steal or engage in corruption, for no statutory order or legal instrument had the authority to judge you. Not even God.

Armed with such a resolve the historian spent the last days of the two weeks visiting, reading papers and speaking to Washaama on the phone. Each moment shared with his family reinforced the need to alter his circumstances forever. The reluctant droplets of oil Maliya used in her cooking, the rugs and worn shoes his father put on every day, the thatched roof of their house unveiling stars at night and leaking in the rain, the old rickety furniture in the living room, the look of dejection and delusion in their eyes as if to say – 'You are to blame for this,' and the gossip in the village about them – 'They have a graduate in that house...yet they beg for salt and other small things!' or: ' His mother was buried in a chitenge because they could not afford to buy a new blanket! What has education come to, if graduates are now walking on foot?' – all attested the fact that something had to be done. Mingled with pity and an understanding that education had lost value, the social perceptions thrust on him deepened his sense of responsibility and loneliness so that, for the first time in his life, Besa understood the existential meaning of social guilt.

Weary with gossip and the family's accusing glances, he took an afternoon away from home and idled at Samfya Holiday Beach as if he had meant to take leave of the place forever. He retraced his past: he recalled the spot where he had first met Musonda and her friend, Gertrude, and indulged reminiscences of their relationship and its tragic end. And he wept for her then, bemoaned her who had loved him well but whom life had denied the chance to see what the difficult years had made of him. Like a candle flame in the wind, her life lasted but a brief moment, leaving only these tears to remember her by. The hour of her flight was the death to all their dreams, for Muzo had returned to the home of shadows, silence, twilight and whirlwinds.

Besa found his way back home when the sun had gone down. Upon seeing him, Maliya gripped his hand and they conferred in the kitchen. There was alarm and anxiety in her young eyes.

'Our father, uncle Bwaale and aunt Chola are in the living room waiting for you,' she whispered. 'I overheard them mention Chama's name several times. Her parents were here in the afternoon.'

Besa did not speak.

'I suspect they'll force you to marry her. But don't make that mistake. Chama has a boy friend and she's not a virgin! They don't understand anything.'

'What else did they say?'

'I heard uncle Bwaale say, "A child whom we tattooed so that he might be protected against evil will listen to us. *The armpit is not higher than the shoulder.*" Were you tattooed?'

'Yes but that was a long time ago. Is there anything else?'

'Nothing. Be careful!'

'I will. Let me see them at once. I'll see you later.'

He left her there and walked into the living room, resolute and firm about his life. After greeting them formally, Besa sat down on a stool and politely said to his uncle:

'Maliya tells me that you were looking for me.'

'Yes, we have waited all afternoon.'

'I was visiting my friends and I also went to the Beach.'

'That is well,' they answered understandingly, moving their heads up and down. 'It is good to visit.'

For some moments no one spoke. A lamp revealed their partially shadowed faces exchanging glances. At last, his uncle cleared his throat and said:

'As you can see, my nephew, your father, your aunt and I saw it fitting to talk to you about our family and your future. It would perhaps have been better to wait a little longer till the funeral fire has been put out, yet we have been overtaken by events, and we don't know when you shall visit again. Anyway, we thought it would be just as well to inform you that the parents of Chama came to see us about your betrothal. They desire to know whether our intentions regarding their daughter being engaged to our son have not changed. They are worried because ever since we paid the dowry, our son has not been to their home. We begged forgiveness and promised to discuss the matter as a family. This is why we wished to speak to you.'

'We desire to know what to tell them after we have heard your thoughts coming from your heart,' his aunt said. 'You promised to think about it the last time you visited?'

A silence settled upon them. Besa wagged his head and answered:

'I don't want to marry just yet.'

'You may not marry her immediately,' replied his aunt with a smile. 'You shall only be engaged until the wedding. Chama will wait for you, of course, but we shall treat her as though she were your wife.'

'I can't marry her. I thought you understood this at the beginning.'

'Yes but we hoped you would change your heart,' returned his uncle.

'My heart is still the same: I don't want to marry Chama.'

'My nephew,' said he in a conciliatory voice, 'perhaps you do not comprehend the seriousness of the matter. You see, we as a family sat down and said, "Besa has grown – he needs a woman to live with after he has completed his studies, for it s not good for a man to stay alone." Then we asked ourselves: "Whose daughter would be suitable for our son to marry?" Your mother said, "I want Besa to marry into the house of Mulonda." After thinking about it, we decided that of all the three daughters Mulonda has, Chama was the best choice. She is a virgin, she is cultured, and she is generous.

'We also considered her family in general and how they would relate to us since every marriage is a union of two families. We also looked at the blood in their clan. They have never fathered albinos, imbeciles or lunatics. Their children have always been without blemish...And then, lastly, we saw that since our son is educated, he needed someone who knew how to read and write. Chama has completed school and we know that she has done well in her examinations...She may not have everything you might like in a woman, yet for us she is the right choice. Moreover, she is from our tribe and she understands all our ways.'

'And she is beautiful too,' added his aunt as a way of encouragement. 'I am certain that she will not cause you to regret. She will be a good wife.'

He held his peace, gravely and tensely drawing eccentric patterns on the ground with the tip of his finger, trying hard to be affected by their well-meant arguments. These were difficult moments – and yet, no matter how much he allowed himself to be persuaded by the loyalty to his family and relatives, Besa could never desert Shantiee for another woman and hope to live unscathed. Her heart was his heart, her life was his cult. The years together had moulded their consciousness of a common destiny, nor was he ignorant of her worth. How could he now shun the worship in her eyes, the music in her voice, the poetry of her body, and the critical influence of her judgement that was so essential to the world of his mind? How could he forsake the promise of their dreams and the inescapable logic that they were in love? Was she deserving of the destruction of these hopes and aspirations, or was he to yield to the influences alien to the quest for a more fruitful life shaped by the dictates of the abstract, that which was always certain and immune to change? That which always remained above the temporary concerns of the individual and the tribe? If only they understood his life's essence and left him alone!

Besa looked up from the ground.

'Uncle,' he said, 'I thank you for choosing this woman for me. I thank you very much for the trouble you took on your shoulders. On the other hand, don't you want me to marry the woman I love?'

'Yes, that is what we all want.'

'Why can't I choose for myself, then? Why can't I marry the woman of my choice?'

'Are you thinking of the woman at University, the one we have rejected as a clan?'

'Yes, that's the one.'

'I had hoped that we had discussed her enough for you to understand, yet it does seem as though our words fell on a deaf's ears.'

'I appreciate your wishes, uncle, but I have my reasons too. Besides, I don't love Chama. I love the woman you have rejected as a clan.'

They turned disappointedly in their seats, much too troubled to speak. Then his aunt cleared her voice and asked:

'What is the name of the woman you say you love?'
'She is Shantiee Perronni. She comes from Mufulira.'
'What tribe is she?'
'I don't know.'
'You don't know? How can you marry someone whose tribe you don't know?'
'That's not very important. I don't care about tribes.'
They stared at him in complete astonishment, shaking their heads several times. What seemed perfectly logical to him was shockingly preposterous to them. Shantiee was half-Italian and half-Bemba: what tribe was that?

'Look,' he said, 'perhaps I made some cultural mistakes like not consulting you about her in the beginning, yet the truth is that Shantiee is the girl I shall marry. She's the right woman for me.'
'Who are her parents?' his aunt said.
'Her mother is Zambian but her father is not.'
'Have you seen them with your own eyes?'
'I've met them several times. Shantiee took me home to see her parents on three occasions, and they do visit her at university once in a while. They are very good people.'
'And they accepted you into their family without being anxious for our consent?'
'They did not see anything wrong with their daughter being engaged to a man she loved. She could do as she chose – because they trust and respect the decisions she makes about her life. Because it is *her* life. *She* may choose what is best for her.'
Another long silence followed.
Besa's uncle said:
'My nephew, I do not know what has fallen upon your head so that you should refuse to see the wisdom in what we are saying, we who raised and educated you. A child who is well cultured must be slow to speech when talking to his elders, and he must do as they say since *fire surrounded by elders does not burn.* Could it be that you are now so educated that you may spit on the breast that fed you? Are we suddenly without sense – and you, a child who was born only yesterday have become wise and deaf to what we are saying?'
Besa did not reply – this was beside the point. His uncle was begging the question and appealing to authority, as if to say, 'Since we are elders whatever we say is correct and must be obeyed without question.' Yet it was precisely this blind obedience to authority and dogma which was totally incompatible with the philosophical awakening of his life. On the other hand (because they were tradi-

tionalists and conservatives) his family would never take the defiance against their wish lightly: the community could not be sacrificed for the happiness of an individual; he would not escape unpunished. He would be disowned and they would obliterate him from their memories. On the contrary, why not take the risk and damn the consequences? By the law of averages, what was the worst that could happen if they cursed him? Were parent's moral authorities on everything that concerned their children? Were they so knowledgeable and sure of their conclusions that their advice (like a trained casuist) could always be relied on and treated as infallible?

As they sat brooding in their seats, and as Besa gazed at them with defiant curiosity, he caught a twitching movement around the corners of his uncle's mouth, followed by a long sigh. Musunga looked dumbfounded and sullen – he had nothing to say. His aunt took in a deep breath and ended the long silence.

'Our child: the matter being discussed here is very heavy, so we cannot forsake our family respectability and honour as if we were fools. But if the dowry were returned, how would Chama and her family feel? How would people see us?'

'We would be a laughing stock,' answered his uncle. 'There would be an estrangement between our two families, as we would have caused harm to Chama's reputation. Other suitors would hesitate to approach Mulonda's homestead.'

'You should have consulted with me first before paying the dowry without my knowledge.'

'Perhaps. But in our culture parents are free to arrange marriages for children, and we did so with good intentions,' interjected his aunt. 'How could the young marry by themselves as though such marriages would not affect the tribe?'

'Marriages are important things,' his uncle rejoined. 'It is for this reason that parents and relatives become involved in such relationships.'

'I understand all your concerns, yet you should also appreciate *my* feelings. How can I reject the woman I have known for almost four and half years and contract a marriage with someone I scarcely know? How can I forsake the woman I love and call myself a man?'

'The woman you speak of is unknown to us,' replied his uncle. 'She is of a different blood and she could only bring harm if she were admitted into our family.'

'Uncle, someone's tribe and cultural roots are not as important as someone's heart. Shantiee is a wonderful woman and you have no reason not to want her. You don't have the facts – you're judging her unjustly.'

'Your mother and the rest of your family desire that you marry into Mulonda's house. If you are a child with ears, you will not invite misfortune into out midst. You will respect our wishes.'

'I should like to do so, my uncle, but you must also accept that I hold freedom in my hands. I may be your child but you must let me lead the kind of life I choose. I am responsible for myself and no one will stop me from choosing. I shall create my own life and bear the consequences.'

A great uneasiness percolated the living room. His uncle's eyes were down cast. His aunt wore a disconsolate look, while Musunga remained strangely passive and silent.

'If I had known that you could have the arrogance and pertinence to speak to us like this,' returned uncle Bwaale, 'I would never have brought myself here to be betrayed by a mere child whose life I have witnessed grow with my own eyes. I would never have born the spittle you have spat on our faces, nor would I have lifted my tongue to speak.' He stood up and announced without ceremony. 'Father of Maliya, I am leaving.'

'No you can't leave like this!' cried his aunt. 'We haven't finished talking!'

'There is nothing left to say. *A breasted woman is not shown a path,* and *a sweet potato cannot be straightened.*'

'*A child is an axe: if it cuts you – you will not abandon it.* Besa will see the wisdom of our words and apologise to us.'

'*That which eats you is seen by its looks.* If Besa could speak to us like this, what more can you expect? Already there are words in the village about this house. People are wondering, "What has *this* child done for his relatives ever since he started work?" His mother dies – and he lets her be buried like a dog in a cheap coffin. He knows the problems we go through, but ask him whether he has ever remembered to send us anything? He is like a seed that a farmer tends but fails to germinate. What good is there in having children who refuse to listen to the wisdom of their elders and neglect their clan? Is this the meaning of the white man's education?'

'Please don't lose your patience. Besa is young and inexperienced. He needs our correction and guidance. He is still our child.'

'What you have said is true, but Besa is not too young to understand our ways. We raised him in the path of our people, and he knows the roots of the tribe. He knows our thinking.'

Besa felt sick and baffled. He wished to say to them, 'I am sorry for what I have done. I'll get over Shantiee and marry Chama and make peace with everyone,' but it was already too late! His uncle and aunt had since left, Maliya was crying, and Musunga had nothing to say to her.

Oppressed by a consciousness of having done wrong, the young historian could not easily fall asleep. His eyes rolled over the walls and thatched roof of his room illuminated by soft light from a candle. He regarded the events of the day: a few acts and steps had collected right where he was, and he was these acts and steps, this frame of mind constituting a crisis in his life. What was he to do now?

A tapestry of a dream unveiled before the eyes in his sleep. His mother, who was attached to Shantiee, addressed her with a surge of pride on her face: 'See not scars on my back. It is I who bore the great one,' and the other responded, 'The graduate occasions transformations of many kinds,' and they danced, singing: 'This is unmistakably our chief. If you see another, he is other peoples'. A passers-by asked: 'What are you dancing for?' 'Our child will be a graduate,' replied Shantiee. 'We're very fortunate!' 'Yes, of course,' said the spectators, 'He who goes to the place of higher learning becomes a chief. You're very fortunate, indeed.' And they fell upon him and fettered his feet and hands with ropes, scrapping off his skin with oyster shells. 'You are hurting me!' he shrieked in terror, as he beheld masses of people demanding, 'Let's take him to the grove and prick his body with tattoos!' a suggestion rejected by his lecturer, Professor Mwila: 'What we need to do is analyse the problem as it stands. You can't bind an individual with your dreams.' Yet someone replied: 'What are you talking about? Do you think it is well for a child to return home empty handed? What has he done for us?' A woman said: 'Let him take a wife.' And a maiden appeared with an ancient manuscript and shoved it in his hands: 'What is in every book can build as well as destroy. Don't shun your navel name and your relatives.' But he denied that such were the contents of the text: 'The book you have brought is by a fellow named Aquinas, and it's about ethics...how to prove that an individual's allegiance to the State is not obligatory if the law is unjust...for in that case, unjust laws cannot oblige in conscience.' Yet at this point, everything seemed to lose their properties and identities, for time and space were frozen or indistinguishable from one another.

Thus when Besa woke up in the morning, his strength sapped by the horrors in the night, he was greatly perturbed and confused. 'What is happening to me?' he shook his head distractedly, reaching for the journal in which he wrote down some impressions of im-

portant events in his life. A thought crossed his mind and he scribbled it down:

*I have had another bizarre dream like the one I had at Inutu's
place. Strange sights, twisted figures and fantastic associations. A
total reverse of my normal experiences. How does one explain this?
How does one ferret out some meaning from the undisciplined me-
andering of the unconscious?*

*Fact 1: The dream content is derived from my experiences in
real life, both mental and physical.*

*Fact 2: The sequencing of events is tragic and centred on me.
There's a way the mind represents truth through distortion. There's
a suspicion that as far as being a graduate is concerned, all are
mistaken.*

A thought calmed him down. What was Shantiee up to these
days? Was she really missing him as much? Besa smiled at the prospects of seeing her very soon. He would smell her tropical odour, enjoy the sunshine of her presence and renew his commitment to her.
'I have failed you by staying out of touch, my darling, but you're always in my thoughts and my dreams. I love you very much!'

A tremor ran up from his feet to his lips: Besa lifted himself on
the elbows and saw his father close the door behind him. He took a
step towards the bed, pierced him with a strange heart rending look
devoid of any fatherly affection, and said gravely:

'Your uncle is here. He wishes to speak to you.'

'What about?'

'Wake up and go to him at once.'

He turned his head away and glanced at the wall for some moments, defiant and unbending, his jaws clenched. Besa looked at
Musunga and suddenly felt hostile: what do they want from me?

'I am not going to discuss Chama anymore,' he replied, 'and no
one will force me to do anything against my will. I am your child,
but even as a child I have the right to decide what is best for myself,
and no one shall take this right away from me, not even when they
have to kill me a million times.

'You are my father, and I acknowledge certain obligations to
you. But I will not do for you what revolts my conscience. I will
not hurt the woman I want in order to please you and my relatives.
I love Shantiee with all my heart, and my life belongs to her. How
could I throw her away just like that? No!'

Musunga froze into silence at once, too astonished to speak.
He seemed suddenly vulnerable and pitiable too, though the words
which issued from his mouth thrust deep into Besa's heart like a

sword, drawing pain and tears from his eyes: 'Now I know, my son,' sounded the words of fate, 'that you have betrayed this land, this Ng'umbo country, for which I am placing a curse on you, you traitor of my own blood.'

And like in a terrible dream where protection, comfort and hope had ceased to light his steps, Besa was again despoiled of home and a blessing, and he would never call his father by name again. Delusion, torment, dejection and dread had racked these moments so that, as he packed his things in readiness to go, he wept deliriously for some time since a certain part of him had returned to the land of silence, shadows and whirlwinds...and he was now alone!

Chapter 14

Concerns some uncertainties,
that is all

She lay propped against two pillows in her bed, muddled and steeped in forlornness, mourning and wishing for his return.

'I am lonely without you, my faith and my heart, and I am longing for you every day, that I may love and tell you all.'

Tears rolling down her cheeks, Shantiee beheld and met her beloved in her dreams: she stirred in her sleep. She opened her eyes. Besa had left their bed.

'What are you getting dressed for?' she asked sleepily. 'Please come to bed.'

'I'll join you later but right now I must do some work.'

'O,' she sighed, disenchanted. 'You never know what time of day!'

'Don't begrudge me the time, I shan't be long.'

She raised herself on the elbows. 'Sweetheart, it's almost midnight. Can't your studies wait until the morning?'

Besa did not reply. He mulled over the question with unseeing eyes, the sort of look he always wore whenever he was engrossed in thought. A strained expression of complete indifference.

'I want to write,' he said finally. 'Apart from that I couldn't sleep a wink even if I tried. I've got to do something to pass the time.'

'You sure love your books. Perhaps you ought to stay engaged to one of them or fuck your writings for a change.'

'Don't hold anything against me. I just need some time to put down a few things on paper while I can. If I don't the thoughts will go away – and Gauss will scream murder.'

'I hate to see you write when we're together in bed. It cheapens me, to say the least.'

She wanted to provoke him, to fight him and claim her rights, yet Besa remained silent and withdrawn. Shantiee turned her back to him, tears welling in her eyes. 'Just when I need him most, he turns round to read his beloved books. He doesn't understand me, really, he doesn't understand women.'

A hand fell on her slender shoulder, and her heart beat wildly in her ears. She made room for him and, snuggling up for warmth and affection, nestled her head comfortably on his chest, firmly holding him in her arms. She felt the touch of his lips on her forehead, and said she had been lonely without him. 'I am very much in the mood tonight,' she whispered. 'Are you?'

'You've got such a crazy mind,' Besa smiled affectionately, stroking her thighs and the flat of her back.

Shantiee gave out a soft moan. The full weight of his body crushed her underneath. She arched upwards to help him in, hungry for love as floods of passion threatened to overflow. She shuddered against him, her arms and legs moving in spasms, surrendering herself to a feeling so deliciously sweet and overpowering. There was more giving and gentleness than they had experienced before, as though the act itself had transcended the physical limits and assumed a spirituality of its own, a new awareness of self and being. Like twin selves inhabiting one body they had recreated and enriched their destiny through love, surrender and selflessness.

'Some coffee?' Besa offered afterward, moving out of bed.

In another moment the water was boiling in the kettle. They were sitting up in bed, drinking their coffee in silence (sated and fulfilled), very happy in each other's arms.

'I have done some Gauss too,' she began suddenly. 'Especially non-Euclidean geometry...The curvature of surfaces, number theory, theory of functions, probability and statistics. His thought is very difficult to grasp. Why are you interested in him?'

His manner had now changed. He was speaking like a lecturer:

'Mine's an epistemological basis of his work. I am interested in his theory of knowledge. I want to know why he thought that knowledge is not absolute. I also want to consider this in the context of what other thinkers have said. It appears that nothing is ever certain and perfect anywhere. Error, or what Gauss might call "the area of uncertainty", is rooted within us, and the quest for certainty lurches away from us every time, from the ancients to the moderns. Given this situation, therefore, what should be our attitude towards the material world if what we know of it, including our methods, is fuzzy, uncertain and remote from the truth – that is, if such a truth ever exists? What constitutes true knowledge, and why?'

He looked a little pessimistic about the paradox of knowledge, yet she hoped that one day Besa would resolve some of his fundamental problems and find peace to his restless mind. He was very intelligent, focussed and ambitious, though there were also times when he seemed utterly confused, disinterested and lacked the power for abstraction (the ability every thinker must possess.)

Shantiee's fancies were adrift. 'This is my man. I shall be glad to spend the rest of my life with him,' and she smiled tenderly at the thought. She would give him some beautiful children to spoil and adore. It would be fun to see them together playing with balls, paints and toys. When Shantiee remembered their estrangement, however, her excitement broke like bubbles.

'You look sulky all of a sudden. Have I displeased you in some way?' he asked her worriedly.

'No.'

'What's the matter, then? I thought you were perfectly happy and content?'

'I am but...' she hesitated, choosing the right words. 'I am not just sure about our future. I am scared that maybe all this will turn out to be something which will have been nothing but illusory. Just some beautiful romance with a boy and nothing more. I want to have a future for us – together.'

Besa lifted his brows. He stared at her with wondering eyes, neither very amazed nor exactly pleased. He took her hands in his palms.

'We do have a future together, and I share your feelings. I want the same things. I want us to marry and perhaps start a family. I want to live my life with you and make the best of it. I want to conquer the world with you by my side.'

She could not refrain from asking, 'What about your relatives? They want you married to a girl from your tribe.'

'Is this why you are upset?'

'Yes. I am afraid to lose you. You're very important to me.'

'Listen,' he said. 'I shall discuss the matter further with my relatives and see what they say. The most important thing, though, is not to worry because you very well know how I feel about you. I love you, Shantiee, and nothing will change this. I love you from the bottom of my heart.'

'What's wrong with me getting married to you, if I may ask?'

'There's nothing wrong. It's just that I happen to come from a place where traditions are still very strong. On the other hand, we'll want their consent to go ahead. I'll try to convince them that you're the best woman for me.'

'And if they say no, what shall we do?'

'We shall take a chance and wed and ask them to go to hell.'

Shantiee turned this over in her mind, and then shook her head slowly. 'Somehow it doesn't sound right. I wouldn't want to stand between you and your relatives as the reason you'd broken away from them. I'd feel very guilty.'

'What would you have us do, then?'

'I am not very sure, but there wouldn't be much sense in continuing with a relationship which had no support from parents. We need them, somehow.'

'Are you proposing that if my parents disapproved you'd break our relationship?'

'Sweetheart,' she said in a plaintive voice, gripping his hands, 'don't get me wrong. I love you and I want to marry you...I think of us all the time...' She bit her lips and looked wretchedly at him. 'But I can't see the future for us if your relatives rejected me as your wife. How would I relate to them? What would I tell our children if they demanded to see their grandparents?'

Triumph and tenderness started in his eyes. 'Dear child,' he said, 'if you love someone very much – the way I think I love you – then you have every right to stand up and defend what you love. If their morality were outraged, you would ask for a justice higher than that of man to judge and absolve you. But if you shunned the love of someone desperately loved, then you have no claim to be loved and protected by those that love you so well: you have spurned the invitation to the absolute and the divine.'

Drying her tears, Besa lowered his voice and continued in the way that made her feel very hopeful again.

'Every time I set my eyes on you, new vistas open up for me. I discover endless joys beckoning to me to give you what I have and what I am. You're incomparably larger than life, larger than me. You're the light of my soul, the vital awareness of who I am. And so,' he quoted John Bunyan, '*Come wind, come weather; There's no discouragement/ shall make him once to relent/ His avow'd intent/ to be a pilgrim...*You shall always be the woman of my life no matter what happens. I shall do my best to make all our dreams come true, and you will be my wife – I promise you!'

What could she say to the sweetest words such as these? The sincerity in his voice – the passion and veneration in his eyes – touched her heart and drove all her fears away. Inspired by an equal love – a strong readiness to risk and sacrifice her for him, Shantiee believed they would survive anything that might prevail against them. She would always stand by him and make him proud of her, although it wasn't easy to live with a man who wrote and lived essays. Besa was too much of a philosopher to care about the ordinary life. Living in a dream, he often forgot – in his shaggy, innocent way – the social responsibilities society expected him to fulfil. She was attached to him, nonetheless, and nothing mattered but him. He was the fruit of her love, the eyes with which she found her way about the world, the steps to all her hopes and dreams, the hands that pained and started tears from her eyes, and the reason to go on!

She lay presently in her bed, inconsolable and dissipated, whispering into her pillows:

'Darling, it's been five months since I last heard from you. You promised to keep in touch – remember? – Yet I've had no mails from you. What has gone wrong? All my friends feel that since you've been away too long, there's no point in waiting for you anymore. You've forgotten about me, so I ought to move on and find someone else.

'In a way they are right. You no longer care about me. Or how do I explain your silence? What am I supposed to do now? I am so confused! Yet I am still a fool in love. I *profess* the love I have for you, even as I toss about in solitary grief. I keep our memories alive and always warm, for I believe that I shall be united to you again. If I could touch you now…if I could…' till her eyes rested and closed in grateful sleep.

Thwarted by loneliness which stalked near and everywhere, Shantiee's will strove to go on (and she did go on), collecting the shattered pieces of her life back in place again. There were lectures, tutorials, assignments, labs, examinations and a research to do in her last year at university. The demands of each day weighed heavily on her consciousness, yet she was glad all the same. Work offered her an opportunity to hide her embittered self from the world.

She was at the General Reference when, as her gaze shifted in the direction of the catalogues to pause from search for data, Shantiee sighted Washaama with a girl leaving the Main Library building. She rushed after them at once, alert and momentarily thrilled – where were they going? – her senses enraptured by a reassuring sweetest of thoughts, that Washaama might perhaps have some news of beloved, and soon caught up with the duo as they descended the concrete steps in the afternoon sun. Her feelings became suddenly dispirited and ambivalent. 'What's the use of it all?' she considered in vexation. She was at the brink of tears. Her features sagged and drooped, and her voice had a quavering touch to it. Futility and pain! 'What's the point of it all? O my dearest, my hopes conspire with fear, my trust with doubt, my love with aversion, and I want to turn back and cry!'

'Hello Washaama,' she greeted him now.

He turned to hug her. 'This is a fine coincidence. Just now we were going to your room to see you. We've brought you some news of Besa!'

'Where is he? Is he all right?'

'In a moment, Shantiee. First you must meet my girl friend, Inutu. You two should get to know each other.'

Shantiee smiled at the girl. She was natural and very pretty. She
wore neither make-up nor ornaments, and couldn't be more than
twenty-five. Washaama's new catch.

'Inutu works for the British Council as a programmer. We've
known each other for about a year now and we're to be engaged
soon.'

'That's wonderful. Congratulations!' Shantiee said, offering her
a hand to shake. She immediately liked Inutu and hoped they would
be great friends.

'Inutu knows you from some discussions we've had about Besa,'
Washaama went on, 'so I need not introduce *you* to her. O, don't be
alarmed!'

'Shall we go to my room?' she suggested. 'We'll have a drink as
you tell me everything I need to know.'

She led the way to her place, throwing Washaama impatient
glances as he skirted around the subject of Besa. He seemed to be in
no hurry to discuss anything yet, so she decided not to rush him and,
instead, briefed him on some recent developments at the institution.

'We have lost a sizeable number of lecturers ever since you
graduated,' Shantiee said. 'Some departments are almost closing
because they are under-staffed. Others have to rely on part-time lecturers. Government under-funds the university.'

'What is your union doing about this?'

'We have a serious problem. The union is not as organised and
focussed as it used to be. There is a lot of in-fighting going on especially over union funds, accommodation and tendering procedures
for the lease of canteens and the Students Centre. Most of our leaders have taken to beer drinking and women. They abuse students'
funds and are corrupted by politicians who use them to destabilise
students. Some of them swindle female students who are desperate
for rooms – or sleep with them on the promise that they would secure them accommodation because they are in the union. It's terrible how women suffer! Others, like some officers at the Bursaries
Committee, are busy using every opportunity to enrich themselves
at the expense of the welfare of students.

'Apart from these problems students are divided. Some are Party
cadres while others are no longer interested in political confronta-
tions with the Government. They just want to graduate and leave the
country. They can't see any future for Zambia.'

'Would you want to leave the country after graduation, Shantiee?'

'I have thought of it many times. As a biochem student the chances that I'll find a good job locally are quite slim, so perhaps I ought to look elsewhere if I don't decide to work for one of my dad's companies. I don't know – and there's Besa, too. He says he likes it here so I'll probably stick around for him. We'll see what happens in a few months.'

She offered them snacks and some fruit juice, a sensation of unease trying her patience. Her armpits were cold and moist, and her hands were trembling slightly. Her manner fearful and restive, Shantiee could bear it no longer.

'Well,' she said, breaking the silence. 'Where is he?'

Washaama did not respond at once. He raised his eyes and began, guardedly at first, to explain the situation, thereby confirming her worst fears.

'I have met Besa twice since the last time I saw you. Things are not well with him. I think he needs help – especially your help. As I speak now Besa is in Samfya for the funeral of his mother who passed away three days ago. He was her favourite child, and he was very attached to her. The death of his mother has changed everything. Besa seems to be newly frightened and all the familiar things no longer appeal to him. The world has lost its lure and glamour. He has no zest for life anymore and his emotions are often suicidal. The deaths of Musonda, his former girl friend, and that of his mother, appear to signify betrayal and abandonment by people who were closest to him. What complicates matters, however, is the fact that Besa is living in squalor in a single room in Chawama. He has been living like that for the last three months. He's a teacher at Lusaka West but has never been paid a kwacha ever since he started work. He has lost weight and looks every bit like a loafer.'

'The first thing I noticed about him,' added Inutu, 'were his cloths and shoes. They were dirty and worn. I couldn't believe that he was actually a graduate from the University of Zambia until I listened to him speak of undergraduate experiences and the like. And he does seem desperate and confused.'

'When will he come back?' Shantiee asked.

'He didn't say, but I am in touch with him. The burial took place yesterday but he needs time to be with his family. I'll find out when I get the next call from him.'

'When he calls, please tell him I need to see him urgently. Tell him –' she broke down and wept: 'Tell him that *nothing* has changed. I love him and I want him in my life. I will not live without him.'

'I doubt whether Besa would come to see you even if he wanted to,' Washaama explained. 'If he were able he would have done so a long time ago. He loves you – yes, but he won't see you.'

'Why not?' cried Shantiee. 'What have I done?'

'You haven't done anything wrong! It's not your fault! I suppose the problem is that Besa has come to the crossroads of life where the expectations of graduates are crushed by the harsh realities of life. He quotes Armah's concept of cargo-mentality to explain his experience. According to his theory, society expects the educated to provide material wealth for their families and relatives, but this is what they can no longer do. The cruel economic conditions in the country will not allow it. How does a graduate feel after realising that his four-year investment in a university education has landed him a job for which he is paid *nothing*? He feels anguished and is in a constant state of guilt. Therefore, you and the rest of us can't share his world because we burden him with expectations. This is why he won't come to you: he's not prepared to offer you explanations or excuses about his situation.'

'I don't understand. Whether Besa is poor or rich is of no consequence to me. He's always been poor, anyway, but I've nonetheless loved him ever since we met. What difference would it make to me *now* if he were staying in a shack? All I care about is *him*! He doesn't have to prove anything to me because I *already* know what he's capable of. This is why I love him. All I ever wanted was his presence. I need him to be near me every time – this has been my wish. I don't care about his money or material things from him. I have everything I need.' She shook her head. 'I am very disappointed in him.'

They all fell silent. Shantiee stroked the ring on her finger. It was a very small thing, yet an important remainder in her life. She could neither discard the ring nor trade it for anything else in the world. It was her longing and her pain.

'If Besa won't see me then I will. Can you arrange a meeting, Washaama? I really have to see him. I can't go on like this. I've got to see him.'

'I am relieved to hear that from you. Yes – a meeting could be arranged as soon as Besa returns. I'll see to it.'

'We thought of inviting him to live with us in Thorn Park. He can't live in a slum as if he had no friends. He's also very disturbed so he needs people around him to help him accept what has hap-

pened. The death of a loved one can be very devastating...emotion-
ally,' said Inutu.

'There is another thing. Inutu and I feel that it'd help much if
Besa resigned from the ministry and found a better job. There are
lots of opportunities for him – he need only make up his mind. However, knowing Besa as well as I do he might resist giving up the profession. The only person who could influence him is you, Shantiee.
We want you to get him to see that teaching is not the only thing a
person can do. He has a liberal arts degree so he could fit in every
situation. We don't want to see him poor and unhappy. There's no
future in teaching in Zambia.'

'We discussed this subject once. He said teaching meant everything to him. He would never give it up.'

'If Besa insists he could also work outside the country where
conditions are better,' said Inutu. 'I have a sister living in Canada.
She's been there for ten years working as an accountant. If I asked
her to put up a friend looking for a job in the country she would only
be too glad to help. She understands what it means to work in Zambia where the value of one's labour means nothing.'

Shantiee was quiet again.

An argument had erupted between them about his career. She
had suggested leaving the country but Besa had refused to do so.

'I wish to work here. My services are more needed in Zambia than anywhere else. Why should I forsake my people and work
overseas? What will I have contributed to Africa if I chose to teach
white kids whose country is already developed?'

'Darling, you forget on thing: we've got to survive. We can't
live here the way things are going. Our country has collapsed. We'll
need to think seriously about our future. Would you like us to be
poor?'

He looked at her indignantly. 'You live above the poverty datum
line. I understand.'

'That's not fair. I just want the best for us.'

Besa paced the room for some moments without speaking.
When he turned again, his countenance had totally changed. An uncompromising expression had crossed over his face.

'As a historian,' he began, 'I have had the opportunity to sur-
vey the general development patterns of Africa since the precolonial times. If I have learnt anything at all, it is that history is made
by men and women who have a vision of what they seek, and the
means by which to realise it. Africa needs such people. We have
to change the exploitation of our human and natural resources for

our own good. Labour, minerals and other forms of wealth have been extracted from our lands and helped make Europe and America richer... One French traveller, after observing the devastating impact of overseas trade in a region we now call Zambia in the late nineteenth century, asked poetically:

> O tender-hearted ladies of Europe,
> as your white hands lightly caress
> the keyboard of your piano;
> as you play with your paper knife
> or the handle of your umbrella;
> do you suspect what blows,
> what tears, what sufferings each piece
> of ivory has cost the wretched Blackman;
> can you imagine the horrible crimes
> and atrocities committed in its name?[44]

'Like David Livingstone he understood the connection between white luxury and black misery. He understood the link between the demands of the industrialised nations for ivory and human beings on one hand, and the diminishing wealth of Zambians on the other hand.'

A grave intent look settled on his face.

'Every African who leaves the country to work abroad perpetuates the same problem. He or she collaborates in the destruction of their people for meagre short-term gains. The question of sending remittances back home as an excuse to live abroad is weak.'

Shantiee was baffled. She stood up to challenge him.

'I don't look at things that way. I have my own life to live. I just want a good life and surely I am entitled to such one.'

'You speak like that because you have no historical mind. You'll do everything to embrace whatever is momentarily pleasurable but destructive ultimately. Like some of our local chiefs who sold their own subjects into slavery for beads, beer, cloth and third rate guns, you're willing to sell your labour for a few dollars and the white man's recognition. You forget this fact: your labour as a commodity will have been exchanged for the wretchedness of your people. How will history judge us a hundred years from today? What sort of education will we have acquired if, as university graduates, we're ill prepared to deal with the legacy of our colonial past?'

Besa picked up a volume from the shelf:

'This book was written by George Simeon Mwase. It is about the life of John Chilembwe, a Malawian who led a Christian revolt against some white planters in British Nyasaland in 1915. To demonstrate the extent of African discontent, he urged his followers to "strike a blow and die" so that, once they were dead and buried, the white men would think that the treatment they meted against Africans was bad.

'You and I have a historical function to strike a blow and die. The forms of protest are different, yet the phenomenon of Western exploitation is the same. The question of migrant labour or the brain drain is one way by which Africa continues to be deprived of this human resource which would otherwise have made a positive contribution to her development. This must be stopped at all cost. Our perceptions must be conditioned by a deeply felt responsibility to alter our present circumstances. It calls for sacrifices and far-sightedness, and I believe it can be done.'

Shantiee walked over to him and put her arms around him.

'Don't be angry with me,' she said. 'I love you very much. Do you love me too?'

Washaama startled her out of her reveries:

'Are you going to persuade him to resign?'

Chapter 15

Concerns the triumph of truth

The morning dawned fresh and clear, after the cloudy, windy night had passed. Amid the garbage, disorder and ugliness of Chawama, there was yet a brutal attractiveness about the place that roused a certain affinity in his heart, a yearning for the scarred human sensibilities in their deepest forms. The public sunrise – those golden threads which united him to the ghetto in poverty, disease and destitution, entangling his feet in tears and shame – bade him onward to meet the day and carry on his shoulders the burden of his destiny, even as a hundred ills bore him reluctantly down, that he might despair and die. He chanted some lines by Rabindranath Tagore – that venerable Bengali Brahmin, poet and philosopher – as though he was a mystic making the last pilgrimage of his life.

Walk alone.
If they answer not thy call, walk alone;
If they are afraid and cower mutely facing the wall,
O thou of evil luck,
Open thy mind and speak out alone.

If they turn away and desert you when crossing the
    Wilderness,
O thou of evil luck,
Trample the thorns under thy tread,
And along the blood-soaked track travel alone.

If they do not hold up the light
When the night is troubled with storm,
O thou of evil luck,
With the thunder-flame of pain ignite thine heart
And let it burn alone.

Besa boarded a bus and reached school at half past seven. After exchanging pleasantries with some teachers in the staff room, he proceeded to the Head Teacher's office to hand in a copy of an official letter of resignation from the Teaching Service. The secretary, whom he remembered as Mrs Phiri, greeted him warmly and pointed a helpful finger in the direction of the 'Big man's door. He found himself in a spacious office crowded with pupils' textbooks, chalk, teaching aids and sports wear. The man in a grey suit was pleased to see him again.

'Please take a seat,' he invited. 'How are you?'

'I am fine, thank you.'

'Did you have a good journey?'

'Yes, sir.'

'How is the family getting on now?'

'Very well, sir. I think we have come to terms with what happened.'

'Good. We were very concerned about you. You seemed very devastated when you left. A friend of yours – a Mister Washaama came to inform us that actually your mother had died. As a school we would like to express our deepest condolences to you and your family on this tragedy.'

'Thank you, sir.'

'How do you feel now?'

'Well I am okay. I loved my mother very much, but nothing will bring her back. I have accepted this as a fact and I am ready to pick up my life again. I have to move on.'

'You're a courageous young man,' he said. 'Your pupils will also be very pleased to see you again and resume lessons with you. It appears that you have made a very big impression on them despite the fact that you have only taught at the school for about three months. You have the makings of a good teacher.'

'Thank you, sir.'

'As a matter of fact, we had serious problems when you left. Your pupils rejected the teacher who took over your classes. They didn't want him and they nearly rioted. It took some time to calm them down.'

'What did they find wrong with mister Ngosa, if I may ask?'

'From what I gathered it seemed your pupils had little confidence in him. They said his lessons were generally boring and that mister Ngosa was short-tempered and not as good as you. They said you understand the subject. Some parents of these pupils even took the trouble to come to this office to protest on behalf of their children. They demanded assurances that the change was only temporal – that you would take over again.'

Besa was speechless for some moments. Sentimentality was out of question, and there was no turning back!

'Sir, I am afraid that I am not going to take over from mister Ngosa. I came to place in my letter of resignation with immediate effect. I am stopping work today.'

'What?'

'I am...I am resigning from the Teaching Service. I'll not teach again – ever.' He produced an envelope and handed it to him. 'There's my letter.'

The Head Teacher was visibly taken aback. 'But why?'

'My reasons are contained in the letter. I've explained everything.'

'Do you mind if I read the letter now?'

'No, sir.'

He waited for some time, his eyes roaming from the portrait of the president to pictures of children in uniforms. There were a few sports trophies, too, glittering in the light, and large, beautiful maps hanging from nails by white cotton threads. An idea crossed his mind. He darted a quizzical look at the man and asked for the use of the telephone.

'Of course. Feel free.'

Besa punched the number and Washaama's voice broke through.

'Washaama, this is me – Besa.'

'Besa? Where are you?'

'I am at school. I came back last night.'

'Are you working?'

'Not really. Look I'll be at your flat in the late afternoon and we'll talk. I just wanted to inform you that I am back. How's Inutu?'

'She's fine. We're all fine.'

'Send my regards to her. I'll see you later.'

'One moment. Are you sure you're coming?'

'Yes, why do you ask?'

'You're in the habit of breaking appointments – that's why I asked. Anyway, we'll be waiting for you.'

'I'll see you then. Goodbye.'

'Goodbye, mwana.'

Besa replaced the receiver on its cradle.

The Head Teacher raised his eyes and let out a desperate sigh.

'Your reasons are genuine – I understand you, but the children truly need you! How will I explain to them? Who will teach them if you resign?'

'That's not for me to say. You'll find a way around the problem.'

'Don't you realise what this means? I was just saying to you that mister Ngosa had a serious problem with–'

'Excuse me, sir. I have thought very deeply about this matter. I love teaching and I hate to have to resign. Resigning is like the betrayal of my soul. But I can't help it. I've got to go. I can't work for the ministry anymore. I am fed up.'

'Things will improve and your salaries will soon be paid out to you. The Permanent Secretary gave me these assurances last week.'

'I doubt whether change will come soon in the Government machinery. But even if it did come the conditions of service of teachers would still be very poor. How would I fend for myself if I were perpetually in debts? How many of your teachers here can afford not to borrow money from their pupils? Where is the dignity of labour if one's salary is not enough to sustain one? What about my relatives and family who expect me to help them? Did anyone in the Government produce a cheque or anything when my mother died? Do you know how much it pains to see your parents who sacrificed so much for you live under a leaking roof? Do you know how much it pains to see your mother buried indecently because you're poor? Do you know that my own mother was buried with *nothing* but a chitenge material?

'I am not asking for riches but for a decent life. I want a meaningful existence because I am entitled to it. I can't sacrifice myself any longer. I have been living on borrowed money and I have reached a limit. It's time I put a stop to this once and for all. I am ashamed of the life I am living.'

Besa was still full of excitement by the time he was home. A huge weight had been lifted off his mind. The Teaching Service Commission would receive a copy of his resignation through the post in a week's time, and they would close his file and add his name to the statistics of resignations. As for the pupils and how they would react – well, that was not his problem anymore. He would miss them, of course, and he hoped for their understanding and forgiveness. Besa would always wish them well.

He spent the entire morning reading through the second draft of an unfinished manuscript titled, *'Tighten up your belts': A study of the social, political and economic crisis in Post-colonial Zambia.* The work was clearly unsatisfactory, as it required further research, yet Besa was still amazed by the spirit and composition of the script, often wondering whether he was the one who had actually created it. The volume was, however, his handiwork. It was the rainbow in which he had invested all the elements of unity even when his mind was crazed with pain, sadness, sorrow and gloom. Like Herodotus, Thucydides, Polybius or any of the historians before him, Besa was impelled to leave a statement behind him. However, what difference would this particular work make given the large number of books on the same subject lying on the shelves without being read? What debate would the work stir and what place would it occupy in the historiography of post-colonial Zambia?

Besa leafed through the first pages. Here was a brief discussion of Zambia's prehistory on the basis of archaeological and ethnographic evidence. From the material culture of the earliest inhabitants he traced the social, commercial and economic patterns of the Stone and Iron Age peoples, respectively, and then dwelt on the more powerful Bantu migrants from the Congo region. The latter introduced into their new settlement areas centralised systems of government built around the institution of king. By 1850 AD the most significant of these kingdoms were that of the Lozi, Bemba, Luapula Lunda, and the Ngoni who had fled from the Mfecane[45] in South Africa. Besa also mentioned the Portuguese, Arab and Swahili factor in the development and decline of these kingdoms, and emphasised the negative impact of slavery and ivory trade on the societies of South-Central Africa.

The penetration of Western capital (especially after the discovery of diamonds and gold in Kimberly and Witwatersrand in the latter part of the nineteenth century), altered the history of the entire region forever. Besa wrote of the British Imperial expansion from the Cape Colony through the British South Africa Company. By means of deceitful demands for exclusive mineral and land rights in exchange for 'protection', Cecil Rhodes' chartered company managed to subdue the people of Zambia and impose a colonial government on them. However, the exploitative character of the white settler regime inevitably gave rise to resistance, nationalism and demands for self rule from the British. Complete independence was granted officially on October 24th, 1964.

The main focus of the book was an attempt to explore factors that had led to Zambia's economic collapse, and these comprised many extensive chapters. Besa opened this part with songs of triumph against colonial rule, of festivities and great expectations for the fruits of independence. The mood was contrasted against the realities of the times: a critical shortage of skilled manpower, high illiteracy levels, a poor economic infrastructure, the liberation struggles in South Africa, Angola, Namibia, Zimbabwe and Mozambique (for which Zambia paid heavily,) the precariousness of the economy which was solely dependent on copper, and the integration of the country into the global economy.

The nationalist leaders had fantastic dreams of expanding the education sector, nationalising all mining activities, building a strong industrial base, diversifying the economy and stimulating real economic growth. Unfortunately, the gross mismanagement of financial resources, the cost of liberation wars, diminishing copper revenues, and rising oil prices in the context of the rising costs of government imports (among other factors), all combined to introduce distortions into the economy so that, by the mid-1980s, Zambia had started experiencing real economic stagnation and an inflationary trend which the central government could not arrest. The country's reserves were exhausted. The national debt from the International Monetary Fund, World Bank and other donors shot up significantly as savings of public workers and the value of the kwacha shrunk to almost nothing in terms of their overall impact on economic growth. Foreign currencies became scarce; prices fluctuated by the day; unemployment and crime rose dramatically, and public workers were reduced to pauperism. Sensing the downward plunge of the country, some highly qualified professionals such as doctors, engineers, bankers, nurses and teachers packed their bags and left in search of greener pastures abroad. Those who decided to remain behind became, in one way or the other, effigies of Franz Fanon's *Wretched of the Earth*. As criticism of government economic policies and the role of international capital (such as the World Bank and International Monetary Fund) mounted every day, President Beyani admitted publicly for the first time that Zambia had reached an economic crisis. Yet the social discontent was already so high that the people opted for political change. Would the President and his Party be able to contain this tide of change whose roots were embedded in the high levels of poverty and the economic chaos of the nation? What was the future of a country whose Gross Domestic Product had ceased to grow?

Besa set the manuscript aside. It was 12:15 hours. Even though he was hungry, the idea of cooking struck him as somewhat tiresome. Besa squashed it and, instead, decided to eat at a restaurant in town before meeting Shantiee face to face. He would present her with flowers and say: 'Shantiee, I know I must have caused you much anxiety and hurt the last five months. This was unjust. For this reason I am to blame for everything – for having failed you. If our relationship at the moment were irredeemably lost, I would be very grieved but would also let you go. What have I done is cause you embarrassment, humiliation and disappointment? I do not deserve to be with you now, yet I only ask you to allow me share with you the story of my experiences the last few moths. Perhaps you will then understand what my heart has been. Perhaps you will see in this solitude my grief sculptured in stone. You will hear my sighs and then pardon me – and may you believe that in my inmost self I have always delighted in no one but you. I have aspired to love you well.'

As Besa was enwrapped in these thoughts (or would she throw him out and banish him from her life forever?) there was an impertinent knock on the door. He went over to open it: who could it be?

Three stout, young men stood near the door with menacing expressions, their reddened eyes impatient and ominous. They wore muscle T-shirts and looked every bit like dangerous juveniles from the streets. A woman got out of the cabin of a light Toyota truck packed a few metres away from this rectangular block of rented rooms. He recognised her instantly. She advanced nearer with unfriendly, determined steps. Some curious neighbours drew about them to witness the spectacle.

'We have found you at last,' remarked Mrs. Tembo in a swaggering manner. 'I am happy we shall bring the matter to an end today.'

Besa suddenly felt sick and weak. At the same time he was tired of living a life of excuses, a life of falsifying himself. Why must he account for everything he did to a shylock? When would he be free from this kind of debasement? *Let the worst happen this very minute*, he thought. *I have nothing to lose!*

'I wasn't hiding from you,' he answered. 'I was away in Samfya because my mother had died. This was why you could not find me.'

'You should have informed me.'

'There was no time. Everything happened unexpectedly and I was confused.'

Mrs. Tembo dismissed this with her hand. 'I did not come here to listen to you. I have listened to you enough. I came to collect my money. Do you have my money ready?'

'Frankly, no.'

'This will be the fourth time you will be telling me the same thing. I shall not accept any apologies from you. I just want my money.'

'I am not yet paid. Give me some time.'

'What kind of work do you do that does not give a salary at the end of *each* month? Didn't you and Mister Mwabba Kauseni assure me that you are a graduate?'

'I am a university graduate.'

'Did we not agree that you would return the money after *one* month?'

'Yes.'

'How many months have passed since then?'

'About three-'

'And during this time you have never been paid?'

'No.'

'Do you take me to be a fool?'

'I am saying the truth. Phone my employers if you like. Why should I lie to you?'

She thought this over for some time. 'Listen. When your friend brought you to my house you seemed sincere and I pitied you. I considered you just like my own son – and I remembered saying to myself, "I don't lend money to strangers, but this young man does look honest and he has just graduated from the University. He'll soon have a good job; he will have no difficulty in paying back the money." See what you have now done. You have inconvenienced me!'

'I am very sorry, madam.'

'Suppose you were I, how would you carry on your business if your customers did not pay on time? How would you live?'

Besa was dreadfully guilty. He had nothing to say.

Mrs. Tembo eyed him resolutely:

'I hate doing this but I really have no choice. I am confiscating a few things from your home. As soon as you have found the money you will collect the items.' Then she gave instructions to her men: 'I want the bed and mattress, and kitchen things!'

Besa looked at the woman in horror. When he tried to bar the doorway the men pushed him violently back, and he landed on the floor with a thud. Spectators were chanting with relish: 'Bailiffs, bailiffs, bailiffs!' as the juveniles overturned things and messed up the room. One of them kicked the small table with a right foot, spilling the precious manuscript and some textbooks on the floor. Watching valuable documents desecrated like that was more than he could bear. It was as if Besa was stripped of existence. Struggling on his feet again, he faced his intruders in rage:

'Take anything you please but don't dare touch my books. Get what you want and leave me alone!'

'Fuck you,' retorted one of them. 'Mother fucker.'

'Just collect your things and clear out or else I'll call the police. You act without any knowledge of the law.'

They loaded the items in the truck, much to the excitement of a crowd of spectators already gossiping about him:

'He can't be a graduate,' they said. 'Where did you ever see a university graduate who lives in a small room and goes to a money lender for kalooba?'

'He must have received his degree certificate from Matero where anybody could buy one. *Nina kuuza kale kuti munyamata uja ni wafeki!*'[46]

'What a pity! He won't be able to cook tonight.'

'The graduate will now have to sleep on the floor!'

Besa could not repress his tears. He wanted to retaliate, to fight back and reassert his dignity and pride, yet he allowed himself to suffer these things in silence. The genius in him had already fathomed the historical dimension of these events, assessing their literary form and aesthetic value. He was not just a fact that exalted its existence now. He was also that accumulated fact that represented the human process since the prehistorical past. He was the historical result that required an explanation and a justification, a question mark that needed to be made manifest in the light of the unitary structure of what history had been.

Besa locked up the room and took a bus into town. An exhilarating triumph percolated through him like frenzy. His life was in ruins. He was heavily in debts. He had no investments anywhere. He had neither a job nor a decent home, and he stood like someone at fault with having chosen a career without a future. And yet – despite the circumstances – he had vowed to ride on the wings of the storm. Having fallen down, he must now stand up and turn his losses into gains. He must face the world and bring it to his command.

He got some roses and hurried through lunch at a restaurant along Cairo Road. He checked his time – it was 14:16 hours. What would Shantiee think of him after all this time? Perhaps she would say, 'I waited for you all these months and you were nowhere to be seen. I thought you'd lost interest in me so I found someone new. You shouldn't blame me – it's your entire fault!' And she would be quite right! On the other hand, 'Was what Washaama said about Shantiee still being in love with me correct? If this *is* the case, I am a very lucky man indeed.'

Besa left the restaurant and emerged into the Lusaka crowds again. A mass of black faces swallowed him as he wormed his way to Kulima Tower. Each of these faces wore the stamp of its own prospects, anxieties and dreams, and each person weaved their own plot that altered according to circumstances. They woke up every day to unfold the drama of their lives like characters in Sophocles' plays. They acted out each line every moment of the way, unresistingly drawn to the passion and tragedy of life, and would then vanish from the stage as suddenly as they had entered upon it. A historian would come. He would see the footmarks scattered in different directions and perhaps discern a general pattern, and he would ask, 'Where were they going?' in an attempt to reconstruct their collective destiny. Yet this reconstruction, in so far as it depended on the historian's subjectivity and selective purpose, would not duplicate their lives in their entirety, nor would he reproduce experiments to test some hypotheses. There were no eyewitnesses, no measurements, and no possibility of working with material in its original state. As everything was changing, the course of history was an elusive concept that could not be completely pinned down. Like the river of Heraclitus[47], the flurry of historical events (the beliefs, desires, hopes, losses, pains and achievements of ages), were always passing away and would never return. Humanity was engulfed by the contingent and unforeseen, by that from which no one could escape. 'Therefore, Besa, what are you thinking?' He scratched his ear. He remembered the manuscript, that narrative of events that purported to explain some aspects of these people's history, *their* history, then considered in desperation, 'Can any history ever be objective?' and could neither affirm nor deny. Yet Shakespeare devastated him in Macbeth: 'Life's but a walking shadow, a poor player that struts and frets his hour upon the boards / and then is heard no more. It is a tale told by an idiot, full of sound and fury, signifying nothing.'

Wedged between two women on the back seat, Besa watched people and buildings 'pass' as a mini-bus pulled out of Kulima Tower. Across his thighs were the roses he had bought Shantiee as a present. He wanted to relax – tried to prevent his mind from running too far ahead of itself, as was typical of him, yet he couldn't. Images of the book and of Shantiee slid into consciousness in vast whirls that he thirsted for her more tenaciously than ever before, while he also reflected on the question which disconcerted him most – the philosophy of history, its theory of logic and explanation.

By now the bus had half circled Kabwe roundabout and turned into Great East Road. Besa paid his fare. They passed over some potholes. He closed his eyes, resigning himself to the sense of something dramatic unfolding in his life. Would Shantiee be glad to see his slovenly looks? Would she still regard him as handsome, a genius and worthy of her love? Would she touch her lips on his and say, 'Why did you let us so long pass before we could meet again? Why are you such an ass?' or would she recoil and spit in his face?

The bus made the first stop at Northmead. Besa leaned forward to catch what the two men were saying about the looming nation-wide strike for teachers – and thought: 'It's quite a pity. How can people in their right frame of mind postulate that teaching is not production in every sense of the term? Is not a classroom, or indeed any environment in which effective learning takes place, a factory in which learners – as human capital – are imparted with values and skills that become the engine of any nation's economic development? Would there be development without a meaningful investment in education?'

'These teachers believe they are special. They think they may hold Government to ransom through continued strikes. If I were the President I would cut their salaries to a quarter and have all of them suspended.'

'You're right,' rejoined his friend. 'The problem is that they want to compare themselves to professionals like bankers, miners and engineers. What teachers forget is that they are not producers. They don't make money, so they should be satisfied with what the Government is offering them. You earn as you work!'

'That's right. There is no way this nation will progress if we rewarded people for not doing very much. Teaching is a kind of work – yes, but you can't use it to increase the Gross Domestic Product. This is why I support our minister of education for saying that these people have gone too far. They should be disciplined or think twice before continuing with their strike.'

The bus jerked forward and cut into the highway. It made three stops before Besa disembarked at university. Still distraught by the vulgar opinion of the men, he crossed Great East Road and beheld the Ruins, Workers' Canteen and New Education Bridge Building in the distance. The familiarity of the place induced a vague feeling of homecoming in him. Had those years of intensive thought and study been worth the sacrifice? Besa answered in the affirmative, despite what he was going through at the moment. Staring about him, the historian saw some students – both male and female – carrying themselves with the same kind of enthusiasm, ambition and hope that had fired him ceaselessly to hard work. Theirs was a very hard road to travel, and there was no certainty that they would ever finish their studies. Given any misunderstanding between the students, Government, university and the lecturers' union, the institution would go up in flames any minute. The police and military would rush in, beat up students and steal their property, and then close the place indefinitely. Because of disturbances and the disruption of learning, a programme that was scheduled to run for four years would take longer to complete! In Besa's case, his four-year Bachelor of Arts degree had taken him five and half years (without failing!). He had witnessed four riots and two closures!

Besa ascended the stairs of Shantiee's block, October 3, dreading every step he took. Would he find the girl in her room chatting with friends? How would she react? Suppose that she -? The will to go on nearly deserted him, as he did not wish to countenance abandonment. Yet he had to live through this ordeal. The comedy of his life would soon be over.

Grasping the roses in one hand, Besa climbed the stairs as though his fortitude had been stifled by impassioned grief. At this moment he discovered that his heart was in a tumult, beating wildly, anticipating the worst. For a long moment Besa paused at the door before he could bring himself to knock.

'Hold on,' answered a voice he could hardly associate with Shantiee's. 'I am coming!'

Besa waited. It was now too late to retrace his steps!

A key turned in the lock. The door opened, exposing an inquisitive female face. Probably Shantiee's new roommate.

'Hi,' she greeted. 'Can I help you?'

'Sure. I am here to see Shantiee. I am an old friend of hers.'

'Sorry she's out. She's with the boy friend.'

'What? Has Shantiee got a boy friend?'

'Of course she has. Don't you know this already, being her friend?'

Besa was speechless. He looked at her in perplexity.

'When will she come back?'

'I don't know. She said she might spend a night at his place. She wasn't very sure. She's been away since morning. Would you like to leave a message?'

There was nothing more to say. The facts spoke a plain sentence: 'You're dumped.' Besa groaned, dropped the roses on the floor, and beat his head wildly with his fists, begging her not to leave him. How could Shantiee break her vows? How could she throw away their life just like that? 'For shame, Shantiee...What is your life trying to prove? Had I known that your lips would lie a thousand times, I would never have offered myself to betray!'

What followed were moments in which Besa was petrified with deep mourning, disquietude and a dozen regrets, for a light had gone out of his life. Grievously aware of the pangs and empty spaces reigning in his heart, he stumped downstairs leaving the girl completely amazed and rooted in the doorway. The mind's logical character had since diminished, and he gave free reign to emotions and vain regrets. To imagine Shantiee in the arms of another man was frightfully distressful. Nonetheless Besa projected them. Her lover kissed her and thrust his phallus between her thighs. Her eyes were still shut but welcoming, and from her throat escaped sighs and groans of contented pleasure. Then the man pumped harder, their breathing quickened as they approached the end of their emotional summit, and she sung out to him, 'I love you, darling,' without any remorse or remembrances of things past. Nor was this the only image that crossed his harried state of mind. He saw his relatives beg him to consider marrying the woman of their choice. Despite their good intentions, however, Besa was obstinate and unyielding. He risked propriety and decorum in a false belief that Shantiee loved him as much. How could he have been so blind? On the contrary, how was he supposed to get on without someone he truly loved?

Besa wept like a child. It didn't matter that his swollen, reddened eyes, as he made it back to town on foot, stunned people. He had lost his only love, the most important investment in his life, and nothing mattered anymore. He was in the region of death and darkness.

Three times he was nearly run over as he crossed the road. Drivers threw their heads out of their car windows and flooded him with abuse. Besa did not care. Why should he care? His first love – Muzo – who had a zest for living was never allowed to kiss him goodbye the moment the spectre of death bore her reluctantly down. Nor did his mother return from the land of solitude and whirlwinds. Death had rendered them both beyond reach and rebuke, and they had left him rootless and dejected. Why should he cling to this life when he must die anyway? Besides, he had no job to go back to, the moneylender had dispossessed him of some household property, his father had disowned him and wished death to possess his feet, and Shantiee; Shantiee in whom Besa believed completely had now forsaken him and found someone else. Why should he care to live if there was nothing worth living for? Why should one go on living if one felt like *nothing*?

Thus for almost two and half hours, the graduate plodded back to Washaama's flat in Thorn Park in a confused state of mind. He was a *nonentity*, a *nobody* that she had chosen to ditch in preference for someone else. Now he understood the existential aloneness of men – their attempts to express their agony through the arts to lighten the burdens of their souls. The load was heavy, the future was the next step, and the heart bled from the wound of her betrayal. At a time Besa needed her most, Shantiee deserted him and broke his life into a million splinters. Considering what he had been through up to this point, the historian felt that the dark clouds that had swamped him completely would never disperse. The darkest days would never pass! Tragedy knocked insistently at his steps, and Besa doubted whether he possessed the inner strength to live to see another day.

Thin clouds of dust occasionally whirled about him. Wherever his eyes fell, Besa saw around him objects that appeared to have suddenly acquired an enigmatic quality about them, as though their interior content was deceptive and fragile. Everything was essentially breakable, destructible and alterable save the law of change. Was this why the mystics had taught all to distrust social relationships and the material things of life? Besa remembered that it was. On the other hand, there seemed to be no reprieve from living as existence entailed radical transformations of many types. Death, growth and decay were the ground in which humanity was situated. There was therefore no freedom from hurt, anguish, disappointment and other crushing misfortunes. If all events had to pass, then there was some comfort in knowing that whatever the circumstances, no burden or pain could be carried forever.

Besa located the flat without any difficulty. A security guard admitted him through the steel gate. As he walked down a brick lane to the door of the house, the historian cast glances at the flowers and green lawn adorning this enclosed space. There were two cars in the garage – a Telka Construction van and a new, black nissan saloon – a sign that Washaama was already home and waiting for him. Besa touched the button and heard the bell ring inside the house. The door was swung open. Besa embraced his friend for a long time.

'Thanks for everything, man,' he said. 'I don't know what I could have done without you!'

'Don't start that again,' Washaama reproached him. 'We're childhood friends and that's what friendship is all about. Shall we go in inside now? The girls will be very excited to see you.'

'The *girls?*' he asked suspiciously. 'What girls?'

'O, I should have warned you! Shantiee is here. She's been here since morning. She's in the kitchen with Inutu. They're preparing something special for you!'

'Wha...what are you saying?' he asked in utter disbelief. 'Do you mean to say that my fiancée is *here?*'

'Yep.'

He blinked in confusion. 'Is Shantiee in *here*?'

'Yes, that's what I said. Come on, let's go inside.'

Besa did not believe it. It was too good to be true! How could life be cruel to him this minute and then reward him so generously in the next moment? How was one to oscillate between sorrow and happiness, desperation and absolute joy? What was he supposed to feel?

Washaama led the way into the living room, ordered him to relax on a sofa and disappeared into the kitchen to inform the girls. Besa was fidgety, guilty and insecure, but he was also very excited! Was this one of Washaama's bluffs?

He heard Shantiee's voice – this was truly *her* voice – and stood up instinctively, raising his eyes in the direction of the kitchen door. Besa was overcome by great incredulity. As happened in those fantastic visions he had experienced in the recent past, he saw the love of his life running up to meet him. Unable to believe his eyes yet, he caught her in a long passionate embrace and wept. Shantiee wept, too, holding on to him least circumstances separated her from him again. Then Besa broke the embrace and hugged Inutu for some moments.

Washaama ended the silence.

'Listen. Inutu and I will take care of the cooking while you two try to catch up on each other. Your bedroom is over there.'

Besa followed her into the bedroom. He turned to her and met her honey-coloured eyes. She rose on her toes to be kissed, and she wanted him again and again as if her need would never fill. He caressed her long hair, her shoulders and her slim back. It was ironical that he should now wish to commit himself to loving this incredible young woman when, only a few hours ago, he had longed to die to end the pain and futility of living. What did this teach about the meaning of life? *You must hold on no matter what happens!* Besa fell on his kneels and entreated her for forgiveness.

'I don't know where to begin, Shantiee,' he said. 'I've done everything wrong. I've caused us so much pain. I am unworthy of your love, but I would like to be readmitted into your life. Will you forgive me? Will you tell me *this* minute that you love me? I'll do anything to atone!'

She knelt down beside him. She took his head in her palms.

'*You are* the most handsome and wonderful man in my life. I've always felt this way about you ever since we met. Yes – *I* still love you and want you in my life. As for the atonement,' Shantiee smiled

mischievously at him, 'I'll ask you to do me *two* things. First, you'll
let me see where you live. I want to spend some time with you at
your place. I'll leave campus and be with you for about two weeks
or so. Washaama has offered us his flat but I want to be where you
live. I want our own place.'

'It's not much of a place. It's a single room in Chawama.'

'I don't care what size it is. All I want is to be with my man in
our home. I don't mind where we live so long I am with you. I also
want to have a sense of what your life has been like. I don't want appointments or arrangements. I want to be with you *every* day.'

'What about your studies? Don't you suppose I might be disturbing you?'

'I've worked everything out. Every weekday I'll be at university between eight and twenty-one hours in the evening. After that I
come home. There won't be any disturbance.'

'Twenty-one hours is a bit too late. There's a question of catch-
ing a bus.'

'I figured that one out, too. I won't need to catch a bus because
we have a car now. I asked my dad to buy me one for the research
and he's done so. It's in Mufulira right now but one of our drivers
will deliver it to this place by twelve tomorrow. So we won't need
to take a bus unless we want to! We have our own brand new car
now! Can you drive?'

'No,' he said, confused. 'I've never driven in my life.'

'Well, you'll have to learn because sometimes you'll be the one
to take me to university and back. Washaama will give you some
lessons, or would you prefer to go to a driving school?'

Besa was aghast.

'Are you alright, darling?' she asked.

'Yes, I am all right. What's the second thing that I have to do?'

'The next thing is – we must sit down to make a budget of all
the things we need for our home. We'll get some money from my
account and go shopping. These are the *two* conditions you should
meet, Mister Musunga.'

Besa nodded approval and kissed her on the lips, inhaling her
odour. He got her up on her feet and laid her on the bed. She moved
to make room for him and embraced his body again, digging her
hand between his thighs. She fondled him with her hand, squeez-
ing and caressing his erection. Besa caught her hand but she fought
off the grip. They quickly undressed and dived behind the covers.
Their lovemaking was very passionate and intense. Afterward, Besa
narrated his unhappy misadventure a few hours ago, as Shantiee lis-

tened with interest. She rolled over him and coiled her arms round his neck. Then she said softly, tears sloping down her cheeks:

'I'll never leave you nor run away from you. I'll be with you *always* for as long as you need me. I am yours forever. I cannot love another man. I am content with what I have. You're all I ever need in this life. There's no room for anyone else.'

Besa believed her every word.

She was questioning him at the moment. 'Don't you trust me by now? How could you possibly think I'd gone to meet another man?'

Besa sheepishly cast his eyes down, saying nothing.

Then Shantiee narrated everything that had happened on the two occasions that she had met Washaama. 'If you love me at all,' she said at last, 'we owe this reunion to Washaama and Inutu. They took the trouble to make it possible for us to meet today. When you phoned Washaama that you'd see him at his flat, he instructed Inutu to pick me up from university so that we should prepare for you. Since I was sure to meet you, I did not hesitate to tell my roommate that I would be out and probably spend the night at my boy friend's place – at *your* place, because I really thought we needed time together. I've missed you and my life's never been the same without you. I needed to be sure you were all right.'

'I've had a terrible time. I didn't want you to see the life I was living as a teacher. I have absolutely nothing. I wanted to spare you the shame of seeing the kind of person I had become. I live like a vagabond and I didn't want you to see that.'

She shook her head. 'Honey,' she said, 'it didn't have to come to this. If you'd told me about your problems I'd have given you some money and we could have found a nice flat for you. I honestly don't care about anything so long as I am by your side. I couldn't run away from you even if you lived in a shack. Have I ever told you the story of how my parents met?'

'No.'

'Well, let me narrate it to you now. Perhaps it'll help you understand my attitude to life and the way I feel about us. My father came to this country without a ngwee in his pockets. He was a foreigner and didn't know the country. He had lost his papers, too, so he couldn't get a job because no one was prepared to give him one. For days he hadn't eaten what you'd call a proper meal, and white people in Mufulira shunned him. He slept in the open and the police twice arrested him. He wandered about worse than a vagabond did. He remembered Italy and his life in Sicily, but he couldn't go

back! How'd he go back empty handed when he'd promised his
parents and relatives that he'd bring wealth from Africa? How'd
he take the shame and start all over again? He had borrowed from
friends to pay for his passage, and he had to pay back! He had to do
something, yet the more he thought about his new life in Zambia,
the more difficult everything looked. He had now reached the crossroads of his life. He gave up and contemplated suicide. Then, when
it was darkest, he met a woman who was to change his life forever.
That woman was my mother.

'He saw her at the market place where she was selling vegetables. He was hungry, lonely and poor, and he asked her to lend him
money. She was at first shocked, but when he explained everything
to her she decided to help him. She was nineteen and had dropped
out of school, and he was thirty-two. She had a vegetable stall at
the market place and the two teamed up together and started a mod-
est business buying and selling vegetables. After about a year, they
decided to marry and lived in a shack! My parents were a laughing
stock everywhere. My mom was jeered at for marrying a poor white
man. As for my dad, his fellow whites rejected him because he was
poor, Italian and married to an uneducated black woman. It was a
very difficult time for them, but their problems brought them closer
together and made them even more determined to succeed.

'At my dad's insistence my mom enrolled for night school
classes and completed her secondary education. Then he sent her
to South Africa to read a diploma in marketing, and then she read
some more and got a master's. Ten years after they had met, my parents could not but marvel at their achievements. My dad was running a very successful business with four subsidiary companies. He
had invested into mining, hotels, transportation, agriculture and pe-
troleum. My mom had risen to the position of managing director of
Barclays in Ndola. She also sat as a board member of all our family
business locally and abroad.'

She stopped and went on.

'My parents are very successful people, and perhaps we may
learn something from their lives. You and I could start almost *anywhere*. I'll cook for us, I'll make the beds, I'll scrub the floor, and
I'll do anything to build a home for us. I want us to do something of
our own from small beginnings so that, after some years, we'll look
back and say, "This is where our dreams began; this is where we
came from." We have *everything* it takes to succeed. I am blessed to
have a man with the most amazing mind I have ever met. I believe
in you and your abilities. There are no limits to what we can choose

to be. We need only have a dream and seize the world in our hands. Life will give us success and happiness in proportion to our belief! When we think big we shall achieve *anything!*'

'You think we can make it?'

'Yes, sweetheart, we can! You have a degree and I'll soon complete my studies in six months. We're very young, intelligent and healthy, and we have people who can back us up – we have my parents! We could ask for a loan from them to start up something. Why don't you build your *own* schools and make your own money instead of waiting for someone to put you on their pay roll system? You could also partner with Washaama to start a construction firm! Do we really need to run around applying for jobs with all the skills we now have?'

Besa laughed out aloud. This was the first time he had heard himself laugh in a very long time. Shantiee was very right. They had so many skills and it was possible to use them in some way.

'You're right, Shantiee. We can do it.'

'Another possibility is to leave the country. Why don't we go and work in America, Australia, Canada or some place for some time? What do you have against this idea? I want to live with you in another country. We could be happier there!'

Besa pondered this and it made sense. 'Maybe I need time away from all this. I need to be in a completely different place. Yes, I suppose you're right. Let's leave the country and see what happens. But that will be after you complete your studies in six months. In the mean time we could start making travel arrangements.'

Shantiee was instantly overjoyed. 'Are you serious about this, darling?'

'Yes. Where would you like to go? I'd love to live in Australia.'

'So would I! Let's go to Australia then!'

'Right. I'll visit the Australian High Commission for information on emigration.'

'We will,' she corrected him. 'I need to be there too. I just hope we're serious about this.'

'Of course we are. Remember the first time we discussed the subject? I condemned you for suggesting that we go abroad to work, but I now feel differently. We need to go away and embrace other experiences. The situation here at home is not so good. But,' Besa looked at her seriously now. 'There's something else.'

'What.'

Besa hesitated a moment. 'Shantiee, are you thinking of marrying me?'

'No,' she laughed. 'Are *you*?'

'Yes. Will you marry *me*?'

'I couldn't risk it,' she said in jest, tears of joy brimming in her eyes. She gazed into his eyes and mumbled: 'Yes, sweetheart, I will marry you! I could marry you right now – if you wish. It's all in my heart.'

Besa turned her over and kissed her lips.

Shantiee held him lovingly in her arms. She parted her legs and received him deeply inside her. Her face was flushed and enchanted. She moaned from his downward thrusts. The magic and passion of her sweet loves was ever new. Imploring him to reach the deepest shades of her being, she locked her arms round him, arching upward as he pumped harder... and then faster until, gaping at him in happy disbelief, she held him proudly in her arms and told him how much she loved him. Their breathing was short, quick and intense. Shantiee wiped sweat from his brows and kissed him again and again. 'Don't ever leave me,' she warned, 'Or else I will strangle you.'

'I won't,' he replied. 'I need you *all the time*.'

'So you are serious about marriage?'

'No,' he smiled. 'I can't take the risk.'

She pinched him in the ribs. 'I am serious, Besa. Are you thinking of marrying me?

'Yes. I made the decision when I was home. We've gone through a lot together and I think nothing could be better than living as husband and wife. We've got to be man and wife.'

'Yes,' she said. 'I'd love to marry you! I dream of it all the time. Nothing could be more perfect than this. I think of the time I'll live with you in our own house with children of our own. Yes, I would like to marry you! But we'll have to wait for me to complete my studies in six months. Can we wait until next year, honey?'

'Yes. Next year would be very fine. It'd give me enough time to reorganise my life and plan for our future – I mean the wedding and leaving for Australia. Bye the way, I resigned from the Teaching Service this morning. I have to start looking around for a better job.'

'Did you resign because of me?'

'No. I made the decision when I was home. I've had to ask myself basic questions about life. I've to be practical and realistic. You can't live by ideas alone. You need to put food on your table for your wife and kids. There's old age too. How will you live when you're too old to work? I also want to help my family. They'll always be my family. But I suppose I'll never give up reading books.

Who knows? Perhaps I'll publish something and make a name. The most important thing, however, is that I want to give you, my wife, a good life.'

'You will, my husband,' she said, kissing him with great pride. Then she moved out of bed naked and said, 'Let's take a bath and go for supper. Inutu and Washaama must be wondering what we're up to. Bye the way, you'd better start having tutorials on how to proceed with marriage negotiations with my parents. I'll give you one or two hints and then you'll be on your own!'

Besa laughed with great delight. 'I love you, Shantiee. I'll always love you.'

'You're my sweetheart, and I'll always be yours till the end of time. Nothing will separate me from you since you have immortalised my soul.'

'You have strengthened and pulled me up, my love, and I'll walk with you a billion miles. I'll never tire nor let you walk this path of life alone. I'll be with you always till the sun loses its light, and the stars fall from their perch. This is my solemn commitment to you, love of my life!'

Chapter 16

Concerns the last word of Musunga Fyonse

Everything that has a beginning has an end, and nothing that *is* ever lasts. The seeds of change have wormed through all existent things so that there is a death to every birth, and a beginning to every end. Death and decay have touched the very roots of things.

How can I forget that life is essentially change? I have seen the working of this truth ever since I was a child. I have seen it working in myself as a person, and I have seen it working everywhere around me. Things do come to an end. This is the certainty and meaning of life. Plants and animals suffer the same fate. They grow and live for some time, and then they slip beyond the edge where light and darkness are one.

This certainty relates to our land as well. We have endured floods, famines, droughts, earthquakes, diseases and pests, and there have been wars, too. Conflicts over land, resources and trade led to civil strife between clans and tribes. Chieftaincies and kingdoms rose up and collapsed. Wars resulted in the loss of lives, property and the displacement of people. We also witnessed how the Arabs captured children, women and men, and forced them into slavery. Entire villages were sometimes annihilated, and thousands of lives were lost. Survivors fled and abandoned their works.

As though this was not enough, Europeans also came and, in the breath of the moment, demanded our land, minerals, forests, wildlife and labour. They dispossessed us of our rights as human beings. We became nothing but beasts that could be killed or abused as they wished. Because of taxation and the threat of imprisonment, my people became labourers: they migrated to Tanganyika, Zimbabwe, South Africa, Congo and the Copperbelt for work. Yet it were these terrible conditions of life which inspired them to fight for the freedom of their land. Independence was won from the British in 1964.

But who could have guessed that our own leaders would behave in the same way as the Arabs and Europeans? Who could have imagined that they would steal wealth from their own people and create a government whose repressive nature made it nearly indistinguishable from the cruelty of the invaders? Who could understand why our leaders set out to defend the values of the people who had oppressed us?

They quickly forgot that no matter how well they imitated the ways of the oppressors, they would never be *them*. They also forgot that our life was rooted in the *shrine*. The *shrine* was our past, our present, and our future. It was the wisdom of our life. It was everything that was us. It was a sacred fount at which we drunk shared visions that we would always be Black.

But the shrine is no more, and our gods are dead. Our people have now taken to worshipping the gods of the Arabs or Europeans, despite the truth that these people have never loved us for who we are but for our wealth. Yet we have not learnt from our past. We have befriended those that have always stood against us, and we imitate their ways. We have lost our path by allowing them to destroy us. Without a vision of our own, we are doomed to perish. We shall blame no one but ourselves. A people that choose to be led by blind leaders can never prosper.

I cannot comprehend these times, and I will not fill my heart with any thoughts of an earth I have perhaps never been able to understand at all. It has been difficult to seek wisdom in everything, and I have now ceased to question life for fear of inviting madness upon my head. My body is very weak – and the senses by which I guided my feet about are failing me every time. I have no excuse to live on. Time has come for me to go, and I must meet the silence, shadows and the half-light in the world beyond. I must merge into nothingness and dream no more.

Why should I linger on *here* and pretend that I am necessary to anyone? I am nothing at all. This truth comes about with time. As seasons pass in great circles of the sun, the physical body of man loses its vitality and good health, suffering disease and weakness every time. Soon the eyes lose their sight; the head sheds its hair; the back slumps forward; the legs refuse to walk; the skin wrinkles in every part, and the spirit in us senses its final return to the world beyond. I have lived a life – for good or for evil – and I am now leaving this world without any bitterness in my soul.

O Spirits of my Fathers, my life has broken like a potsherd. My breath has finally been cut. Just as you guided me in the ways of the tribe, so should you do so now, when the path of my end has finally opened up before me. Take me now into your presence, O you that protected me from the storms and burdens of this earth. May my will to go on wither like an elephant grass, and may the senses through which I understood life be mute forever. I who was married to this end at my birth, I cannot flee from it any longer. All that is born possesses within it the seeds of its end. This is my end; this is my beginning. My eyes are now closed, and my tongue has clung to the roof of my mouth. I have a beginning and an end.

Notes

1 A tribe in the Luapula province of Zambia who live on the shores of lakes Bangweulu and Chifunabuli, respectively.

2 The government administration area of the district.

3 An owl.

4 Civil disobedience activities against the white colonial leadership of Northern Rhodesia prior to independence.

5 The Public Order Act. First enacted in 1953 to control the freedom of movement and assembly of Black freedom fighters who agitated for the dissolution of the Federation of Northern Rhodesia, Southern Rhodesia and Nyasaland.

6 The Primary God.

7 Street vendors who sell cigarettes, cloths and roam bus stations to make money

8 Bats

9 female marketers who sell bread, buns, tea and other things at bus stations and council markets

10 A concoction of faeces, urine and herbs that is given to a victim accused of witchcraft to drink. His or her death, upon drinking, is seen as a confirmation of guilt.

11 Colonial Governor of Northern Rhodesia (now Zambia).

12 The station building.

13 Teachers.

14 A honey bird.

15 Ukupesha cibola kumupengwila.

16 Ukupesha ilungu kwendamo.

17 This song is sung to express great joy at seeing the Chief (Mankangala)

18 This song informs the people that the Chief whom they see is the *only* Chief for them; the song expresses unfaltering loyalty to someone popularly acknowledged as a political authority in a kingdom.

19 A type of beer made from millet that is usually drunk warm and with a drinking stick.

20 A type of much organised music and dance very popular in the Luapula Province of Zambia.

21 Bwanga bwandi lala, tumone imicitile ya bakaya.

22 The song teaches the bride or groom not to have a cold, indifferent and even hostile attitude towards visiting relatives from both sides.

23 The song teaches the bride or groom to welcome relatives from both sides in the *same* manner. Not to treat one's parents or relations more kindly.

24 A tribe in the Democratic Republic of Congo.

25 A white substance in powdered form that is used in many rituals to symbolise peace, blessedness and luck.

26 Jesus Christ

27 University of Zambia Students Union.

28 Kalingalinga Township

29 Ba-monko means 'monks'. Male students without girlfriends and who are reputed for being radical and very serious with their studies. The term may also apply to any male student at university.

30 Christopher Akigbo, the great Nigerian poet who published *Labyrinths and the paths of thunder*. He died in the Biafra War in 1967.

31 The Constitution of Zambia Act, Cap 1.

32 The Penal Code, Cap 146 of the Laws of Zambia.

33 Under the regulations, the President may detain indefinitely anyone considered a threat to the government. The detained are given grounds for detention, and the tribunal is set up to review their cases within a month and thereafter at half-yearly intervals; but the President may turn down the tribunal's recommendation to release or continue detention if he/she wishes... In this regard, Presidential powers are above the tribunal or the courts.

34 The place where the Zambia Secret Service operates from. Institution of torture against perceived enemies of the State.

35 Francis Bacon (1561-1626) wrote of the doctrine of the idols in the *Novum organum*. The 'idols' are basically the errors, preconceptions and prejudices that distort judgement and our interpretation of experience. Bacon's 'idols' prepare the mind for the acquisition of knowledge through induction.

36 October car park

37 Graduation dais

38 Derogatory: Party and Its Government.

39 Ruin Police: an association of very staunch student radicals who believe in Unzasu and act as its security wing. They are based in the Ruins or Old Residence.

40 Francis Bacon.

41 Dialectics means physical process of transformation from one being to another.

42 This official government figure has now (2005) been disputed by Dr Y. Chondoka, lecturer in History at the University of Zambia, who puts the figure for the number of graduates at independence to be over 146.

43 Bemba proverb: When fishermen decide to go on the lake when there is a breeze, it is because they have *already* judged it to be safe. When they are on the lake and there is a storm, then they *know* they won't be able to contend with it because it has come about *suddenly*. You may therefore only sail with the wind that you know.

44 Roberts, Andrew. *A History of Zambia*. London: Heinemann, 1976.

45 The wars of the expansion of the Zulu nation under Shaka (1818-1828).

46 Translated from Nyanja: I told you a long time ago that this young man was fake.

47 A Greek philosopher who taught that everything changes: you cannot bath in the same river twice. Reality, therefore, is change, war or instability, or transformation.

Printed in the United States
144928LV00002B/111/A